'He more or less said I couldn't come back here,' I
...ning to drop.

...ge...ous and ...o difficult
...id that they'd have to
...he ...achers w...uldn't

...l Cleo
...s in

Lois Keith is a writer and teacher and a supporter of civil rights for disabled people. She is the editor of *Mustn't Grumble: Writing by Disabled Women* (The Women's Press, 1994), winner of the MIND Book of the Year Award 1994, and the author of *Take Up Thy Bed and Walk: Death, Disability and Cure in Classic Fiction for Girls* (The Women's Press, 2001), as well as a book for children, *Think About People Who Use Wheelchairs* (Belitha Press, 1998), shortlisted for the Nasen Special Educational Award in 1999. *A Different Life* (Livewire, 1997), was selected for Book Trust's 100 Best Books of 1998. She lives in London with her husband and their two daughters.

Lois Keith

a
different
life

Livewire

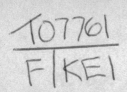

First published by Livewire Books, The Women's Press Ltd, 1997
A member of the Namara Group
34 Great Sutton Street, London EC1V 0LQ
www.the-womens-press.com

British Library Cataloguing-in-Publication Data
A catalogue record for this book is available from the British Library.

ISBN 0 7043 4946 9

Typeset in Bembo 12/14pt

Printed and bound in Great Britain by
Cox & Wyman Ltd, Reading, Berkshire

Acknowledgements

Firstly, I would like to thank Laurie Critchley and Kathy Gale of The Women's Press for encouraging me to believe I 'had a novel in me'. Dr Ron Benson from the Intensive Treatment Unit of St Vincent's Hospital, Sydney, unwittingly gave me the title, telling me two days after 'the accident' that I would have 'a good life but a different life'; and Mr J I L Bayley and his team at the Spinal Injuries Unit, the Royal National Orthopaedic in Stanmore, helped me to see how this might be true. Thanks also to the real-life Trudy and to Fiona Barr and Dr Brian Moffatt for supplying and supervising some of the medical details in the book. The campaigning organisation Surfers Against Sewage, based in St Ives, Cornwall, were both helpful and informative. Many people told me stories from their own lives, and I am particularly grateful to Cassandra Lewis from Wales, Joanna Owen and Barbara Saunders. And of course, thanks and love to Colin, for encouraging me to take time out to write this book and for much more.

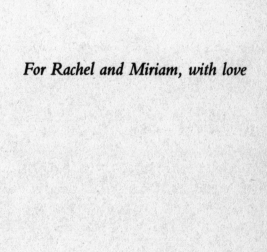

For Rachel and Miriam, with love

Part One

Part Two

Part Three

Part One

Chapter One
Libby

On the 16th of July last year when I was fifteen years, two months and four days old, the questions in my mind were:

1. Was I going to get a seat on the back row of the coach tomorrow when we went on the Year-10 trip to Littlehampton, or would Cleo blank me (again) and make sure it was filled up with the latest crowd she hung around with?

2. When was Mum going to stop seeing Robbie as the sweet, little, innocent, perfect child and me as the difficult, moody teenager?

3. What was I going to wear tomorrow? Jeans and T-shirt (baggy? skimpy?)? Denim shorts and the black shoes with clumpy heels? Red shift-dress? And how come other girls seem to know about these things and I don't?

4. How had I done in the exams? (Terrible probably but I honestly, really, truly was going to work harder next year for my GCSEs.)
5. What did others (especially boys) think of me? Stupid, pretty, ordinary, ugly? Did they think about me at all?
6. And last, but by no means least, was Jesse ever, ever going to look at me and think I was special?

A week later, it was impossible to believe that this was all I had to worry about.

My name is Elizabeth Alice Starling and I live at 41 Crowndale Avenue, London NW9. My mum says she called me Elizabeth so I could have a choice of names and decide what I wanted to be called when I was older – Liz, Lizzie, Beth, Betty – but it never worked out that way. Dad started calling me Libby when I was a baby, so that's how I see myself now and always will, I imagine.

From the outside I lived the most ordinary of lives, at least then. Mum, Dad and two kids in a semi-detached house in an area where all of the houses appear to be the same. I really loved our house – still love it, actually. It was just the right size for our family. Upstairs there's a toilet and bathroom and three bedrooms. Mum and Dad had the biggest one, I had the second biggest and Robbie had a tiny, squashy little room but he didn't seem to mind. We used to live in a little one-bedroom flat above my dad's parents' shop and we moved into this house when I was ten and Robbie was just a little baby. When we first moved in I couldn't believe how big my room was and I couldn't believe I could have it all to myself. I persuaded

Mum to have it all decorated in lilac (my favourite colour then): lilac wallpaper with ballet dancers on, lilac paintwork, frilly lilac lampshade, etc. I lived to regret it.

Downstairs there are two living rooms knocked into one, a kitchen, quite a big garden which Mum has always talked about improving but never does, and a garage on the side. In this garage lived Dad's pride and joy, his link with his long-lost youth – a red 1972 MGB-GT.

Every weekend he'd be out there fiddling away with it, changing the spark plugs (or whatever men do with semi-vintage cars), polishing the hub caps, trying to stave off the rust. He thought it part of the family's equal opportunities policy to try and interest me in this car, to rouse my enthusiasm in mechanical craftsmanship, but it never worked. I liked the look of the thing, but I couldn't see the point of just lying on the floor gazing at the underneath of something and getting your hands filthy. To me a car is something to get you from A to B in the quickest possible time. I think this was about the only way I was a disappointment to my dad. He was never the sort to find fault in his kids. He was more successful at getting my seven-year-old brother Robbie interested in spare parts and vintage rallies, so that was alright.

'Nellie', as my dad called it – called *her* I should say – was a major bone of contention between my parents. What Dad thought of as a thing of beauty, a romantic link with the days when motoring was still a pleasure, Mum thought of as a waste of space and money. She tried to pretend that she didn't think like this and that it was 'nice for a man to have a hobby'. But then, on the very Sunday he'd promised to help her in the garden, Dad would decide that he had to drive all the way to Manchester to spend a hundred quid on a water pump he'd been looking for for ages. Then things could get pretty nasty in our household.

My dad never actually lost his temper or shouted; that was Mum's special talent. And he'd always try to find a way round it.

'Look pet,' he'd say sweetly (you could almost see my mum clench her teeth when he called her 'pet'). 'I'll get up early and leave at six. It's only a two-hour drive to Manchester' (he always was an optimist, my dad) 'and I'll be back at eleven, twelve at the latest and then we'll all go to the garden centre together. That'd be nice, wouldn't it love?' And he'd give Mum his big-brown-eyes, lopsided-grin look and more often than not she'd end up laughing.

When things really got going at home after some great scene – Mum silent with rage, Robbie howling in the corner, me having said something awful and wishing I could swallow it right back down my throat – the most he would do was raise his eyebrows and sort of look down his nose and say, 'That was a bit much, don't you think Libby? I think you'll have to find a way to sort this one out.' And you knew he was right.

In many ways my mum and dad are like the proverbial chalk and cheese. I've never understood that expression now I come to think of it – chalk and cheese, how weird. My dad is like those nice kind of dads you see in children's story books. Not drop-dead gorgeous but all comfortable and safe. He's average size and has always got a rumpled sort of look, even when he tries to dress up smart. Partly he looks like this because of his hair, which is always untidy, black and curly with the odd bit of grey which he doesn't like you mentioning – and his eyes, which are dark brown and deep set under craggy eyebrows. I think he must have been more than your average spotty adolescent because he's got lots of pockmarks all over his face but it doesn't really make him look horrible or anything because he's got a lovely big grin. Easy-going is the word I'd use to describe him, unlike Mum and me. He says clothes are for being comfortable in and wears some pretty revolting things in the name of comfort like brown suede Hush Puppies, baggy ribbed jumpers and not-quite-fitting jeans.

Once when I was little, we went to a holiday camp and I forgot my 'shooshie blanket', an old piece of blue blanket with a piece of satin ribbon just about intact. I was inconsolable and said I couldn't go to sleep without it. Dad took off his jumper – it was a kind of beigy, cream colour – and said, 'There you go poppet, this'll do just for tonight.' And it did.

That's how I thought of my dad, as a big comforting shooshie blanket. It took me quite a while to realise that I never really talked to him, well not about important, difficult things. It was my mum I'd always turn to if I needed to get something off my chest. That's funny really, considering that I argued all the time with my mum and never with my dad.

Where my dad is comfortable and round, my mum is small and thin. Mind you, you don't realise how short she is because she's got a lot of what you might call presence. You always know she's there. Not that she's got a very loud voice or is always shouting or anything; you just know she's there.

She goes for the dramatic look, my mum. She's got a face like a bird, pale skin with big grey eyes and a longish straight nose, and now that she's dyed her hair black and had it cut really short she looks even more bird-like. She's into dramatic colours at the moment like red, black and white and she'll suddenly appear in something she's dragged out from the back of her cupboard – like a brocade jacket she used to wear in the seventies – saying proudly, 'Look at this – I used to wear it before I met your dad. Not bad for someone who's forty, is it?'

It's no good telling her that no-one goes around in that kind of thing any more because the truth is she'll usually look rather good in it. I've got to admit she's got a bit of style and she's good at making nothing very much look like something, which is a good thing because there's never any money to spare in our house.

My mum left school when she was quite young and went into Marks and Spencer's to be a trainee manager because 'that's what girls did then'. I know that one of her ambitions was to go to university and be what she calls 'a very mature student'. She worked part-time as a volunteer in the local Citizens Advice Bureau so that she could be around for Robbie and me. I should think she'd be quite good at sorting out other people's problems, bossing people about. She's like a whirlwind, organising everything and everyone, but she's still a huggy kind of person. When she was feeling a bit down or we'd had one

8

of our 'misunderstandings', she'd look around and say, 'Now who fancies a cuddle?' Even though I've been taller than her ever since I was thirteen and even though most of my fights with her were about trying to get her to see that I wasn't a child anymore, I'd still like to climb on her lap and wrap my long legs and arms around her. She gave the best hugs in the world, my mum. I miss that now – those long pretend-to-be-a-baby hugs.

I don't know why we argued such a lot. I suppose I'm a lot like her, although I don't really like admitting this. We've both got bad tempers. The frightening thing about her is that you could never really see it coming. One minute you'd think you were having a reasonable grown-up sort of discussion about school or friends or something (usually about school, come to think of it) and that you could both say whatever you think and the next minute she'd be screaming, 'Honestly, Libby, you really are the limit. You're a lovely girl but why must you always be so negative about everything?' It always started with her telling me how she thought I was clever, intelligent or pretty but it soon moved on to her saying what a disappointment I was.

'Why can't you just . . . ' and then there would follow one of the many items on her list of things she wished I were but was disappointingly proving not to be. Things like – keeping my room tidy ('There aren't any servants in this house, you know.'). More organised about work ('Sometimes I feel like I'm doing your homework, the way I have to keep on at you. And look at your last report. It's a disgrace that someone of your intelligence gets a report like this. I don't enjoy nagging you.'). Less dreamy ('I've been calling and calling you, Libby. I can't believe you haven't heard me.'). Less selfish ('Robbie is only a little boy and he adores you. Couldn't you let him use your paints just this once?'). Or more sociable ('I don't like to see you all on your own like this. Why don't you give one of your nice friends a ring and see if they'd like to go and see a film with you?') Yes, the list of the ways my mum would like to change me, mould me into something more easy-going, more like-she-was-when-she-was-my-age, was pretty long.

This business about not being 'negative' was a favourite cry of Mum's. It was no good trying to make her see that being negative about things was practically the only way a fifteen-year-old could be. After all, there are so many things you don't like about your life – appearance, school, friends, boyfriends, sex (or in my case the lack of it) – but you are powerless to change anything. Take friends, for example. Other people I knew seemed to have the knack of making friends and keeping them. Groups of people just seemed to hang around together, meet each other on the way to school, phone each other on the weekend in a natural, seamless way like the way tropical fish of the same colour swim around together in the tanks in dentists' waiting rooms. I often felt that I was the only fish of my kind in the tank. Not a funny colour or anything but destined to swim around all on my own.

When I was in primary school I used to wish every night for one best friend. That's all I wanted – still do in a way. Sometimes I would think I'd got one, but then everything would go wrong. Like Vanessa. We were inseparable for a year when I was about seven. We played with each other every playtime, went to each other's house after school, told each other our secrets. But then her parents decided to move to Hove, 'where the schools were so much nicer, not so rough, you know'.

Then when I was about ten, there were kids who I thought were my friends until I realised that they used the things that I told them, my secrets, to make fun of me in the playground when the teacher wasn't looking. Sofia was the worst. When she was little she had the kind of looks most little girls were taught to long for, the looks of a china doll. She had curly blond hair, porcelain skin and deep blue eyes. She was one of the cleverest kids in the class, brilliant at drawing and good at sport – teachers all loved her. But Sofia could be nastier than any other girl I knew. Because she was so pretty, all the kids wanted to be her friend, and she took this power and used it to make other children unhappy, even the ones she called her friends. It was her that always took Cleo away from me. Made it seem like she'd chosen Cleo from all of us to be her special, bestest friend.

She invented a game called 'spying'. During class she'd make sure that all the kids who had been playing together for the last couple of weeks knew that they were not allowed to ask me (it could be someone else) to play with them next playtime. Then when I was on my own in the playground trying to pretend that I didn't want to join in anyone's games, that I didn't care at all, they'd suddenly appear behind a bench and start whispering about me. Sometimes they would call out my name and I'd turn around hopefully to hear them giggling stupidly before they ran away. Perhaps the cruellest variation of the 'spying' game was when Sofia would choose someone – often it would be Cleo – to come and sit next to me on that bench and pretend to be my friend. I would always fall for this one because it seemed so nice to have someone to talk to, someone who wanted to listen to how I felt, but of course they'd just run back to the gang and tell them everything I'd said. I would bite my lip and try and try so that they wouldn't see how much I wanted to cry, but they always knew they'd got me. Spying – perhaps it doesn't sound like much but it still hurts me when I think about it, the ways in which little girls can be horrible to each other.

Boys' cruelty was always so much more obvious. They'd kick each other or push someone over because they'd taken their football away and the teacher or helper would intervene, tell someone off, stick a plaster on the cut and by next break the boys seemed to have forgotten it. Girls' cruelty was always more subtle. If I tried telling a teacher they'd say, 'Oh, they're just being silly – I'd ignore them if I were you.' As if I'd just made it up.

If I had been able to make a wish come true and choose who would be my best friend, it wouldn't have been the lovely, cruel Sofia. It would have been Cleo. Cleo was a curious mixture of brave and fearless about some things, like speaking out if she thought a teacher was being unfair, and shy and awkward about others, like if she was praised about her work. Her stories were better than anyone else's but she seemed to be embarrassed about being clever. She had that typical English, brownish, fair hair and small, even features. At times she'd run in big bold strides and at others she'd be awkward and clumsy like someone who was pretending they were invisible. Although she could laugh and giggle as loudly as any other kid in the playground, there was something sad inside Cleo. I felt I understood her. There were times when we were good friends. Sometimes we'd both offer to do a job for the teacher at lunchtime – I loved talking to her – or she'd come round and play after school and we'd do really good make-up games or just watch telly together. I never found her boring.

But at some crucial moment just before we got to the point where other people saw us as 'special friends', she'd back off from me and be lured back by Sofia to some new subtle variation on the spying game, and Cleo would be the cruellest one. It could happen in a single day, this withdrawal, from morning play to lunch or from afternoon play to hometime. It always made me feel I'd done something wrong but I never knew what it was. I'd have imaginary conversations with Cleo where I'd ask her why she didn't want to be my friend any more and why she wanted to hurt me like this. In my imagination she'd say sorry and promise to be my best friend forever.

I know I'm making myself sound like a junior misfit but it wasn't like that all the time. I think a lot of people didn't realise how lonely I felt – well I hope so anyway. I had birthday parties and people came to them. I got invited to other people's parties, even Sofia's and Cleo's parties. It was just inside that I felt different from other kids. Friendship seemed so easy for them. Why was it so hard for me?

I developed a knack of hiding myself away but this just

resulted in me getting accused of being antisocial at primary school. At parents' evenings the teachers would say, 'We're really pleased that Libby is doing so well with her reading, Mrs Starling, but I do think it's important for her to go out and get some fresh air at playtime. It isn't good for her to be cooped up all the time reading and reading.' Of course my mum understood what it was all about and I think that she was pretty pissed off that the teachers couldn't see what was going on under their noses.

'Do you think there might be any reasons why Libby doesn't want to go out into the playground?' she'd say in her most reasonable-sounding voice, while I would wish I could disappear under the table. 'Has anyone looked to see if she's alright or anyone is picking on her? Girls do have their own ways of bullying other girls.' I could have murdered her for saying this, although she meant it for the best. At least I knew she was on my side.

My mum has always been the sort to give advice whether you want to hear it or not. She always used to say, 'You don't have to be friends with those girls, you know. There's lots of other people in school who'd love to be your friend. Why don't you ask someone like that nice Joanna to come round?' But the truth is, I didn't want to be friends with the sweet, placid, boring Joannas of this world. I wanted to be friends with Cleo and the strong, spiky ones – the kind who made my life a misery.

When I started secondary school, it felt that finally things were going to go right for me. In London, most people agonise over the school they're going to send their little darlings to. They discover Christianity because that's the school with the smartest uniform and they think it's bound to have better discipline. Or they want to send their daughters to an all-girls school so they won't be dominated by ego-maniac boys, or their sons to an all-boys school so they won't be distracted by the girls. If they're rich enough they touch Granny for a bit more cash and ship them off to private school, or they get a tutor in and cram them for a place at the last free selective-entry school, even though it's ten miles, two buses and a train journey away.

As a result of all this high-anxiety pushing and shoving, only three girls from my school went to Dupont High Co-ed School, even though it was the only school in walking distance from where most of us lived: me, Cleo, who I still wanted for my friend despite what she'd done to me, and sweet, wouldn't-harm-a-fly Joanna. It didn't have a brilliant academic reputation, but my dad felt loyal to it because it was the school he'd been to when he was young and growing up with Grandma, Granddad and Uncle Richard in the same house we live in now. He thought if it was alright for him it would be alright for me. My mum was still treating me like a baby and didn't want me going on the dreaded public transport if I didn't have to, so it was just decided. Cleo's mum was going through a really hard time. She'd just split up with Cleo's dad, and Dupont High seemed the safest choice because no-one knew where they'd be in a few months' time. And Joanna – well, Joanna just smiled about everything and nobody knew what was going on beneath that mop of light-brown curly hair.

You were allowed to choose one person you wanted in your tutor group. For the first time, they both chose me and I thought my day had come. But it didn't last for very long. It only took a term for Cleo to decide that there were other, better fish to fry. Of course it wasn't enough for her to just dump me, she had to go back to the old, primary school habit of mocking me in front of others, making me feel stupid. I knew the best response would be to laugh it off, pretend I didn't care or to do what Mum said and go for a different kind of friend, the ordinary, nice, easy-to-please sort, but I didn't know how to do it. Anyway, they seemed to be out to stop me from making new friends, at least with anyone they considered to be part of their crowd.

Once, in about the second term, I got quite close to a girl called Asfah. I liked her a lot and asked her home one day after school. At this stage Cleo had moved out of her mum's house and was living with her dad so she used to get the train along with a lot of other girls. As we were walking past the station, Cleo called out, 'Where you going, Az? Aren't you coming on the train?'

'No, I'm going home with Libby.'

'Libby – ugh! You must be joking!'

'You must be mad,' someone else shrieked. 'God, not her. How could you? You're not that desperate!' They rolled around in mock laughter as if I was some sort of contaminated creature, and I felt terrible inside. Asfah tried to laugh it off, and she even tried to give me advice on how to get along with the gang, but she never came round again and I never asked her.

For a while I lost all my confidence and went back to

my old tricks of spending dinnertime in the library or in the tutor room. It did wonders for my homework but not much for my self-esteem. This bad patch lasted until the beginning of my second year, Year 8, and then I did start to make my own friends. Trusty old Joanna, Esther and me. We weren't the most dynamic bunch in the world but I was pleased to have them to hang about with. It's not much fun being on your own.

But friendship was still a bit of a mystery to me – why people click, why they stay together. When I looked in the mirror on a good day, I didn't see anything that looked any different or any worse than other girls my age. I had the right amount of eyes, ears, arms and legs. My nose was a bit pudgy but not especially so. I had nice breasts – 34B, what girls my age were supposed to have – and long legs. I wasn't too thin or too fat. I had knobbly knees and size 7 feet, but that didn't seem any reason for not being popular. My hair did what hair was supposed to do – it was long, slightly curly and a middling sort of brown – and I was a bit spotty but what teenager isn't? I didn't know what it was I hadn't got, what magic ingredient I was missing which made others popular, and I learnt the art of pretending not to mind.

My mum with her endless stream of 'good advice' used to say when she saw me looking unhappy, 'Friendship isn't easy, love: you've got to work at it, try not to be so defensive. If one of them says something you don't agree with sometimes it's best just to be quiet.'

I knew she was right. I used to watch others nodding and fitting in, making sure they didn't stand out in the crowd. I wished I was like that. I knew that sometimes I could be a pain, butting in on other people's conversations, saying things like, 'Actually, that's not right. The vast majority of people in this country do eat meat. Only 4.5% are vegetarians and most of those are women', and they'd all turn on me and groan, 'Oh shut up, Libby.' Being quiet wasn't my style. I knew it would probably make me more friends but I couldn't be someone I wasn't.

When I got to Year 9 there was that other ingredient to complicate my life even further. Boys. Longings about boys, fantasies, dreams, being silly, hanging around after school. But very rarely did real live boys enter my life. By Year 10 most of the girls in my year had boyfriends, but not me. Of course the adults in my life tried to make me feel good about myself. Mum would say, 'Things will start to go your way, you'll see. It doesn't happen for everyone at the same time.' And Dad would say, 'A gorgeous girl like you? They'll be queuing up; I'll have to beat them away from the door.' I knew they meant well but it didn't help much. In fact it didn't help at all.

And then, of course, there was Jesse. It's funny that I've left him to the end, because at that point in my life I hardly seemed to think about anything else. Ever since Easter I'd been dying for the 16th of July to come because that was the day of our school trip to Littlehampton. The number of fantasies I'd invented about what was going to happen between me and Jesse that day would keep the film industry in ideas for years. We would be walking romantically along the beach or we'd find a lonely, quiet spot while the others would be screaming their heads off on one of the big rides. There would be us on the ghost train together with me pretending to be scared so that he would comfort me. We would be on the dodgems, laughing and being part of the crowd.

My favourite fantasy of all was the one where I got hurt – not too badly, of course – and Jesse would look after me. That's ironic when you think about what really did happen to me after that trip. Perhaps we'd be running along the pebbly beach and he'd trip me up for a laugh and I'd go crashing down and really hurt my ankle so that I couldn't even stand up properly. Jesse would be terribly upset and insist that it was all his fault. He'd sit in the ambulance with me, holding my hand, and we'd have a wonderful, clever conversation. I wouldn't cry or anything even though I was in terrible pain. Later, he'd come and visit me in my hospital bed when I was looking all pale and beautiful and tell me that he'd always really liked me and he would kiss me and . . .

At this point beyond *Just 17* romance, I wasn't exactly sure what would happen next. I'd never had a real boyfriend, just a bit of stage-one snogging at summer camp last year and a single date with Ben, the son of my mum's best friend, who I'd known since I was born. I think we only went out together because we both felt we needed to be able to say that we'd had a date. We went off to Wembley to see a rubbish film and he tried to put his arm round me but it didn't work. We both felt so silly and decided we'd be better off kicking a ball around in the back garden when he came over with his mum for Sunday lunch like we'd been doing for the past fifteen years.

19

But Jesse — Jesse was different from any boy I'd met before. It really annoyed me how much time I spent thinking about him considering I probably didn't even exist in his world. But short of a brain transplant there was very little I was able to do about it. I wasn't a complete idiot and I knew that there were loads more important things in the world to worry about (even in my own little world), but somehow knowing that didn't seem to help at all. When I woke up in the morning he was on my mind. When I walked to school I was dreaming that I was going to bump into him and say something brilliant and funny which would make him notice me for the first time. When I tried to do my homework I wrote his name a dozen times in the margin and had to throw the paper away.

I'd had lots of crushes on film stars and boys in the sixth form, the kind of boys that all the girls liked, but what I felt about Jesse was different. He'd only been at our school since the beginning of Year 10. Usually there are two sorts of kids who transfer to Upper School from other schools. There are the soft ones who've probably been bullied or have overanxious parents worried about their little darling's exam results. Then there are the hard cases who've probably been in loads of trouble in their last school and the Head has 'suggested' that a move might be a good thing. Jesse didn't seem to belong to either of these categories and I didn't know him well enough to ask him his story. He seemed to fit in really well and had already made a lot of friends in school — boys and girls. If he was sitting in the hall at lunchtime someone would always go over and just sit down at his

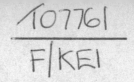

table with a slice of pizza or a baked potato and start chatting. He made it look so easy. He never seemed to have a special girlfriend, or even a particular friend, but he always had people around him.

For a kid his age, he was incredibly comfortable in his own body. He didn't go strutting around the school to show you how big he was and he didn't shuffle around trying to hide himself under layers of clothes. He just walked around in a quiet, confident way not making a great fuss about anything, just friendly and straightforward. I really liked that. He seemed to leave it to other people to stop him in the corridor or start a conversation with him. Cleo for instance. Cleo always seemed to be starting conversations with Jesse although he wasn't the kind of person she usually talked to.

He was clever in class, too. We were only in one of the same groups, maths, and he was brilliant at it. We did that system where you were supposed to get on with work individually from cards 'at your own level' and then ask the teacher for help when you'd finished a group of cards. Of course, the teacher was never actually there when you needed her — she was always helping someone else — and it was amazing who'd ask Jesse to give them a hand. He'd sit down and work with really tough kids. They'd come up to him and say, 'Jesse — you've done this matrix — giss a hand with it, will ya?' And afterwards they'd just slap him on the back and say, 'Thanks, mate' or 'Safe', and go back to their seats. He got a bit of respect for doing that and managed to escape the boffin, teacher's-pet insults.

He had a lot of friends too because he was good at sport. Everyone loves people who are good at sport. I was

21

pathetic at games and if I ever committed a crime it would be for murdering the PE teacher who said to me, 'No-one can be that uncoordinated without trying, Libby. Come on, pull yourself together and have a go.' Ugh! I hated games.

Jesse played in the Upper School football team with kids practically twice his size and ran the 100 metres pretty well. I thought he was great. I was surprised that loads of girls didn't fancy him really. I suppose if there's any accounting for taste it was because of his red hair that he wasn't more popular. Girls in our school, well some girls anyway, liked the flat-tops with big boots and jeans, and there were others who fancied the kind who went in for ultra-white trainers and expensive, casual, designer clothes. Red hair and freckles wasn't everyone's taste. But he had a wonderful smile and I knew he was the sort who could be your boyfriend and a really good friend, too. Jesse. Yes, because of him I spent even more time than usual in my own dream world.

In our school if you liked a boy and wanted to go out with him it went like this: You told a friend of yours you liked him, she told a friend of his, this friend told him and if he liked you, he'd tell this friend, who'd tell your friend, and twenty Chinese Whispers later, you'd hang around in the same place at lunchtime for a first meeting. Then, before you'd even arranged to swap phone numbers, your friends and his friends and practically the whole of Year 10 would be talking about it. Of course in my case I didn't have anyone to tell. It wasn't any use telling Esther or Joanna; they didn't know anyone who knew Jesse. And someone like Cleo – I could just imagine what she'd do with a piece of news like that. She'd already started listing all the most revolting boys in the school, the real creeps, telling me that they fancied me. Her idea of a joke. She'd love to know who I really liked. But the main reason I couldn't bear him to know was that I was scared that he'd just laugh and say, 'Oh, Libby. Yeah, she's alright, I suppose, but I wouldn't wanna go out with her.' I couldn't bear just being invisible to him.

And tomorrow was the Year 10 summer trip to Littlehampton. Sun, if we were lucky (but the weather forecast was good), sea, sand (well pebble beach actually) and fun fair. Not quite on the Disneyland scale but pretty good fun. And no teachers. They usually dropped us off on the beach, told us what time to meet up again and disappeared off to the pub for the next five hours.

It's hard looking back and seeing what was important to me then. It isn't that I don't still worry about all these things – friends, boys, clothes, family (Mum!), exams, the future. It's just that I have a whole new lot of things to think about, new priorities. Things I could never have imagined would be important to me.

Chapter Two
Becoming Ill

It was still dark when I woke up. Not pitch-black dark but the kind of grey that meant it was not quite dawn. I felt awful, really awful. Worse than the time at Esther's house when someone had produced a bottle of Southern Comfort and I spent the next two days throwing up.

I wanted to open my eyes to see the luminous numbers on my alarm clock because I wanted it to be day but it felt like they had weights on them. How could eyelids feel so heavy? I needed to get up and be sick but my body wouldn't move. I needed a pee. I must have drifted back into sleep because I dreamt horrible dreams. Short dreams, each one nearly the same, with weird creatures looking down and pointing at me. I carried on dreaming the same dream for months.

'Get up, you lazy lump, it's nearly eight o'clock. Mum says you're going to be really really late and what did you bring me back from the seaside?' Robbie's sweet high voice sounded as if he was calling me from a long way off, but he was climbing into my bed, trying to wrap his bony little seven-year-old body under my duvet. It was an old game we played. He'd come into my room asking me loads and loads of questions, usually things about himself like 'What's my name?' Or 'What colour are my pyjamas?' And I'd ignore him and pretend to be asleep. Then he'd gently prise open my eyes one at a time and I'd act as if I was really surprised to see him and say, 'Who is this completely strange boy in my bed? Where do you live? Do you have a mummy and daddy? Do you have a big sister?' All the time pretending to be astonished that he seemed to know me and my family and even claimed that he lived in the same house as me.

After a few minutes he'd be shouting, 'You do know me, you do, you're my sister Libby!' It would be a fine line between pleasure and hysteria until I gave in. I'd open my eyes really wide as if I'd just remembered who he was.

'Oh yes, I have met you somewhere before but I can't really remember. Now where was it?' By this time he'd be jumping up and down on me nearly going crazy until I'd give in and hug him tight saying, 'You're Robert Richard Starling aged seven and you're my brother and I'm Elizabeth Alice Starling aged fifteen and I'm your sister and we both live at 41 Crowndale Avenue, London NW9.' Then he'd laugh and shout with joy until I'd have to chuck him out.

Sometimes, now that I was older, I minded him coming in like this, but usually it was in these early mornings that he was still my completely sweet little brother. Later on he'd be irritating, complaining to Mum about how I wasn't fair and wouldn't let him play with my things and he'd get Mum on his side.

'Libby, he's only a baby. Can't you just let him into your room for a little while?' A baby!? He was pretty big for a baby and he certainly knew how to get his own way.

Still, this was 'our time' in the morning and usually I enjoyed our little game. But this morning I couldn't bear him near me. I wanted to tell him that he needed to get off the bed because it was hurting me and that I'd bought him a disgusting set of dayglo-coloured sugar false teeth from Littlehampton which he would love and Mum would detest but I couldn't make my mouth move. My tongue felt enormous as if it was taking up all the space in my head, and my whole body felt so peculiar.

'I'm getting in now,' Robbie said, wriggling and wriggling under the covers.

'Please,' I whispered. 'Don't Rob, please. Get Mum for me. Now.'

Robbie stopped still and leant up on one elbow, looking at me. He sensed that something was different.

'Please,' I said again, and this time he jumped up and ran downstairs calling, 'Mummy, come quick, come now.' Then she was there by my bed.

'What's the matter, darling?'

'Mum – Mummy, I . . .'.

She looked worried suddenly as if she sensed this wasn't an ordinary cold or period pains.

'Tell me where it hurts, tell me how you feel.'

'I don't know . . . it's, it's everywhere. It hurts, I feel weird.' It was only as I said this that I realised how very strange I did feel. It was as if someone had injected me with a metal liquid which had flowed down my veins in the night without me knowing, making my whole body heavy. So heavy.

'Are you hot? Try to sit up a bit.' Her soft, familiar hand stroked my hair back from my forehead like she'd done all my life. It felt good.

'Do you feel sick?' I nodded pathetically and felt tears stupidly come into my eyes.

'Do you want to be sick?' I nodded again. She had to know that I needed to be sick now but I couldn't move. Couldn't even sit up.

'I'll go and get a bucket.'

'Mum,' I said weakly.

'Okay. Robert, be a darling and go and fetch me the brown plastic bucket from the bathroom.'

I was sick and then I was sick again all through that first long day. Each time I thought I'll be better now, but I wasn't.

'What's the matter with Libby, Mum?' Robbie said loudly.

'Just go downstairs for a minute please, love. I'll be down soon.'

'Why Mum? Can't I stay here and watch? I'll be very quiet. It's a funny smell, isn't it, puke? Sick I mean.' He explained in case we hadn't understood.

'Robbie – go downstairs now and wait.'

'But Mum, Libby bought me a present from the seaside. Can I just ask her where it is? I know it's here somewhere.'

'Robert,' Mum said quietly but with ice in her voice. 'Downstairs. Now.'

I don't remember all that much about that day. Robbie must have got to school somehow but I don't remember Mum leaving me. She kept trying to make me drink water but every time I swallowed a drop, I was sick again. Usually if I said I was ill, Mum seemed to think that I was just making it up. She'd ask me what she thought were subtle questions like 'What lessons have you got today?' or 'Did you have a row with anyone yesterday?' to try to establish what psychological reasons I might have for wanting to bunk school. Unless I was coughing and sneezing all over the place or covered in spots she'd say, 'I think you'll be better once you're in school. It'll probably clear up by midday.' Thanks a lot Mum.

Today she didn't say anything like that. She was just there, sponging me down when I felt boiling hot and, ten minutes later when I was shivering and my teeth were rattling, wrapping me up tightly in my duvet to get warm again. I had terrible pains in my stomach and my head. It was like someone had put an iron circle around my head and was tightening it and tightening it.

Later that morning she called the doctor. I could hear her on the phone in the next room.

'It's a bit worrying. I've never seen her like this before. She can't keep anything down and she's running a really high temperature; one minute she's in a cold sweat and the next minute she's like fire. She's got terrible stomach-ache .... Well, yes, I'm trying to make her drink but it's hard because she just keeps throwing up .... It's a kind of greenish colour .... Headache? Yes, she has, it's really hurting her. I've tried giving her some paracetamol but she can't keep anything down .... No, she hasn't complained of feeling ill before. She was on a school trip yesterday — to Littlehampton. I'm not sure there's any point in asking her what she ate. She hardly seems to be able to hear me, she's obviously feeling terrible . . . . I'm sorry. She isn't well enough to come to you. Her legs feel all numb and heavy. I've tried rubbing them to bring the feeling back but she can't bear me touching them. I don't like to bother you but I've never seen her like this before. I'd be really grateful if you could come and see her . . . . Okay, about twelve then. Thanks very much.'

By the time the doctor did come Mum had stopped asking if I'd like something to eat or drink and was just sitting by my bed watching me. This in itself was peculiar. Usually if I wasn't well and she had to stay at home with me, she'd take the opportunity to wash the curtains or catch up on her phone calls and you'd hardly see her all day. Today she just sat looking at me and didn't move until she heard the bell.

The doctor was new to the practice and young. He was tall and thin with rimless specs. He looked like everyone's idea of a maths teacher. Without speaking to me he took my temperature then my pulse, holding my wrist with one hand and looking at his watch with the other. Then he took my blood pressure. I couldn't bear the feeling of the black rubber band getting tighter and tighter around my arm. It was only after he'd done all this that he began to ask questions — about my stomach and my head and my limbs. Everything seemed to hurt me but I hardly had the strength to tell him this.

'When did you start feeling ill, Libby? Were you unwell yesterday?' Was I? Yesterday seemed years ago. I'd felt a bit sick on the coach going there but that could have been because of the nervous state I'd got myself into. And I'd felt a bit sick on the way back but that wasn't surprising considering how much rubbish I'd eaten during the day and everything that had happened.

'Can you remember what you ate?'

My mum answered for me. 'She had some cereal and milk for breakfast before she went and then when she came home, she said she didn't feel hungry and just had one of those soups you make in a mug. Do you think it's food poisoning?'

'I don't really know. We'll have to try and work through all the possibilities, Mrs Starling. She's certainly not at all well. Can you tell us what you ate during the day, Libby?'

What hadn't I eaten? Ice-creams, crisps, sweets and that fresh-made doughnut Jesse had bought me from the van on the sea front after we came out of the water. I'd saved the little greaseproof paper bag it came in, knowing it was silly but thinking that I'd never, never throw it away. It must still be in the pocket of my denim jacket.

'Did you eat any seafood at all? Prawns, scampi, mussels?' I'd bought some fish and chips at lunchtime but it was disgusting – the batter the colour of wet cardboard and the fish inside it slimy and grey. I'd just tasted it and thrown it in the bin. Could that one bite have made me so ill?

'She must have gone for a swim at some time,' said Mum. 'Because her towel was damp. Do you think she's caught a bad cold?'

'Did you go to a swimming pool, Libby?' asked the

doctor, leaning towards me as if the reason I was so slow in answering his questions was because I couldn't hear him. 'Or did you swim in the sea?'

We'd been in the sea, all of us – Cleo, Esther and Joanna – and Jesse.

'Was it just a paddle or did you go right under?' In my head I could see what had happened yesterday but I couldn't find a way to say the words out loud. Every bit of my head hurt – my ears, my eyes, my jaw, even my teeth seemed to ache and down the right side piercing into my eye, a hot gnawing pain like something had heated up and expanded inside my brain.

'Was there anything funny in the sea that you saw – any seaweed or algae?'

We'd been playing water handball, boys against girls. I'd been pleased they'd asked me to join in, Cleo and her gang, I mean. It was hot and sunny, the teachers had disappeared off somewhere. I'd put my costume on underneath, 'just in case'. We were jumping up, shouting, mucking about. I knew I'd never catch it, I'm hopeless at things like that, but I'd jumped around screaming 'Throw it here, throw it here,' like everyone else did. By some miracle the ball had come in my direction and I'd put my arms up in the air and actually caught it. Then, in a second, Jesse was diving down under the water, catching my legs, pulling me down with him.

For a minute I thought I was going to drown. I came up coughing and choking, my nose and mouth and chest full of sea water.

'Who d'ya think you are, Jesse? Jonah Lomu or

31

something? It's supposed to be water play, not a scrum half. Or are you trying to get her swimming costume off, you dirty bastard?' I couldn't seem to be cool about anything. I must have looked a complete idiot, coughing and coughing until my eyes were streaming and my nose running.

'God, I'm sorry, are you alright?' Jesse asked. I'd have said something clever and funny if only I'd been able to breathe. 'Do you want a pat on the back? No better not, it'd probably just make things worse. I'm really sorry, I thought it would be alright.'

That made me feel even worse. 'I thought it would be alright.' Meaning, I thought you were like everyone else and could take going under the water for a few seconds. Meanwhile, Jesse was still holding the ball.

'Jesse. C'mon you idiot – throw us the ball,' everyone shouted. 'Libby, you drowned or what?'

'Chuck us the ball.'

'I'll just get out for a minute, I think. I'll be alright in a second,' I said, feeling stupid and embarrassed. I waded back to the beach, half walking, half swimming, trying not to cough or look too stupid, but before I reached the edge, Jesse was there by my side.

'I'm really sorry Libby – are you okay now?' I nodded. 'Do you want a drink or something? That'd make that sea-water taste go away. It's horrible I know, when the water goes up your nose before it gets in your mouth.'

'Yes thanks,' I nodded, afraid that if I spoke I'd splutter some more.

'What do you want – Coke, Fanta? I'll get it for you.'

'I'll come with you,' I said. He picked up his money

from one of the poor kids who'd been deputised to sit there taking care of everyone else's things and we put our T-shirts and boots on and wandered along the concrete promenade. That's where he bought me the drink and the doughnut from a funny little stall like an old caravan which had a sign saying, 'Cold Drinks, Earl Grey Tea Served in the Pot, Freshly Fried Doughnuts Hot and Delicious'. He didn't ask me if I wanted one; he bought two and handed me one in the little square paper bag which I kept in my hand until we got back.

Everyone else came out of the sea not long after that, but it felt like we talked a lot. I don't know what we talked about. School I suppose. He asked me if I was friends with Cleo and I asked him where he lived. Then suddenly we were surrounded by people laughing and shouting, flinging towels about.

'Libby, Libby, can you hear me? Open your eyes a second.' The doctor's voice and Mum's worried face brought me back to the bedroom again.

'Try to answer the doctor, darling, even if it's just nodding.'

'Tell me about the sea, Libby. What did you do after you'd been swimming? Did you come home in your wet costume?' I shook my head.

It had been a beautiful hot afternoon and we sat about on the beach until the sun had dried us off. I'd hoped Jesse would stick around for a bit but some of the boys pulled him up for a game of football and they were soon followed by Cleo, Kelly, Bea and the rest of them.

'Don't be so sexist, you lot. Football is a girls' game too.'
As Jesse went to join them, he turned round and smiled.

'Bye Libby, thanks.'

It was a familiar feeling for me. Wanting to join in, not understanding why I'd been left out, not knowing how to become a part of the in crowd. I wandered off to find Joanna and Esther, who seemed neither pleased nor reluctant to see me. We chatted for a bit and then wandered back to where the coach was waiting for us.

'Best not to be too late,' said Esther sensibly. 'Otherwise we may not get a good seat.'

'Have you been to the toilet today, Libby?' asked the doctor. I shook my head again.

'Do you want to go?' I didn't know. I felt too ill to think about it. It was weird not to know whether you needed to have a pee or not.

'Okay. Let's just have a quick look at your chest. Can you sit up for me please?' Mum helped me to sit up and pulled up my nightie. I could feel the cold stethoscope on the top of my back. I had to concentrate hard on the doctor's instructions.

'Breathe in now. Good. Breathe out. Little cough. Good. Breathe in again – out now. Good girl.' As the stethoscope moved further down my back, it stopped feeling so cold.

'Okay, that's it. It doesn't sound too bad.' He put my nightie back down again.

'Okay, you can lie down again if you feel more comfortable.'

'What do you think it is?' asked Mum when it became

clear that the doctor wasn't going to ask me any more questions.

'I know it's not very helpful, Mrs Starling, but it's hard to be sure at the moment. There isn't any point in giving her anything until I'm a bit more certain what it could be. We'll have to keep a careful eye on her and I'll probably come and do a few blood tests tomorrow. Just try to keep the liquids up; that will help her go to the toilet regularly. Try to keep her cool to get the temperature down a bit and give her some paracetamol for the pain. Give me a call if you're worried.'

During the afternoon I started to feel a bit better. I stopped being sick and even managed a bit of Heinz tomato soup, our family's solution to all problems, mental or physical. I still felt funny and achy but definitely more human. Mum had arranged for someone to bring Robbie home from school and I gave him his present – an enormous set of boiled-sugar false teeth in luminous pink and white which, as predicted, delighted him and appalled Mum. I persuaded her that I wasn't going to die in front of her eyes and with some relief, she'd gone downstairs to start cooking. I could hear the radio in the kitchen playing the six o'clock news and Robbie in the front room talking to himself.

I tried to recapture my feelings about yesterday – walking along with Jesse, talking, just the two of us. He'd nearly held my hand, I was sure if I'd been more confident perhaps I could have done it first. Had he purposely pushed me under the water as a way of getting to know me? I wished I could just think about this bit of the day and not the part where Jesse, Luke and Jason with

Cleo, Kelly and some others had all walked towards the coach, arm in arm, singing and laughing, and pushed past us all to grab the back seat. I thought I saw Jesse turn round and look at me but who knows what that look was supposed to say? Who knows if I'd even imagined it?

I must have drifted off to sleep because I woke in terror – the sight of all those weird creatures with distorted, ugly faces like gargoyles still alive in my mind. I felt terribly sick and the pains in my head and down my back were worse than they'd been before. I called weakly for Mum but she was downstairs in her own space, chopping onions and mushrooms, putting on pots of boiling water. I knew that I had to get up and go to the bathroom. My head felt twenty times worse as I sat up. It felt like there were burning wires inside my brain. Waves of sickness came over me but I was determined to get to the bathroom. My legs felt so heavy. When I tried to stand and walk it felt like there was nothing to hold me up. Nothing.

I must have fallen with a terrible crash because within seconds there was Dad who'd just come through the door, then Mum, then Robbie.

'What happened?' Dad asked, then, stupidly, 'are you alright?'

'Libby. Libby. Libby,' said Robbie in a little scared voice.

'Go downstairs, love. Libby's just fallen over, she'll be alright. Someone will be down in a minute.' Dad's voice sounded as calm and even as always. He lifted me up as if I was still a baby and put me back to bed.

I don't quite remember what happened to the rest of the evening. Mum didn't leave me again. Robbie was taken off somewhere. The doctor came back, felt my head and took my pulse again. Then he asked me about my legs but I didn't know how to answer his questions.

'Can you feel this, Libby? Close your eyes and tell me where you can feel the pin.' It felt like he was trying to reach me through layers of material. I could feel him but the sensation was vague and distant.

Then everything seemed to change. People were moving in and out of the room. Everyone looked anxious and busy. It was Mum who finally remembered that no one had spoken to me.

'The doctor thinks it's for the best if we take you to the hospital now,' she said as if she was explaining why I needed to wear gloves on a cold day. 'They're going to do some tests and find out what's really the matter.' Her voice said one thing; her face said another. My eyes filled with tears. Perhaps I'd been pretending I was worse than I really was just to get attention. I tried to convince her.

'I'm feeling a bit better now. I don't feel so sick. Couldn't we leave it for a bit? I'll probably be better tomorrow. I must've eaten something.'

'No, love, we need to get you to the hospital so they can find out what it is and give you the right medicine.'

'Why can't I take the medicine here?'

'They need to do tests we can't do at home and they might have to give you medicine through a drip.'

'Why?'

'So that it gets into your system quicker.'

'What's the matter with me?'

'I don't know love,' said Mum. 'I hope we'll soon find out.'

I was going to say that I needed to go to school

tomorrow or find a hundred reasons why I couldn't go but then they were there. A man and a woman, both big people in enormous uniforms. They were lifting me onto a white stretcher. I was terrified.

'Mum — Mummy. Don't let me go. Let me stay here.' I was like a baby again.

'I'm coming with you. I won't leave you alone, I promise.'

'What about Dad?'

'He needs to stay with Robbie. He'll come and see you tomorrow.'

It was dark outside. They wrapped me in a large, white, cotton blanket, like a baby's blanket, and lifted me into the back of the ambulance. Then, just as they were about to shut the ambulance doors, I could hear Robbie's urgent, piping voice through the dark night air.

'Libby, where's Libby? I want to give her this, she needs this.'

Dad must have lifted him up because there he was in his pale-blue spotty pyjamas and bare feet, with his hair sticking up.

'You have Morris, he'll make you feel better when you feel sad. I know he will,' and he threw his beloved toy into the back of the ambulance. Morris was a brown-and-white toy rabbit with bare patches where Robbie'd hugged all the fur off and with a little, worn, red felt waistcoat which Mum had made to try and save it from falling apart completely. Robbie had taken it to bed with him every night since Gran had given it to him for his second birthday.

'Thank you,' I managed to say and made a kiss with my

38

mouth for him. I knew I loved Robbie more than I'd ever done before. I was sorry for all the times I'd been cross and impatient with him.

Then, with a sudden, painful jerk we were off. The sirens sounded with a loud, juddering noise and we seemed to be roaring through the streets. Mum was there holding my hand but I felt scared and alone.

Chapter Three
Hospital

The next few weeks aren't easy to describe. I do remember things but not in any logical order. I can't say that the first day I was here this happened and then in the second week that happened. Everything is confused and muddled. Odd incidents stand out clearly in my mind but I don't know which of them happened first. I could hardly tell day from night. People came and went, mostly people I didn't know. They spoke to me, poked and prodded at my body, whispered about me from the end of my bed and then went away again. Then there were the people I did know – Mum, Dad, Grandma and Granddad and once, Robbie. Whenever I opened my eyes someone who loved me would be sitting there, holding my hand, hardly saying anything.

Mostly what I remember is that every bit of me seemed to hurt. My head ached, my back hurt, my eyes were hot and sore all the time. When I opened them, everything seemed fuzzy and distant. I didn't care about what was going on outside my own enclosed world of pain and confusion. The worst thing was the nausea. Waves of pain would roll up from my stomach round my body and I would feel so sick. That must be the worst thing in the whole world, retching and retching and nothing to bring up. I had no energy, no will to do anything. It felt like the old me, the Libby I had once known had disappeared. I didn't know who I was anymore.

I was weaker than a baby. When Robbie was a baby, when he was just born, he would open his mouth and you would hear his cries down the road. They would cut right through whatever you were doing and everyone would rush to see what he needed. He'd wave his arms and his legs in the air and with his hand he could grip onto your finger so tightly, you'd have to prise him off, one tiny finger at a time. I didn't even have the energy of a baby. Someone seemed to have attached lead weights to my body. I was frightened and pathetic; I'd forgotten how to make a noise, how to make demands.

There was nearly always someone there in the day but at night I was alone in the long dark ward with curious noises from other patients and the occasional click clack of nurses walking up and down. Then the horrible, half-waking dream would come back to me. In the dream I was as ill as I was in real life, lying in the same bed in the same hospital. All around my bed looking down at me were grotesque creatures with crimson shiny eyes like marbles and hideous, scornful expressions. They leaned over my bed pointing at me and laughing, a nasty high-pitched scream. The ones nearest me were little but they got bigger and bigger. The creature at the end of my bed had long, long arms. When he pointed at me, his finger practically reached my nose. I thought I would die if it touched me. I couldn't call out for help. Somehow my voice was trapped in my throat. I couldn't move. I wanted to call out to one of the nurses to come and touch me. If someone would come close or speak to me, just hold my hand, I would feel them touching me and know that I was real. I had to fight off these creatures to keep myself alive.

I would try reciting things in my head – lists of facts about myself. My name is Libby Alice Starling. I live at 41 Crowndale Avenue, Kingsbury, London NW9. I am fifteen years old. My mum is called Claire and she is forty years old. My dad is called Michael, but everyone calls him Mike; he is forty-one years old. My little brother is called Robbie; he is seven years old. My grandma's name is Eva Starling. My granddad's name is Daniel Starling. They live in a flat above the shop in West Hampstead where we used to live. I go to Dupont High School . . . . And so on. It was as if by listing all the things in my life, I could make the creatures smaller until they nearly disappeared. I could become myself again.

In the day, doctors and nurses came and went, doing things to my body. They would wash me, roll me over into a different position, take blood, help me to have a pee, change the sheets. I couldn't really tell one from another. Most of the time I couldn't even remember if I'd seen them before but they all talked to me in the same bright, jolly tone which suggested that they knew me very well.

Every morning, someone in a white tunic with navy blue round the edges and blue trousers would come and roll the bedclothes back and work on me. They would stretch my legs, move my knees up and down, bend my feet backwards and forwards and wriggle my toes. Usually they did it without saying anything to me as if I was a large lump of Playdoh that they needed to keep warm in case they wanted to make something with it in a few days' time. These were the physiotherapists – physios, who would prove to be a big part of my world over the next few months.

There was a particular one who was around a lot in those first few horrible weeks. Her name was Trudy. She had a nice face and dark curly hair. Trudy – I liked that name; it sounded comforting, like something out of a children's story-book. She was the only one who always spoke to me, telling me what she was going to do.

'Am I hurting you?' she'd ask, holding the sole of my foot against her stomach and moving each leg smoothly towards me and away again as if we were practising rowing techniques.

'Did it hurt me?' It seemed an easy enough question. How could I not know the answer? Sometimes I could feel sharp pains down my leg as if someone had put razor blades inside me. At other times, there was only the merest tingle. It was like someone else's legs had accidentally been attached to my body so that it was a stranger's legs Trudy was moving up and down. There was a vague tingling feeling like an electrical impulse which meant there must be some connection with me, but nothing more. If I shut my eyes, I'm not sure whether I would even have known what she was doing to my body. My eyes would fill with tears.

'Don't worry love,' she'd say kindly. 'You're probably a bit numb from all this lying still. The feeling will come back once you're up and walking again.'

I couldn't imagine being up and walking. I couldn't imagine being better again. My head, however sore and aching it was, definitely belonged to me. The top half of my body was mine and so was my heaving, gut-wrenching stomach. My arms? They seemed to be part of my body. I could move my shoulders a bit and use my elbows to get into a more comfortable position. My hands looked just like they used to, and I could give a rather feeble wave when I saw someone coming to see me. I could wiggle my fingers and hold a cup to drink even though I didn't seem to have a lot of strength in them. But my legs and my feet. They just didn't seem to belong to me at all.

Every day Mum or Dad would come to see me; quite often they'd both be there together. Sometimes it would be my grandma and a couple of times my mum's best friend, Joyce. Being ill means that you only ever think of yourself, so I didn't stop to wonder how they managed to get time off work or who was looking after Robbie. I just expected someone to be there looking out for me; I needed them to be there. I especially needed my mum. I liked finding her there when I opened my eyes. Even if she was reading or doing some sewing, she'd look up and smile at me as if she could sense when I needed her. She still looked the same in her neat, bright clothes and her silver earrings but her smile was different and her eyes were sad and worried. She'd try to talk to me in a happy way but her face had a sort of screwed-up, concentrated look about it as if she was trying to keep something inside her.

My dad was just like he always is. You can never tell from his expression whether he's sad or happy because the bottom half of his face is always smiling and cheerful as if he's just thought of a really good joke that he's about to tell you, but his eyes have got a kind of turned-down-in-the-corner sad look about them like a dog who had a really delicious bone but can't remember where he put it. Dad would sit by my bed and try to tell me funny things that Robbie had done or cheer me up by telling me stories about things that had happened at his school.

My dad was a CDT teacher – craft design and technology. 'What they used to call woodwork and metalwork in my day.' He'd only trained to be a teacher a couple of years ago and we were all proud of him really. 'You see, you *can* teach an old dog new tricks,' was one of his favourite lines, although he's only just over forty-one which isn't *that* old. And then he'd roll on the carpet panting with his legs and arms sticking up in the air waiting to have his stomach tickled. He could be a real idiot, my dad, but you couldn't help laughing.

But I'm losing track here. I suppose that's because I can't remember all that much about those early days in hospital. I've had to piece things together from hearing other people talking about that 'terrible time when we were all so worried about you'. It felt like I was going to

45

be ill forever and it was scary not knowing what was happening to me or what all these people in uniforms and white coats were doing to me. Perhaps they thought I was too ill to understand. Perhaps I was. I know that they were doing their best and trying to protect me, but I wish that someone had told me why they were doing these endless painful things to my body.

I must have had a million blood tests. It didn't hurt all that much but I hated them coming and I couldn't stop myself from watching another syringe filling with my sticky, dark red blood. Everything they did to me seemed to involve some kind of prodding or pulling me about. I couldn't take the pills because I couldn't swallow and even if I did manage it I'd just chuck them up again so that was another reason to roll me over and stick something in my bum.

Of all the things that happened to me in those first few weeks the lumbar puncture was the worst. This memory is a nightmare which I don't think will ever go away. One morning, two nurses and two men I'd never seen before came and lifted me gently on to a trolley. It was early in the morning, too early for Mum and Dad to be at the hospital. The nurse told me the name of the thing they were going to do to me, but I didn't know what it meant. No-one said, 'Don't worry, this won't hurt,' like they always did before a blood test – and at least that was honest of them, because it hurt like hell. I wanted to ask them to wait until Mum or Dad came but I couldn't seem to make my mouth say anything. My heart was banging away in my chest, not like it does when you've run a race but like it feels when a Head of Year comes to get you out of a classroom and you know you're going to be in a lot of trouble.

They pushed me down the corridor. It seemed like we went a long way away, but it's hard to judge distances when all you can see is the fluorescent light strips on the ceiling. The two nurses were talking about someone they really seemed to hate.

'I don't care if I never see her again. If you want my opinion, I think she's a right cow.'

'Yeah, but he's no better, is he? If I was stuck with someone like him, I'd run away too.'

'Some people think she's pretty, but I don't. She's got a really hard face. And another thing, I'd never leave one of my kids no matter how much I hated my old man.'

It took me until we got to the room at the end of the corridor to realise they weren't talking about real people but Cindy and Ian from the telly.

The doctor's eyes smiled at me. That's all I could see because he had a white mask on, covering his mouth and nose. Like everyone else in the hospital he knew who I was, but I didn't know if I'd ever seen him before. I was moved again on to another bed and all the time I was terrified that I was going to throw up all over them even though I knew I didn't have anything in my stomach. Then it started. They knew that it hurt me to move but I was curled up into a ball like a baby in the womb.

'We have to get you into this position so that we can get at your spinal cord properly,' the doctor said. I imagined my spinal cord like one of those translucent green plastic tubes they make skipping ropes out of, the sort that manages to be stiff and bendy at the same time. I didn't exactly know what the spinal cord was but I knew it was important. Christopher Reeve, the actor who played Superman, had broken his spinal cord falling off his horse and it had been all over the papers that he would never walk again. Was this what they thought had happened to me without me knowing about it?

Before I had time to think about this properly, the doctor started trying to get the needle in. It's impossible to find words to describe pain like this. Agony, excruciating, sore, sharp, relentless don't begin to describe what it felt like. I suppose if you think about your spinal cord as being the place which is the centre of all the sensations and imagine your nerves spreading like narrow rivers on a map right round your body, down to the tips of your fingers, up to the top of your head, round your eyeballs and then try to imagine that someone put a bomb or an electric impulse in that centre so it exploded through your whole body – then that's what it felt like when the doctor put that needle in my spine.

He told me it wasn't supposed to feel like that – that the first injection was supposed to have made everything go numb. Then he told me that it was very difficult to get it just right and that he would have to try again. I think he said there wasn't a big enough gap between my vertebrae. Each time it hurt more. I tried to be brave and not make a noise but I couldn't stop myself. By the third time he attempted to get the needle in I was screaming and screaming.

'Please, please don't hurt me anymore. Don't do it anymore.'

'I'm sorry,' said the young doctor, sounding as if he really was sorry. 'Just lie really still, Libby. I've got to do this; it's really important.'

'You're making me hurt everywhere, I can't bear it. Please, please don't do it again,' I begged. 'Do it again tomorrow. You can try again tomorrow.'

'Just this one last time, I promise,' he said without much conviction in his voice. 'If you keep really still we'll get it in properly this time.'

'It hurts everywhere. Please stop,' I said, desperately trying to sit up.

'You must lie still, otherwise you'll just make it worse. I'm going to put in a bit more anaesthetic. You'll just feel that first needle a little bit and then you'll go numb. You'll probably have a nasty headache when it's over.' I knew I had no power to make him do what I wanted. He must have known he was lying to me when he said it would only hurt when he put the needle in.

The nurse who had been worried about Cindy's shortcomings held my hand and patted my arm. She looked as if she was about to burst into tears too.

'Oh God. Please don't, please stop!' It felt like a bomb had been detonated inside me. The pain reverberated through every bit of my body. My head was splitting open with hot pain. 'Mum!' I screamed. 'Mum – where are you?'

'Calm down now, love. Just lie still for a few minutes, then we'll take you back to the ward.' Calm down! How dare they tell me to calm down after what I've just been through. My head still hurt like hell but the pain in my body was slowly beginning to ebb away and as it did I realised how sick I felt.

'Please,' I said faintly, trying to move my head a bit. I wanted to tell them to fetch something for me to throw up in.

'Just lie still, there's a good girl. You'll begin to feel better in a few minutes,' the doctor said. The next two things happened simultaneously. I retched and out came a stream of bilious green vomit straight over the doctor's hand and arm, and my mother burst through the door.

'Where is she?'

'Mrs Starling, it's best if you . . .'

'What are you doing to her?!' my mum screamed. This was angrier than she'd been at the worst offence I'd ever committed at home.

'We've just done a lumbar puncture, as Dr Singleton told you yesterday,' the doctor said. 'I'm afraid it was a bit awkward but . . .'

My mum didn't let him finish. 'You had no right to take her off without one of her parents being with her. They told me yesterday they'd let one of us come in with her. They didn't say you were going to do it today. Why did you have to do it so early?'

'Well, Dr Singleton is off at a conference,' the doctor said nervously. 'And he thought it was important to get the sample of spinal fluid as quickly as possible, so that we can see whether there's any infection in the central nervous system. We need to eliminate the possibility of meningitis.' I could see my mum was about to give him another mouthful but then she caught sight of me.

'Oh, Libby darling, you poor thing.' I'd hardly ever seen my mum cry but this was one of the few times she did. A mixture of rage and panic, I think. She'd arrived on the ward a bit later than she'd meant to – I don't know what kept her but she was probably pretty exhausted herself. When she found that my bed was empty, she had asked the first nurse she saw but they hadn't known where I was. Then she'd heard my screams. You could probably hear them all over the hospital.

'It's alright, sweetheart, I'm here now.' She spoke to me in the voice she sometimes talked to Robbie in, but that felt okay. I was glad she was there. My head still felt like it was clamped in a vice but I wasn't on my own anymore.

I think that I had only been in hospital for a few days when that happened. It still gives me the heebie-jeebies to think about it, but I remember it as an isolated incident in an otherwise foggy and confused time – like the way an English teacher once explained haiku poetry to us.

'Imagine that everything is completely dark,' she'd said. 'Outside the window there is a flash of bright light and suddenly everything is absolutely clear, but only for an instant. That's what I want you to do when you write these short poems. Use your words to make an image or a feeling that's completely clear even if all around it is darkness.'

I remember Robbie's visit like that too. I don't know how long I'd been in hospital, perhaps a week. They'd stopped asking me whether I was hungry because the answer was always no. They'd stopped bringing me plates of food that went cold before someone took them away.

It must have been just before they started to feed me through the tube they put up my nose and all the way down my stomach. Robbie didn't come to see me while I had that; I suppose they thought it might scare him. At that time I just had a drip feeding liquid into me – glucose or saline or something to make sure that I didn't dry out completely.

Robbie came one afternoon with Grandma. He was wearing a blue-and-red striped T-shirt and a pair of blue shorts. He looked so sweet. He carried a little old-fashioned brown suitcase which had belonged to Granddad, the sort with silver clips which you press with two fingers on the side and then they fly open. He was crazy about that suitcase.

'I've brought lots of things for you,' he said, trying hard not to show his excitement – they must have told him to talk quietly. He pulled them out one by one. He'd brought me a pencil with a mongoose clip on the top, a black-and-white rubber shaped like a panda, a toy red-and-yellow stethoscope from his medicine kit and his prize gift – the clock he'd had for Christmas. It was a powder-blue plastic bed and when the alarm went off, a pig sat up and went 'oink'. It was true, I'd been envious of it when he'd got it – even though I knew I wasn't supposed to want things like that.

'Thanks Robbie,' I said, wishing I felt strong enough to sit up and look at them properly.

'What's that?' he said, pointing to the drip.

'It's just something to make sure Libby keeps her strength up, because she's not feeling hungry at the moment,' Grandma explained. He followed the line from the stand, up to the clear bag of liquid and then down my arm to the place where the square white plaster covered the needle, which fed the liquid into me.

'Poor Libby's hand,' Robbie said in a tight little voice. And then, trying to imitate Dad, 'Does it hurt you? Never mind, I'll soon make it good again.' And then he bent down and kissed it to make it better.

There's one other thing I can remember. It wasn't really scary or sad but just weird. I know now that it was an MRI scan. I think they were doing it to look at my brain but perhaps I haven't remembered that right. I'd practically stopped speaking by this time – I certainly wasn't saying anything sensible, so perhaps they thought they'd be able to tell whether I was going to be permanently brain damaged.

At the time it seemed like something out of a science fiction movie. Everything was white. The walls, the ceiling, the uniforms, the machines. I was lying on a bed and my head – all of me, in fact – was moving backwards into an incredibly narrow white tunnel. There was a little mirror above me and when I opened my eyes, I saw them staring back at me, less than two inches from my nose. I don't know whether there were really flashing lights but I remember a weird clunking sound with an uneven beat as if drummers were tapping on the walls of the tunnel. I was completely engulfed in this round, enclosed world. I suppose I should have been freaked out by it but somehow it seemed a safe and calm place, as if I was dreaming. I felt a strange, rested happiness there.

* * *

I don't remember a particular time when I began to feel better; perhaps it was a few weeks. My recovery certainly wasn't like in those old-fashioned story-books I used to read, where the character has a terrible fever that 'turns' in the night and instead of dying they make a complete recovery. It was slower and more confused than that. I started being aware of when it was night and when it was day. I began to look forward to Mum and Dad coming to visit each morning, and I could recognise the doctors and nurses who I'd seen before. I still felt tired all the time and I couldn't concentrate on anything for long, but my brain began to de-fog and the world almost began to make sense to me again.

Chapter Four
When Will I Go Home?

I was in a ward of about ten or twelve beds and I was at least fifty years younger than the next youngest patient there. They'd taken the tube out of my nose and were bringing me things to eat again, although I still didn't feel hungry. Grandma used to bring me flasks of her special chicken soup and I'd try to eat a few mouthfuls just to please her, but I still felt that horrible vague sickness all the time. Every day loads of people came to see me – the physios, the nurses who continued to take more blood and give me injections or take me down to the radiography department for X-rays and scans, and the doctors who came with serious faces to take Mum or Dad away to 'have a bit of a talk'.

Then, suddenly, they stopped doing the tests. Lots of people still came to see me every day but they weren't the doctors. Those serious, half-heard conversations seemed to stop altogether. Trudy was about the only one who still came to do her 'passive movements', which consisted of flexing my feet and bending my legs. I liked her coming; it was something to look forward to.

'We've got to keep your joints and muscles moving so you don't stiffen up too much. That won't help when we get you up and walking again.'

'When do you think that will be?' I just couldn't imagine how I could get out of bed with these heavy legs but Trudy, as always, was brightly confident.

'Oh, pretty soon I should think. You're getting stronger all the time.' I looked doubtful.

'Yes you are, Libby. A couple of weeks ago you couldn't even sit up on your own or hold a cup. Now look at all the things you can do for yourself.'

'What things?' I asked darkly.

Trudy laughed. 'Well, you can brush your hair for a start. You never know who's going to walk through those doors.' The most exciting thing likely to walk into the ward was my dad or the nurse with the pill tray, but she was right — I hadn't thought about my appearance for weeks. Once or twice Mum had tried to wash my hair over the side of the bed using a wash bowl, practically drowning me. She'd bring a hair dryer from home and tie my hair back with some brightly coloured scrunchy, talking to me all the time. When my head wasn't hurting too much I liked having Mum touch me, but I felt too ill to care about what I looked like. I hadn't looked in the mirror for weeks; I didn't want to. To please Trudy, I got out my hairbrush and gave it a few lacklustre pulls. My hair seemed to have grown a bit whilst I was doing all that being ill. I wondered whether it would be easier to have it all cut off. If I was going to have to be here a long time.

'Okay, that's a *bit* better, I suppose,' Trudy said. 'Now let's go through our usual procedure, shall we, and then we'll do some of those arm-strengthening exercises, so you can take up wrestling when you get back to school. Okay, now sit up properly.' She put out a bent elbow for me to hold on to and plumped up the pillow so I could sit up straight. Then the questions started. We went through the same set of questions every day and however bright and positive Trudy tried to be, I dreaded them more each time. If it had been anyone else I think I would have lied.

'We'll start with your toes.' Out would come Trudy's pin with a little blob of colour on the top. She kept a supply pinned to her pocket for this purpose. 'Can you feel this?'

I wish I had a pound, or even ten pence, for every time someone stuck a pin in me and asked if I could feel it. It was like a trick question. I thought I could feel a vague, tingly, shivery sort of feeling, but I wasn't sure if I was imagining it or not. When Trudy told me to shut my eyes and tell her which toe she was sticking the pin in, I always gave her an answer but I couldn't be positive I'd got it right because Trudy went on saying, 'good, that's good' all the time anyway.

'Now wriggle your toes. Left foot first, now right foot. Good, that's good.' I made a brave attempt at wriggling my toes, but I could hardly make them move at all. Since I'd been in hospital, my feet had gone all floppy. When I lay in bed they didn't stick up like they used to; it was as if they'd become too heavy for my ankles.

'Now your heels. Bend your foot down towards my hand so that it's flat against it. Now up so that your toes face the ceiling.' If Trudy put her hand under my shin and thigh, I could make my heel move up and down, just a little bit.

'Good, that's good,' she said. Next Trudy would run one finger down the back of my calf. This would make my toes jump as if they were saluting her, but it didn't seem to have anything to do with me, they just seemed to do it on their own.

'That's a spasm,' Trudy explained, 'an involuntary movement, but it's good because it keeps your muscles working whilst you're lying in bed.' I wasn't entirely convinced.

Things got a bit easier as we moved up my legs. I could make my knees bend a bit and was much more certain I could hit the spot when Trudy stuck a pin into my thighs. If I was lying on my back, I could lift my buttocks off the bed and roll from side to side still keeping my shoulders flat on the bed.

'Good, that's great,' Trudy said, this time with some real enthusiasm in her voice.

'Why am I like this?' I would ask. 'When am I going to get better?' Trudy was about the only person on the staff who didn't say, 'We'll have to leave that one to the doctors, I'm afraid,' as if the doctors were some kind of god-like creatures who everyone had to obey. But I felt that even Trudy was avoiding telling me something.

'There's improvement all the time, Libby. You're

definitely getting some of your feeling back. Let's concentrate on your arms today – you're getting more movement and strength in them every day. Come on, let's get those hand weights going.'

Deidre, pronounced 'Deer-Druh', was another regular visitor. She had bright chestnut hair, pink-and-white skin and a soft, Irish accent. She visited me on Tuesdays and Fridays. She was dressed exactly like Trudy, in dark trousers and a white tunic which buttoned down the front, but her uniform was dark green in all the bits where Trudy's was dark blue. I wasn't absolutely sure what Deidre's job was, but it seemed to be to give me things I didn't want to do and to insist that they would do me good. Perhaps she was worried that if she didn't keep me busy my brain would stop working along with my legs. I'm just guessing here, but her title was Occupational Therapist, so maybe she was just doing her job – trying to keep me 'occupied'.

'I've bought some things to keep you busy during the day. Just until we get you up and about.' She would have her arms full of giant jigsaw puzzles of 'A Golden Labrador and her Ten Puppies' or 'Friends of the Earth, Wild Animals in Danger'. Sometimes she brought me tiny coloured felt shapes you could stick on to a background to make pictures of parrots or flower arrangements. Deidre was a very nice person and I tried to be polite to her but she could tell I wasn't very interested.

'Come on now, Libby. It's not good to moon about all day.' What did she think I should be doing? My body wouldn't move, I felt sick all day long, I was miserable and homesick, exhausted from doing nothing. I honestly couldn't see how a bit of fuzzy felt was going to help me. Still, I didn't want to seem too rude, so Dad or Grandma would help me by working out the dog basket or the endangered panda bits of jigsaw when they came to visit. I think my visitors liked it; it gave them something to do.

One Tuesday morning, Deidre came without a craft activity. Instead she had a wheelchair with her. I had been in a wheelchair before when they took me off for all those zillions of X-rays and scans but this one looked new and bright and was sporting a red tag with my name on it. I was absolutely horrified.

'Why do I need that?'

'It's to get you up and about. We'll be starting a proper rehab programme soon – strengthening you up, getting you walking again – and you'll need this to get you down to the gym or into the swimming pool. We'll soon get rid of it.'

Gym? Swimming? I couldn't even do a pee on my own and they seemed to imagine me doing step aerobics. What was 'rehab' anyway? I didn't like to ask. It sounded like 'pre-fab', which I knew was a kind of temporary house my gran had lived in just after the war, but I couldn't see how it had anything to do with that.

'How am I supposed to get into that thing?' I couldn't imagine getting out of bed.

'We'll lift you in the first couple of times and then I'll show you how to do it on your own.' She caught sight of my face again. 'But don't worry, you won't need it for very long. It's just until you get a bit stronger.'

The next morning Deidre and Trudy lifted me into the wheelchair together, Deidre on the legs and Trudy under the arms.

'One, two, three – go!' I hated the feeling of being in it. I felt sick and dizzy and I just wanted to get back into bed. I could hardly sit up, let alone push myself about. They took it in turns to push me up and down the ward and all the old ladies smiled and waved at me from their beds or armchairs. I tried to smile back, but I couldn't.

'Hello love, it's good to see you up and about. Fancy a Murray Mint?' Olive adjusted her teeth with her tongue and waved a sweet at me.

'No, thanks. Not at the moment, Olive.'

'Go on, take it for later.' There was no point in refusing Olive, as everyone on the ward knew. I already had half a drawer of unopened mints and boiled sweets.

Olive looked older than anyone I had ever seen. In the day she was pleasant and cheerful to everyone, but at night it was as if some other force overtook her. She would talk and shout in different voices as if she was acting out arguments she'd had a long time ago. The nurses would try to stop her, sometimes they'd even shout, but it only kept her quiet for a few minutes. Then she'd start her chanting. 'Oh dear, oh dear. Oh dear, oh dear.' She'd sing over and over in a flat voice making a kind of tune of it like the sound of Big Ben on the ten o'clock news. I would be kept awake for hours listening to it. It would seep into my brain and I would find that I had Olive's rhythm in my head. Oh dear, oh dear. Oh dear, oh dear.

'Are they taking you out for a little ride, dear? That's nice.' That was from Mrs Gates in the bed next to Olive.

She must have had a first name but nobody would dare call her by it. We went up the ward and down it again, people waving at me and smiling.

'Ooh, you're doing well,' called out Agnes from the end bed. 'You'll be taking your driving test soon, ha ha ha.' Suddenly the world started to disappear – everything went black.

'Whoops, I think that's enough for today,' said Trudy. 'Let's get you back into bed.' It couldn't be soon enough for me. At least in bed I was safe. I could reach out for the buzzer to call the nurse. I could get myself a drink of water or a magazine. In that wheelchair I couldn't do anything.

A couple of days later Mum and Dad both appeared. This was unusual; mostly by this stage I only had one visitor at a time. If I'd thought about it, I suppose I'd have realised they looked nervous but I wasn't thinking about anyone else's feelings at that time. My own were enough to cope with.

'Hello darling,' Mum said, kissing me. 'How's everything?' I'd got the nurses to take the wheelchair away from the side of my bed, so she pulled up one of the mock leather, blue armchairs and sat down. She was wearing her little black suit, a white shirt and her shell earrings. She was wearing make-up; something was obviously going on. Dad looked exactly like he always did except that he was wearing wool trousers and brown leather moccasins instead of his usual loose jeans and trainers. Mum had clearly had a bit of a go at him.

'We've got a meeting with the doctor now.'

'What doctor?'

'Dr Singleton – I think you might be supposed to call him Mr Singleton because he's the consultant. He's the doctor in charge of you.'

'Why does he want to see me? Is he going to tell me what I've got?'

'Well,' said Mum, sounding unusually hesitant. 'I think that it's going to be a kind of review meeting.'

'What does that mean?'

'He wants to talk to us about what the tests have shown and how well you're doing – and what they're going to do next.'

'Do they know what's the matter with me?' I asked anxiously. Before Mum could answer, the doctor's head appeared around the curtains.

'Good, you're all here,' he said in a jolly I'm–in–charge–here kind of voice. 'Trudy's joining us as well, so I thought it would be more private to talk in my office. Oh,' he said, looking round, 'where's the wheelchair?' At that moment Trudy appeared.

'I found this at the end of the corridor,' she said, pretending (I think she was pretending) to look cross. 'You can't get rid of it that easily. Shall we try a transfer?' I wanted them to all sit round my bed and talk about me like they usually did, but I knew they weren't going to let me choose.

'Come on, you can do it Libby. You're getting better at it all the time.'

I was terrified of transferring from the bed into the wheelchair; it was like being asked to walk the tightrope. That probably sounds like an exaggeration but it was exactly what it felt like. All my balance had gone and although my arms were getting stronger, I had no confidence that lifting my bottom and swinging it round would land me in the chair. It felt just as likely that I would nosedive towards the floor and crack my head open. I sat perched on the side of the bed unable to move. I could feel myself starting to cry; tears came easily to me these days. I could also feel Dad moving forward and I knew that he wanted to take over and lift me up. He hesitated, not knowing what to do for the best.

'Come on, I'll give you a hand. This will be the last time though,' Trudy said, stepping forward. I put my arms around her neck like a clinging monkey and in half a second we were on the chair. 'For that, you can push yourself down to Dr Singleton's room,' she said brightly. It felt like I was trying to manoeuvre a tank. My hands stretched over the cumbersome arms of the wheelchair and I pushed the cold, silver metal rim – a tiny little push at a time. Each bump in the hospital lino floor felt like a hurdle. I couldn't understand what I was supposed to be learning from this. If someone would just give me a push, we'd be there in half the time. Mum and Dad walked on either side of me. I could tell from the way Dad was moving that he was itching to take hold of the handles but he didn't. Perhaps he thought it was doing me good too.

Dr Singleton was sitting behind his desk by the time the rest of us arrived. His office was small and untidy. On it there were two brown folders, an enormous one with X-ray photographs in it and another folder not quite so big, full of various bits of paper. He laid his hand flat on the smaller one and smiled at us all.

'Right, now these are Elizabeth's – Libby's – notes and the results of all the tests we've done. I've talked to you about most of them as they've come in but I know that you wanted to look at all of them together to see if we can draw any conclusions. Trudy is going to chip in on Elizabe . . . , Libby's progress in building up her strength again. Now, is there anything you'd like to ask before I start?' Mum and Dad looked at each other, then they both looked at me. I hoped that I wasn't expected to say anything – I didn't know what to say. Mum, as always, had to get her word in.

'I think it's better if you tell us what you know and we'll ask questions if there's anything we don't understand.' She bit her top lip. This was probably to stop herself interrupting every ten seconds. Or perhaps she was dreading what he had to say.

'Okay. Fine. Well, as you know when Libby was first brought into hospital six weeks ago she was very poorly indeed.' Six weeks? I didn't know whether it felt like six days or six months.

'We looked at a whole lot of possibilities then. Severe food poisoning was one idea at that time. I know she'd had a day at the sea and we couldn't trace everything she'd eaten, but the blood and faeces tests seemed to rule that one out.' Dad opened his mouth as if he was going to say something, then closed it again.

'We also looked at various gastro-intestinal disorders at the beginning. She had terrible sickness and the runs.' He laughed nervously. 'And very bad pains. Some of those symptoms went fairly quickly.' The doctor turned towards Mum. 'I know that you were very concerned

65

about bacterial meningitis at the beginning and that was another possibility we looked at. We put Libby on a very strong dose of antibiotics on a drip on a "just in case" basis but again, the blood tests and the lumbar puncture showed us that wasn't the problem.' The idea of the lumbar puncture still filled me with horror. I certainly hoped he wasn't going to suggest I had another one of those. They'd have to kill me first.

Dr Singleton gave a long sigh. For the first time it occurred to me that he might be about to tell me some terrible news. For a moment I could hardly breathe – I didn't want to hear what came next. Mum moved a little closer to me and held my hand. Did she already know what he was going to say?

'The truth is – and however long you've been doing this, it's always very hard for a doctor to admit it – we don't exactly know what is the matter with Libby. It's clearly some kind of viral infection which has got right into her system and is affecting her quite badly. We've been treating this with anti-inflammatory drugs – steroids – and they do seem to be having some effect, although not as quickly as we had hoped.'

Well, at least he wasn't going to tell me that I had an incurable disease, I thought, but it hadn't occurred to me that they wouldn't know why I was so ill. How could they make me better if they didn't know what it was? I looked at Mum and Dad, expecting them to ask the questions the doctor would be able to answer. Surprisingly, they were silent.

'What *is* the matter with me then? Why can't I move my legs properly? Sometimes they really hurt inside but when you touch them on the outside I can hardly feel a thing. And I still feel so sick all the time.' It didn't sound like my voice but it was coming from me. 'I can't do anything for myself. I can't stand up, I can't walk. I can't even push myself in the wheelchair.' Mum held my hand tighter as my voice began to squeak with tears.

'Well Libby, I'll explain it as best I can, but some of it is a bit difficult.'

'I'm not a baby!' I said in a voice that sounded like I probably was. 'If I don't understand what you're saying I'll just ask.'

'I'll try my best, although as I said, a lot of what I'm saying is explaining what you haven't got rather than what you have. But still, it will help to understand things a bit better. We think you have some kind of viral infection which has affected your spinal cord.' He looked around to see if we could understand what he was saying. I knew I had heard all those words before – spine, spinal cord, virus, infection – but put together they didn't mean anything to me.

'Your spine is all those bony rings which run down your back.' Instinctively, the three of us started feeling for the sticking out bits at the top of our necks.

'Your spinal cord is a round, flexible column which runs from your brain to the lower part of your back. If you imagine your brain as a kind of telephone exchange: the spinal cord takes incoming calls about feeling and sensation – that's how you feel pain or tickling – and also outgoing calls like movement. Your spinal cord takes messages from the brain to the muscles, for example, to scratch your nose or wave your arms about.' Dr Singleton simultaneously scratched his nose and waved his other arm about in case we hadn't got the point. 'It also takes messages from all over the body to the brain about feeling, touch, pain, hot and cold etc. Are you with me so far?'

We all nodded. I tried it out for myself. Without having to consult the spinal telephone exchange, I could wiggle my thumb whenever I wanted. I tried it now but so that they didn't see what I was doing. 'Now, wriggle the toes on my left foot,' I told my brain. Nothing moved. The message wasn't getting through.

'What we think has happened is that a patch of inflammation has passed across Libby's spinal cord. We call this "viraemia". It's a kind of viral infection and as you know it can make you feel pretty lousy. It acts as an insult to the spinal cord and it stops it working properly.' Again, he stopped talking and looked at us. We all waited for him to continue but it seemed that he had finished. There were several seconds of silence. 'Viral illness' sounded a bit vague even to my ears. Once again I wondered how I was ever going to get better if they didn't really know what was wrong with me. I thought that after all those tests they'd know what pills to give me or even what operation I'd have to have. I'd put up with anything if only I could be better again.

Mum and Dad both started speaking at the same time.

'Is that it? Is that all you can . . .'

'How did she get it? I mean, did she catch it from . . .'

They both stopped talking. Then Mum started again.

'Is that it? Is that all you can tell us about it?'

'I'm afraid that is all we know at the moment.'

'What actually caused it? Wouldn't it be easier to treat her if we knew how she'd caught the virus? Wouldn't it be easier if we knew what kind of virus it was?' This was Dad's question. 'She'd been fine until the day she went to the seaside. You said it wasn't any kind of food poisoning and even if it was, I expect she'd be better by now. We know she went swimming that day. What about the sea – do you think she could have caught something from the water? You hear such a lot about pollution these days.' Dad spoke in a quick, excited voice quite unlike his usual, calm self.

'Well, we could contact the local Public Health Department to look into these matters, Mr Starling, but even if it is that, it wouldn't affect how we treated it.'

'How are you going to treat it?' Mum and Dad asked at exactly the same time.

'Physiotherapy is going to be the key to the treatment we give Libby from now on, that's why I asked Trudy to join us.' Trudy, who had been sitting silently so far, nodded in agreement and the four adults began a discussion about exercise and rehabilitation, eating better, swimming, and building up my strength. They seemed to have forgotten I was there. Perhaps I'd become invisible; perhaps no-one could see me. Why weren't they asking me what I wanted to do? I wanted to scream at them but it was like I'd forgotten how to be angry. As if Mum could read my thoughts, she stopped mid-sentence and turned to me.

'Are you okay, love? Do you want to ask anything?'

Yes, I did; I had lots of things I wanted to ask.

'Why can't I come home now? I want to go home.'

My voice sounded wobbly. Everyone stopped and looked at Dr Singleton to answer this.

'I understand how you feel, Libby, but it is best if you stay here for a while. It's important for you to build up your strength, and Trudy and the physiotherapists and lots of other people will work out a whole programme of things for you to do.' I tried so hard to stop myself crying again that the lump in my throat really hurt. Suddenly I couldn't control it anymore and I just blurted it out.

'I hate it in that ward. I hate it here. How can I get better if I can't sleep? Olive calls out all night long. I know it's not her fault but I hate it. I can't eat anything if I feel sick all the time. It smells revolting in there. Everyone's so old in that ward and I'm lonely at night. I want to go home. Why can't I go home?' I was really crying now. Mum came over and squatted down beside the chair and tried to hug me. No-one said anything for a while, then Trudy spoke in her usual calm, kind way.

'I honestly think it's best if you do stay for a while Libby. I know the doctors want to keep a close eye on you and there's lots of work to do getting you up and walking. We need to get you moving again – your joints have become stiff lying in bed all this time and we need to build up your muscles. We've got the equipment to help you here – and the staff.'

I sat silently. I couldn't have spoken without making ridiculous snorting noises like you do when you've been crying and anyway, I knew no-one would listen.

'It is very miserable for Libby in that ward,' said Mum. 'There isn't anyone for her to talk to. Isn't there another ward she could go to?' The doctor looked at my notes.

'How old is Libby?' he asked rhetorically. 'Fifteen. Well, we could transfer her to the Children's Ward. It's quite unusual at her age – she's a bit in between you see – but it might be pleasanter for her there. She'll be the oldest rather than the youngest and it certainly won't be quieter at night.' He laughed, as if he'd made a good joke. 'It might suit her better.'

'What do you think?' Mum asked me anxiously.

'How long do you think I'll have to stay there?'

'Well, it depends on how quickly you get on, but at a guess I'd say at least as long as you've already been here.' Another six weeks? I thought of everyone starting back at school for the final GCSE year. That world seemed a million miles away. Then I thought about being in a ward full of little kids. Still, it would have to be better than where I was.

'Okay, I'll move to the Children's Ward,' I said. Mum and Dad both looked relieved, although I was surprised to see that Trudy wasn't smiling.

Dr Singleton started shuffling his notes around. He was probably trying to tell us that the meeting was over. Nobody had asked the real question. Why hadn't anyone asked what we all really wanted to know? They were all talking about physiotherapy and exercises, about building up my muscles and getting me back to normal, but I was the one sitting in this wheelchair in a body that didn't move.

'Am I going to get better?'

It was as if we were playing musical statues. Everyone in the room stopped moving and everything went quiet. Dr Singleton didn't look at me.

'Well, I can understand why you want to ask that

question, Libby,' he said as if he was stalling for time. 'We have to look at it in terms of where we've come from.'

We? *He* hadn't come from anywhere.

'At the beginning, the viraemia, the virus you caught, had clearly affected all of your body, your brain, your upper body, your bladder and bowels, your legs, even your liver. Now, we can see that there's been a lot of improvement in the last six weeks. Your brain has cleared – you're thinking and speaking clearly. You can feel when you need to use the toilet. You've got most of the movement and strength back in your hands and arms, and our tests show that your liver is clearing up nicely.' Here he paused. 'So it seems like there's every hope for a good recovery.'

'Seems like there's every hope.' I repeated those words in my head.

'Seems like.' 'Every hope.' What did those words mean? They were the kind of words that might mean nothing at all. They were the kind of words that the wind could blow away.

Trudy, Mum and Dad stood up with the doctor. The meeting had clearly ended. Dr Singleton left the room with us and was about to walk off in the opposite direction when Dad started speaking in a voice which was unusually firm.

'Could I have a quick word, doctor?' He went on quickly before Dr Singleton had time to answer. 'I still feel that we need to know how Libby caught this virus or whatever it is. I think it needs to be looked at. We shouldn't just sweep it under the carpet. The day before she got ill she swam in the sea on the south coast and the next day she was critically ill. Now I don't think that's a coincidence. I think that's pretty scary.' Dad's voice was rising. Dr Singleton put his hand back on the door handle.

'Why don't you come inside and we'll have a chat about it, Mr Starling.'

I heard the door close quietly behind them.

Chapter Five
The Children's Ward

I moved to the Children's Ward in the afternoon of the following day. Before I left, I had another visit from Danielle (call-me-Denny-everyone-else-does) Watson. Denny was the hospital dietician and it was her job to make sure that you kept eating hospital food. Denny was in her early thirties, I think; she was medium height with red cheeks and shoulder-length thick blond hair which she usually wore in a ponytail. She was also very bony. Nevertheless, her purpose in life was to get me to eat more.

Denny had been to see me at least once a week since I'd been in hospital – or at least since they had removed the tube through which they used to feed me. When I'd been lying flat on my back, I used to be able to recognise her by her shoes. They were always plain high heels in extraordinary colours. I used to wonder whether she'd had them specially made. Denny was a victim of the idea of colour co-ordination – everything she was wearing matched something else. Today it was 'The Colour Purple' with a few 'ecru' touches to lighten it up a bit. She was wearing purple leather slingbacks, a purple wool straight skirt which ended just above her knees and a purple-and-cream striped leather belt with a gold buckle. Up top she had on a beige silk blouse with little purple and black paisley squiggles and a purple waistcoat. She wore large gold earrings studded with amethyst glass beads and (I'm not kidding here) large glasses with thin purple frames. Denny had glasses to match every outfit.

'Well, Libby, I hear you're off to Ward 5 this afternoon,' she said brightly. 'They won't like to see you not eating down there, you know. They keep a much closer eye on you.' I kept quiet. 'Now, how about the egg-nogs? How are they going?'

The whole time I'd been in hospital I'd felt sick. At first it was seriously throw-up vomit sick with agonising pains and I couldn't keep anything down. Since then it had been that vague kind of nausea, a bit like you get when you've had too much of something and can't imagine ever wanting to eat again. I would try to eat soup and things that Mum or Grandma brought me, but it was more to please them than because I really wanted to. Mum and Dad must have been worried but they never made me feel bad about it. They just smiled and looked pleased if I ate something. Denny's approach was more direct. Her job wasn't to wait until I got better. Her job was to tell me that I wouldn't get better unless I ate more.

'The egg-nogs, Libby, are you eating them? They're full

of vitamins and protein and calories.' She emphasised the word calories. 'Perhaps I should order you two a day instead of just the one.' Denny's egg-nogs were thick drinks the colour of Bird's custard powder when you stir in the first tablespoon of milk. I'd never drunk a single glass but she didn't know that. Dad was my secret ally in the matter of Denny's egg-nogs. They'd sit on my bedside table all day until he came, then he'd wink at me and drink it down in two gulps. We never spoke about it but I knew that he did it because he didn't want me to get into trouble. On the days he didn't come, Mum would usually bring me something from home to eat, so I'd tell the nurses I was full up. I think they knew but they didn't tell me off about it. I don't think Denny the Dietician was their favourite person.

'I know you've been very sick,' she said, puckering up her mouth a bit. 'But I also know that a lot of girls your age get a bit silly about food.' She said the words 'a bit silly' extra slowly. 'You see pictures of supermodels and you want to look like them, but it's not good for you, you know. Especially in your condition, you need to build up your strength. Now, when you get to the Children's Ward, we're going to look at the week's menu together and pick things that you'll enjoy eating.'

'It isn't that I don't want to eat,' I said irritably. 'I do, but I just feel sick all the time.' I thought of all those Mars Bars and Cadbury's Mini Rolls Joanna and I used to stuff our faces with on the way home from school. The one job around the house I'd usually been willing to help Mum with was the cooking, because I liked eating so much.

'That's what they all say,' said Denny, raising her eyebrows, 'and that's often the beginning of anorexia. Now, I expect you've heard that word before, haven't you?'

'Of course I have.' What did she think I was, a baby? She sat down on the edge of my bed with a different expression on her face. I knew that expression. It meant – 'I'm going to give you a little lecture now, but it's for your own good. To do this, I'm going to pretend that you're grown up and talk to you in a VERY SERIOUS VOICE.'

'When there's a reason for young people, especially young women, to stop eating,' Denny said, 'for example when they've been ill like you have – it's very easy to just get out of the habit of eating. You get thinner because your body has been burning up all those calories to keep you going and you haven't been putting much back in, so you've lost a lot of weight.' Here she eyed me from top to toe to emphasise her point. 'Because there's so much stuff now about how great it is to be extra skinny, you probably like the look of yourself now. You probably think you look better than you did before.' She stopped talking, waiting for my response. I kept my eyes down on the bed covers. She wasn't going to be able to make me look at her.

'These girls may look good but they aren't healthy. It's impossible to look like that without half starving yourself. Now in your case it's even more dangerous to think like that because you need lots of strength to build yourself up again. When you go to Ward 5 they'll have you up and about in no time. But to do that you need

ENERGY and to get that energy, you need FOOD.' She pronounced these words as if she was saying them in a foreign language I might not understand. 'So, Libby.' She dropped her chin and looked over the purple specs. 'So, Libby, what are we going to do about it – hmm?'

I just kept my head down. What was the point in answering her? I wasn't eating very much because I felt sick. When I stopped feeling sick no-one would have to tell me to start eating again.

'Is there another problem here that we ought to talk about? I know you think of me as someone who just makes you eat when you don't want to – but you can think of me as a friend, too.'

'Yeah, sure,' I thought nastily. 'Perhaps we could talk about colour co-ordinating my nightie and slippers.'

'Just tell me about your problems and little worries because often those things stop you wanting to eat. What about boyfriends, for example. Have you got a boyfriend who you're missing at the moment? I know a lot of girls think boys only like very thin girls, but it's not true, you know.' She laughed a little, tinkly kind of a laugh. 'In my experience, boys are much more interested in a girl's personality than we sometimes give them credit for, and in your case, it's going to be personality that counts.'

What was that supposed to mean? I thought. That I should forget about ever looking good again and be one of those bright, cheery creatures that go around doing good things for other people like you get in wet girls' comics? Anyway, this conversation was getting out of control. One minute we were talking about egg-nogs; the next she thought she could get me to tell her things I didn't talk to anybody about. Short of wearing a T-shirt which said 'I'll start eating again when I stop feeling sick', I couldn't see how I was going to get her to leave me alone, without being really rude.

Luckily we were saved by Trudy, who swept along the ward as if she was in a terrible hurry and stopped sharp by my bed as if someone had put the brakes on. Trudy was usually a lot more relaxed than this.

'Right, Libby,' she said as if there was no-one else but me to talk to. 'I volunteered to take you to your new accommodation so let's get going, shall we? Are you all packed up or do you want me to help?' I felt a bit confused, because I knew that Dad was coming to help me move, but there was no stopping Trudy and I was very glad of the chance to get rid of Ms. Purple-Gear.

'I'm glad we've had a good chat, Libby,' Denny said as if we were the best of friends. 'I'll come and see you again when you're all settled in and we'll talk some more. In the meantime, remember what I said about keeping up your energy and not thinking about those silly super-models.' She looked at Trudy for support but Trudy was busily gathering up the cards from my bedside locker. 'Your new physio will be on my side, too, you know. We're all using our special expertise to get you fit and healthy again.' And with that, she gathered up her food charts and breezed off. As she turned her back, I saw the big purple velvet bow stuck to the back of her head.

It was only when her high heels had stopped clicking down the corridor that her words began to sink in. Not the stupid words about eating more, but what she'd said about the new physio. Trudy was looking at me sadly as if she could read my thoughts.

'I'm sorry, Libby,' she said. 'I wanted to tell you myself – that's why I volunteered to come and help you move. I didn't want you to hear it from her.' The way she said the word 'her' told me that she probably felt the same way I did about Denny.

'What did she mean – are you leaving or something?'

'No, I'm not leaving. It's just that in the Children's Ward they have a different team of people – different nurses, occupational therapists, different physiotherapists.' She stopped for a minute and gave me a wry smile. 'Unfortunately, they don't have different dieticians.' We smiled at each other. 'I work just with adults and there are different physios who work with children. They've already decided who'll be working with you. She's very experienced – in fact she's had a lot more experience than me. I've already talked to her about you and she knows what we've been doing together.' Once again I could feel my eyes fill with tears. I seemed to cry at nothing these days.

'Don't you want to work with me anymore?' I knew that was a stupid thing to say but it was how I felt.

'I'd love to if I could. We've done such a lot of work together and I know that you're going to do really well with your new physio.'

'Why can't you ask someone if you could carry on with me this time? Couldn't they make an exception just for me?'

'I don't think it would work – it's the way things are organised around here. They wouldn't let me – honestly.'

'Why didn't someone tell me this before? If I'd known,

I might have decided to stay where I was. I don't want to go to the stupid Children's Ward anyway. I'm not a little child.' I realised why Trudy had looked like she had when we had that discussion with Dr Singleton. I didn't think it was fair that she hadn't told me then. Trudy was the only person in the whole hospital who was helping me to get better. All those stupid blood tests and scans, eating plans and jigsaw puzzles – they didn't help me at all. Every little thing was so hard for me – balancing on my own, learning how to dress myself as if I was three years old, learning how to transfer from the bed into the wheelchair. And now we were starting the really hard part – learning how to walk again. I didn't want to have to begin all that with someone else. It wasn't fair.

Trudy had seen me crying before but this time she didn't seem to know what to do with me.

'I'll come and see you whenever I can – honestly. You'll be in good hands with Mrs Blood – Pauline. She's very good – she's the head of the whole department – she knows what she's doing.' Pauline Blood wasn't a very reassuring name; it sounded like something out of a horror film. I sniffed loudly, trying to get control of myself again. Trudy pulled a tissue out of the box on my bedside table and handed it to me. She didn't actually say 'Go on, have a good blow, it'll make you feel better,' but that was the look she gave me.

'Come on now, we'd better get going. They're expecting you downstairs. Just do one, final, brilliant transfer for me.'

I was determined to do this well for Trudy, to show her how much she'd taught me even though the thought of it was still terrifying. I shuffled my bum sideways to the edge of the bed and put my left hand onto the wheelchair cushion and my right hand flat on the bed. When I sat up without anything at my back, I had no balance at all. As usual I froze, unable to move. It felt like I was suspended in mid-air and if I let go of anything, I would go crashing down.

'Use your arms to lift your bum and SWING!' Trudy said firmly.

I gritted my teeth and willed myself to do it. Silently I counted, one, two, three, four, five, six, and with enormous concentration, I stretched my arms and lifted my bum in the direction of the seat. A quarter of an inch of me connected with the cushion.

'Lift, don't shuffle,' Trudy said for the twentieth time.

I tried again and this time I was near enough to lean backwards and grab the far wheel with my hand so that I could yank myself across.

'I thought I said lift,' said Trudy, but there was a smile in her voice. 'You need to be careful doing it like that; you'll do terrible things to your skin on those wheels.'

With my bum safely on the cushion, I positioned my legs on the square metal footplates which stuck out like non-stick baking trays – first one, then the other. Then I looked at Trudy for approval.

'Almost brilliant,' she said, grinning broadly, and I did indeed feel like someone who had completed a dangerous and difficult journey.

Trudy gathered up my things. There wasn't really all that much. I'd forgotten what real clothes felt like. For the past six weeks I'd been living in oversized T-shirts which were more comfortable than ordinary nighties, slippers and the odd sweatshirt when I felt cold. Mum took them home to wash and brought a different one back with her when she came. I'd got a few toiletries – soap, shampoo and a nice tube of moisturising cream from Grandma which smelt of peaches and cream. There was a pot of pale pink flowers someone must have sent and, of course, Morris the toy rabbit who had sat faithfully at the end of my bed all the time I'd been in hospital. Trudy had opened the drawer in my bedside cupboard and was putting things into a cardboard box.

'Gosh. Did you know that you had all these in here?'

'What are they?'

'All these cards and letters. I bet you didn't know you were so popular.' There must have been forty envelopes there, all addressed to me. I vaguely remembered them arriving. Mum had tried to interest me in one or two but I'd turned my head away and refused to listen. I suppose they'd just been put in there until I was well enough to read them. It made me feel like I'd returned from the dead.

'You'll have fun reading these in your spare time – between physiotherapy sessions,' Trudy said. 'But I'm not sure how we're going to manage all this. I could plonk it all on your lap and push you or you could push yourself – what's it to be?' I settled for pushing myself – I was lazy but I was starting to realise how much I disliked the feeling of having someone behind me taking me where they thought I should go, even someone as nice as Trudy.

'Do you want to say goodbye to everyone?' Suddenly I felt young and shy. I didn't know how to say goodbye to people who were probably never going to leave this ward. Anyway, I wasn't exactly leaving.

'I'll tell you what. I'll hold on to one handle and you can push with one hand and give a regal wave with the other.' I wheeled down the ward waving to Mrs Gates and Agnes, accepted a final lemon sherbet from Olive, said goodbye to the nurses and left.

The Children's Ward – or Ward 5, as most of the doctors and nurses called it – was actually called Beatrix Potter Ward, and you could see why. Some artist had gone berserk with lopsided copies of Peter Rabbit, Jemima Puddleduck and their friends. They bounced all over the walls of the ward. Every inch where there wasn't a window or a temperature chart had a Benjamin Bunny frieze or a Mrs Tiggy Winkle poster. Perhaps it was called Ward 5 because it made you feel five years old again. For a minute I thought of wheeling straight back to the land of Olive's Murray Mints and Big Ben chanting, but then a cute little boy with bright red, soft, curly hair and about a million freckles came up to me. He had a curious walk – shoulders first, followed by his legs, and with his head on one side, but he walked towards me with tremendous speed.

'Hello, I'm Brian and I'm three who are you and why are you in that thing?' he said all in one breath, pointing to the wheelchair.

'I'm Libby and my legs have stopped working properly.'

'Oh dear,' he said very seriously. 'That's no good is it – never mind. Would you like to see my plaster?' He lifted up his yellow top to show me an enormous plaster cast which went from his neck right down to his waist with holes for his arms which stuck out a bit. That explained his curious walk.

'It's very interesting, isn't it?'

'Yes it is,' I said, trying not to laugh. 'Very interesting.'

'I must go and do some expertises now. You'll have to do them too, I s'pose. Bye bye.' And off he waddled like a little penguin, as cheerful as anything. He's like a mini Jesse, I thought, and for the first time in ages I smiled.

The nurses were much more relaxed than they'd been upstairs. They wanted you to call them by their first names and they seemed to have more time to just stop and chat. One of the nurses, June, who was to be a good friend to me while I was there, came up and put a hand on my shoulder. She was quite tall and round, with the kind of figure you hear people describe as 'motherly', warm, dark-brown skin the colour of cedars and wavy black hair arranged in a bun at the back of her neck. She had a rich, fruity voice and when she spoke it sounded like she was laughing underneath.

'Hello lovey, we've been expecting you. I see that you've met young Brian – he's quite a character; he has us all in stitches. Now you're going to be in this room for a while. We thought it would be nice for you to have a bit of privacy as you're the oldest one here. Can't promise that you'll be able to stay forever – it depends on who comes in. We might get someone who's infectious and needs to be in isolation or someone who needs intensive care nursing but we'll let you have it as long as we can. You'll be glad of having a door to shut, believe me. It's supposed to be a hospital ward but sometimes it feels more like an adventure playground. And it doesn't get quieter at night – oh no.' She gave a low, rich laugh and shook her head.

The room she led me to was little more than a cubicle. It had the usual single bed, bedside cupboard and dark-blue vinyl armchair, but there was also a thin wardrobe with a few hangers in it and a little wooden table with a grey, moulded, plastic chair like the kind you get in school. The walls were covered in slightly grubby, pale-green paint which was peeling off in a number of places, but at least Jemima Puddleduck and the Flopsy Bunnies were absent. With me, the wheelchair, Trudy and June, the room was completely packed – there was hardly space to turn round in.

'I'll take this one out, I think,' said June, picking up the grey chair. 'You won't need it and it will give you a bit more space. Have you got any clothes in there?' She peered into the box which Trudy had put on the bed. 'Probably your mum will bring some with her when she comes. She said she'd be here about three o'clock. I'll be back in a tick to make you comfortable. I think they're going to let you have an easy day today. They'll start torturing you tomorrow, I expect.'

'Thanks a lot, June,' said Trudy, only half laughing. 'That's not very good for our image.' Trudy took a step backwards. She was holding her arms awkwardly at her sides as if she didn't quite know what to do with them.

'Will you come and see me again?' I asked anxiously.

'Yes I will, but I'll see you in the Gym anyway.'

The Gym? This sounded too much like school to me. 'Where's the Gym?'

'It's on the top floor. It's the place where you'll be doing all your rehab work and exercises – all the physios use it.'

'If we're all going to be there, why can't I work with you?' It seemed to be worth one last try.

'Sorry, Libby, it doesn't work that way, but I will see you again, I promise.' Before I could say anything else, she was out of the door.

Almost immediately June was back with another nurse.

'Would you like to get into bed for a little while? You're looking a bit tired.' I realised that I was exhausted. I'd hardly done anything and it felt like I had been working all day. June took my top half and the other nurse grabbed my feet.

'One, two, three – lift.' They swung me up like a sack of potatoes and put me firmly onto the bed. Still, at least they weren't telling me how I had to do everything for myself. June patted the covers over me in a comfortable sort of way.

'Now you just have a nice rest, lovey, until your mummy comes. Is there anything you want?'

'There's a whole lot of cards and things on the top of that box. Could you just push it a bit closer so that I can have a look?'

'Good gosh,' June said, peering in. 'Is this all your fan mail? What a girl!'

I spent the next hour or so looking through the stack of letters and cards. Some of the envelopes had been opened, but most of them were still sealed. This must have taken superhuman effort on Mum's part because usually she can't keep her nose out of my business. I tried guessing who they were from by looking at the writing and the postmark. It was easy to tell the difference between the cards from people my own age and the ones from friends of my parents, aunts and uncles and from older people like Grandma's friends. I wondered whether handwriting somehow got curlier as you got older or whether the way people were taught to write had changed. Gran's friends and distant relatives I hardly knew had chosen cards with flowers on the outside and 'Get Well Soon' poems on the inside. I also had a few of those ghastly cartoony sort which had people in hospital beds with all their limbs in plaster suspended from the ceiling. My mum's friends and my aunties (both the real and the courtesy kind) had mostly chosen those kind of cards that have a photograph or painting on the outside and are blank in the middle so you can write your own message. I had loads of Monets and Matisses, plenty of landscapes and even more cats. Every sort of cat: tabby cats, fluffy kittens, painted cats, even cats in flower pots. I had quite a lot of postcards, too. The whole summer holiday had passed without me even knowing about it. Joanna and Esther had both written to me lots of times — they'd sent postcards from places they'd visited with their families, a little note from Joanna camping with her family in Yorkshire, a postcard from Esther in Spain. They sent me cards with sweet pictures of teddy bears holding 'get well' banners and cards with Biff cartoons. Nearly every card they sent said they would like to come and see me when I was feeling a bit better.

I was surprised to see that there were two cards from Cleo. One was one of those postcards that you can tear out of books of cards. It was a picture by that weird painter, Escher. It was grey and yellow and pink and when you looked at it closely there were hundreds of identical insects all fitting together. Cleo had written:

Well Libs – trust you to get sicker than anyone I've ever known. Sounds like you've gone a bit ape-shit there. Hurry up and get just a bit better so I can come and tell you about my summer holiday which has been so TOTALLY BORING even yours will look like you've been having fun. Your mum tells me I can't come and see you until you've stopped up-chucking SO STAY COOL AND GET REAL. Cleo

The other card was something I assumed she'd made herself. It was a piece of plain paper folded over with one half covered in a mad, complicated pattern drawn with a fine, black pen. Inside it said:

Hi again Libby-Libs. I was just settling down to a bit of neurotic doodling when the doorbell went and who do you think was there? Well of course you won't know till I tell you, will you? It was your old mate Ben and his new mate Jesse. Well, Jesse was asking all about you and I told him what I know which is nearly nothing and he said he wanted to write to you but he isn't grown up enough to get his own card and pen so I've lent him mine.

Under Cleo's uneven scrawl, in scrupulously neat, almost square handwriting, it said:

Dear Libby,
I'm really sorry to hear that you've been so ill all summer. Ben's been giving me some news about you which he's heard from his mum and it sounds like you've been having a really bad time. I'd like to come and see you when you're feeling a bit better. Perhaps I could come with Cleo, would that be okay?

Love,

Jesse

Love, Jesse. For a whole term I'd thought about him practically every minute of every day and for the last six weeks I hadn't thought about him at all.

I didn't know how these letters made me feel. It was a new sensation having all these people thinking about me and wanting to come and visit me, but it made me feel anxious. Before, when I'd dreamt of Jesse coming to visit me in hospital, I'd thought of it as interesting, even romantic – me looking beautiful and sad, perhaps with a badly sprained ankle or wrist. But it wasn't like that at all. I wasn't sure I wanted anyone to see me like this, especially Jesse.

I felt completely exhausted. Half an hour reading and the words were swimming on the page and my arms felt too tired to hold even the lightest card. I closed my eyes and was soon dreaming that I was back at school. I could

90

see Jesse at the end of the corridor. He lifted one arm to wave at me and smiled. I smiled back. I tried to walk towards him but my legs wouldn't move – they seemed to be stuck to the ground and however hard I tried, I couldn't lift my foot off the ground. With extraordinary effort, I managed to do it – one step, then one more. I had to look at the ground, otherwise I was sure that I would fall over and when I looked up, I saw that Cleo was standing next to him, very close. They were both waving at me, both smiling, and as I got closer, I realised that they were holding hands.

Chapter Six
Pauline Blood

'Libby, Libby, wake up! Don't sleep now, look what I've got!' Robbie was so excited that he was hopping up and down, his little hand tugging at the sleeve of my T-shirt. I opened my eyes slowly. Robbie was holding a very ordinary package two inches from my nose. 'You don't know what this is, do you? It's magic stuff for sticking your cards on the wall. And look what else I've got.'

'Hold on a second, Robbie,' Mum said. 'Give her a chance to wake up.' She leaned over the bed and gave me a kiss. 'How are you feeling darling? I'm sorry we weren't here to help you move down. We tried to get here earlier but Dad's Head of Department called and asked him to go in for a meeting. His new term starts tomorrow and Robbie's the day after that so we had to go and get him some . . . '

'New shoes,' he screamed, interrupting her. 'Look at

these, Libby – magic straps!' Robbie proudly stuck a leg up on the bed, showing off his new blue leather shoes with velcro fastening fronts. Chrrr, chrrr, chrrr, he ripped them back and forth with great pride. It was a horrible noise, the kind seven-year-old boys love. 'And,' said Robbie with great emphasis, 'we bought some big ones just like it for . . .'

'Would you please just calm down and be quiet for a few minutes,' Mum said sharply. 'Libby's only just woken up. Sorry love, he's in one of those moods. He's a bit overexcited about going back to school.'

'What's all that about sticking things on the wall?'

'Well yesterday, after we agreed you'd come down to this ward, Dad and I came to have a look and the nurse said they'd try to give you this room if they could. I thought that would be great for you, especially when you start to get visitors. I just thought you could brighten it up a bit. What do you think?' This was my mum's way of going about things. She'd decide that something was a good idea and then put it to you as a question to try and make you think that you'd thought of it yourself.

'Can I start putting the cards up now? Please Mummy, please Libby.'

'The other reason we're so late is because I wanted to go out and get you some new things to wear. There's hardly anything decent in the shops this time of year.'

Of course I was pleased at the idea of getting some new clothes because money was always a bit tight in our house, but it had been a while since Mum and I had shared the same taste. Also, Mum was looking nervous and this wasn't a good sign. First of all she produced two new T-shirts from Gap. They weren't my colours exactly – I usually wore fitted tops in black or grey and these were big, one in lemon yellow and one in dark pink – but they weren't bad and I could see why she thought it would be good for me to wear bright colours. But then things got worse.

'As if!' I screwed up my face as if I wanted to spit something out. 'I'm not going to wear those! I wouldn't be seen dead in things like that.' Mum looked really startled. I hadn't raised my voice above a whisper for weeks.

'Just calm down a bit and let me explain,' Mum tried to interrupt.

'Oh God. Look at those shoes. I'm not wearing those, they're not even my size – they're way too big.'

'But they're just like mine,' Robbie said sadly.

'And why on earth did you buy these, Mum? These are the sort of trousers nerdy boys wear. Why couldn't you just bring my jeans from home? These are revolting!' I flung them down on the bed in disgust – a pair of light-grey leather trainers with velcro fastening fronts and two pairs of shiny, turquoise-blue, nylon jogging pants with elasticated waists and white stripes down the side.

'Just listen to me for a minute,' Mum said with unusual restraint. Talking to her like this would usually have resulted in full-scale war. 'Daddy and I have spoken to your new physiotherapist and she said that you need clothes which are comfortable and easy to get on and off. She doesn't want you to wear tight clothes or things which have zips or buttons because they can cut your skin and cause damage because at the moment you can't . . . '

'Can't can't can't' I yelled at her, feeling uncontrollable, endless anger rising in me without warning. 'Can't move. Can't feel anything. Can't dress myself. Can't walk. Can't go to the toilet. Can't go home. Can't go back to school. Can't even wear decent clothes. What is this?' I picked up the track-suit bottoms from the bed. 'A kind of uniform for cripples? And these shoes are the kind of thing eighty-year-old men wear. I suppose they'll go well with the grey wheelchair – I might just as well dress like I'm ready to die.' Mum went pale.

'It's not for ever, darling. Just try and be sensible for a minute. They're just comfortable, practical clothes to wear until you're up and about a bit more. It's important that you've got some clothes that you can get in and out of on your own and these are the easiest kind of things to wear. The nurses will be busy with the younger children, they won't be able to spend much time with you in the mornings. I tried my best, Libby,' she said with a sigh. 'These clothes weren't cheap, you know – they cost quite a lot of money.' Mum and I looked at each other without speaking. I knew she thought I was making a stupid, selfish fuss but for once, she wasn't going to say it to my face.

Robbie saved the day – funny that. In the past he'd always used arguments between Mum and me to his own advantage – me the selfish, unreasonable teenager, him the perfect, unfairly treated little boy, but recently he seemed to have become a bit of a diplomat.

'Shall we do it now, then?' he said, holding the packet of Blu-Tak in the air as if nothing had happened. 'You give me a card and I'll put a little bit in each corner. I know how to do it,' he said proudly. 'Daddy showed me at home.' I didn't trust myself to speak and Mum pretended that nothing had happened. The anger washed out of me as quickly as it had come and I just felt tired again.

In the end we had quite a good afternoon decorating the grubby blank wall with all my cards, reading them again as we went along. Not the one from Cleo and Jesse though – I put that in the bedside drawer so I could look at it again when I was on my own. Mum stuck the high ones and Robbie the low ones and I sat in bed and gave orders. It almost felt like the sort of thing ordinary families do together. When Dad came in, we were all admiring our hard work. It looked like some kind of mad art gallery.

'Wow,' said Dad. 'Look at all that. I didn't know you had such a big fan club. How are you feeling love – this is a bit of an improvement on the old ward, don't you think?' He bent over the bed and gave me a kiss. He felt all scratchy, obviously leaving the boring business of shaving until he had to start work again. 'Did Mum give you your new clothes – how did you like them?

Mum and I looked at each other. She raised her eyebrows at me but smiled at the same time. I tried hard to smile back.

'What's the matter with you two then – some joke I don't understand? Look, I've bought you a couple of things myself. This isn't a box to share.' He looked at Mum and Robbie as if they were about to steal them. 'It's a box just for Libby – a special treat.' Dad produced a box of Terry's Neapolitans, the kind where each tiny bar of chocolate is wrapped in a different colour paper to show their different flavours – Devon Milk, Dark Seville, Cafe au Lait, Orange Silk. They'd always been my absolute favourites but usually they were something we had to argue over. When I was little, Uncle Richard, my dad's brother, had always brought us a box when he came to visit. That was before he died. 'I've bought you something else too because I thought you might need it for tomorrow when you start your army training with Mrs Vampire.'

'Mike,' Mum said sternly.

'Sorry,' Dad said. 'I mean your physiotherapy with Mrs Blood. I'm sure she's wonderful but I thought you might like this.' He fished in his bag and pulled something out which made me smile.

'Oh thanks, Dad,' I said, giving him a kiss. 'I'll take care of it, honestly.'

'Well make sure you do. I'm only lending it to you, mind – as soon as you're better I'm going to take it back again.' I took out what looked like a crumpled grey ball and opened it up flat on the bed. It was an old, washed grey American T-shirt with UCLA printed in big navy-blue letters on the front. I'd always wanted it but Dad had never allowed me anywhere near it. It had been Uncle Richard's from the time he'd been a student in America. I knew how much it meant to Dad.

The next morning no-one came to visit me. Dad and Robbie were both about to start back at school and I expect that Mum was organising the whole family. The routine was obviously going to be very different here. I had to be up and dressed before nine o'clock and was expected to sit at the table in the main part of the ward and eat breakfast with all the other children. Little Brian with the plaster jacket was my personal alarm clock. He was also a talking menu.

'Libby, it's time to get up,' he announced on that first morning. 'There's munchrooms and toast today and there's scrambled eggs. You can have eggs and munchrooms together but it makes the eggs go a funny colour. My best is bacon but they haven't got it today.' I'd never been a great one for breakfast even at home, but under Brian's watchful eye I managed to eat a piece of toast, and the hot chocolate was a great improvement on Denny's egg-nogs.

'Hello chicken,' June said, coming into my cubicle just after Brian. 'Did you have a good night then? Now let's get you up and dressed and you can just have a quick wash this morning and then we'll think about a way for you to have a shower later on. Is that okay?' I nodded. I couldn't see how I could have a shower – you had to stand up to have a shower – but I didn't say anything.

Mum had laid out socks and underwear along with the unspeakable new track-suit bottoms and velcro-fastening trainers.

'Oh, new clothes,' said June. 'You lucky girl.' I kept my thoughts to myself. Watching June dress the lower half of my body was like watching someone dress a dummy model – the kind you see in those sessions where people are taught the kiss of life. She expertly lifted one foot and put a sock on it, then the other. She put each leg into a hole of a new pair of bigger knickers and then smoothly rolled me from side to side to pull them up, talking to me all the time in her deep, rich voice. Then she did the same thing with my trousers. I hated to admit it even to myself, but I could see what Mum had meant – it was easier to put on these sorts of clothes. When my feet and legs and bum feel like they belong to me again, I thought, that's when I'll start dressing in clothes that I like. June wanted me to put the new yellow T-shirt on but I chose the grey one. I thought I might need it for luck.

The idea of the Gym had hung over me like a dark cloud ever since Trudy had mentioned it, so I was glad that June offered to accompany me there on that first day. In the lift and along the corridor, she laughed and joked with me.

'That little Brian's fallen for you, you know. You'd better watch out. He can be a little devil.'

'What's the matter with him?'

'He was born without all his vertebrae formed in the right way and he has to keep having new plaster casts while he's growing to make his spine as straight as possible.'

'Does it hurt him?'

'Yes, sometimes he's in a lot of pain.'

'Will he be alright when he's grown up?'

'It's hard to say. He'll always look different. It's a good job he's got such a strong spirit. He knows how to make people fall for him!'

Even June seemed to shrink a bit as we went through the door of the Gym. It was an enormous square room on the top floor of the hospital. Out of the huge picture windows, you could see all the small factories and shops nearby, then out over the thousands of red-tiled roof-tops of suburban northwest London. The houses seemed wedged together like identical twins with small squares at the front and long green rectangles at the back. One of these houses could be mine.

It wasn't anything like the gym at school, where big groups of people would all be actively pursuing the same task, somersaulting, jumping over stools or throwing balls at each other with a teacher telling you all what to do. It wasn't anything like the kind of gyms they have in sports centres, either, where there are loads of exercise bikes and people 'pumping iron' and everyone is doing their own thing. Everything seemed very spread out and there was a lot of stuff I'd never seen before.

In one corner there was an old man strapped to one of those beds you see in the doctor's surgery, but the whole thing had been tilted up so that his body was vertical. His skin was a ghastly unhealthy grey, and poking out of the bottom of his green striped pyjamas was a bag full of orange-colour pee. Revolting. There were a few people lifting weights in a half-hearted way, and a woman about Mum's age sitting on a mat on the floor with someone in a uniform throwing large, brightly coloured balls for her to catch. None of the kids had come up from the ward yet. I felt miserable and lonely and it was good to feel June's hand lightly touch my shoulder.

'Ah, you must be Elizabeth; we've been expecting you. I'm Pauline Blood, the senior therapist on the paediatric team, and you'll be working with me at least at the beginning. Dr Singleton tells me you've been getting on quite well with young Trudy but there's lots of work still to do. Lots of work. And of a different kind.' She spoke in a PE teacher's kind of voice – well, PE teacher with a bit of army sergeant in it. It didn't seem worth mentioning that no-one called me Elizabeth – I couldn't have got a word in anyway. 'Now today you'll be with us for just two hours and then we'll build the time up each day until we've got you here full-time.' She laughed as if this was some kind of joke. 'We'll work out a programme of activities for you to follow so that you can get on, even if I'm working with someone else. Ah, nurse,' she said, as if she had just spotted that someone was with me.

'June,' June said.

'I'm sorry – June. You can come and get Elizabeth.'

'Libby,' June said.

'You can come and get *Libby*,' she said with sarcastic emphasis, 'at twelve o'clock. I expect she'll have worked up quite a good appetite for her lunch.' June gave me a final reassuring squeeze on the shoulder and disappeared.

'Right, we'll get going straight away. I don't have anyone else coming for an hour so I can give all my attention to you.' I wasn't at all sure I wanted Pauline Blood's undivided attention but I didn't have a lot of choice. She took out a little blue book where she'd already written quite a lot of notes and looked like she was about to write some more. 'We'll start seeing what you can do and then I'll put you on the tilt-table when George goes back to the ward.' She nodded over towards the grey-green elderly bloke I'd spotted earlier. 'It's a long time since you've stood up and we need to get you upright so that the blood starts circulating properly. We'll do that for a few days and then I'll really start working you hard. We're going to get you walking, you know. Oh yes,' she repeated in a tone which suggested that some invisible person had just contradicted her. 'I'm not saying it will be easy – it takes a lot of effort and determination, but we're going to get you walking again. Very soon.'

That first morning we went through all those tests I'd done loads of times before. 'Squeeze my thumbs as hard as you can. Push your hands against my hands. Try to wriggle your toes. Can you feel this? Can you feel that?' PB, as I started to call her in my mind, asked these questions like she was drilling me in my twelve times table which she was sure I hadn't learnt properly. It was horrible going through this all over again. The answers were exactly the same as those I had given to Trudy. Why couldn't she have spoken to her? Perhaps she already had it written in her little book and was just testing me. She didn't say anything when I answered her questions, just carried on poking and prodding and writing things down.

After about twenty minutes of this, somebody wound down the tilt-table and two porters bundled George into an enormous grey wheelchair and took him off somewhere. He looked at them vacantly as if he had no idea where he was. Under instruction I wheeled over to this contraption and was helped onto the slightly padded red vinyl bed. I was strapped down and fastened with three wide belts. No-one explained what was going on, but I was getting used to this. The hospital seemed divided into two kinds of people. Those like Trudy and June who talked to you all the time and explained what they were doing to you, down to the minutest detail. And those like PB and some of the doctors who did things to you while saying as little as possible.

PB pressed a button on the side of the bed and the whole bed began to tilt upwards until it felt like I was going to fly straight out the window, out over the roof-tops of suburban London. Fortunately she stopped it before I turned completely upside-down. Actually, it stopped when I wasn't even completely upright but it still felt weird to see people's heads rather than their belly-buttons. I could see further out of the window, and I could see my feet (not that I wanted to look at those revolting trainers) without practically falling out of the chair. I'd forgotten what it felt like to be this tall. But it didn't feel good, it felt horrible. I wasn't really standing up – I certainly wasn't walking. I was just strapped to a hospital bed at an angle of 65 degrees and I must have looked stupid. Before I had time to get really depressed, I was wound down again and put back into the wheelchair by two guys in blue uniforms who seemed to be standing around just for that purpose. This time PB set up some machine and instructed me to pull down these weights looking at the timer so I could work out how many I did in a minute. 'The more you can do, the stronger you'll get,' was her idea of a conversation.

Somehow a whole morning passed like this and I was exhausted by the time June came to get me. Back in the ward, Brian was announcing loudly, 'You can't sit here, I've saved this place for Libby – she's got to have her lunch next to me.' I smiled and June manoeuvred me into the place at the lunch table. I could have done it myself, I suppose, but it was nice not to have to think about it. To my surprise, I actually felt hungry. I'd felt sick for so long that I almost didn't recognise the sensation. This was just as well since Brian had clearly decided to be my self-appointed minder in the matter of eating. He went through the menu like he was reading from a book where the writer had forgotten to put in any full stops.

'First of all you can have tomato soup or you can have little bits of great-fruit with a cherry on the top but have tomato soup that's what I'm going to have then you can have sarndeens with lettuce and tomato and stuff or you can have chicken with rice in it and have chicken 'cos that's best and tastes lovely and then you can have chocolate pudding like me.'

Fortunately there were only three courses, because Brian was completely out of breath by now. He stopped talking and took a deep breath, looking very pleased with himself.

I'd never known such a small child to eat so much – Robbie wouldn't have eaten a third of what Brian got through and that was without an enormous plaster jacket. He ate rapidly with a spoon with his head on one side as if it was too heavy to hold itself straight for long. I didn't exactly tuck in but nevertheless ate more than I had for weeks and weeks. Brian had been right, the soup was familiar and comforting and the chicken was warm and tasty. I couldn't manage the chocolate pudding so Brian and I silently swapped plates and he ate all mine, too. That was the first day in a long time that had felt remotely like a normal day – getting up in the morning, getting dressed. A day of activities punctuated by mealtimes and then going to bed in the evening feeling tired, or in my case, absolutely exhausted. I hadn't exactly enjoyed myself but at least it seemed like real time rather than the endless dream/nightmare of my first weeks in hospital.

The next morning, I was pleased that June's was the first face I saw. In the adult ward, I never seemed to see the same nurse two days in a row.

'Hello chicky–chick. I'm going to get you dressed because we're a bit late today and I don't want to get a smack from her up there in the Gym.' She winked at me. 'But when your mummy comes this afternoon one of the nurses is going to show her how to help you have a proper shower and wash that lovely hair of yours.'

I didn't mind her talking to me like I was a baby. I didn't have to think about things when June was in charge. She certainly got things done quickly and before I knew where I was, I was dressed, hair and teeth brushed. Under Brian's watchful eye, I'd eaten a piece of toast and drunk half a cup of tea and was now in the Gym waiting for PB to appear. I couldn't help noticing the look of relief on June's face when she realised we'd actually arrived early in the physiotherapy department. Old George was lying on the tilt–table again still looking like he didn't know what he was doing there, and there were a couple of other people doing their exercises in a half–asleep sort of way so that their yawning and stretching both seemed to be parts of the same movement.

Pauline Blood came in like a whirlwind, speaking to the world at large, rolling up her sleeves and getting her notes from her bag all in one movement.

'That traffic, it's just ridiculous. I left home an hour ago – an hour for a twenty-minute journey. One heavy rainstorm and the whole of the road system is in turmoil.' She spat out the word 'turmoil' as if it had two parts – TUR MOYLE. 'This country – don't they realise some of us have an important job to do?' It seemed that I was PB's important job to do because as she talked, she scooped up a plastic sheet, a big roll of something white and an enormous pair of scissors and nodded in my direction.

'Right,' she said. 'Let's get going. We're late and I want to get you started on a proper programme as soon as possible.' The 'you' was obviously 'me'. I pushed myself slowly over to a bench where she was smoothing out a large, white, plastic sheet.

'Oh,' she said irritably. 'They should have told you not to wear trousers this morning, we'll have to get them off. I trust that you're wearing clean knickers.' She made a rough grunting sort of noise to acknowledge her own joke.

Before I knew where I was she'd got my shoes and trousers off and lifted my legs onto the bench like they were heavy bags someone had annoyingly left in the wrong place.

'Okay,' she said. 'One hand on the bed, one on the chair and a nice clean lift – one, two, three – over.' Before I had time to think about it, I was there. It was the neatest transfer I'd ever done. PB was tying herself up in a large plastic apron and putting on thin rubber gloves. She looked like she was about to start dissecting something messy. She called over to the young woman who

106

yesterday had been throwing the coloured balls. It took me some weeks to work out who did what job in the Gym, and eventually I learned to tell by their different uniforms, but it was obvious from the way PB spoke that she was used to giving this person orders.

'Sandra, I need thick white stockings and a large basin of warm water. Then you can come and give me a hand.' Sandra was back within a few minutes, a basin in her hands and a packet of something tucked under her arm. She placed them carefully on the trolley next to the bench. 'One isn't any good to me,' PB said irritably. 'I told you I need a pair.' Sandra looked as if someone had hit her but went off and returned swiftly with another packet.

I had no idea what she was doing to me but assumed that, when it suited her, she'd let me know. Sandra pulled a thick white stocking onto each leg and rolled me onto my stomach. I turned my head and watched in amazement as she cut a strip off the thick white roll, dipped it into the water and smoothed it onto the back of my legs, from the top of my thigh right down to my ankles. It felt like I was a pie and they were covering me in pastry – Libby en croute.

'What are you doing to me?'

PB looked at me with some interest, as if she'd forgotten there was anyone there.

'Can you feel this at all?' I was beginning to feel a pleasant warm tingle all the way down the back of my legs. 'It may start to feel uncomfortably hot but we'll only leave it on for another ten minutes.'

'What's it for?' I felt a bit scared asking her the same

question twice but I was beginning to understand that unless I did, I wasn't going to know.

'I'm making you some back slabs.'

'Sorry?'

'Back slabs,' PB repeated slowly, as if my problem was that I hadn't heard what she'd said. 'Now you just lie there quietly. I'll be back in a few minutes and see how you're getting on.'

'What is it on my legs?' I asked Sandra when PB'd gone. 'Do you know what back slabs are?'

'Erm, erm . . .' Sandra began nervously as if I'd asked her to tell me some great secret. 'What it is, it's like that plaster stuff they put on you if you break your leg or something.' She spoke in a tight little voice as if she was afraid of the sound of it but was fine once she got going. 'What they do is, they wet it so it becomes soft and then they press it onto you so that it moulds into the shape of your legs and when it sets it's like a plaster cast, erm, only they don't have to cut it off or anything, they can just lift it off because it's only on the back of your legs.'

'What are they going to use them for?'

'Oh,' she said, as if this question had taken her by surprise. 'I'm not sure exactly. I'm just the assistant here; I haven't done my training yet so I don't think you should ask me.' Her voice trailed off to a whisper and she busied herself clearing up the plastery mess.

Chapter Seven
Visits

I learned what they were for a few days later. I'd begun to settle into an uneasy routine – get up, have breakfast and a little chat with Brian and phone home from the plug-in phone on the ward if there was time and if it was free. Then I'd go up to the Gym and stay there until lunchtime. After lunch I was supposed to be doing 'education'. The hospital teacher had come to see me and talked about getting work from school but quite honestly after two hours or more with PB the only thing I was fit for was getting into bed and sleeping. Grandma sometimes used to say she felt 'bone tired', and I began to understand what it meant. After the evening meal or sometimes a bit earlier Mum or Dad would come bringing news about a world I could hardly remember. I still hadn't seen anyone from school.

I was in a state of limbo somewhere between being

very ill and getting better. Inside me, everything seemed as confusing and frightening as it had been when I was really ill. I still didn't understand what had happened to me or what would happen in the future. I just went along with what other people told me.

When PB started what she called the 'real work', I had no alternative but to go along with that, too.

'This is the first stage towards getting rid of that wheelchair,' she said briskly. 'We'll take it one step at a time and you'll see how much progress you're making.'

From a nearby bench she took up what looked like two creamy-coloured drainpipes which had been cut in half lengthways and a large roll of crepe bandage. I could just about identify them as the 'back slabs' – the braces for my legs that they'd made the other day. Then, wordlessly, she pulled my bum forward in the wheelchair, slipped the half tubes up the back of my legs one at a time and wrapped the crepe bandages round them to keep them in place. I was the sausage meat and they were the pastry. Hey presto, two stiffly baked, extra-long sausage rolls.

Next she began to fiddle around with my feet and what looked like a large catapult. It had a circle of elastic at one end, a circle of canvas at the other and between them a strap with a buckle on it. PB fastened the canvas circle around my knee, put the elastic loop under my foot and pulled hard on the buckle. 'Right, that's got rid of the foot drop,' she said, as if she were talking about the kind of disease farm animals get.

It was a mystery to me what would happen next. My legs stuck out straight in front of me and I held on tightly to the wheels, terrified that I would tip out. PB had no alternative but to speak.

'This is just your first try at standing up. Now you really have to concentrate on keeping your balance. Let's see how far you get on your own. I'll move the footplates of the wheelchair out of the way and you move your bottom forward and get yourself into a standing position by holding on to these parallel bars.'

It was like telling me to do a triple somersault. Mrs Blood waited. I stayed stuck to the chair. She pursed her lips and raised her eyebrows as if she couldn't believe anyone could be so pathetic. 'Sandra, come here a minute please.' Sandra stopped what she was doing and came forward nervously. 'You stand at the back and help this young lady move forward and I'll stand here until she's upright.' Between them, they manoeuvred me forward and one pushed and one pulled until I was standing up with my hands clutching the parallel bars like a drowning man clinging to a life raft.

I don't know if you've seen that video of Wallace and Grommit, *The Wrong Trousers*, the one where Wallace invents a pair of metal trousers that are supposed to walk on their own. Instead of flexible knee joints that bend when you walk, these are stiff, metal leg-shaped tubes that stick out horizontally. When Wallace tries to walk in them the legs go straight out in front then down again, one after the other. That's what I felt like – someone in the wrong trousers, or more accurately, the wrong legs. PB's 'leg braces' had got me standing up stiff as a post, but I didn't know what I was supposed to do next.

'All I want you to do is let go with one hand, then let

111

go with the other,' she said, trying to prise the fingers of my left hand away from the bar. She said it as if it was the easiest thing in the world. I tried, I really did, but it felt like I was holding on to my own life. I concentrated on the large coloured ball lying at the other end of the parallel bars. Suddenly all the colours started to merge together, first into pale grey, then into black.

'I think that she's . . .' I heard Sandra's little voice from a distance.

'Okay, I suppose that's enough for today,' PB said, trying, I suppose, to sound encouraging. 'We've made a start anyway. More tomorrow.'

All the tomorrows slid into one another over the next few weeks. Pauline Blood and I developed one of those relationships you sometimes have in school with really strict teachers. You think they are loathsome human beings, but they get you through the exams. Sometimes I really hated her but I felt that she was my lifeline – if I worked hard with her, I'd get rid of the wheelchair, I'd be able to walk again, I'd be able to go home. Everybody tried to convince me that I was making progress but if I was, it was achingly, unbearably slow. After about a week, with the leg braces on, I could get myself into a standing position on the bars and hold on just one hand at a time. After two weeks, I could swivel my hips and move one leg at a time but it took ages more for me to get anywhere near the end of the parallel bars. I couldn't get rid of the image of *The Wrong Trousers*, programmed to take Grommit the dog for a walk – disembodied, stiff legs moving one creak at a time.

PB's manner was either barely controlled irritation or a kind of bright jolliness which I found unconvincing. Even her words of encouragement made me feel worse.

'Last month I had a boy who was badly injured in a car crash. At first he couldn't walk at all. The doctors said he'd probably have to be in a wheelchair for the rest of his life but I've never seen anyone so determined to make progress. He'd make the nurses bring him up first thing in the morning and then he'd be on those parallel bars up and down, up and down, there was no stopping him. Within three weeks I got him from the bars onto the rolling frame, then crutches, then a stick, and by the time he went home, you wouldn't think there'd ever been anything wrong with him.' She paused in satisfaction at her story and looked at me. I could guess what was coming next.

'I'm not saying it's easy, Libby. You've been very ill and you're still weak, but you must try as hard as you can every single day, otherwise you'll never get on.'

Perhaps it was true. Perhaps a stronger, braver, more determined person than me would make better progress but I was so tired all the time and I didn't see how you could make legs work when they had no life in them – no life and no feeling.

The thing I liked best was being in the water. Once a week, I'd go down to the hydrotherapy pool. It was quiet and calm down there and the water was as hot as a good bath. PB never came with me. Sometimes I'd work with a different physio and I'd be able to walk along, holding on to the side of the pool. Sometimes I'd be left alone with a foam collar under my neck with a float on either side and there I'd lie in the warm half light and dream about being home, about going back to school and everyone wanting to be my friend, about wearing nice clothes again, about not feeling so sad any more.

Some weeks into what my dad still called my army training – it must have been the beginning of October – Dr Singleton came to see me in the Gym. He was surrounded by a team of young people in white coats. I was lying on one of the plinths with my left leg up in a big canvas sling. At the top of the sling was an enormous butcher's hook which was attached to metal mesh which hung down from the ceiling. The idea was for me to move my leg backwards and forwards to build up the muscles in my hips and thighs, but I'd learned that by moving the upper part of my body, I could give the impression that I was working hard. It wasn't the most elegant position to find yourself in.

'Hello, Libby. I've brought some students to see how you're getting on. Would you mind taking us through your paces?'

'Oh, Dr Singleton, how nice to see you.' PB had appeared from nowhere and spoke in a voice I'd never heard before, heavy and sweet at the same time. It was typical that she'd known he was coming and hadn't said anything to me about it. 'You're a bit earlier than expected,' she said. 'I'm just setting up the parallel bars and then she can move onto the walking frame. I'm afraid we haven't progressed to the crutches yet, but we're still working at it.'

Dr Singleton gave a silent nod in her direction, and his students moved round me in a semicircle.

For the next thirty minutes I felt I was on show. Well, I *was* on show. There was the doctor, his five students with their pens and notebooks, Sandra, who looked as though she might cry any second, and PB hovering around like a hostess at a cocktail party. And me. I really tried as hard as I possibly could. I wanted to show him how much I could do and I felt that if I failed, I would be letting PB down. I don't know why I cared about this but I did. I went through everything I'd learned. I put on the leg braces, lifted myself upright by holding on to the parallel bars and stood there for a few seconds trying to get my balance. I took a few steps forward and then two steps backward. The students were busily writing. Dr Singleton looked at me and then at his students. I was certainly being judged.

'That's very good, Libby. Now let's see what else you've learned.'

Sandra brought over the rollator. It was the sort of thing you see on the TV news in items about falling standards in old people's homes. There was usually an old dear in furry slippers and a pink cardigan rolling the frame along the corridor. I'd been heavily resisting using it up to now but I wanted to show how well I was getting on. Sandra held it steady whilst I let go of the bars and clung on to the handles. You had to move in a different way in this frame. You had to roll your shoulder, hip and leg all in one movement. I must have pushed too hard with my shoulders because the wheels stretched away in front of me and I couldn't move my leg quickly enough. I felt myself falling, not in a gentle heap but splat, straight forward onto my face with my stiff legs sticking out straight behind.

Everyone rushed forward and PB caught me just before I hit the ground. I heard someone laugh then try to cover it with a cough. There was nothing funny about it to me, nothing at all.

'I'm sorry,' I said foolishly. I was completely exhausted and near to tears.

'Don't be silly. You're doing your best.' PB sounded as if she really meant it, and it was the nicest thing she'd said to me so far.

When Dad came to see me that night I could hardly bear to tell him what had happened. Still, Dad didn't often ask me about difficult things. I think he was worried it might get me all upset and he saw his job as cheering me up. He was also very caught up in the whole business of what had made me ill in the first place.

'I got this pamphlet today called "Murky Waters" and it says that almost half of Britain's coastline can be considered polluted and it's getting worse. Do you know that every day, every single day, around 300 million gallons of raw sewage is discharged into the seas around Britain? This research shows that ninety per cent of the sewage going into the sea hasn't even been treated. There's all sorts of cases where people have become really ill after being in the sea even for a short time – hepatitis and ear infections and heaven knows what. There's beaches that have been passed as safe to bathe in by the authorities because there isn't any evidence of ordinary bacteria in the sea-water – Littlehampton where you were, that's one of them that's supposed to be safe – but this report shows that they know there are enteroviruses in the water and they can be much more dangerous. That's what they say you've got, a really nasty virus.'

I just let him run on. There wasn't any point in interrupting once Dad got a bee in his bonnet. He's always been a bit of a hobbies man. Old cars was just one of them – there'd also been collecting wild mushrooms, fishing, making musical instruments, tennis. It seemed like pollution in the sea was one more of his hobbies.

Mum's visits were very different. Looking back on it now I can see that she must have been worried out of her mind the whole time and trying not to show it, but I wasn't in any state to think about anyone else's feelings. She tried bringing me books to read or tapes to listen to but I couldn't bear other sounds or other worlds in my head. I didn't even want to watch the television. I looked forward to her visits more than anything but when she came I was irritable and grumpy.

'How did you get on with physiotherapy today?'

'What's the point in asking me that all the time? I don't "get on" with it at all. I just do it. I just do what she tells me. I strap the bloody casts round my legs – that takes forever – then I try to stand up, then I try to walk. I walk two or three steps up the bars too scared to let go and *she* says, "I'm sure you can do a bit more than that" and I say, "No I can't, my legs hurt too much" and then I sit back down in the wheelchair and I'm too tired to do anything else all day.'

'It's bound to go slowly darling, you've come a long way. Don't forget that you've been really ill.'

'I haven't *been* very ill, I *am* very ill. Why does everyone talk as if it's all in the past and I'm better now? If I was better I'd be up and walking, I'd be going home. I can't do a fucking thing for myself.' Mum winced but didn't say anything. 'Everyone talks as if they know what's best, as if they know what I should do. But they don't. If they felt like me they'd soon stop talking all this crap about making progress and having come a long way. I haven't come anywhere, I'm not going anywhere.'

Sometimes Mum would try a different tactic. 'Esther phoned yesterday to see how you are. She and Joanna would really like to come and see you. She said they've got lots of cards and things for you from people at school. Can I tell them they can come this Saturday? I'll tell them they can't stay long – even half an hour would be nice for you; it would be a change.'

It was strange seeing them again – like visitors from another planet. They were ever so sweet and a bit shy, like little girls visiting a rather scary great aunt. You could tell from the way they came in together that they'd become closer now. They were quite different. Esther was tall and slim with lovely, caramel skin. Her hair was parted in the middle and arranged in braids which made her look sweet and rather old fashioned. Her glasses made her look more serious than she really was. Everyone thought of Esther as a bit of a star student, hardworking, top marks, Grade 6 piano. All the teachers liked her. Joanna, on the other hand, was a bit of an airhead. She wasn't stupid or anything but it was hard to get her to take anything seriously. Even when Esther challenged her, she'd just laugh and say, 'Well, you know me. I don't know anything about anything.'

They'd brought me good presents — thoughtful, sensible ones. Esther bought me a great big T-shirt to wear in bed — white with a red and black Minnie Mouse on the front — and some fruity-smelling shampoo and conditioner from the Body Shop. Joanna had bought me different pairs of brightly coloured socks and some nearly matching hair ties. We were all awkward at first but once they realised they didn't have to talk about me, things relaxed a bit.

'We didn't know what to get you, but we thought as you've got to be in here all the time it would be best to get some useful things. We thought about getting some chocolates or something but your mum says you haven't been eating all that much so we didn't know what to do. Is this okay?'

'No, honestly they're great presents, I really like them.'

'You've lost ever such a lot of weight. You'll have to get all new clothes when you get home.'

We all looked at what I was wearing now. No-one said anything. There were so many things not to be mentioned — the wheelchair for example, the fact that I stayed in it for the whole of the visit. Joanna had never been the most talkative of people but now she sat almost in silence. Whenever she looked at me and tried to speak, her eyes welled up with tears.

'I'm really sorry. I've never been very good in hospitals.'

Well, why did you come then? I thought but stayed silent. Esther tried to keep the conversation going. She told me what was going on in school, who was going out with who, who was getting into trouble, who was bunking off. We never talked about me other than the first, polite 'How are you?' which didn't need any more reply than 'Oh, not too bad, thanks.' As they went to leave, Joanna could no longer hold the tears in her eyes; they rolled down her face.

'I feel so sorry for you, Libby. I wish I could do something to help.' She practically ran from the room. Esther bent over and gave me a firm kiss.

'Take no notice, she's always been like that. She does worry about you, but if it's alright, I'll come on my own next time.'

I had a small, regular band of visitors. Mum or Dad would come every day, Gran and Granddad, sometimes 'auntie' Joyce and now Esther. The second time she came, she brought me an enormous card signed by everyone in our tutor group and a nice letter from my tutor. Robbie would usually come once or twice a week, sometimes after school with Mum and sometimes for a little while on the weekend. I liked seeing him but his energy wore me out. He seemed so noisy and loud in the little confined space of my room. Brian still followed me around like an enthusiastic puppy dog. His favourite time to come in and see me was on a weekday in the afternoon. After a morning in the Gym, my head and my legs and every bit of me would be aching and often I would get into bed, sometimes too exhausted to fall into a proper sleep. Brian would wait outside my door and I'd hear June or one of the other nurses trying to shoo him away.

'Libby's trying to get some rest. Why don't you go to

the playroom? You can see her when it's teatime.' But he'd just sit there patiently until he heard me say, 'It's okay, I'm awake, he can come in now.'

'Well, you just sit there quietly, Brian. Libby needs to build up her energy.'

'I'll be very, very quiet. Promise,' he'd say in a whisper that didn't convince anyone.

Brian was a child who liked to talk. For him, there was no difference between thought and speech. As soon as something came into his head, he'd say it out loud so that listening to him was like being in someone else's brain. His favourite pastime was to pick up something off my locker, a pen or a hairbrush, whatever came easily to hand, and to offer a stream-of-consciousness monologue about the still growing collection of cards on my wall, pointing to each of them in turn, making up stories about them as he went along.

'Here are two cats, their names are Sammy and Polly just like my cats at home. The big cat's more big than the little cat. The big cat is ginger like my cat and the little cat is brown and it's got stripy bits on it. The big cat is poorly, he had to have a plaster jacket on but now it's taken off and he's better. They're sitting on a big pillow sort of thing, I think it's red. Is it red? This one's got a table and lots of flowers, I like flowers but I don't like the smell 'cos it makes your nose go all funny . . .' He could go on like this for ages without expecting me to say anything and I would lie there listening to him, half sleeping, half listening. It was curiously restful.

'Hello love, you awake yet?' Mum stuck her head round

the door and Robbie ducked his head under her arm and wriggled into the room. 'I've got an appointment to see the doctor. Is it okay to leave your brother with you for a little while? Should be back in fifteen minutes at the most.'

Robbie looked at Brian like a cat who has spotted a stray tom climbing a tree in his own garden. Brian stopped mid-stream and looked back in surprise.

'You shouldn't take things if they don't belong to you.' Brian stood very still. 'That's Libby's brush, it's not yours. Give it back or I'm going to tell my mum when she gets back.'

'Robbie, it's alright,' I started, but he had already moved forward and sharply grabbed the hairbrush out of Brian's hand.

'And you shouldn't be in here anyway. This is Libby's room and she's got to be quiet. We had to go and get a drink when I came out of school because my mum said she hadn't finished her rest yet and I couldn't come in. And I'm her brother.'

Brian's eyes opened wide. He looked at me for guidance.

'Don't speak to him like that,' I said sharply. 'I don't mind him having my brush; he isn't causing any trouble.'

But Robbie continued to hold his ground.

'He shouldn't be in here, he should go somewhere else, go to his own room, not this room.'

'Okay, Brian,' I said, trying to sound consoling. 'Don't worry. You go off now and I'll see you later.' He backed out of the room without taking his eyes off Robbie.

'Why did you speak to him like that?' I said as soon as

Brian was out of earshot. Robbie looked at me and didn't say anything. 'He wasn't doing any harm. He just gets bored spending such a long time in the hospital. His family live a long way away and they can't come and visit every day so he likes to come and be with me. That was really nasty what you just did.'

'He's always in here, I hate him. He shouldn't be in here all the time. He's not your little brother, I'm your little brother!'

'Oh Robbie, come here.' I put out my arms and he climbed up onto the bed. I made him sit at my side and tucked the blanket over him. He was crying now, big noisy tears running down his face. 'I don't love him like I love you – you're my brother. But Brian hasn't got any brothers or sisters and he's only a baby really, he's not a big boy like you, so sometimes I let him come in and look at my things. It doesn't mean I don't love you anymore. I'm still your same sister even though I'm in hospital.'

'But you can't play with me like you used to, can you?' he said, with the painful honesty of the young. 'You can't give me piggybacks any more or play bouncy-bouncy.' I tried not to show how much that hurt. He was still only seven and he wanted me to be the same as I'd always been. I understood that.

'I'll tell you what we'll do. You just hop down for a minute and I'll get up.' I pulled on the sky-blue shiny trousers and allowed Robbie to velcro up my trainers. 'How would you like to go for a taxi ride?' I swung fairly easily onto the wheelchair. 'You tell me where you want to go.' I slipped a tenpence coin into his hand. 'I hope you've got some money on you.' It took him a moment to get the hang of what I was on about, then his face opened up into a delighted smile.

'Taxi, taxi,' he called, sticking out his arm. 'I want to go to the shops.'

'Well, climb on then,' I said, and he clambered onto my lap, completely forgetting Mum's frequent warning to be careful not to hurt me. I pushed us out of the ward and along the corridor towards the lift, suddenly feeling more energetic than I had for months. Robbie didn't care that there was nowhere to go; he was happy just to go up and down, up and down saying, 'Taxi, I want to go to the park – taxi, I want to go to the seaside' whilst the ten-pence coin changed hands again and again.

'Libby, Libby, hi, it's us.' I stopped abruptly by the lift doors and looked up. Cleo and Ben stood side by side and, slightly to their right, was Jesse. It was lucky that my face was more or less hidden by Robbie because I can't imagine what I must have looked like. I couldn't have been more amazed.

'I didn't know you were coming today,' I stumbled into conversation. 'My mum must have forgotten to tell me.' Ben looked uncomfortable.

'Is it okay to come?' He turned to Cleo. 'I told you we should have asked someone first. Sorry. Cleo said it would be alright just to turn up. She didn't think you got a lot of visitors in the week.'

'It's fine, honestly,' I said, trying to cover up my embarrassment and everyone else's. 'It's just a surprise, that's all. My mum always wants to organise everything for me so that I can be prepared.' I stopped. This was just making everything worse. I tried a smile instead. 'It's really nice to see you. Do you want to come and see my room? Robbie, you get off now.' Robbie willingly hopped off my lap in Ben's direction. He'd always liked Ben.

'Do you want a push?' I felt my jaw set against Cleo's question, although almost everyone who came to visit said the same thing.

'I'm fine, thanks,' I said, but I felt small and self-conscious, pushing along beside them. Ben seemed to have grown enormously tall and Cleo had gained three inches in a pair of black, thick-heeled leather shoes. I was suddenly aware of how ungainly it was pushing along, compared to the easy business of walking.

We all squeezed into my cubicle/room. Jesse sat on the chair, Cleo on the bed and Ben hovered.

'Robbie, if you go and ask one of the nurses, they'll give you one of those small grey chairs.' He scurried off with Ben behind him, pleased to have something to do. There was an awkward moment of silence.

'Where's my cards then?' Cleo said, studying the collection on the wall. 'You must have got the card from me and Jesse.' I wasn't sure how red I went; I hoped the heat was just coming from within.

'She's only put proper cards up; I don't suppose she wanted your manic scribbles on the wall when she was feeling so ill. Are you feeling a bit better now?' This was the first thing Jesse had said. He smiled at me and I smiled back, grateful that he'd found a way to get me off the hook.

'Yes, thanks. I think so anyway.'

'What do you do all day? Do they make you do schoolwork?'

'Most of the day I do physiotherapy in the Gym and sometimes I go swimming in the hydrotherapy pool. The children here do schoolwork in the afternoon but I'm usually so tired I can't do very much after lunch. I couldn't work here anyway; I think it's better if I wait till I get home. I must be really behind. I don't know how I'm ever going to catch up, especially in maths.'

'Oh, don't worry about it,' said Cleo, butting in. 'Jesse'll help you as soon as you come back. He's brilliant at maths.'

'What kind of thing do you do in physiotherapy?' Jesse asked, ignoring the interruption.

'Well, they get me to do weights and things to build up the strength in my arms, and they make me throw and catch balls to improve my balance. Then most days I have to put these braces on the backs of my legs and get up on the parallel bars or on a frame with wheels.'

'Is that to get you walking again?' I was surprised at the directness of the question. Walking. The favourite word in physiotherapy departments; the forbidden word elsewhere.

'Yes, but I'm not doing very well at it.' This was the first time I'd said anything like this to anyone other than Mum. How strange that I was saying it to Cleo and Jesse, two people who I'd thought would be guaranteed to make me feel tongue-tied and self-conscious. They looked at me sympathetically.

'Did they say how long it'll be before you can go home?'

'They never tell you things like that. They just say, if you keep working hard on the parallel bars, you'll soon be able to use the frame. If you keep working on the frame, you'll soon be able to walk with crutches, then you'll just need a stick. Things like that. They never say how long it will take.'

No-one knew what to say next. I looked at Cleo. She looked even more extraordinary than the last time I'd seen her. Her hair was very short and dyed a sort of greeny red as if two separate colours had merged together in the wash. She now had about seven earrings in each ear and a new acquisition, a nose stud. Lots of girls in school had nose studs but it was a cultural thing. I was surprised Cleo's mum had let her. She looked back at me in a peculiar way and I was suddenly excruciatingly aware of my appearance.

'Are those shell-suit bottoms?' Cleo asked with her usual level of tact and diplomacy. Jesse turned towards her with what I hoped was a 'what does it matter what she's wearing' look. I found myself laughing.

'I know, they're revolting aren't they? Mrs Blood . . .'

'Mrs *Blood*!?'

'Yes, Pauline Blood, my physio, she told my mum that I had to wear loose comfortable clothes and this is what she bought me.' I tried to make light of it. 'Great shoes, don't you think?' We all looked down.

'My granddad's got some just like it,' Jesse said. 'He said they're the most comfortable things he's had since his army boots.' We all convulsed in giggles, part genuine, part nervous. I was glad I hadn't known they were coming. I would have worried myself sick but now they were here, it felt okay. More okay than I could have imagined. Ben came back into the room with Robbie and chair.

'What are you all laughing about? I saw your Mum

down the corridor, Libby. She said she'll be along in a couple of minutes – she's just going to talk to Mrs Flood. What have I said now? I don't know what's the matter with you lot.'

We all went off again. Ridiculous childish giggling about nothing at all. Robbie caught the infection even though he didn't have a clue why we were laughing.

'It's Blood, not Flood,' Cleo said, gasping for breath.

'Where's the blood? I don't know what you're all on about,' Ben said crossly, and that started us up all over again.

'Well, you sound as if you're having fun,' Mum said, coming into the room. Her presence changed the atmosphere and we suddenly felt young and a bit silly. 'Sorry, I didn't mean to put a damper on things. I think I'll go away again.'

'No, it's alright, we better be going soon anyway,' Ben said, looking at Cleo and Jesse. 'I didn't tell my Mum I was going to be late; we just decided to come at the last minute.'

'Yeah, Jesse bought a present for you and asked Ben if he could give it to his mum and we just decided we'd all get on the bus and give it to you ourselves.' It was Jesse's turn to go red now. I saw how freckly he'd gone in the summer, freckly and tan at the same time. His hair had grown longer and less schoolboyish, and although he was wearing his school blazer, he still managed to look pretty relaxed in it. 'And I got you something as well,' Cleo continued. 'I'm not sure what your mum will think of it though.' But Mum had diplomatically disappeared again, this time with Robbie.

Cleo produced her gift, stuffed into a brown paper bag. I pulled out a small cellophane packet of black, red and white tattoo transfers, everything from a rose to a skull and crossbones.

'I thought they might brighten things up a bit, not sure they'll go with the outfit though. But it doesn't look like we can do them now, shall I come another time? Oh, there's something else in the bag too.' I fished inside it and pulled out a tiny, ruby-coloured stud and a small, round piece of metal. I must have looked confused. 'Don't you know what it is? Here, let me show you.' She leaned over me in a familiar way and stuck something in my nostril with one hand and something outside with the other.

'Ouch, that hurts!'

'There you go, that will give Mrs Blood something to talk about.' She stood back and admired her own work. 'That looks pretty cool.'

'Is that what yours is?'

'Naw, mine's the real thing; yours is magnetic. My mum only let me have my nose pierced because I threatened to have my navel done. These pretend ones are a bit naff really but we can go and get yours done properly when you get out of here. Nose I mean, not navel.'

'We really need to get going now,' Ben said, fiddling with the door handle. 'I didn't bring anything for you because my mum said that when she came to see you she . . .' He trailed off awkwardly.

'That's fine, honestly,' I said. Ben had always needed reassurance that he was doing the right thing and not hurting anyone's feelings. 'Thanks for coming. Really, it's been great.' They all headed for the door.

'This is for you.' Jesse fished in his bag and pulled out a rather crumpled but brightly wrapped parcel. I opened my mouth and closed it again. Speech seemed to have left me entirely. Jesse smiled one of those smiles. 'You can open it later. It's a bit soppy but I hope you like it. I chose it myself.'

'Thanks' was all I managed to say. He stood in the doorway as if he couldn't decide whether to leave or stay.

'By the way, I meant to say it before. My aunt works here in the hospital and asked me to ask you if it would be alright if she came to see you. Would you mind? She's cool.' I nodded again. I wasn't mad keen on seeing anyone's aunt but I wasn't going to say that to Jesse. 'Right, I'll tell her to come then. See you soon, bye.' He smiled at me again.

As soon as they were gone I opened his present. It was a little teddy bear with curly old-fashioned fur, wearing a knitted navy-blue jumper with 'get well soon' stitched on it in red. I hunted around for a card or something but there was nothing else there.

'That was nice, wasn't it?' Mum said, coming back into the room. 'Did you mind them coming in like that without any warning?' She burbled on. 'That Jesse seems like a really nice boy. Joyce told me that Ben had got a new friend from school. He only started last year, didn't he – do you know where he'd been before? I hardly recognised Cleo, she looks so different. I'm glad you don't want to look like that. Is she going out with Jesse? I wouldn't have thought they'd go for each other, but what do I know?' She paused for a second to catch her breath. 'My God, Libby, what's that in your nose?'

Chapter Eight
Failing

On November 5th, the 'Friends of Queensbury Hospital' organised an indoor fireworks display for the patients on the Children's Ward. They brought in jacket potatoes donated by Spud-u-Like and hamburgers donated by McDonald's. Then they turned off the lights and those who were well enough waved sparklers around. Benjamin Bunny, Flopsy, Mopsy and Cottontail scuttled round the walls in the flickering light. My job was to go around and collect up the used sparklers so that the little kids didn't touch the hot ends and burn themselves.

'You're a big, brave girl. Now what happened to you, did you have a nasty accident?' I looked round to see a middle-aged woman in a flowery printed wool skirt and a white blouse, smiling down at me and nodding. 'Do you get out of that at all? You poor thing, you must have to have very strong arms to push yourself around in that. Let me give you a hand.' She moved behind me and I felt a jolt as I was pushed forward.

'Don't do that,' I said more sharply than I had intended. It had given me a fright being pushed when I wasn't expecting it. 'Could you let go? Please.'

'Well, I was only trying to help you my dear,' she said huffily. 'I've worked as a volunteer in this hospital for nearly twenty years and mostly I find people are very grateful for the helping hand I give them.'

June appeared from nowhere.

'Libby, Brian's asking for you again,' she said, putting her back between me and the offending woman. 'He's feeling all sore and itchy under that new plaster. Could you go and talk to him?'

'I could go and read him a story if you like,' the woman said. 'That's what I'm here for today.'

'Thank you very much, Mavis, but he'll only have young Libby, I'm afraid. He's been in and out of hospital so much over the last couple of months and he'll only let people he really trusts near him now.' June smiled sweetly as if she couldn't imagine having said anything to offend. I was grateful for the chance to escape.

I was getting used to people seeing me as an object of pity. I felt sorry for myself. I had been in hospital for three and a half months and sometimes it was impossible to imagine that I would ever go home. How could I when all I could do was to take a few steps clinging to a frame as if it was a life support machine or wash myself with a hand shower sitting down in a waterproof chair? I was sick and angry at how hard everything was. Endless,

endless exercises for such little progress. Everyone said I should take it one day at a time, but if I looked at it like that it seemed worthless to even try.

Joanna hadn't come since that first visit and even Esther hadn't been to see me for a long time. The journey to the hospital wasn't easy, and when she got here I wasn't much fun to be with. I didn't really want to hear what they'd been doing. What was the point? I couldn't share their world and they didn't want to talk about mine. I was miserable and I suppose visiting me was a miserable experience. I still spoke to her on the phone sometimes and that was better. We seemed to feel more comfortable with each other when it was just our voices.

I hadn't seen Jesse since that first visit. I'd thought about writing to him to thank him for the present but I didn't know his address and I wasn't going to ask anyone for it. Cleo hadn't been back either, but she'd taken to writing me long letters in her mad scrawl with gothic drawings in the corners and down the margins. Things weren't going too well for her. Her mum was in hospital in Maida Vale and Cleo was staying with her Dad, who lived quite a long way from school. She never really told me what it was about but I got the impression it was to do with depression. I remembered hearing Mum and Joyce talking about Cleo's mum and her 'problems' a long time ago.

Her letters were surprising and truthful, full of details about her life now and how she felt. She was unhappy living with her dad and his new girlfriend, even though she admitted they were nice to her, and she was worried about her mum. She was in a bit of trouble in school, too

– not keeping up with her homework, not wearing school uniform, cheeking the teachers. She was fine with the teachers who could be bothered to take some time and trouble with her, but she didn't feel the need to hide it with the teachers she didn't like. She told me they were getting twice as much homework now that they were in Year 11 and the teachers were always going on about 'only two more terms until the final GCSE exams.' At the end of every letter, she said, 'I seem to have spent this whole letter going on about ME. I'm sorry, I do think about you and hope you're getting better. I double promise I'll come and see you as soon as you get home. Love and hugs from Cleo.'

It was as if she'd forgotten that she'd ever been mean and nasty to me and just remembered us back in primary school in the days before Sofia came on the scene. It gave me a tight knot in my heart to think about the cruelty of those days; I could still remember that feeling. When someone you think of as your friend bullies you, then there is nowhere else to turn.

I'd stopped thinking about Jesse's promise to send his aunt to see me. I mean, I'd expected her every day for the next week, but it had been a long time since their visit and I assumed that she'd forgotten all about it. When she did eventually arrive, I was sitting up in bed, browsing through a magazine. I had three kinds of shock.

The first shock was that she was young, not like I'd imagined when he'd said the word 'aunt'. She had neat hair pulled back tight in a velvet band and she was wearing tight, chocolate-brown stretchy trousers, beautiful, shiny, short leather boots and a cropped, cream, ribbed cardigan. The second shock was that she was black. I wasn't completely stupid about mixed-race families – Esther's mum was from Trinidad and her dad was white and she looked much more like her mum – but thinking of tall Jesse with his shiny auburn hair and freckles and this neat, dark woman – it was hard to imagine the family connection. The third shock was the biggest one of all. Barbara pushed herself into my tiny room in a smart, sporty looking, black-and-red wheelchair.

'Hello, Libby,' she said in a confident, warm voice. 'I'm Barbara, Barbara Simons. Jesse may have mentioned me to you; we're related. I'm one of the hospital social workers but this isn't official business, I've just come for a chat. Is this a good time?' I nodded. 'How are you getting on?'

'Oh, okay I suppose.'

'You don't sound too sure.'

'Mm', I said evasively. 'What kind of work do you do here?' I didn't want to have to start off by talking about me and anyway, I was fascinated by her. She wasn't like anyone I'd seen before.

'All kind of things, really. I work with the patients or I help their families. I sort out benefits people are entitled to, housing problems, things like that. It might be a mum who has got to be in hospital for a long time and there's no-one who can look after her kids – I can help to organise foster care. Or someone needs help with organising a care package so that there will be someone to help them when they get home. Sometimes people just want to talk through their worries. I don't really need to do anything very much then, just listen.'

'How are you and Jesse, erm, you know . . .?'

She laughed. 'How are we related? Well, Jesse's mum is married to my big brother, Malcolm.' I must have looked confused because she laughed again. 'I know, it's a bit confusing, isn't it? Malcolm's not his birth dad, but he's looked after him since he was really little so they're like father and son in every way but looks.' That explained quite a lot about how Jesse got on with everyone at school and never seemed to take sides.

'Did they have any children of their own, Jesse's mum and your brother?'

'No, he's the only one. Do you like Jesse?' I must have gone scarlet. She laughed again.

'Sorry. Sorry. Dumb question. I've got a reputation for sticking my nose in it. Tell me something about you now.'

I found it really easy to talk to Barbara. I told her the whole history of the last few months, everything from the school trip to the sorry state I was in now.

'My dad's trying to prove that it was pollution in the sea that made me so ill. He's collecting all this research which shows how much raw sewage goes into the sea and how even when they test the waters, they're not doing it properly so the kind of viruses that make people ill don't show up on the tests. He's talking about getting a lawyer and taking them to court and everything.'

'And how do you feel about that?'

'I don't know how I feel. It *is* important if the sea is making people as ill as this.'

'But?'

'But, I don't think about it as much as he does. It isn't really helping me at the moment. It's like he's just trying to find something to do so that he doesn't have to talk about what's happening now. I can't really understand some of the things he tells me.'

'What about your mum?'

'My mum's been great, they're both great really. We used to argue a lot when I was at home, but we never seem to argue now. She tries to be cheerful but she just looks worried and upset when she comes to see me. Everyone treats me like I'm going to break into little pieces. She's always sneaking off to talk to the doctor or someone but she doesn't really tell me what they say. I don't want to have to think about other people's worries. I know that sounds selfish.'

'It doesn't sound selfish to me, it sounds human. You've got enough worries yourself. How are things going here?'

'Sometimes it just feels like people are getting at me. The physio gets at me because I'm not walking enough. The diet woman gets at me because I'm not eating enough. The occupational whatsits because I'm not jigsawing enough.' She smiled at me.

'*Are* you eating enough?'

'I'm eating as much as I can eat. I just don't feel that hungry, especially with most of the hospital food.'

'Well, I can understand that.' Barbara reached behind her into the bag on the back of her wheelchair. 'Would you like some chocolate?' She broke a bar of Cadbury's Fruit and Nut in half and we ate in silence. 'What are they saying in physiotherapy?'

'Do you know Pauline Blood, the chief physio?'

She smiled ruefully. 'Yes, I do.'

'Well, sometimes I feel that she's the only person who's helping me and sometimes I feel like she's just a big bully. She's always telling me stories about people who started off worse than me but did better. She wants me to be able to walk with crutches before I go home.'

'How much movement have you got in your legs?'

'I can stand up fairly easily if I hold on to something with both hands, and I can walk a little bit holding on to the parallel bars or that rollator thing, but if I try to stand up on my own, my legs just buckle underneath me. She makes me feel as if it's all in my mind, not in my body, like it's all my fault. Even if I just stand up, I feel exhausted and achy afterwards; it takes such a lot out of me.'

'It's good to be able to do that, though, stand up. I can't move my legs at all.' I stared at her in astonishment. She looked so fit and healthy.

'Well, how do you manage?'

'I use my arms – and this thing.' She patted the side of the wheelchair affectionately. 'This is my legs, this is my independence. I'm not saying it wasn't hard getting used to it. It was, especially at first. I spent months crying and crying all the time. I felt unbelievably sorry for myself before I realised how much I can still do without walking.'

'What happened to you?' I asked, and then a shadow of a look on her face made me ask, 'Do you mind talking about it?'

'I don't mind talking to you at all. Sometimes I feel it

138

isn't anyone else's business, but they're usually the kind of people who ask you just so they can say, "Oh you poor thing, I'll say a little prayer for you in church tomorrow."' She said this in a little squeezed-up voice and it made me smile.

'I was in an accident when I was eighteen, in the summer I was due to go to university. I was riding a bike with my boyfriend; we were going to Hampstead Heath. I was pushing my bike across the road at the crossing just by Whitestone Pond when a young guy in a flash car came speeding up the hill and ran me over. He said that he couldn't see because the sun was shining in his eyes. I don't remember the next bit but I was knocked flying and the result is, I broke my spinal cord just about here.' She pointed to a spot somewhere between her waist and her breasts. 'It was different for me because they told me straight away that I wouldn't be able to walk again, and after I came out of intensive care, the help I got was all about teaching me how to get on with life using a wheelchair.'

'Were you in this hospital?'

'No, I was in a special Spinal Injuries Unit in Pinner – it's not far from here actually. Everyone there was in more or less the same situation, although a few people who hadn't broken their spines completely were doing walking things like you.'

'Did you go to university?' I knew that I was asking too many questions but I wanted to know everything about her.

'Yes, I had to take a year out but the next year I went to Sussex to do a Social Studies degree just like I'd planned. They have rooms adapted for disabled people on the campus. Then I moved back to London to stay with my mum and dad and did my social work training.'

'Where do you live now?'

'I've got my own flat in Cricklewood. It's a housing association flat. Perhaps you could come and visit me one day. Would you like to?' I nodded. I was trying to imagine what her life could be like. I'd never seen anyone like her. I could only imagine people in wheelchairs in connection with hospitals. Or really old people.

'Do you have . . .' I stopped myself. I knew that there really should be a limit to my questions. Barbara threw back her head and let out a whoop.

'Do I have boyfriends? Yes I do, and shall I tell you something?' She leant towards me and opened her eyes very wide. 'Sometimes we even go to bed together.' Then seeing the look on my face she added, 'I'm sorry, I don't mean to tease you. I'm just saying that I have a pretty normal life for a single woman in her twenties. Not perfect, not always easy, but surprisingly normal. But it took me a long time to get my life how I want it. I had the kid-glove treatment for far too long, people wanting to overprotect me. I know it was because they loved me but sometimes it felt like my mum thought because I used a wheelchair, I was gonna be her baby forever.'

'How did you manage when you were living at home?'

'It wasn't as bad as it could have been. My parents live in a flat in Willesden and there's a lift in the building. Of course when the lift broke down, it wasn't much fun. It was pretty cramped but I had my own room. We had to have the bathroom and toilet all put into one, to make enough space for me to get in. They took out the bath and put in a shower with a shower chair – the council did that for us. My mum didn't like that very much, but it's just a little flat. Where do you live?'

'We live in a house in Kingsbury. All the bedrooms and the bathroom are upstairs. I don't see how I can go home until I can walk properly.'

'Yes, I see.' Barbara looked at me hard as if she was about to say something but then she changed her mind. 'All you can do is your best. It's still early days to be thinking about going home. I was in hospital for over five months before they even let me home for a weekend.'

'Five months?'

'Yup. I expect they'll want to see what progress you make in the next few weeks before they make any decisions. Would you like me to come and see you again?'

I nodded. 'Will you come soon?'

'Yes, I will. I'll come next week, I promise.'

She began to come regularly after that. One day she came a bit later so that she could see Mum, and I could tell Mum liked her. You couldn't help getting on with Barbara. She made things easy. There was something different about talking to her and it took me a while to realise what it was. It was that I didn't make her feel nervous and she didn't talk to me as if she was worried about each word she said.

All through November and into December I battled away with my walking and swimming exercises. I was getting fewer headaches and my arms were stronger but it still didn't feel like I was 'getting better'. PB had a couple of weeks holiday in early December and I hoped that they'd let me work with Trudy, but no such luck. Occasionally one of the other physios would come and help me, but mostly I worked with Sandra. She would whisper encouragement to me as I stood clinging onto the bars, inching my way along. But if I said I was too tired to do any more, I think she was as glad as I was to stop.

PB returned from her holiday in Malta, tanned and ready for action.

'Right, let's see how you've been getting on without me,' she said with typical briskness. 'Let's try you on the crutches. I hope you've been working on those.' I wasn't sure whether this comment was aimed at me or Sandra. Sandra looked like a frightened rabbit, but that wasn't anything new.

'I haven't been using the crutches,' I started. 'I can't really . . .' PB looked exasperated.

'Well, what have you been doing while I've been away? Just messing about?'

'Actually, I haven't been messing about. I've been trying to walk but I'm getting fed up with . . .'

'Fed up,' she repeated sarcastically. 'It's not supposed to be fun, Libby.' She said it as if we were talking about why I hadn't done my history homework. 'You're getting too used to that wheelchair. That's just taking the easy way out. You don't want to be stuck in that thing all your life, do you? You're never going to make any real progress unless you put in a bit more effort.'

Suddenly I couldn't take any more. All those months

and months of trying and trying as hard as I possibly could, however much it hurt and however little progress I made. I felt as if something had exploded in my brain.

'Shut up. Just shut up!' I screamed. 'You can't say that to me. "Make a bit more effort." Don't you think I've been trying and trying as hard as I can all these months? You don't seem to have any idea how frightening it is to try to stand up, to try to walk when you've got nothing to hold you up. You just make me feel as if I'm nothing and nobody and that any silly idiot half my age could do better than me and I'm fucking sick to death of you all. Don't you think I want to get better? Don't you think I want to walk again? That I want to go home? I'd do anything to get out of this stinking dump. Look at them. Just look at them.' I hit my legs hard with my hands. 'They feel like they're dead. Like I'm living but they've died. I wish for one minute you could get inside my body and see what it feels like. Then perhaps you'd stop making me feel like I'm useless and stupid. Then you'd stop going on and on about how I need to try harder. I am trying, I am. I've done nothing else but try.'

Suddenly all the fire and energy left me. Pauline Blood, Sandra, Trudy – in fact everyone in the whole Gym, patients and staff – had stopped what they were doing and were staring at me.

'I want to go back to the ward now,' I said quietly. 'It's alright. I can go on my own.'

I didn't start to cry until a few hours later, when Mum came. It still wasn't lunchtime so I suppose that June must have called her.

'Hello darling' was all she said, and she looked at me

with eyes so full of concern and love that I just cried and cried as if there was no way to stop. She held me in her arms and stroked my hair back from my head, saying nothing very much except, 'It's alright, it's alright. We love you; that's all that matters.'

When it was almost dark, June came in to say that she was going off duty now and she'd see me tomorrow. She'd brought Mum a cup of tea and me some hot chocolate and a couple of dried-up sandwiches on a plate. We ate them in silence.

'What am I going to do now?' I asked.

'I think it's time you came home,' Mum replied.

Part Two

Part Two

Chapter Nine
Home

It was a funny Christmas. Mum and Dad really wanted us all to be a happy, normal family again but it felt like everyone was trying just a bit too hard. Usually I loved everything about Christmas: opening all the cards as soon as they came through the letterbox, buying presents, wrapping them up, putting tinsel and paper chains everywhere. I loved all the special things we had to eat: spicy olives from the Greek delicatessen, sausage rolls, prawn toasts and the big Christmas dinner, turkey, roast potatoes, parsnips and all the trimmings. Mum and I always laid the table on Christmas Eve; it was the only time all year that we used a tablecloth and matching serviettes. Everything about Christmas was something to look forward to. But this year I sat and watched everyone else getting excited. It was like looking through a thick sheet of plate glass. I could see them and hear them but I was in a different space. I was like a visitor in my own home. I wouldn't have been at all surprised if Pauline Blood had knocked on the door and said, 'We're taking you back to the hospital now, Libby. Say thank you to these nice people for having you to stay.'

A week before Christmas, Dad went off to Wembley market and came home with an enormous Christmas tree and a box of coloured fairy lights in the shape of Victorian lamps. Mum turned up her nose when she saw them but Dad was very pleased with himself.

Decorating the tree was usually my favourite job. I loved getting the box down each year and dusting all the coloured baubles and the little toys. Mum and I had made some of them together when I was younger. Silver birds with tissue-paper wings and 'stained glass' bells and trees and angels with wings. These had been a mad craze one year. You could get them from the stationers in Kingsbury Road, and every day on the way home from school I'd nag Mum to buy a new one. They came in little boxes with tiny envelopes of plastic coloured crystals. You fitted them into little metal frames and baked them in the oven so that all the colours melted and shone. This year I watched Robbie stand on a chair and put the fairy at the top of the tree.

Grandma and Granddad came round for Christmas dinner as usual and we had the treats we always saved up for: sausage rolls when we opened our presents and chocolates and pale, pastel-coloured sugared almonds for after the meal when we were watching the Queen's speech on the telly. Granddad made us do it even though he said he was against the monarchy. 'It's a nice habit,' he always said. 'There are some traditions it's good to keep.'

It was funny about presents. Usually there were millions of things I really wanted and I'd make huge lists and hope for the best on the day. This year I didn't really need anything. I wasn't doing anything, I wasn't going anywhere. Mum and Dad bought me a Walkman with a radio in it. I knew they'd spent a lot on it and I didn't want to seem ungrateful but I couldn't build up much enthusiasm. I only really liked listening to music when I was on my own, but I never was on my own these days.

On weekdays I slept downstairs in the back part of the sitting room, on a sofa-bed mum had borrowed. I washed in a bowl in the kitchen and if I needed to go to the toilet, I'd have to use the commode the Social Services had brought round. It was revolting but it was surprising how quickly you got used to not having any privacy. I was scared Robbie was going to blab about it to his friends at school, but his new-found tact seemed to be lasting. He seemed to have grown up a lot in the last few months, too.

On the weekends when Dad was at home, or sometimes in the week if he wasn't teaching the first lesson of the day, he'd take me upstairs in the wheelchair, bump, bump, bump, or carry me in his arms like a baby. Up in the evening and downstairs again in the morning. At least then I'd be able to use the bathroom and sleep in my own bed. It was a surprise to see my bedroom again. It was still a child's room, lilac and white, full of cluttered girly things. Tiny china ornaments of teddy bears and cats curled up on cushions, glass bottles full of coloured swirly sand, stuffed animals, a dusty old doll's house full of little animals dressed up as people, a pin board full of postcards and pictures I'd cut out of *Just 17*. My room from another life.

The first weekend I was home, Robbie hung around outside the bedroom door.

'Libby, are you awake? Can I come into your bed – can we play our game?' I could hardly remember what he was talking about. 'You know. The one where you pretend that you don't know who I am and you say . . .' Mum interrupted before he had time to finish.

'Come away Robbie,' she said gently. 'Libby doesn't want to be disturbed. She needs to rest.'

'But Mu–um. Libby likes that game as well. She always used to let me . . .'

'Come on. Come downstairs now. You can watch some telly.' She led him away, quietly but firmly, and Robbie didn't ask anymore.

Mum had stopped working to look after me. Our relationship had really changed. She never shouted at me or told me off these days, even when I was really nasty to her. And sometimes I wasn't very nice at all. I'd shout at her for no good reason – like if she brought the wrong jumper from upstairs or made spaghetti when I thought we were having chicken. And then I'd feel so bad I'd burst into tears. She'd look at me sadly as if to say that she understood why I was acting like this – because my life was bloody awful, wasn't it? I'd feel guilty afterwards but I couldn't help myself.

Mum and Dad, and Robbie in his own way, worked hard to make us all into an ordinary family again. On Saturday nights we'd have takeaway pizza and Dad would go and get a video, usually a rubbish video. On Sunday, Gran and Granddad would come over for tea. I would try to join in – to get back that old familiar feeling of being part of a family – but sometimes I felt like an alien in my own home. It was as if I was an observer, looking in on something I wasn't quite part of.

I'd come home in the middle of December. It's not as easy as you might think being discharged from hospital, especially when everyone else thinks you ought to stay. Dr Singleton came to visit me the morning after my showdown in the Gym. He pulled up the chair and sat down.

'I hear you're not too happy, Libby.' I didn't know what to say so I kept quiet. 'Mrs Blood tells me that you're feeling rather negative about the progress you've been making with her.' More silence. 'Is that true?' I nodded. He looked at me for a few seconds. He was a nice man with a kind face and I didn't want him to think I was being rude on purpose but I honestly didn't know what to say. He took a deep breath and tried a different tactic. 'Try telling me why you got so upset yesterday.'

'I don't know what to say really,' I started. 'I have tried to do what she tells me but it doesn't seem to get me anywhere. I just couldn't take it any more, her bullying me.' I wasn't going to apologise to him for how I'd behaved and I certainly wasn't going to apologise to her. I wasn't sorry for what I'd said; she deserved it. 'I just want to go home and my parents think the same. I've been here long enough.'

'I understand how you feel,' he began. People were

always saying that to me – it drove me crazy. 'I'm just not sure you are ready yet.'

'It doesn't feel like I'll ever be ready,' I said gloomily. 'I'm not getting any better in hospital. I'd be better off at home.' I said this without much conviction. The truth was, I couldn't imagine what it would be like to be at home now everything was so different. But I knew I'd go mad if I had to endure one more day of PB's torture regime.

'You can't just stop doing physiotherapy and exercises though, Libby.'

'I know that.'

'Well, how about this for a compromise? I'll let you go home for Christmas – that's about two weeks away – if you promise to do some standing and walking with your mum each day. It will take a few days to get some equipment sorted out that you'll need at home. Then you can come and see me again in the new year and we'll look at it again. How does that seem?' I nodded, glad that he hadn't given me a lecture about causing such a scene on his territory. He stood up to go and then, as if he'd thought better of it, stuck his hands in the pockets of his white coat and looked down at me.

'You mustn't give up, you know. Rehabilitation takes a long time after such a serious illness as you've had. You need to keep on trying, even though . . .' He stopped again.

'What do you mean, "even though"?'

'You're a very direct young lady, aren't you?' he said, sitting down again. 'I can see I can't pull the wool over your eyes.'

'Well, what do you mean?' 'Even though' didn't sound like the start of an encouraging sentence. He looked me straight in the face. I knew he wasn't going to lie to me. It seemed like he was genuinely trying to work out what he was going to say.

'What's happened to you is very unusual. Rare even. There are other rare viruses that start like colds or flu and quickly cause complete paralysis – almost like someone breaking their spinal cord in a car accident. Then I have to tell them quite quickly, "This part of your body is going to be permanently paralysed." And the physios work with them to make the most of the parts of their body that still work. In your case, it's not so clear-cut. We haven't been able to pin down the exact virus and you still have feeling and movement in your legs.'

'Not very much,' I interrupted.

'No, not very much,' he repeated. 'The physiotherapist's job is to be as positive as possible – to make the best of what they've got. That's why Pauline has been working you so hard.' I made a face. 'I know you think she's been too hard, but the way she sees it, she's just doing her job.' I made a worse face but said nothing. I knew that if I stayed silent he'd eventually get to the point.

'It's nearly five months since you became ill. Usually I would want to wait at least a year until I made any pronouncements about how full the recovery was going to be, but there isn't anything usual about you, Libby.' I had to bite my tongue not to speak. I wanted to ask him to tell me the truth. No bullshit. No pretence any more. 'I can't give you any definite answers, I'm afraid. There is obviously some paralysis.' He paused again and we sat

153

there in silence. 'This is very difficult for me. Doctors never want to give negative news, especially when the patient is as young as you are. We always want to say there's a good chance – carry on trying, let's hope for the best. In a case like this, there aren't any pills we can give you to make you better. The best we can hope for is that with exercises your muscle strength will build up again.'

'They don't seem to be working so far.'

'No, they don't.'

'Are you really saying that things will never be the same as they were before?'

'It does look that way.'

'And are you saying my legs won't get any stronger?'

'No, I'm not saying that. I'm saying it's important to keep on trying, keep on exercising. But I'm also saying I don't have all the answers.'

I felt confused and upset. On the one hand he seemed to be telling me something new, but when I tried to think about what it was I'd learned, there seemed to be nothing there.

'Have you talked to my mum and dad about this?'

'No. It's very unusual for me to talk to someone as young as you like this, but you are a very unusual person, Libby. Would you like me to speak to them?'

'I think you should. They won't listen if it comes from me. But tell them after Christmas, when I come back from my check-up.'

He smiled at me, kindly. I took a deep breath.

'Is it my fault? Is it because I don't work hard enough in physiotherapy?'

'No,' he said very firmly. 'It isn't your fault. Whatever

you believe, you mustn't believe that.'

The last few days dragged by slowly. I had to wait until Barbara organised for someone from Social Services to come and pay a visit to our house. PB wanted me to go home with a walking frame and a pair of crutches. They didn't want to lend me a wheelchair at first, but Barbara persuaded her that it was a good idea. I wouldn't have been able to get anywhere without one. Social Services lent us the commode – 'until you can get upstairs on your own' – and a metal ramp for the step into the front door.

I didn't go to the Gym in those last few days in hospital. I stayed in my little hospital room, pretending to read and thinking about what it would be like to be home again. I felt scared and excited. I'd been a terrible coward about telling Brian. I'd become part of hospital life for him and he just expected me to be around. A few days before I went home, he was unusually quiet, as if he knew something was different.

'It's your favourite breakfast today,' he said as I moved towards the table. 'Scrambled eggs and munchrooms, but you can eat it all up 'cos I'm not very hungry now.' This was a sign of something serious; Brian always felt hungry.

'Oh dear,' I said. 'What's up?'

'June told me somefink and I don't know if it's true.'

'What is it?'

'She said you're going home and you're not coming back but you're not, are you?'

'Yes, it is true. I'm going home in a few days,' I said as gently as I could.

'But you're not better. Can you go home if you're not better?'

'Perhaps this is as better as I'm going to be.'

He looked at me very seriously. In fact, it was almost the same look as Dr Singleton had given me.

'Will you be in that chair thing all the time then?'

I didn't know how to answer him. 'I'm not sure. Maybe I will.'

'Mmm.' Brian nodded sagely as if nothing more needed to be said on this subject. 'That's alright then.'

I spent as much time with him as I could after that. He helped me take down all my cards from the wall and I let him choose some of his favourites to keep.

'You take the one of the two cats that you like. You know, the one you said used to have a plaster jacket on. The one that got better.' He took it down and carefully placed it on the table.

'There isn't a picture of a cat in a wheelchair,' he said.

'No, you'll have to draw one for me. What colour will you draw it?'

'I'll make it all the colours of the world. Not grey like your one.'

'That'll be lovely.'

'I like this a very lot. Are you going to take it home with you?' Hopefully, he held up the teddy with the little blue jumper – my present from Jesse. I fought with myself. I was too old for cuddly toys and I would have liked to give it to Brian but I couldn't. It was too precious to me.

'I tell you what I'll do. I'll send you some crayons with all the colours in the world in it and you can send me your picture. Will you?' He nodded gravely and I kissed my hand and placed it on his curly ginger head.

'Do you promise?' he asked.

'Yes, I do.'

'Okay then, that's fine, that's nice,' he said as if confirming the deal. He took my hand. 'Shall we see if dinner's come? I hope it's lamb chomps and peas.'

I only bought two Christmas presents that year. A red plastic case with loads of different colour wax crayons for Brian and then, feeling a bit guilty, I sent Mum out again for an enormous pack of felt pens for Robbie.

A little while after Christmas, Barbara came to visit me at home. It wasn't really an 'official' visit because I'd been handed over to the local Social Services since I'd been home and I wasn't Barbara's 'case' anymore. Funny word – 'case'. Like I'd been packed up in a box for someone to open when they thought there might be something interesting inside. Barbara had done a lot for us while I'd been in hospital. She'd been really helpful to Mum and Dad, advising them about who to contact and benefits I might be entitled to. But she'd also become my good friend.

She had a neat car. It was a purple metallic Nissan Micra, all shiny and new. I sat in the doorway and watched her get out – it seemed like a miracle to me. First of all she leaned over to the passenger seat and lifted the frame of her wheelchair onto the kerb. Then she took each wheel out and clicked it into place. In a second she'd put her bag on the back, opened the chair out and lifted herself into it. It was like a dance, smooth and easy. I wondered if I'd ever be able to do anything so accomplished.

After a bit of a chat and the ritual of making the

coffee, Mum left us alone in the front room.

'It's great having a few days off work. I went to Brent Cross to see if there was anything good in the sales but it was so crowded I nearly turned round and went straight back home again. There weren't any orange-badge parking spaces left, either. Well, there was one and just as I was about to turn into it someone beat me to it – a little black sports car, in fact. I couldn't see whether it had a badge or not. I watched this woman jump out in a short skirt and high heels and when she saw me staring at her, she started to limp. Honestly she did, started to drag one leg behind the other. Some people have no shame!' Barbara laughed.

'What did you do?'

'There wasn't anything I could do, really, short of running over her toes. Sometimes I do have terrible rows with people but I wasn't in the mood today. "Mellow out" is my New Year's resolution. I don't know how long I'm going to be able to stick to it, though. Anyway shopping's depressing enough without having screaming matches before you get started. Why is it everything I like costs over a hundred quid? And another thing is, the fashions now seem to have gone all long and that's useless for people like us because everything gets caught up in the wheels. Still, I found this in the sale in Kookai – what do you think?' She reached her hand round the back of her chair and pulled out a short, square-cut jacket in soft, shiny material. It was black with a silver zip up the front and little pockets.

'It's great.'

'Do you think it's too young for me?'

'Of course not, you're not old.'

'Well, I am compared to you. Go on, try it on. It'll look great on you.' There was no mirror to see myself in but Barbara assured me I looked 'fab'. It felt so normal to be trying on clothes and talking about what fashions you liked and what you thought was revolting.

'At the hospital they told my mum that I had to wear loose baggy clothes. They said it was dangerous to wear things that were too tight because they'd cut into me and I wouldn't be able to feel it.' Barbara let out one of her enormous laughs. It made me jump.

'I know. I call it the track-suit mentality. It's the idea that you stop caring what you look like when you become disabled. It's also the idea that other people will be looking after you forever and it'll be so much easier for them if everything's held together with velcro.'

I started to giggle, remembering the scene in the hospital with Mum.

'You'll soon learn what you like to wear and what suits you. If you were the sort of person who liked clothes before, you're not going to stop liking them now. In fact, I think it makes you even more inventive about the things that look good on you. I don't feel happy about looking scruffy these days.'

'Dr Singleton says that I've got to keep on doing the walking exercises every day,' I said, changing the subject abruptly. The way Barbara was going on made it sound like she knew something about my future that I didn't. She stopped talking and looked at me.

'I'm sorry. I suppose I'm just talking about myself, really. I'm always rambling on. You just have to tell me to shut up.'

'I don't want you to shut up. It's just that I don't really know where I am.'

'What exactly did the doctor say to you?'

'I'm not sure. I've gone over and over it in my head. I can remember him saying that I must carry on doing the exercises and I must keep on trying. But what sticks in my mind from that conversation is the feeling that my legs aren't going to get any stronger and I've got to learn to live with things as they are now. I don't remember him saying those actual words to me, but that's the feeling he left me with. I don't feel I can talk about it to anyone. Mum's preoccupied with me doing walking exercises every day because she promised them she would, and Dad's still obsessed with finding out what made me so ill in the first place.'

'And you?' Barbara asked with her usual directness.

'I . . . I don't know what to think half the time. Everything's stopped still for me. I want life to move on but I don't know how to make it move anywhere. I don't know where to start. I don't feel ready to go back to school yet but I don't want to stay at home all day long. When I went back to the hospital last week they were talking about me going back into hospital for some more physiotherapy, but I'm not going to go anywhere where that cow is.'

Barbara smiled. She didn't need to ask who I was talking about.

'Why don't we start with some of the practical things that might make things a bit better for you? I'm not a doctor so I can't help with any of that side of things, but I'm good at helping to get other things moving.'

'What sort of things?'

'Well, the house for a start. I think it would be a good idea to get someone from the borough to come round and do an assessment of changes they could make to the house. It's not easy for you living like this, without even a toilet downstairs. You might be able to get a grant to do all sorts of things. Who knows, we could even get you your own room downstairs. By the way,' she said, changing the subject herself. 'Seen anything of that nephew of mine recently?' I shook my head. 'Funny that.'

'What's funny about it?'

'Well, whenever I see him, he never stops asking me about you.'

Barbara was as good as her word and it wasn't long before we had a visit from the occupational therapist. She wasn't dressed in a uniform like Deidre had been, but was neat and efficient with a clipboard and a whole lot of forms and papers. She addressed her comments to Mum rather than me.

'I moved you to the top of the list when I heard about Libby. I'm afraid that people sometimes have to wait months for an assessment, but we usually try to do a visit quickly when there's a young person involved. I'm going to ask some questions about what Libby's able to do for herself and then have a look round the house to see what adaptations we can suggest. I'll have to wait for a report from her doctor before we make any final decisions because we need to establish how permanent her disability is going to be. I mean there's no point in making significant alterations to the house if she's going to make a full recovery, is there?' She coughed in an embarrassed kind of way. 'If I think there need to be any major alterations, I'll also need details of your income and savings because these days I'm afraid it's all means-tested.'

'What does that mean?' Mum asked.

'It means that we'll work out what we think it's fair to ask you to pay towards the cost of the alterations. The council probably won't – can't – pay the full amount.'

Mum, Dad and I had tried to talk about this the night before. It was a funny, awkward conversation because we were all avoiding talking about what had been so easy for this stranger to say. How permanent was this going to be? Was I going to recover? Dad was the best at putting things off.

'Look,' he said. 'Why don't we let her come and look round the house and see what she has to say? We don't have to make any decisions right now.'

Ever since Barbara's visits I had been thinking about what could be done to the house to give me a bit more freedom. I imagined having my own room, a private space, so that I wouldn't have to ask anyone to help me and where I could be on my own if I wanted. But our house wasn't that big. I couldn't see how it could happen.

The OT looked round and took lots of notes.

'It must be difficult for you, Libby,' she said, speaking to me for the first time. 'I'm sure there's something we can do. As soon as I receive the doctor's report, I'll try and push my recommendations through as quickly as possible.'

Life seemed all about waiting. Waiting to get stronger, waiting for the report about the house to come back,

162

waiting to see if Dad could get a case together and sue the Southern Water's people for damages. Esther was kind and concerned when I did speak to her but, funnily enough, it was Cleo who kept the promise she made to me in her letters and came to visit me as soon as I got home.

Her hair was now cut really short and dyed peroxide blonde. The rest of her looked quite ordinary – big boots, black jeans and a small, tight, dark-green top. My mum said she'd freeze to death in the winter but I thought she looked great.

'Oh god, it's great to escape,' she said as soon as we were on our own. 'I think I'll even be glad to get back to school.'

She was back round the corner now, living with her mum.

'What's the matter? Didn't you have a good Christmas?'

'I never have a good Christmas but this one was even worse than usual. My mum. Well, poor Mum, really, but honestly.' She sighed deeply.

'What *is* the matter with your mum? Do you mind me asking? I never really understood. Is she ill?'

'No, no-one ever talks about it much – except her. She talks about it all the time. She gets really depressed and unhappy and cries a lot. She's not like it all the time but she always seems to be like it at Christmas. Then she gets worried because she can't work when she's in a state and then she doesn't earn any money and that makes her more depressed.' She raised her eyes to the ceiling and sighed again. 'I can't stand it when she's like this, it's so bloody miserable in the house. My dad goes on about how it's not good for me to be in that atmosphere and I should go and live with him and his wife and her kids but then when I get there I just worry about Mum being all on her own and I want to come back again. They're always arguing about me, especially at Christmas, but the thing is, it never feels like they want me with them because they like spending time with me. It's just because they don't want the other one to have me. They can't stand each other.'

'I'm sure that's not right, Cleo. They must both care about you.'

'I don't think they do really. I'm not being horrible or anything but you wouldn't understand because you've never had to go through it. You don't realise how lucky you are having a mum and dad like yours and a little brother who's your own. I used to be really jealous of you when we were at primary school, watching your mum collect you every day, especially when Robbie was born and she'd bring him along in the pram.' She let out a deep sigh and I thought back to those days in the Juniors. Sweet Robbie with those big brown eyes. I'd been really proud of having a baby brother then.

I looked at Cleo with a new understanding.

'Is that why you always used to be so nasty to me – because you were jealous of my family?'

Cleo looked amazed. 'What do you mean? When was I nasty to you? You were my friend.'

'Oh, Cleo, honestly. Don't you remember?'

'Remember what?'

'How you used to treat me at primary school and then

when we got to Dupont how you used to get the others to gang up on me. Remember Asfah at the station? Remember the spying game?' I couldn't quite believe I was saying this. A few months ago, I could never have had this conversation. Dr Singleton had called me 'very direct', but I'd always thought of myself as a coward where these things were concerned. I suppose that I was already beginning to change.

'I don't remember that,' she said as if she was really trying to work out what I was talking about. 'I don't remember us having fights or arguments. I used to come round here quite a lot and we always used to go to each other's parties and everything when we were at Kingsbury Lane and then when we went to Secondary we just had different friends.'

'But you always used to act like you couldn't stand me. And you seemed to enjoy getting others to hate me too.'

'I never felt like that,' she said with such emphasis that I had to believe she meant it. 'I always liked you. I thought you didn't like me, especially when you started going around with Esther and Joanna.'

'What've they got to do with it?'

'Well, they're not exactly my type are they? I thought we'd just grown apart.'

Two sides of the same story. I'd kept my pain hidden because of pride, and Cleo didn't know she was causing it.

'Didn't you wonder why I used to spend so much time in the classroom at break and dinnertime?'

'I just used to think you liked being on your own. I always felt so insecure if I didn't have loads of friends round me all the time and I used to admire the way you

165

were able to spend time on your own. It made you seem really grown up and independent. And you'd got your mum to talk to. I thought that made a difference.'

'But at primary school. All that plotting and whispering about me with Sofia. You must have known how that would make me feel. I used to lock myself in the toilet so you wouldn't see me crying.'

'Sofia was a bitch to everyone. You had to go along with her ideas to keep in her good books, otherwise she'd turn on you. I'd seen her do it to others. I'm really sorry I made you unhappy. I've never known when to stop, everybody's always telling me that. I suppose I was just trying to look clever in front of other people.' Cleo's round face began to crumple. 'You must have thought I was terrible when I just turned up like that at the hospital, when you hated me so much.'

'I never hated you. I always wanted us to be friends. I was surprised to see you, I admit it, but I was really pleased.'

'And what about now? Shall we be friends again?' Her face had gone all lopsided but she crooked her little finger at me in the 'make up, make up, never do it again' shape. We looked each other straight in the face and smiled.

'Yeah, why not,' I said. 'I think I'll need all the friends I can get.'

Grey January slipped invisibly into grey February. Christmas and New Year were over, Dad was back at work, Robbie back at school and Mum was at home worrying about me. We didn't talk any more about me going back to the hospital. Every morning Mum made me stand on the crutches or try to take a few steps on the walking frame, and every day I felt like a failure.

My life had its own routine. It's incredible how much time you can take to do nothing. Everything took longer: dressing, washing, eating. Each short day was filled with little busy-nesses. Gran, Granddad, Joyce – every day someone came for coffee in the morning or tea in the afternoon. Every evening Robbie came home from school, Dad came home from work, we ate our meal, watched the telly and went to bed.

But the nights were long and lonely. The horrible dreams from those first days in the hospital came back to me again. Ugly, inquisitive faces standing round my bed, staring at me and pointing. Every night, I was like a child frightened of the dark, and Mum sat by my bed and held my hand until I fell asleep.

Chapter Ten
On the News

'You won't believe this,' Dad said, waving yet another piece of paper at me. 'Did you know that almost half of Britain's coastline is polluted? Last year the National Rivers Authority – they're the ones responsible for keeping our bathing waters clean – they took samples to detect pollution in the water off a lot of different beaches – Littlehampton is named as one of them. Anyway, despite the fact that they found evidence of viruses in the samples of water they took, all the beaches were passed as safe for swimming and water sports. It's disgusting. Do you know how this happens?' I shook my head. Dad didn't need you to say anything; he just needed an audience. 'It's because in this country we only have to comply with the minimum standards and so even when they know the water is polluted, they still pass the beaches as safe. They ignore the tests for salmonella, enteroviruses, the colour of the water, loads of things. And they're allowed to get away with it. As long as there aren't too many bacteria in the water, it doesn't matter if there's hundreds of thousands of viruses. It's a disgrace. They're supposed to keep the public informed but they don't. People get nasty illnesses – stomach upsets, earache, skin rashes – from the bacteria, but it's these viruses that make people really ill. Hepatitis, paralysis – it's all here.' He waved some papers in the air. 'There's case studies. There's a sixteen-year-old boy and a seventeen-year-old girl went swimming in Oxwich Bay in Wales last year and they're both paralysed, both in wheelchairs. Welsh Water are saying it's not their responsibility. There's all these beaches waving their blue flags of cleanliness about but we don't know what's in the water.'

Dad sat down at the folded-up bit of my grandparents' old table in the back half of the sitting room. When I came home from hospital, he'd found the old doors that divide the two parts of the room and hung them up again so that there were now two smallish rooms and we could shut off the television part from what was supposed to be my bedroom. I was sitting on the sofa-bed trying to read *Of Mice and Men,* which Cleo and the others were doing for English Lit, and Dad was rearranging all his pamphlets and newspaper cuttings on pollution in the sea into different boxes. It was a favourite task of his these days.

'Now listen to this,' he said, holding up a magazine called *Pipeline News.* He held it away from his face and screwed up his eyes a bit. We all knew Dad needed reading glasses but he wouldn't admit it.

'"Every year the Government trot out the same old

statistics – 82 per cent of UK beaches comply with the EC Bathing Water Directive. Surfers Against Sewage have clearly shown that these beaches pass the bare legal minimum standard for only two out of the nineteen criteria laid down by that directive. There is no guarantee of absence or even low numbers of viruses. In fact, Government beaches can often be awash with a slick of human sewage and strewn with panty liners, condoms and other sewage-related debris. Two billion sanitary towels end up in the sea each year."'

'Ugh, Dad – that's revolting,' I said.

'What's sewage?' Robbie asked innocently.

'Shit.'

'Libby, please.' Mum put down the book she was trying to hear Robbie read. She wanted him to finish so she could watch the Eastenders Omnibus on the telly.

'Well, that's what it is.'

'What's it doing in the sea? Do people do a poo in the sea when they go swimming?' Robbie looked really interested now. 'You're not supposed to do that, are you? I mean, you can do a wee if it just comes out, but you mustn't do a poo. That's very naughty.' He giggled. 'That rhymes – do a poo, do a poo.'

'You see what you've started, Mike,' Mum said, but Dad was already off on his favourite subject.

'Sewage is everything that gets flushed down the toilet. It goes down the drainpipes and eventually it gets pumped into the rivers and seas. Now it contains all sorts of bugs and germs and . . .'

'It smells stinky revolting,' Robbie interrupted enthusiastically. There was nothing to get him going like

170

a conversation about excrement. Any sort: dog's, human's, hamster's.

'Yes, that as well,' Dad continued patiently. 'Because those germs can make the beaches dirty and make people ill, it's important to treat the sewage so that it's harmless to humans and other wildlife and keeps the water clean. There's different kinds of treatment they can use. They can do primary treatment where they allow big solids to settle and then they remove what they call sludge and there's secondary treatment where . . .'

'Big bits of poo in the water,' Robbie said with some delight. 'Yuck, I wouldn't want to go to that seaside.'

'No, no-one would. That's why it's so important to treat the sewage properly. Now the best way to do that is what they do in Jersey. They have sewage plants that use ultraviolet treatment and that seems to be the most effective method of killing off viruses.'

Robbie had stopped listening. 'Daddy, how do they stop poo getting in the water? Can it come out the tap when you turn it on? Could you drink it?'

'Mike, for heaven's sake,' Mum said crossly. 'No, don't start going into all that primary, secondary, tertiary stuff again. I've heard it all before and Robbie isn't listening anyway. He doesn't know what you're talking about.'

'But it's important that they understand. It affects us all.'

'Maybe, but not on a Sunday afternoon when we're all trying to relax,' Mum said with some of the old irritation in her voice. I hadn't heard her talk to any of us like that for a long time. 'Give us a break. Go and make everyone a cup of tea.'

Dad wasn't put off by Mum's lack of commitment to his research. It wasn't that she didn't care about what had made me ill, or about pollution in the sea; it was just that no-one could quite share Dad's level of enthusiasm for a project once he got going. He was determined to get a legal case going against Southern Water to prove that they weren't carrying out their statutory duty to keep the beach clean.

Every day when he came back from work, he'd enthusiastically check through the post – to see if any more information had arrived. He had filled in a medical form and sent it to this group Surfers Against Sewage in Cornwall. They'd set up a medical database, monitoring all the cases of people they believed had become ill after swimming in sewage-contaminated water. He'd written to universities who were doing research into viruses in the water. There was a researcher working at Leicester University who had established that there were high levels of viruses in many areas covered by Southern Water. Dad had even written letters to newspapers and radio stations, hoping to get a bit of publicity.

'Look at this,' he said excitedly, coming into the kitchen where Mum and I were sitting. 'Two brilliant letters today. I've got one from Cornwall. They've found a top virologist at University College Hospital in London and a lawyer who's willing to act on Libby's case and both of them are willing to stand up in court and make the link between viral illness and the sea.'

'That's good,' Mum said dryly. She was peeling potatoes and cutting them into thin slices and I was arranging them in a shallow pyrex dish with salt and pepper and little dots of butter every few layers. 'Isn't a legal case going to be very expensive, though – how will we be able to pay for it?'

'We'll cross that bridge when we come to it,' Dad said, looking like a little boy who'd just been told he's got a place in the school football team. 'Look at this other letter first. That won't cost us anything.' He handed Mum a heavy white envelope. She read it out loud.

Carlton Television, St Martin's Lane, London

Dear Mr Starling,
I understand that you are campaigning on behalf of your fifteen-year-old daughter who has become ill as a result of swimming in the sea on the south coast. We are interested in doing a feature for London News which goes out every day at 6.30 pm and I would be grateful if you would contact my researcher Lindi Bancroft on the number above so that we can arrange a time to come and interview you and your daughter. Yours sincerely,
Tony Jobson–Scott
Producer

'What does that mean?' I asked, struggling to understand. 'Do they want me to go on the telly?'

'Yes. Brilliant, isn't it? The more publicity we get, the more they'll have to take notice.'

'Who'll have to take notice?' Mum asked.

'The people responsible. The Public Health Department. Southern Water. The National Rivers Authority.

I'm going to get on to them straight away. No time like the present, that's what they say.' Dad was already heading out of the kitchen to get the phone.

'Hold on a second, Mike. Just sit down and have a cup of coffee or something first,' Mum said quite firmly. 'Don't you think we ought to talk about it? I might have some ideas about this. Libby might have some ideas of her own.' Dad came to an abrupt stop in the doorway.

'Yes, sorry love,' he said to both of us. 'What do you think? It's great, isn't it?'

'I don't know. Is it?' I said, looking at Mum for the answer. I really didn't know. I mean, theoretically the idea of going on the television was exciting, but like this? Looking like I did now? And I didn't know what to say about the sea and whether it was polluted or not. To me, it had been like the sea always is in England – freezing cold, greenish grey with bits of murky-looking seaweed floating about. My image of a perfect sea was warm, clear-blue water where if you looked down you would see the bottom of the ocean. In my limited experience, the English Channel never looked like that.

'Yes it is,' Dad said. 'Think about how many people watch the television at that time of day.' He looked at the letter again. 'And they say they're going to do a feature on it. That means they want to do more than just a quick news flash. It probably means they want to do an in-depth interview. Find out a few facts. They might even go to the water company and make them try to answer a few questions.'

'Yes, I know. But is that okay with Libby? How do you feel about it, darling?' Mum turned to me, waiting for my response. She seemed to think it would be easy for me to say either 'yes, I'd love to go on the telly' or 'no, don't let them in the house'. But I really didn't know. Then I looked at my dad. He was looking at me in a half-joking, imploring way. It seemed so important to him. I bit my lip.

'I think it'll be okay,' I said cautiously. 'It will, won't it? It might be interesting to be on the television.' Dad gave me one of his lopsided grins, and his dark eyes practically disappeared as he screwed up his face with pleasure. I hadn't seen him look so pleased for ages.

'That's my girl,' he said, leaning over and giving me a hug. 'I'll get on to this researcher person right away. I wonder how soon they want to come round?'

They arrived a few days later. I wasn't sure how Mum felt about all this but as I said, no-one ever got as enthusiastic as Dad once he'd got his teeth into something. You could tell he'd really got going about this one because he even arranged for someone else to teach his classes and took a half day off work. Not only that, he actually ironed his shirt, took his best corduroy trousers to the cleaners and polished his shoes before they came to film us. As for me, I'd been worrying for days about what I was going to wear. At least it took my mind off what I was going to say. I'd moved on from the shell-suit bottoms and the geriatric grey trainers, but not very far. My standard uniform was now ordinary navy track-suit bottoms or leggings, white trainers and loose jumpers. I'd talked to Cleo and Barbara and Mum about what I was going to wear but in the end it was Esther who gave me the best advice.

'Just wear what you usually wear,' she said in her calm,

sensible way. 'Otherwise, you'll feel uncomfortable and different and it will make you feel even more nervous.' I decided on my favourite thing – Dad's, Uncle Richard's, old grey UCLA T-shirt. I thought it would bring me luck. Stupid mistake.

We'd spent the evening before they came doing a frantic tidy up. This wasn't an easy thing to do because our house was always full of clutter and there never seemed to be anywhere to put things away. Our sitting room was old fashioned. Not as in Victorian fireplaces, Dado rails and velvet armchairs. I mean old fashioned as in needing a good chuck-out and start all over again. Some people (like Dad) said it had a cosy, 'lived in' look. Others (like Mum) called it scruffy. She was always looking through magazines or the IKEA catalogue, sighing over small, neat armchairs covered in cream linen or bright modern rugs, but we hadn't bought anything new since forever.

The floors of the downstairs rooms and the hall were covered with moss-green fitted carpet which my grandparents had put down when they lived here. Gran often told us how it had been 'best grade, pure new wool' when they'd bought it, but now there were places where there was more straw-coloured webbing than soft green carpet. Under the window and in one corner were two parts of what had once been a three-piece suite – part three having fallen to bits last year after one of Robbie's jumping frenzies. The large sofa and armchair were covered in what you might call 'early eighties fruit and flowers', and there were distinct shiny patches on the back and arms. In various places around the room there were pretty but rather grubby lamps with fringed shades in pastel colours and some home-made cushions with Indian prints from Mum's hippyish days. The only really good piece of furniture was the coffee table. It was made of pale, polished wood and had two levels and beautiful rounded corners. Dad had made it for Mum as a wedding present and he was really proud of it. Today was the first time in years I'd actually seen it. Usually it was hidden under a pile of books, papers, bits of Dad's marking, my homework and old shopping lists.

In the alcoves on either side of the gas fire there were shelves, but no-one ever seemed able to decide whether they were supposed to be for books or ornaments and vases, and everything was just piled up together, fighting for its own space. We had curtains – plain, dark-red material. I liked the colour but the rail was always in danger of coming down and they didn't quite pull together in the middle. Gran could never understand how we could leave the windows bare in the day. She'd say, 'Claire dear, doesn't it worry you, people just being able to look in? I've still got some lovely white nets that fit those front windows perfectly. Why don't you let me give them to you? They're not a bit of trouble to look after. They wash up as easy as anything.' But Mum had grown up in a quiet village with people peeping from behind net curtains, pretending not to be minding each other's business, and she wasn't having any of it.

There were four of them from the TV company: Tony Jobson-Scott, who'd written Dad the letter, a camera and sound man, someone in charge of the lights and a young woman, all buzzy and bright, who went around with a

177

folder full of bits of paper and a felt pen. What with all of them, their equipment, me, the wheelchair, Mum and Dad, you could hardly fit all of us in the front room.

Tony was obviously the one in charge. He had a nice, bright smile and looked straight at me when he talked to me. Most people looked straight over my head. He was quite young – not nearly as old as Dad – with dark-blond, swept-back hair, a long black raincoat and trendy glasses with thin, tortoise-shell frames. He also wore bright turquoise socks, presumably to prove he wasn't boring.

'Now where would you like us all to be?' Dad asked, buzzing around like a waiter in a restaurant trying to take orders and clear the table at the same time. 'Do you want to move any of the furniture out of the way, or would anyone like a coffee or something to eat before we start?'

'No thanks, we're fine,' Tony said, answering for every-one. With the cameraman helping him, he was pulling the sofa away from the window to make a space behind it.

'What do you think about the lighting, Chris? Would it work if we shot from this angle?'

Mum stood in the doorway with her arms folded over her chest. She was wearing a pair of navy leggings, plain flat shoes and a long checked shirt. I thought she looked good in these kinds of clothes but I was surprised she hadn't dressed up a bit more.

'Now, what about you, Mrs Starling – Claire? Would you like to be included in the interview?'

'No, I'm fine, thanks,' Mum said politely but with a bit of a chill in her voice. 'We've already agreed that it will be just Libby and her dad.'

'Okay, well in that case perhaps you wouldn't mind going off with Lindi and she can get a bit of background from you. Is there another room you could go to – the kitchen perhaps?'

Tony suggested that I got onto the sofa and Dad sat on a chair beside me. I wasn't very keen but it would have been hard to say no to Tony. He was so nice and friendly about everything. I was getting better at doing transfers, but I still found it embarrassing to have to do it in front of other people – grab one leg, put it on the sofa, grab the other one, lift my bum over and all that.

'Okay,' Tony said again. Okay seemed to be his favourite word. 'You look fine like that. What about the sound, Kev? Do you want to fit the mikes now?' Kev came forward with a little metal clip-on device.

'I'm just going to fiddle about with you now,' he said in a jokey kind of way. He leant over me and felt for the top of my bra strap. 'I hope my hands aren't too cold.' I laughed, trying to pretend that I was used to this kind of thing.

'Is everything set now?' Tony asked after what seemed like ages of fiddling around with the furniture, cameras and sound equipment.

'Are you going to ask me questions first and then ask Dad or what?'

'Oh, I'm sorry,' he said. 'I should have explained it all to you before. I'm going to ask some questions and I don't mind which one of you answers them. Don't worry if you get it wrong first time. I'll just say it again and you can have another try. It'll probably take about twenty minutes in all – we're hoping to broadcast a three- or

179

four-minute piece. Is there anything else you want to ask?'

'When will they show it on the television?'

'Thursday, I hope.' That was in three days' time. 'Lindi will give you a ring and let you know if it gets changed. Okay. Let's get going.'

Tony was really nice through the interview. If I got muddled, he just let me say it all over again. Not that I said much; Dad did most of the talking. It was mostly stuff I'd heard him say before, except there were a couple of things which really surprised me. They filmed Dad taking me up the stairs in the wheelchair and me wheeling up and down the sitting room. They filmed me doing nothing at all and they filmed Tony doing 'noddies' – just nodding his head up and down as if he was agreeing with something. He explained that this was to fill in any gaps if they needed to do some cuts.

'Libby,' Tony said, looking over into the corner of the room. 'How about filming you walking with those crutches or that frame?' He smiled at me and nodded encouragingly. I didn't know what to say, but fortunately at that point Mum came back into the room. She had one of our old family photo albums under her arm.

'I think Libby's had enough; she looks a bit tired. Would it be alright if we just left it at what you've already done?'

'Yes, sure,' Tony said. 'We've got more than enough already. Thanks very much everyone, that went really well.' He shook Dad's hand. 'Best of luck with everything, Libby. God bless.' He leant over and gave me a kiss on my cheek. I felt myself go pink.

Robbie was furious he'd missed it all. I tried explaining it to him but all he kept saying was, 'If Daddy could have a day off school, why couldn't I?'

We were on the telly that Thursday. Everyone was excited about seeing it. We ate specially early and at 6.25, Mum and I were on the sofa and Dad on the chair with Robbie sitting on the floor at his feet. Dad had telephoned practically everyone he knew, and from a conversation I'd had with Cleo, I imagined the whole of Year 11 at Dupont High would be watching, too.

The first item was about the weather. Apparently it was the warmest February on record and there was a picture of all the flowers in St James's Park and a young reporter was walking through them reciting that silly poem about wandering lonely as a cloud amongst the golden daffodils.

Then it was us. I felt all silly and fluttery inside as they went back to the News Desk and heard the main reporter say, 'And now for something which affects all Londoners, even though it might seem a little way from our doorsteps. Reporter Tony Jobson-Scott brings you the worrying story of Elizabeth Starling, once a pretty and lively teenager, now tragically struck down by a mystery virus which has left her paralysed and confined to a wheelchair.'

Up on screen came a photo of me in a swimsuit taken on holiday last year. I was mucking about, sticking my chest out, pretending to be a fashion model. I gasped. The camera moved immediately to a shot taken from the hall showing Dad hauling me backwards up the stairs. The camera seemed to be aimed at my crotch. Then Tony's voice saying, 'Last summer Libby was a bright, healthy fifteen–year–old, studying for her GCSE examinations at Dupont High in northwest London. In July on a school trip to Littlehampton, she enjoyed a dip in the sea with her friends. That evening she became critically ill with aching joints and a high fever, and now doctors say that they are not sure how long it will be before she can walk again.'

Here the camera showed me parking the wheelchair next to the sofa and slowly lifting myself onto the settee, ready for transfer. It closed in on my stiff, immobile legs. I hadn't realised the cameras had filmed me doing this. They'd told me they were just testing for light.

'Michael Starling, a teacher, is convinced that his daughter picked up the virus from contaminated sea-water and is now campaigning to get Southern Water to come clean.' The camera swung round to Dad, sitting next to me. Over my shoulder you could see my wheelchair, framed like a skeleton against the dark curtains. Dad's voice, sounding unusually strong, began to go through the routine.

'European law requires the sea to be virus free, but in this country we rarely carry out proper tests. Even when we do, the results which the public gets to see often ignore the viruses. So it's possible to see the blue flag which means a clean sea waving on the beach, when in fact, the water may be full of dangerous viruses.'

The camera swung to me. I looked pale, thin and unhappy.

'Tell me about that day, Libby.'

I didn't recognise my own voice. I used to feel confident speaking to adults, but I sounded timid and unsure of myself. I told them about playing in the sea and what I could remember about becoming ill. I didn't say anything about friends or about Jesse, the things that had really been important about that day. Tony asked about what we'd been doing in the water, emphasising the game with the ball. He was trying to make me sound like the captain of the sports team or something. What a joke.

Next came a picture of my medical notes from the hospital, which showed that my illness was caused by a viral infection.

'Has anyone given you any indication you might have contracted this from the sea?' he asked.

Dad replied. 'The doctor did say it was a possibility it had come from the water, although naturally, he's a bit cautious. But there isn't any doubt in my mind that that's where she contracted the illness. What we need is a full investigation.'

'When do the doctors think you'll make a recovery from this?'

A close-up of my face came up on the screen but it was Dad's voice that answered. 'They say that once the muscles start coming back, then they'll come back quite quickly – it'll just take time now.'

I looked over at Dad in amazement but before I had time to think it through properly, there was the hospital gym on the screen. It was Pauline Blood, talking about how she'd specially planned a programme of exercises for me and how in a case like mine it was very important to keep the muscles working, otherwise they might get all contorted and 'a young person like Elizabeth could remain unnecessarily wheelchair bound'.

The picture shifted to a beach full of sanitary towels washed up from the sea and then to a laboratory with a man in a white coat giving lots of facts and figures. But I'd stopped listening. Something was banging so hard in my chest that I could hardly catch my breath. Then the camera was back in our house again.

'What is the first thing you'd like to do when you recover?' I remembered Tony asking me this question. I hadn't known what to say.

'I'd like to get my life back again.'

'That's a good answer but it's rather subtle for some of our viewers,' he had said kindly, making me feel intelligent and rather mature. 'Can you make it a bit more specific?'

I thought for a second.

'How about saying something about going back to school?' He had chewed his lip thoughtfully and suggested that perhaps I could say something about movement. I watched now as the camera came in close to my face.

'And Libby. What is the first thing you'd like to do when you recover?'

'Run?' I heard the sound of my own voice, laughing nervously.

The final shot was of me, sitting immobile in the hall, my hands on the arms of the wheelchair, whilst the camera drew back until I was just a small dot.

'Well, what did you think of that?' Dad asked, letting out a long breath. 'Wasn't bad, was it? I'm sorry they didn't show the interview with the lawyer. He could have told them about that other case from Littlehampton and the business of the . . .' He stopped talking and looked over at me.

'Libby, what's the matter?' The feeling inside me was physical, a great heavy weight in my heart and in my stomach.

'How could you let them come and do that to me? Don't you think I've got enough without all that?' My voice was thin and high.

'What do you mean? I thought it went quite well.'

'You don't understand anything, do you?' I screamed, spewing out the words. 'You've got no idea how I feel. No fucking idea.' Tears and anger distorted my voice into a strangled wail. Robbie gave a start. I was aware of the look of shock and fear on his face. He jumped up and ran towards me.

'Libby, what's wrong?' he asked, putting his hand on my knee. 'Have you got a hurting place?' I pushed him away. All the pain came tumbling out at once.

'That bastard. I trusted him, I thought he was so nice. "You don't have to say anything you don't want to, Libby. We think you're wonderful, Libby."' I mimicked his posh voice. 'And then look at what they did.'

'What do you mean?' Dad repeated, genuinely puzzled.

'The way they made me look. Poor little crippled girl – look, her legs won't move. I didn't even know they were filming me getting out of the chair. Poor tragic victim all alone in her wheelchair.'

'They didn't say you were a tragic victim.'

'They might not have used that word but that's what

185

they meant. Why do you think they ended it with me all alone just stuck in the middle of the room? A pathetic little creature – can't do anything for herself.'

'But Libby . . .'

'You just wanted me to go on the television so that you could spout on about all the stuff you've learned about pollution. It's got nothing to do with me – you just did it for yourself.' Mum stood up and moved towards the door. 'I think you and Dad ought to have a talk about this on your own.' She took Robbie by the hand. His little face looked scared and wet with tears.

'Yes, that's easy for you,' I cried. 'To make out it's all Dad's fault and it's got nothing to do with you. But it wasn't Dad who gave that woman the photo of me in my swimming costume looking like an idiot. Why did you do that? You must have known how they'd use it. Before and after pictures. Before – a normal lively teenager sticking her breasts out at the camera. Afterwards – a tragic victim, wheelchair bound. You didn't even tell me you'd given it to them.' For a second Mum looked as though I'd hit her. Then she looked angry.

'You're being ridiculous. I was in the kitchen with Lindi. We didn't have anything to do and we started talking about how sweet you were when you were little and she asked if she could see some pictures. That's all.'

'That's not all. That's just making me look an idiot in front of the world. How am I going to face everyone in school after they've seen me like that?'

'I think you've got this a bit out of proportion. Dad thought . . . we both thought that it was important to show what's happened to you. I didn't think it was so bad.

They didn't make you look a fool or anything.'

'You just agree with them. You think I'm a pathetic victim too, that's why you think it doesn't matter how they showed me on the television.'

'Libby, we don't think about you like that. You're not going to be like this forever.'

'No. I'm going to be miraculously cured because that's what Dad told the whole world. My muscles are going to come back and I'm going to walk again. Come back? Where have they been then – on holiday?' I turned to my Dad. 'Where did you get that crap from anyway? You know it's not true.' Dad opened his mouth but decided to say nothing. 'The doctor spoke to me before I left the hospital. He told me things were never going to be the same again, I'll never be like I was before. You just made it up for the television because that's what you want to believe. But it doesn't help me.' Nobody spoke for a few seconds.

'You're being very hard on Daddy,' Mum said softly. 'He hasn't lied to anybody. Everything we do, we do because we care about you.'

'All you care about is me getting better.'

'Well of course we do . . .'

I cut her off. 'You just want to make more and more appointments with the hospital and force me to do exercises all day long and all Dad wants is to prove that I got ill because of pollution in the sea. The Water Authority will never admit that they're in the wrong and even if they did, it's not going to change anything for me, is it? Even if they name some stupid virus, it's not going to make me any better, is it?'

'We're just trying to do what's best,' Dad said again. He

let out a deep breath. 'What do you want us to do?'

I put my hand up to my face and covered my eyes. I wanted to storm out of the room, run out of the house, anything to get away from how I was feeling and how they were looking at me.

'I don't know, I don't know,' I said over and over. 'I know you love me. But I can't go on like this any more. I don't want to be carried upstairs any more. I don't want to have to pee into a potty like a baby. I don't care why it's happened. It's happened. I can't walk properly any more. It makes it worse if everyone thinks that's the only thing that matters. Look at Barbara, she's alright. Why can't I be like her?'

I put my hand out towards Robbie. 'Come here,' I said. 'I'm sorry I was mean to you. I know it's not your fault.'

'That's alright, Libby,' he said. 'Don't worry.'

'It's not alright. No-one takes any notice of you any more, do they?' He didn't really understand what I meant but he put his arms round my neck and gave me a hug.

Mum and Dad stood close together looking at the two of us. Nobody knew what to do next. I knew that I was using Robbie as protection against them. I didn't want them to come any closer and I was too angry to forgive them.

'Look,' said Mum. 'Dad and I will have a proper talk. We . . . we'll look at things again, we'll see what we can do.'

Chapter Eleven
It's Good to Talk

Of course, things aren't ever solved simply by an argument, but the television programme was the start of some kind of change. There was a different feeling in the house. It's hard to say exactly what it was but there was a kind of loosening up. I was able to look at Mum and Dad without finding them gazing at me with eyes full of worry and concern, and they stopped giving me that tight, bright smile when they saw I'd caught them at it. I think the truth was that everyone had been scared of me. I'd been like an immobile rocket, fizzing and fizzing but with nowhere to go off. Nobody had known what to say to me or when I was going to explode.

Dad still kept in touch with the campaigning groups but he was quieter about it and it didn't feel like I was being beaten about the head with all his reports and papers. I still did some exercises every day, mostly to

189

please Mum, and whilst I was feeling stronger in myself, nothing had changed in my legs. My muscles certainly weren't 'coming back'.

One interesting thing was that as I stopped being so revolting to everyone and started taking more notice of Robbie, he stopped behaving like the model child and became naughty and irritating. The first thing he did was to go to my room and take back all the things he'd given me over the past few months – Morris the rabbit, the mongoose pencil, his little brown suitcase and lots of other little things he'd wanted me to have. I was amused rather than angry – I hadn't needed any of these things; they were just tokens of love from him. But he was in a rage. He waited until Saturday when I was upstairs, too, came into my room with a grim little face and his lips pressed together in a silent straight line, and gathered them all up. He gave me a look you'd give to a naughty child who'd just eaten all the chocolate biscuits and marched out again. I was speechless. Then he started playing Mum up. He got all fussy about his meals, wouldn't go to bed on time, cried if we wouldn't let him choose the programmes on the TV, said 'it's not fair' at least twenty times a day and was generally obnoxious. It was as if he'd been holding it all in until it felt safe to act like a seven-year-old again.

I had lots of phone calls in the few days after my star appearance on the telly. Of course, nobody else seemed to think there was anything wrong with it. When Cleo rang the next day she said, 'Everyone at school's been talking about you. They're all asking me questions.'

'What do they want to know?'

'Oh, you know the kind of thing,' she said evasively. I did know. They'd have been asking when I was going to get better, or if it was possible that I was never going to walk again. 'Mostly they wanted to know when you'd be coming back to school. And if they could come and see you. Jesse is always asking me that.'

'Is he?'

'Well, he's always going on about whether they've found out what's wrong with you. I've given him your phone number about six times.'

'Do you talk to him a lot?'

'Sort of. We just hang around a bit.' Hanging around in Cleo's language could mean anything and I didn't want to investigate further. Which wasn't the same as not wanting to know.

For weeks Mum had been trying to get me out of the house by suggesting I went to the shops with her or went round to Cleo's or Esther's instead of waiting for people to come and see me, but I was unpersuadable. I said it was because I still got tired so easily but this was only partly true. It seemed like such a hassle to go anywhere. It wasn't like I could go out on my own; I couldn't even get out of the front door without help. I didn't want to have to think about how I'd get into other people's houses or whether they had a toilet downstairs. But deeper than that, I suppose the real truth was that after seeing myself on the telly, I didn't want to be seen, even by strangers. I didn't want to go out being pushed around in a wheelchair.

'Let's go to Brent Cross,' Mum would say. 'It's all accessible there (accessible – new buzz word in our house), and I'll treat you to lunch. You can have that chicken in breadcrumbs and chips you like.' Six months before, I'd have been ready and waiting by the front door before she'd even finished speaking. I used to love going shopping, even when we didn't have any money to buy anything. But I wasn't in the mood for treats. It was easier to stay at home.

It was Barbara who finally got me out of the house. She had a few days off work and invited me to come and pay her a visit in a way that made it impossible to refuse her. It was a Saturday and Mum said she'd take me there and then go on shopping with Robbie. Dad was happily spending the day under the bonnet of the MG and Mum drove me there in the battered old Ford estate known half affectionately in our family as the 'brown car'. I got myself into the seat and Mum folded up the wheelchair and put it in the back. Robbie was already whining about how he never got to sit in the front these days, but Mum gave him one of her looks which could kill a python and even Robbie shut up.

Barbara lived about fifteen minutes' drive from our house. We got lost in Cricklewood and I was beginning to get anxious because my mum, a very organised person in every other respect, had a blank area in the part of her brain usually called 'sense of direction'. I was relieved when she stopped and consulted her *A to Z* and, with it upside down on her lap, we drove away from the busy shops of the High Street, past some industrial buildings and turned into a long straight line of small, modern red-brick houses and low-rise flats. It wasn't much to look at from the outside – the road was bare and treeless without so much as a tub of tulips to brighten things up – but I knew that inside her flat it would be different.

I was worried that Mum was going to come in with me and stop for a cup of coffee and then take up all my visit, but Robbie was being so difficult she had no alternative but to take him away. For the past week he'd refused to wear his nearly new school shoes on the grounds that 'blue was for babies', and she'd finally given in and promised him some new trainers. He certainly wasn't interested in adult conversation especially since Toys R Us had been mentioned, so Mum just helped me out of the car, waited until the door opened and drove off.

The person who answered the door wasn't Barbara but a tall, good-looking bloke with very short black hair, a close-cropped beard, jeans, leather jacket and Timberland boots.

'Hi,' he said. 'You must be Libby. Come in. I'm just going, but don't take it personally.' He gave me a dazzling smile. Of course, I blushed. He laughed and I felt myself go even redder. 'Babs, I'm off,' he called down the hall. 'Give me a call as soon as you've read that file.'

'Babs?' I said, raising my eyebrows at her.

'Don't,' she said laughing. 'I've told him that's not my name but he doesn't take any notice.' She manoeuvred her chair alongside mine and leant over and gave me a kiss on the cheek.

'Is he your boyfriend?' I asked. This was the sort of thing you could ask Barbara.

'I wish. Still, you never know your luck in a big city. Right now, he's just a friend. He works in the law centre up the road. Sometimes he asks my advice about things.'

There were so many things I wanted to know about Barbara but I couldn't ask them all before I'd hardly got through the door. Fortunately she wasn't one for holding back.

'I'm only just getting over a relationship and it's not a good idea for me to start anything new for a while. It was a bit of a disaster towards the end.' She screwed up her face in memory of the mess. I looked at her encouragingly, hoping she'd tell me more. 'Yeah, two firsts for me in the lover line. He was white and he was disabled. Not that they were the reasons things went wrong. Unfortunately he was also a two-timing, egotistical creep, but it took me a while to work that out.'

'How did you meet him?

She smiled rather grimly. 'Well, there's a funny story. I met him in the gym in the leisure centre up the road. I got this leaflet through the door saying that they had new equipment for disabled people and you could get a free session with an instructor who'd show you how everything worked. So I went along to see what it was like and the instructor was this incredibly fit, muscley, weight-lifting guy who was in a wheelchair himself. I went to the gym a couple of times and he was always there and we had a coffee together and then we went out for a meal and one thing led to another. At first it was great. He was good fun and it was brilliant going out with someone who was disabled. I thought it might be embarrassing but actually I felt really strong being out with him. There was so much rubbish you didn't have to go through. There were a lot of things we shared.'

'What went wrong?'

She sighed and laughed at the same time. 'Oh God, what went wrong? Let's see. He was a twenty–seven–year–old guy who still lived with his mum who treated him like a prince so when he stayed the night with me, I felt like I was kidnapping her little boy. Then, he was jealous of my job because he'd never been to university and the more I tried to encourage him to go back and study if that's what he wanted, the more annoyed he got with me. But mostly it was because we had different ways of dealing with being disabled. He was always talking about keeping himself fit so that if they find a cure for spinal cord damage, he'd be the first to go for it. I think that's like waiting for them to invent wings so humans can learn to fly. He couldn't accept himself as he was and I found that difficult to deal with. Also, he didn't have any other disabled friends and I did. He hung around with all that fitness crowd and I didn't have a lot in common with them. One day I turned up at the gym when he wasn't expecting me and sitting on his lap was a skinny nineteen–year–old in a leopard-skin leotard and leggings. Need I say more?' She smiled at me. 'Come on, that's enough about me. Let me show you where I live. My mum's baked you some of her special chocolate and banana pastries and she'll kill me if you don't eat at least half of them.'

Her flat was brilliant, different to anything I'd ever seen, even in magazines. You came into a square hall, and on the right there was a large room full of light and a small kitchen fitted out with low units and cupboards. This had a door that led out into a little garden. On the other side was a bathroom and a bedroom. Everything was painted white and there was only the minimum of furniture, all in plain, bright colours. In the corner of the main room, there was a pine wood table with a couple of chairs, and a shiny brass table lamp with a big cream shade. On the opposite wall was an emerald-green sofa, raised to wheelchair height with neat wooden legs, and an armchair with a loose cover of deep purple. There were lots of cushions – cream, sunshine yellow and deep red with patterns on them of little dots or wavy lines. The floor was plain wood without any rugs or carpets. In fact, the only rug in the room hung on the wall, a big African print full of deep jewel colours and intricate patterns.

'Wow,' I said, loving it all. I wheeled backwards and forwards. 'No friction.'

'That floor was a labour of love. My dad got it from a school where he was doing some decorating. They were throwing it out and he removed it in strips; cleaned it all up and laid it piece by piece like a jigsaw puzzle. My mum thought we were both mad. She couldn't understand why I didn't have a nice fitted carpet with autumn leaves or flowers on it so it wouldn't show the dirt.' As she talked, she moved around the kitchen with a tray on her lap and put together the tea and cakes.

'Come and sit at the table and tell me about you.' I realised why there were so few chairs. 'How are things going?'

'Fine,' I said in that automatic way I'd got used to answering that question.

'Fine?'

Without any warning to myself or her, I burst into tears. 'I'm sorry. I don't know what's the matter with me. It's not you or anything, I'm really pleased to be here.'

'Don't apologise. You don't have to say sorry about anything,' she said gently. 'Just start where you want. Tell me how things are going at home.'

I sniffed loudly. 'I don't know why I'm crying. Things are better at home. It's just that I feel like I'm in some kind of in-between land. Everyone's waiting for me to get better, to get up and start walking again, but here's my body, exactly the same as it's been for months. You heard what Dad said on the telly. He seems to think it's just a matter of time and then my legs are going to get strong again. Mum doesn't say all that much but I know they want me to go back into hospital to "build up my muscles". That's the expression they all use. Whatever I do, I've hardly got any feeling or movement in my legs, that's the truth. I think in their hearts they know that my legs have been paralysed permanently. Dr Singleton practically said as much when we saw him after Christmas, but everyone's clinging to the idea of some kind of miracle.'

My voice was all choked up and I couldn't talk for a bit. Barbara waited patiently. 'I don't want to go back to hospital and have to work with Pauline Blood or even with one of the nice physios and feel like a failure all over again. Everyone says I musn't give up, that I should keep on trying. But I don't know what to do with myself. I can't just carry on like this.'

Barbara waited for a minute before she began to speak. 'You have to make these decisions for yourself. People around you do what's best for you – it's just that their training, their goal in life is to restore you to a state that's as near to normal as possible, and for them "normal" means walking. That's not their fault. It's the way society looks at the world. They want everyone to be "normal". Normally average. They think a wheelchair – using a wheelchair – must be the end of the world. I didn't have any choice in looking at things in a different way. The day after my accident I was told that I wouldn't walk again. It's harder for you because thing's aren't so clear-cut, but you have a choice, too.'

'What is my choice?'

'You tell me.'

'I could do nothing except keep going to physio classes all day and keep trying to walk using crutches. Or I could use the leg braces and a frame to help me walk. But if I do that, I can't hold anything, I can't do anything. I just move around so slowly, it takes about ten minutes just to get across the room and it just wears me out. Or I could be like you and ...'

'Don't think about it being like me. Think about it being like you. Like Libby Starling.'

'Okay. I could just admit that this disease or virus or whatever it is has permanently damaged my legs and they're not going to get any better and if I want to be independent it will have to be by using a wheelchair.'

'And how does that feel?'

'It feels bloody awful.'

'I know it does,' Barbara said, her own eyes filling with tears. 'But what feels worse?'

'Waiting and waiting and never getting any better.

Being bullied at physiotherapy and always feeling a failure. Not being able to get anywhere on my own.' I stopped for a moment. 'And do you know what I really want to do?'

'What?'

I smiled, surprised at myself. 'I want to get back to school.'

'You seem to have made a decision,' she said. 'Now let's get on with your life.'

Barbara poured the tea and handed me a plate with a wonderful little cake. It had a dark chocolate shell and inside was banana, sponge cake and whipped cream. We sat quietly for a few minutes eating and drinking, both thinking about the implications of what I'd just said. Suddenly the doorbell rang so loudly that I gave a start, spilling some tea on my lap and making my leg jump all on its own. Barbara looked surprised, too.

'Is that your friend again?'

'No, I don't think so. Oh gosh. Oh my gosh. I'd forgotten. Honestly I had. I really, honestly, truly did forget.'

'What?'

'It's Jesse. He's come to do a few odd jobs for me. I meant to ring and put him off but it went right out of my mind. Don't worry, I'll send him outside, he can tidy up the garden.' She went to answer the door whilst I rummaged around for a Kleenex, hoping I didn't look too bad. Crying made my eyes look even bigger and greener but it also made my nose look red and swollen.

'You'll never guess who's here,' Barbara said brightly as she led him into the room.

'Oh, Libby,' he said, Two large, bright pink spots spread

199

quickly across his cheeks, clashing terribly with his hair. Then he recovered and looked genuinely pleased to see me. 'I didn't know you were gonna be here. How are you?' He leant forward and gave me a kiss on the cheek as if it was the most natural thing in the world.

'I'm fine,' I replied automatically. Barbara laughed and Jesse looked puzzled and amused as if he'd like to be let in on the joke.

'I saw you on the telly. And in the local newspaper. Miss Brady brought it in and showed it to the class in tutorial period.' I groaned. After the piece on London News, a couple of papers had rung up for an interview. I'd absolutely refused to have anything to do with it but they'd still run a piece about my 'terrible problems'. Most of it was based on the programme and other people they'd talked to about me. This included pollution experts, doctors – even the awful Pauline Blood 'had her tuppence worth', as Grandma would say. They'd interviewed the Head of my school (horrible man) and I suppose it was him who'd given them our class photo for a 'before' picture.

'What's the matter? Didn't you like the way they did it? I wondered about what you'd think about it when I saw it.'

'I didn't like it much,' I said as neutrally as I could. 'What did *you* think about it?'

'Well, I thought parts of it were good. It was interesting that stuff about pollution. Your dad put the argument forward really well but it was a bit, erm, schmulzy. You know, a bit poor victim stuff.' I was impressed. Even if he'd had a conversation with Barbara about it, I thought it was brave of him to say anything. 'I thought that some of it was over the top. That last frame was a bit much. The one where the camera drew back and there was a long shot of you all on your own.'

'There speaks a true media studies student,' said Barbara. Either she didn't want us to dwell on this topic of conversation or she was keen to keep her promise and get Jesse out of the way.

'Are those by any chance Grannie Phyllis's chocolate banana cakes? Yum, my favourites.' He stuck his hand out and then remembered his manners. 'Can I have one?'

'You great stomach on legs. You can have one now and one when you've tidied up the garden,' Barbara said, joshing him. 'I've still got the conkers from last autumn all over the place and it's nearly time for the blossom. It's too early in the year to mow the lawn but you could scrub down the paved bit and clear out all the window boxes and tubs.'

'Tyrant,' Jesse said affectionately, stuffing a whole cake into his mouth.

Once he was out of the way, we settled down to talking about what had been the original reason for my visit, although it was hard for me to concentrate what with the thought of Jesse out there in the garden with his sleeves rolled up, just beyond where we were sitting. I wanted to talk to Barbara about the letter we'd received from the council about having the work done on our house. However many times I read it, it didn't seem to make any sense. It wasn't just the complicated words – it was that none of us had a clue about what we were supposed to do next.

After the occupational therapist had come to visit us when I'd come home from hospital, we'd all felt quite enthusiastic about what could be done to our house. Dad had spent ages filling out a thirty-two-page form for something called a Disabled Facilities Grant. It was like writing down his life. 'Big Brother is Watching Me,' he'd said only half jokingly as he pored over the pages. He had to tell them his salary, Mum's salary (even though she only received expenses for what she did), our savings (we didn't have any), any benefits I received or was likely to receive in the future, who owned the property we lived in (us), any children still living at home and any other dependents. He'd sent off copies of his pay slip, tax forms, building society books and bank statements to make sure he wasn't making any of it up.

A couple of weeks after that first visit, the OT had come back again, with someone from the council's Housing Department. He was a big, round-faced bloke with a big loud voice.

'Hello. Nice to meet you all. I'm called Jack Planner. Great name for a building surveyor, don't you think?' They'd gone round the house together opening doors and tapping walls, and he made lots of notes and drawings in this big form he had.

The letter had arrived a few weeks later. 'Dear Mr and Mrs Starling and Libby,' it began. I thought it was nice that she had included my name, too. 'Following my last visit to your home with Mr Planner, I am writing to let you know the state of play re: your application for a Disabled Facilities Grant. I have now received a reply from Dr Singleton about Libby's prognosis and with the Housing

Department, I have devised a plan for adaptations to your home.' There were three things listed underneath: A paved ramp instead of the small step to the front door. A stair-lift. Adjustments to the bathroom which included knocking down the wall in the toilet to make an all-in-one bathroom and putting in some grab rails.

Then the letter became confusing. It talked about sending the full report to something called the 'Housing Renovations Grants Section'. It said that due to a terrible backlog, we might have to wait at least a year until they did something called 'processing the grant application'. The letter finished with these gloomy-sounding words: 'Even though the grant is mandatory, it is likely that you will be asked to make a significant contribution towards the cost of the adaptations. For example, in a case I dealt with recently where the family finances were similar to your own, the works were assessed at £12,000 and the family were asked to contribute £10,000 towards this, which they did by raising a charge on their mortgage.'

Barbara listened to me telling her the story and read the letter herself.

'Wow,' she said, sucking in her breath. 'That's not very good news, is it?'

'What does it mean?'

'Well, it's true what they say. They are incredibly short-staffed and it does seem to take them forever to get anything done. But I'm not very happy about what they say you need. I wouldn't have thought a stair-lift was the answer. You'll need two wheelchairs, one at the bottom of the stairs and one at the top. It's very tiring making all those transfers and it's a bloody pain if you leave something downstairs. They're just suggesting that because it's the cheapest way to do it.'

'But they say we'll have to pay for it anyway. I thought that the council paid for the work if you were disabled. What does "mandatory" mean?'

'It means that they're obliged, in this case legally obliged, to adapt your house as long the work is "necessary and appropriate". Unfortunately, these days they work out how much they think you can afford to pay and sometimes they think you can afford to pay more than the work actually costs!'

'But where are we supposed to get all that money? Dad doesn't earn all that much and we haven't got anything in the bank.'

'They don't look at it that way. There've been so many cutbacks, sometimes it seems like they try to get money out of stones.'

'Why do they come and visit you then and spend all that time talking to you about what they can do to help you? They just build up your hopes for nothing.'

'It's that old question of money. Not enough money. One OT said to me, "They give us good lines and then they gag us so we can't speak them." It's also about attitude, of course. What they think disabled people deserve.'

'What do you think we should do?'

'You could always apply to a charity for some dosh,' Barbara said ironically. The last time I'd seen her she was wearing a black T-shirt with 'What do we want? Rights not Charity' printed on it in luminous pink capital letters. 'I found some incredible ones when I was trying to get some money to send one of my clients to the seaside for a couple of weeks. There's one called "The Ancient Parish of Kingsbury Charity for People in Need" who give money for you to go to Lourdes, and there's another one for "Poor Sick People of Wembley". You can apply for a grant of £200 towards a neckline.'

'What's a neckline?'

'Haven't a clue. There's a charity in Kenton called "Invalids at Home" and they sometimes give money for adaptations but they turned down over 400 people last year.' She took one look at my face. I wasn't finding this funny. 'I'm sorry, Libby. I know it's not a joke. I wish I did have a serious suggestion to make. I'll talk to someone I know at work next week and see if they have any ideas.'

I folded up the letter and put it back in my bag.

'Time for cake number two and three,' said Jesse, coming in from the garden. 'I've put all the stuff in plastic bags. I'll take it through when I go.'

'Finished already? I don't believe you. I'm going to do an inspection. Don't eat any more of those cakes before I've checked.' Jesse looked at me and smiled. Then he pulled up a chair and sat down so we were on the same level.

He held a cake in his hand as if he couldn't decide whether to say something to me or eat it. There were a few seconds of awkward silence.

'I wanted to call you after I saw you on the telly.'

Why didn't you? I thought.

'I spoke to Barbara about what she thought and I knew you'd probably be upset. I wasn't sure you'd want to talk to me about it.' I didn't know what to say to him. Why couldn't I just say something, light and easy? Surely other girls didn't find it hard to make conversation with boys. But then this wasn't exactly small talk. I plunged in at the deep end.

'Yes, actually, it was horrible. I was really upset about it at the time, especially as I knew it wouldn't occur to anyone at school that there was anything wrong with it. I had a terrible argument with my mum and dad about it afterwards.'

'Why?'

'I thought Dad was just doing it for his own benefit. He was obsessed with all that stuff about pollution in the sea and . . .'

Jesse cut into what I was saying. 'Have they found any proof that it was the sea that made you ill?'

'Not really. I was okay the day before and then the next day I was ill so it probably did have something to do with it. But nobody else at school got ill.'

'Only I've been really worried. You know, I pushed you under the water when we were mucking about and I've felt really bad that I might have done it to you.' I was amazed. It hadn't occurred to me that he might think like this. I didn't know that he'd even remembered.

'I'm sure it wasn't your fault,' I said when I'd recovered from the shock. 'Other people went under the water.'

'Does your dad blame me?'

'Of course not. I never even mentioned it to anyone.'

'Oh,' Jesse said.

'It's not that I haven't thought about that day,' I said, plucking up the courage to say something directly for once. 'I think about it a lot.'

'Do you?' he asked, giving me one of those grins.

'There's something else I wanted to say to you. If . . . when . . . erm, I don't know what your plans are about coming back to school. Do the doctors say you should wait till you're better?'

'The doctors don't really say too much about my prognosis,' I said, showing off my new word. 'I'm only just starting to think about what I'm going to do about school.'

'Have you stopped working with the frame and crutches you talked about in hospital?'

'Looks like it.'

'Only, when you do come back to Dupont, I'd really like to help. I was only nine when Barbara had her accident – she's a brilliant person you know, Barbara is – but since I've been older, we've all been on holiday together and things and I'm pretty good at getting the wheelchair up stairs and whatever.' He ended, half confident, half embarrassed.

'Thanks,' I said. 'We'll have to make an appointment to talk to old Blakemore. I'm not sure what's best, but I'll let you know when we've decided.'

'Will you ring me?'

'Yeah, I will.'

'Do you promise?'

I laughed, more relaxed now. 'Yes. I promise.'

Barbara came back into the room at the same time as Mum rang the doorbell. I couldn't believe how quickly the time had gone. I didn't want anyone else to be in that bright, sunny room. I wanted it to be just Jesse and me. I felt him do a subtle shift from this new half-confident, anxious-to-please Jesse to the more familiar popular, cool Jesse I'd known at school. He stood up and turned to Mum.

'If you're going back towards Kingsbury, Mrs Starling, is there any chance of me getting a lift?'

'Yes, of course,' my mum said. 'You're a friend of Ben's, aren't you? We met at the hospital.' Jesse put out his hand just like a real grown-up and suddenly I was aware of his height, nearly two feet taller than me.

He watched me transfer into the car and offered to put the chair in the back for Mum. I felt funny about him touching it. He sat in the back with Robbie and as soon as he had discovered Robbie's enthusiasm for American basketball, charmed the pants off him, too.

'How many NBA teams do you know?' he asked. 'Let's do it together. I'll say the city and you give the name. Chicago?'

'Bulls!' Robbie yelled.

'Orlando?'

'Magic.'

'Seattle.'

'Rockets.'

'No, you're kidding me, aren't you? Try again.'

'Super-Sonics,' Robbie said, grinning madly.

'Right. How about Los Angeles?'

'Lakers.'

'New York?'

'Knicks.'

'What a lovely young man,' Mum said as he got out of the car. I looked out the window at him.

'Don't forget what you promised me,' he mouthed silently through the glass.

Chapter Twelve
Goodbye to Nellie

When we got home I was surprised to see Grandma and Granddad there and the table laid with an old-fashioned high tea – salmon fish cakes, hard-boiled eggs, tomatoes, beetroot, sticks of celery in a glass, cheese and a plate of crusty white bread and butter. There was a big apple pie for afters. In recent weeks, my gran had taken to bringing round cooked meals already arranged on her crockery with lacy paper doilies. I hadn't been to their flat above the old shop since I'd been home.

Dad was in the kitchen, washing his hands, and Robbie was showing off his trainers and the new addition to his collection of Batman toys. Usually we'd have eaten at the big table in the back part of the sitting room, but what with my bed and Dad's 'office' in there now, we all had to squash into the kitchen. I wasn't hungry after Barbara's cakes but I enjoyed everyone being there. It was exactly the same meal Grandma had cooked for us once a fortnight ever since I could remember. The only thing that ever changed was the pudding and even that had its timetable. One visit she'd make apple pie and next time it'd be trifle. It was one of those rituals of family life.

After our meal, Robbie went in the front room to watch telly and Granddad produced a bottle of whisky he'd brought back from Scotland. I was surprised. This was strictly a funeral or grown-up's birthday drink in our house. Mum, Dad, Grandma and Granddad all cleared their throats at the same time as if they were going to make a communal speech. It was Mum who started off.

'You've probably realised this isn't just an ordinary meal, Libby. It's a family conference.' Of course I hadn't realised. Why should I? We'd never had anything so formal sounding as a 'family conference' before. 'Your dad and I listened to what you said about things after the television business and we think you're right. We need to look forward to what you can do now, not backwards to how things were before. We were all disappointed with that letter from the council but we've got to face facts. It doesn't look like they're going to help us with anything and there doesn't seem any point waiting a whole year and then being told they're not going to pay for any of it.'

'Barbara says she'll talk to someone at work,' I interrupted.

'I've already talked to some people I used to work with and they don't think there's any point in holding out too much hope. Anyway, even if they did, none of us thinks that a stair-lift is what you need. You need somewhere for yourself, downstairs. Your dad and granddad have done a bit of reckoning. It looks like it wouldn't be too complicated to convert the garage into a room for you and we could build a partition and you could have a shower with one of those fold-down seats and a toilet and a little sink in the back part. Dad and Pop would do most of the work themselves to save costs. What do you think?'

'Where are we going to get all that money from?'

Mum looked at Dad.

'I'm going to sell Nellie.'

'Oh Dad, you can't do that.'

'Why can't I?'

'Because you love it so much. Because of all the hours you've spent on it.'

'I'm not a kid anymore. It's time I grew up.' He winked at me, showing it hadn't quite happened yet.

'But how much is your car worth?'

'Well that's some good news. I rang up the MG Owners Club this afternoon and they reckon a 1972 MGB-GT in good condition is worth at least £5,000. And you've got to admit,' he turned to Mum with a wry smile on his face. 'I've kept it in good condition.'

'£5.000. Wow.' That seemed an awful lot of money to me, but then I had no idea how much it cost to build things. 'Is that going to be enough to make the garage into a room?'

'We haven't done all the calculations yet but we reckon that if we do most of it ourselves, we can get it done for about £10,000.'

'Where are we going to get the rest of the money from, then?'

Granddad gave a little cough as if he was going to give a talk at one of his British Legion dinners. 'Your grandmother and I have talked this over and we both agree this is what we want to do. You never really knew your Uncle Richard and that's a shame because he would have been proud of you.'

Richard was Dad's older brother. He'd been the first person ever in the family to go to university. I'd seen pictures of him in the sixties when he was a crazy left-wing hippie at the London School of Economics. Then he settled down and got his degree in law. Everyone said how clever he was. 'Much cleverer than Dad' was what they seemed to be thinking, although they never said so. He got a brilliant degree and after a few years he was offered a job teaching in a university in California: UCLA. We've got pictures of him there in the late seventies looking all tanned and sporty with a tennis racket in his hand. When he was twenty-eight he learned he had cancer and he came back to England and Gran looked after him till he died. He was thirty years old and I was two. His death wasn't like a hidden secret or anything. Gran liked showing me old photos and telling me stories about him, but it was a sadness you could feel had seeped into the family and could never be removed.

Granddad continued. 'Uncle Richard had a small life insurance policy, very sensible for a man his age, and when he died the money came to your granny and me. We always intended to save it for you and young Robbie when you were older and there's no reason why you shouldn't have it now when you need it. Also,' he tried to inject a bit of cranky humour into things. 'Your grandmother is always saying that since I sold the shop, I get under her feet all day. She's got our little flat all tickety-boo and there's nothing for me to do all day.'

'Except play bowls and bridge,' Grandma said.

'Don't be cheeky, you,' Granddad said fondly. 'Anyway you don't want me around all the time. I'm having DIY withdrawal symptoms. There's nothing I'd like better than to make a room for the best granddaughter in the whole world.' Here his wrinkly grey eyes did begin to look a bit watery. He took a deep breath and tried to sound cheerful again. 'I'm going to get some catalogues on Monday. There's specialist firms that do all those things for . . . hm . . . for . . .' He couldn't get the word out.

'Disabled people?' I suggested.

'Yes, of course. Perhaps that friend of yours could give us some advice. We'll need to look at windows and things and we ought to inquire whether we need to get planning permission. I'll do that straight away. It won't be difficult to take off the garage doors and put in a nice big window in the front. I know someone whose nephew is in the business. We'll have to get someone in to do the plastering, that's a hell of a job.' Granddad was off. I could see where Dad got it from.

'I get to choose all the colours and the fabrics,' I said, thinking of the differences between Barbara's sitting room and ours.

'Of course,' Granddad said solemnly. 'You can be the . . . What do they call them? Interior something or other?' He was humouring me now.

'I'll be the design consultant.'

'That's a deal. You can do all the easy bits like deciding

213

whether to have flowery or striped wallpaper and we'll do the hard bits like building it in the first place.'

'Aren't the council going to do any of the work then?'

'We can't wait a year for them to make up their mind and then decide they're not going to give us a grant anyway,' Mum said. 'It's not fair on you.'

'The first thing we'll do is the front step. It'll be easy; it's only small. I've got lots of friends who'd love to help. My friend Bill from the Bowls Club. He used to be a builder. His son Chris took over his business. They've all been asking me what they can do to help.'

'I see,' I said, more sharply than I'd intended. 'I'm going to be their charity project, am I?'

'Now, now, my dear,' Granddad said, dabbing his eyes with a white, perfectly ironed handkerchief. He and Gran were the only people I knew who still had real hankies. 'People just want to be kind.'

'I hope I don't have to listen to them going on about how they're so sorry for all my troubles like the people next door do all the time.'

'Libby,' Mum said quietly but with her eyes flashing the clear message: don't be rude to your grandfather. 'These people are proper craftsmen who'll help us to do a good job. It's the only way we'll get things done. The important thing is your independence and this is the way we'll do it. And don't worry,' she added, with more than a touch of sarcasm in her own voice. 'I'll write the thank you letters.'

After they'd gone, Mum insisted on taking me upstairs on her own. She was determined to show Dad she could do it too.

'Are you sure, pet? I don't mind doing it.' I don't know why Dad never learned that calling Mum 'pet' was not a good idea.

'Just go away,' Mum said, nudging Dad aside and taking hold of the back of the chair. 'I'll be fine. Look at her, she's as slim as anything. Remember, I'm the one who used to get the buggy up and down all those stairs when we lived above the shop.'

'Oh, thanks very much, Mum,' I said crossly.

'What?'

'Is that how you all see me now? Like a great big baby in a great big baby buggy.'

'Of course not. That's not what I was saying.'

'Well don't talk about me like that then. You're the one who's always going on about how important words are. You ought to think about what you say.'

I waited for Mum to have a real go at me about my attitude problem but she didn't say anything. Instead I had to let her get me upstairs which she did easily and efficiently, help me get into our narrow toilet and then pass me things in the bathroom because everything was too high or too awkward. I thought about having my own place where I could reach everything and do everything. It couldn't come soon enough.

Mum handed me my nightie and watched as I brushed my hair and got into bed. She'd lost weight, too, and for the first time I saw tiny, fine wrinkles around her eyes.

'Mum?'

'Yes, love.'

'You know downstairs. Was I very rude to Granddad?'

'You were a bit but I think he understands how you're

feeling. He tries to anyway. Don't be too hard on him and his chums, though. They don't mean to be patronising – they probably don't even know what it means. They're just trying to be kind.'

'Was I rude to you?'

She smiled and raised her eyebrows. 'I can take it.'

'You never used to take it, though. If I was rude before you always used to have a real go at me.'

'If you're still talking to me like this when you're in your new room and everything's settled down, I'll start having a go at you again.' She was only half joking. 'What do you think about it all?' I felt excited and uncomfortable at the same time. I felt bad that Dad was going to have to sell his beloved Nellie and also that Gran and Granddad were going to spend all of Robbie's share of Uncle Richard's money on me.

'Don't worry about either of those things. Dad really wants to do this for you and so do Ma and Pop. Anyway, there'll be certain pay-offs for Robbie. He gets your room and he gets to choose the decorations. I hope he's gone off Batman and Robin by then.'

'What do people like me do if they haven't got family who can help them out?'

Mum looked serious. 'I suppose they just have to wait until the council get round to deciding if they're entitled to a grant. If they're already living in a council flat they might hope they'll be rehoused into something more suitable. There must be lots of people out there living in appalling circumstances.' She shook her head sadly. 'Perhaps you'll find a way to help people in that situation when you get older.' She leaned over and kissed me on the forehead. 'Don't worry about it now, though. Tomorrow, I'm going to go out and buy loads of magazines and you can think about good things like paint colours and bathroom tiles.'

I was dying to tell someone about the plans for my new room. I rang Cleo the next morning to tell her but she wasn't in and there was no point asking her mum where she was. I told Cleo most things these days and she told me a lot, too. I was the only person who knew that she was going out with someone called Ed who was much older than her. He lived near her dad in Willesden and she used the fact that her mum and dad never talked to each other to spend time with him. Her mum thought she was with her dad and vice versa. He appealed to Cleo's wild side but I think she was a bit scared of him, too. He worked in Waitrose supermarket in the day and played in a band in the evenings. She'd shown me a picture of him standing outside his beat-up blue van. He was tall and skinny with extraordinarily white skin and long, dark-blond dreadlocks.

Like me, Cleo had a private side, and she didn't tell me what they got up to in the back of that van and I didn't ask. I knew that most of his mates had girlfriends who were in their twenties and I couldn't imagine what that felt like. I hadn't told her how I felt about Jesse. I thought she might laugh at me, and I suppose I still didn't trust her 100 per cent with my secrets.

Esther rang me later in the day, Sunday afternoon. She was busting to tell me the gossip. I'd never heard her sound so excited about anything.

'Anita had a party last night for her sixteenth birthday.

It was great. It was the best party I've ever been to.' The best party? It was probably the first party. 'I was really pleased she asked me. I don't even know her all that well.' I had that familiar sensation I thought I'd got used to over the years. That hard, dull feeling of knowing you'd been left out, excluded. Obviously no-one had thought to tell me about it. As if she could read my mind, Esther said, 'You know Anita. She lives in those flats on Fryent Way. Second floor, no lift.' As if that made it alright.

'Libby, you okay?'

'Yeah, sure,' I said. 'I couldn't have gone anyway. We had a family thing on.' Esther paused on the other end of the phone, unsure whether to continue. Perhaps they all thought it was impossible for me to go to a party on the second floor. Or perhaps they didn't think about me at all. The silence didn't last long because her need to tell me the news overcame any worry that she might have hurt my feelings.

'You'll never believe what Joanna did. She got completely smashed on Hooch, the blackcurrant-flavour one. She didn't even know it had alcohol in it; she thought it was fizzy Ribena. She drank four cans and was sick all over the place. It was a disgusting mess, you should have seen the colour. Fortunately she did it in the kitchen and not on the carpet.'

She continued without stopping. 'Guess who I danced with? No, guess. Ben! He's had his hair cropped really short and it feels so nice when you rub it the wrong way.' Her voice went all dreamy. 'God, I really like him, you know. I never even thought about him before. Do you think he likes me? Did he ever say anything to you about me? He took my phone number. I hope he rings. I used to think he was a bit of a nerd but he's so cute when you get to know him.'

She paused momentarily for breath and dramatic effect. 'And you'll never believe what Cleo was up to.'

So Cleo had been there too? That was a surprise.

'Go on, guess who she got off with?'

She waited for me to ask, 'who?' but I didn't need to. That sinking feeling in my stomach told me already.

'Jesse!' Esther squealed. 'Can you believe it? Jesse! You've never seen such a snogfest. They were absolutely all over each other. First of all it was when they were dancing — tonsil gymnastics or what? Then they were well away on the sofa; no one else could get anywhere near it.'

Snogfest? Tonsil gymnastics? Nobody actually talked like that. It was so unlike the serious, calm Esther I knew; she'd obviously been reading too many teen magazines.

'Anyway, after that they just disappeared. It was so embarrassing what happened then. I took Joanna into Anita's bedroom to have a lie down because she was feeling sick and they were in there! Only they weren't snogging any more. They were sitting on the edge of the bed holding hands and talking. Jesse just looked at me as if he wanted me to disappear. God, I could have died! I wouldn't have imagined those two together. Did you know about it? I thought Cleo already had a boyfriend. Asfah told me she'd seen her with this older guy . . .' Her voice continued but I'd stopped listening.

'Libby? You still there? What do you think I should do?'

'Sorry?'

'About Ben.'

I tried to guess what she'd been asking me. 'I'm sure he must like you if he asked for your number. He's a bit shy, though – he hasn't had a girlfriend before. Give him a bit of time and just be friendly at school. You know what boys can be like – they panic.'

Esther laughed. 'Thanks, that's good advice.' There was a pause. I wanted her to get off the phone. 'Libby, are you okay?' she asked. 'You sound a bit low. Can I come round and see you?' She was sweet really, Esther.

'I'm a bit tired now,' I said, hoping it sounded convincing. 'I'll give you a call in the week. Good luck with Ben.'

The little place inside me that went tight and hard was really hurting now. I wasn't going to let myself cry, even though there was no-one to see me. It felt as though if I started, there would be no reason to ever stop. Esther, Ben, Jesse, even Joanna had all been invited but nobody thought about me. It was too much trouble for people to think about including me in their plans. I mimicked Jesse's voice in my head. 'I'd really like to help. I've had lots of experience getting people in wheelchairs up stairs.' So much for promises. But when I thought about it, he hadn't promised me anything, he'd just made me promise to ring him. I'd have to get used to the idea that if he thought about me at all, it was as a friend. He was nice to me because he was worried that he might have been responsible for me getting ill, and he'd offered to help because Barbara was his stepdad's sister, so the thought of people in wheelchairs didn't frighten or repulse him. That was all. I'd been stupid to think there was anything else in it.

As for the thought of him and Cleo together, I could hardly bear it. I shut my eyes tight to get rid of the picture Esther had created in my mind. I was so pleased that I'd never told anyone how I felt about Jesse. At least now when Cleo told me about it, I could pretend that I didn't care. I could just wait for her to tell me.

I needed something to take my mind away from all this. I tried listening to music but I couldn't bear all those songs about love going wrong. I tried looking at the decorating magazines Mum had bought but that didn't help. I used to like reading but I couldn't get into other people's stories. For the first time in my whole life, the idea of having some homework to do seemed rather appealing. I wished I had a geography project to do, an English essay to write or a page of maths problems to solve.

When Cleo called in to see me a couple of days later, she looked pale and anxious but I pretended I hadn't noticed. I had lots of news to tell her and I was determined to be cool about everything. I was not, definitely not, going to ask her about the party. She listened enthusiastically, especially when I told her about the idea of converting the garage.

'I know what you should do: you should paint it gold with a black ceiling with silver stars and moons stencilled all over it. I'll come over and do it. I've just made a box like it for Art.' I laughed.

'And we've finally made an appointment to come and

see the Head about when I can come back to school.'

'That's brilliant. When are you coming?'

'Friday, 10.30, before break. It's just going to be me and my mum. Dad can't get the time off work.'

'I'll look out for you. Where will it be, in Blakemore's office?'

'Yeah, I suppose so.' There was a long pause which was unusual for a conversation with Cleo. I didn't know whether she was going to say anything. Then suddenly, she got up and closed the door.

'Is anyone going to come in?'

'No, we should be okay. Robbie's at a friend's house and Mum will leave us alone.'

'Have you spoken to Esther or Joanna?'

'Esther rang me on Sunday.'

'Oh, well, you've heard then,' Cleo said biting her nails. 'What did you think?' What did I think? Why was she asking me that? 'I've got myself into such a mess,' she continued, running her hands through her hair and pulling it nervously at the neck. 'If I tell you about it, do you absolutely, totally promise you won't tell a living soul?'

'You know I will. I mean I won't.'

'It's all about Ed really. I saw him Saturday afternoon when he finished work. He'd really been stressing me out. I've known for a long time that he's too old for me. I thought I could keep up but I couldn't. His friends, they all do drugs and that's okay, I smoke as well. Don't look surprised. My mum started me off; I smoke dope with her sometimes. She says her therapist thinks it's a good idea for relieving tension. But Ed's friends do lines of coke and some of them do crack and I was in there way

above my head. And then there was the whole sex thing.'
She chewed hard against the skin on the side of her nails.
'I'd hardly even kissed anyone before I met him. I know
people at school think I'm right in there but it's all an act.
I just try and pretend to be hard.

'At first I was crazy about him. He was really sweet to
me. He said he wouldn't have sex properly with me until
I was sixteen and then he promised he'd be responsible
and use condoms and everything. I thought it was great
to have someone to show me what to do. He was so
gentle and he used to touch me and kiss me everywhere
and call me baby-woman and say how pretty and soft I
was. And then, when I was sixteen, on the day of my
birthday in fact, we actually did it. It wasn't brilliant or
anything but it was alright. Then things began to change.
He always wanted to be on his own with me and we
never saw his friends. He wanted to do it all the time –
the second he saw me, he just wanted me to get in the
back of the van. Then something changed in me. I don't
know what happened but suddenly I didn't fancy him
anymore. I started to find him repulsive. His mouth
seemed all wet and slobbery and I couldn't bear him
touching me. Every time he came near me, I couldn't
stand it. It used to make me feel physically sick. He
started waiting for me outside school when he wasn't
working and we were hardly down the road when he
wanted me to do it. I used to try to make excuses and say
I'd got my periods or a bad cold or something.

'Anyway, it got worse and worse and on Saturday he
was waiting for me in the van just down the road from
Dad's house, about seven o'clock. He knew I usually left

at about that time. He'd already rolled a joint; I suppose he thought it'd make me relax. I'd made up my mind I was going to tell him, but I wasn't really prepared to say it then because I didn't know I was going to see him. I tried telling him I was too young for him and I had my exams coming up and everything and I thought it was best if we stopped seeing each other. He just laughed – he was already stoned – and he put his hand here, not gently.' She touched her breast. 'It just felt so horrible, like he was trying to take over my whole body, and I pushed him away and said I was going. He locked the door and started being really horrible.' Cleo caught the expression on my face. 'He wasn't physically violent or anything but he was saying how I was just a tight-arsed slag and I didn't know anything about having a good time. He said there wasn't any pleasure in being with me anyway; he'd just been wasting his time. I wasn't a baby-woman, I was just a pathetic stupid baby.'

'What did you do?'

'I was really scared. I just sat there absolutely still and eventually he opened the door and told me to get out because I was just a "fucked-up little bitch". I felt really dirty then. I went home to Mum's and had a shower and changed and then without really thinking about what I was doing, I went off to Anita's party. I hadn't even thought about going before then.' Cleo looked straight at me and I looked straight back at her. 'When I got there, the first person I saw was Jesse. He came up to me and you know what he's like, he's so friendly and nice to everyone. And then he started on about you. "Did I think we should have asked you if you wanted to come to the

224

party? Did I think you'd mind?" And I felt awful because I knew you should have been there, and what kind of friends are we if we don't even tell you what's going on? So I started to cry and he looked really worried and he put his arm round me and asked me what was wrong and I couldn't tell him, could I? I suppose I must have been a bit stoned because I just pulled him towards me and started kissing him. And he is *so* nice to kiss. He wasn't wet and disgusting and all over me and I didn't feel scared any more. I just wanted to forget everything. Poor Jesse. I was all over him like a rash. I don't think he knew what hit him.' She smiled a weak kind of smile. 'Did Esther tell you what happened next?'

'She just said she saw you talking in the bedroom.'

'She ran out like a frightened rabbit when she saw us. Perhaps she didn't know what had happened to me. It was so weird. In the middle of kissing Jesse, I suddenly got incredibly upset and started shaking all over and I couldn't catch my breath. I got really terrified; I thought I was going to die. He looked just as terrified as me at first, but then he seemed to know what to do. He didn't panic or anything; he just took me into the bedroom and made me put my hands over my mouth and take little breaths in and big breaths out. When I eventually calmed down, I said I was sorry I'd behaved like an idiot and explained a bit about what had happened. Not everything, just enough to get him to see I didn't usually carry on like this.'

Poor Cleo. I couldn't help feeling sorry for her. She looked absolutely awful, pale and tearful, with black kohl streaks on her face and her short, white-blonde hair stuck out from her head. She had no adults in her life who she could talk to or who would help her with her problems. I put out my hand across the table and touched hers. She looked up and smiled at me. For a second I thought she was going to ask me how I felt about her kissing Jesse, but she didn't.

'Do you think Ed's going to make trouble?' I asked her.

'Naw, I don't think so. He made it pretty clear what he thought of me. I don't imagine he'll want to come anywhere near me again.'

'Well, let me know if anything happens.'

'Thanks. But I've made up my mind – I'm going to be a reformed character from now on. No more blokes for a long while. I'm going to try and help my mum sort things out, finish all my coursework on time and . . . ' She paused for emphasis. 'Be a good friend to you.'

After she'd gone, I went through it again. I was glad I knew the truth, or at least Cleo's version of the truth, but it didn't really make me feel much better. After all, I didn't know what Jesse thought about all this. Maybe he saw it as an opportunity for him and Cleo to get it together? Like Cleo, I made some resolutions. Three, in fact. First, no more thinking about Jesse as a potential boyfriend. I had quite enough real problems in my life. Second, I was going to concentrate my energies on making sure my room and all the things I needed to be independent were right for me, and that included getting a really good wheelchair like Barbara's and not this cranky old NHS thing. Third, I was going to get on with my education.

Chapter Thirteen
School Visit

Mum drove into the car park outside what we called the 'old building' and we came in through the main entrance, the one usually used by teachers and visitors. It was so strange coming back to school after all this time. Nothing had changed but nothing seemed the same. Even the journey in the brown car had been weird. I'd been up to the shops a few times since I'd been ill, but there was only one reason to turn off Kingsbury Road, down into Brooke Lane, past the quiet houses with their small, scruffy gardens and then right into Duke's Avenue, and that was to get to Dupont High School.

I felt a bit like a visitor from the planet Zog. A Zogian who had spent almost a thousand days in these buildings but who, through some mysterious happenings outside her control, had now become an outsider. Nine months is a long time for anyone to miss school even if they come back looking and feeling exactly like they did before. I knew that I had changed, inside and out.

I'd forgotten how nice the old building was. It was a lot more interesting than most school buildings you see, except for those posh, private ones. It was long and low, only two storeys high, and built of dark-red brick with curved wooden windows, and it had a big double oak door in the middle like an old castle. There was a crescent-shaped garden outside, just in front of the teachers' car park, and it was full of bright tulips and pansies.

The main entrance led into a spacious hall known as the 'vestibule' (whatever that meant), and the Head's office was just on the left. Dad told me that when he and Uncle Richard had been at this school, when it was still a grammar school, if a teacher told you to 'go and wait in the vestibule', you knew it meant you had to stand outside the Headmaster's office until he saw you there and then he'd take you into his 'study' and give you the cane. He never even asked what you were doing there; he just assumed you'd been in trouble. I often wondered what would have happened if someone had been sent to tell him something else, like the school was on fire. Presumably they'd have had 'six of the best' while the school burned down.

Everything was unnaturally quiet and calm as we waited for our meeting with the Head. His office and the general office were still in the same place and there were corridors straight ahead and to the right and the left. There was no way you could make yourself invisible here, not in Dad's day and not now. I had hoped we'd be in and out again while everyone was still in their lessons but the Head didn't appear for ages and when the pips went at the end of period 2, the quiet corridors erupted with the noise and movement of hundreds of kids moving in every direction. The other two buildings, the 'new building' and the gym, must have been completely empty. Somehow, the entire school needed to walk, shove or run past where I was waiting.

I didn't want anyone to see me, especially people from my year, but there was nowhere for me to go. The idea of imagining I was an alien from the planet Zog was not such a bad way to get me through the next ten minutes. Outside I was someone who looked a bit like the old Libby Starling but inside there was a metal robot sent to observe the strange encounters that took place between ordinary teenage mortals and an alien creature who occupied a small vehicle with large, round wheels.

The Libby-Zogian in the wheelchair – dressed not in the regulation brown skirt, brown jumper and cream top but in her own uniform of trainers, navy track-suit bottoms and sweatshirt – noted several different reactions. The first response was nice. This was from the people who had sent Libby cards when she was first in hospital. They came up with smiles on their faces; some gave her a kiss or a hug, even though it's not that easy to hug someone in a wheelchair when one is standing up and the other is sitting down. They asked her how she was and said they hoped she'd come back to school soon.

The second response was from people, lots of people, who acted as if they thought that Libby couldn't see or hear them. They pointed at her and whispered loudly to each other that this was the person who had been on the telly and who couldn't walk anymore. They said they had heard she might be in that wheelchair forever and wasn't that terrible?

The third response was peculiar. People came up to Libby and asked her if she wanted any help. Some even went behind the chair and tried to push her, but they couldn't move her because the brakes were on. Libby tried saying, 'Thank you, but I don't want to go anywhere', but people didn't seem to hear her voice.

The fourth reaction was just as strange. People walked towards Libby as though they were going to go past the office but when they saw her, they turned round and went back the way they had come as if she had a strange smell or some disease they could catch.

'Hello, Mrs Starling Hello, Libby. I'm so sorry to have kept you waiting. Bit of a problem with some intruders from another school. Do come in.' Mr Blakemore's booming voice brought me back inside my own body. He was a large man with a big red face and thinning brown hair arranged in what Mum called the wraparound style. He was wearing a dark, slightly shiny suit, white shirt and his trademark – a maroon spotted bow-tie.

'Now do come in,' he boomed heartily, a bit too heartily for my liking. 'I've invited a couple of other members of staff to join us. I thought it would be useful if Mr Warren came along. He's our Head of Science as you probably remember but he's also the Health and Safety Rep. I've also asked Miss Benjamin – Mizz Benjamin, I should say . . . ha, ha, ha – Libby's Year Head. Oh, here she is now.'

Ms Benjamin gave me a nice, warm smile. 'Hello, Libby. It's good to see you again. How are you?'

'I'm okay,' I said. 'Thanks for the cards you sent. They were lovely.'

'Did you enjoy the book?'

'I haven't read it yet.'

'I see,' she said and smiled at me again. She turned to the Head. 'Mr Warren asked me to send his apologies but he can't make the meeting. Both of the science technicians are away and he has to help one of his teachers.' A look of extreme irritation flashed across Mr Blakemore's face. 'Oh dear. Well, never mind. Take a seat everyone. Not you Libby, of course. You've already brought your seat with you. Ha, ha.' He pulled some chairs forward and then went round and sat behind his desk on a big leather chair.

Mum looked over at me and raised her eyebrows. I smiled back nervously. None of the kids I knew liked Mr Blakemore. Nobody trusted that laugh.

'First of all I'd like to say, on behalf of all the school, how pleased I am to see Libby again,' he said in the kind of voice he used in school assembly. 'We've all been following the difficult time you've had and I'm very pleased to see you looking so well. I'm sure you've been very brave. Now, Mrs Starling. You asked me to arrange this meeting, and perhaps you'd like to start off and tell us what you have in mind for your daughter.'

Mum took a deep breath. She was wearing her good black suit and neat, gold earrings. Compared to the size of Blakemore, she looked really tiny, but her voice was strong and firm.

'We want to talk about arrangements for Libby

coming back to school. I don't mean right away. There's still some things to get straight at home and I know her year group are getting ready to do their GCSEs. But we've talked about it as a family and we all agree that it's a good idea for her to start thinking about school now, so that she can begin again in September. One of the things we want to know is whether there is any work she could be doing at home to help her get up to date?'

Mr Blakemore gave a startling cough, which made me jump. I looked up and saw that his face was even redder than usual.

'Ah, yes. I see. Well, I'm afraid it's not going to be as simple as that. There's quite a lot of things we're going to have to look at before we can even think about giving Elizabeth any schoolwork to do.'

'I'm not sure what you mean,' my mum said quietly. Mr Blakemore didn't know what that voice meant, but I did.

'Well, let me start by asking you a few questions,' he said, regaining his jolly tone. 'First of all, Libby's medical condition. What exactly is the latest state of play from the doctors?'

'It's the same as I explained to you in my letter,' Mum said evenly. 'But I don't think we need to discuss her medical condition in any detail. She can bear weight through her legs, which is helpful for some things, but from the school's point of view it's best to think in terms of her using a wheelchair all the time. She'll need to be taught as far as possible in the downstairs classrooms.'

Blakemore gave that funny cough again. 'Oh dear,' he said. 'We had hoped there would be some improvement in her health.'

Mum looked up at him sharply. 'There won't be any problems with Libby's health by the time she starts school again. She's very well now and she has full use of her arms and her brain. It's just that she can't walk any more.'

'I'm afraid it's not quite as simple as that, Mrs Starling,' he said with a theatrical sigh. 'I only wish it were. There's nothing I'd like better than to be able to say to you "There's nothing to worry about, she can come back whenever she wants, we'll arrange it all". Some Heads might say that, but much as I would love to be able to welcome Libby back to Dupont High, I don't think it would be honest of me if I didn't say that this young lady is presenting us with some very serious problems.' He gave me an entirely unconvincing affectionate smile.

'What exactly are these problems?' Mum asked. Her voice was still quiet but it was now ice-cold quiet.

'There are so many. I'm afraid the architects didn't have wheelchairs in mind when they built this school.' He shook his head and gave another irritating little laugh. 'Both of the main teaching buildings have stairs and no lifts. The new building is especially difficult, being four storeys high. I'm not going to try to spin you a line about making alterations to the school, either. I've already been on to the authority and you can guess what they said – "No funds available in the foreseeable future." And as for our own school budget, what can I say?' He opened out the palms of his hands. 'The coffers are almost bare; we hardly have enough money for books and other essential equipment.'

'Why can't lessons be organised so that Libby can be taught in the downstairs classrooms? This building seems pretty accessible to me. All the entrances to this floor are completely flat.'

'Yes, we have thought about that. Please don't think we haven't looked at it carefully but it's not as simple as it might seem.'

'Oh, yes?' Mum's eyebrows couldn't have gone any higher up her head.

'You see, all the departments have specialist equipment which would have to be brought down just for these lessons. Take maths, for example. That's taught on the third floor of the New Building. All the maths rooms have stacks of filing cabinets holding all the separate worksheets needed to teach a mixed ability class. It would be impossible to bring all that downstairs to teach one lesson.'

'Have you asked the maths teachers what they think? Maybe it would be possible to bring some of the work needed to one of the classrooms downstairs so that . . .'

Blakemore cut across her. 'It's a great shame Mr Warren couldn't be here with us today. There are some particular problems in the science department and I would have liked him to talk about them himself. Still, I'll do my best. As you know, science is a compulsory subject in this school and it requires specialist equipment. It would be quite impossible to bring a science laboratory downstairs, as I'm sure you understand.' He laughed again.

'Could Libby be taken upstairs for those lessons?' Blakemore knitted his brows together and looked at Mum with a 'well really, I don't think so' expression on his face.

'That brings me to the next point Mr Warren was

going to talk about. As I said, he's also the Health and Safety Representative for the school and there are some relevant issues here for all the staff and indeed the students if we attempt to incorporate a disabled student into our system.' He started talking in gobbledygook. 'It is essential that we carry out procedures commensurate with the law and the authority regulations to the maximum benefit of all the participants in our institution.'

'I didn't understand any of that. Could you please just say what you mean?' Mum said rudely. Usually I wanted to curl up and die when she spoke to people in that voice, especially at school, but I felt strangely removed from it all, as if they were talking about somebody else, not me. He shuffled some papers uneasily around on his desk.

'Since you ask me to be clear, I will indeed try to be. This isn't easy for anyone.'

'It's Libby it isn't easy for, but it would help us all if you just say what you want to say.'

'Well, bear with me a minute. You must understand that I have to look at things from the teachers' point of view as well. Their job is quite difficult enough. The school is organised in department bases and I don't think I would be very popular if I suggested moving that about so that we had one maths room here and one maths room there and so on. Second, I don't think I could ask teachers to carry your daughter up and down the stairs all the time. What if there was an accident? What if someone put their back out? I'd have the unions on my back in a minute.'

'If need be I'll come in and take her up the stairs myself. It's not difficult, you know; she hardly weighs anything.'

'Then there's the safety issues,' Blakemore continued as if he hadn't heard the interruption. 'What would we do in the case of a fire? We can't put the other students at risk.'

'I don't see how they'd be at risk. Surely there are cases where . . .'

'I've been a teacher for over thirty years and I can tell you that even in a fire drill, never mind a real fire, it's very hard to control a crowd of several hundred children. This school just isn't designed for wheelchairs.'

'Even when those people in wheelchairs are members of your school?' Mum's voice was so clear and so full of passion that everyone stopped dead. Even Ms Benjamin lifted up her head and looked at her. 'We're talking about a person here. My daughter, Libby, who is ready to come back to school and study for her exams. We came to meet you today hoping to talk about how you would include her in the school. Instead everything you have said is negative; I haven't heard a single positive remark from you. What you're saying is just blatant prejudice. This is the kind of attitude that kept ordinary disabled people locked up in asylums for their whole life because other people who had power decided they were too dangerous to go out.'

I knew Mum. I knew that deadly calm in her voice meant that she was near to explosion point. I didn't want her to break down because I didn't want her to feel embarrassed and I couldn't bear the thought of how

Blakemore would react if he found a weeping woman in front of him. Somehow her distress helped me to feel calm and removed. Ms Benjamin looked at me and caught something of what I was feeling.

'Do you want to say something, Libby?' she asked softly. I turned to Blakemore and looked him straight in the face.

'Where do you think I should go to school if I can't go here?'

He shuffled some more papers and revived a bit. 'Yes, well, I've done a bit of research on that one.'

'That's very kind of you,' Mum said sarcastically.

'The college over at Wembley, you may know it. They have a new building with a lift in it and they've just opened a unit which caters for students with special needs like Libby. They'd be very happy to have her, I'm sure. I recommend that you at least go and visit. How does that sound?'

'I really wanted to stay here, where I know people and where my friends are,' I said uncertainly.

'Well, that's another point isn't it?' he said patronisingly. 'You wouldn't be with your friends, would you? Even if you stayed here, you've missed a whole year of school and would have to start with the new Year 11 whilst all your old friends went into Year 12 and started their A levels. They'd be allowed to use the Sixth Form Common Room so you wouldn't even see them at break. Did you think of that. Hmm?'

'Of course we've thought of that,' Mum said, her voice calmer again. 'But they'd still be around and they'd be able to help her out. And it's her local school. It's a long way to get to Wembley every day.'

'I wouldn't worry about that. They might well have a special bus.' Mum and I looked at each other.

'The other thing that worries me is whether Libby would be able to do the same options as she's been doing here. Apart from the main subjects, she's been studying Geography and Textiles and Spanish for a year. It wouldn't be fair to ask her to start a whole lot of new subjects. We don't know what kind of courses they offer. Libby's a clever girl and we're hoping that she'd be entered for the Higher Level in her GCSEs. We don't know what kind of students she'd be with at college and whether they'd encourage her to do well academically. The teachers here have always been very keen for her to do well.'

'Ah, here it is!' Mr Blakemore had finally found the piece of paper he'd been looking for.

'What is that?'

'Libby's end-of-Year-10 report.'

Oh God. Those exams I'd taken a week before we went to Littlehampton. I'd been so worried about them then. It seemed ridiculous that he was going to give me the results now.

'I'm sure that Libby's a bright girl, but I'm afraid it doesn't always show up in her results. She was always a bit of what we call an underachiever.' He waved the report in the air. 'Almost all her teachers say here that they were disappointed with her grades and thought she could do a lot better. She had problems with concentration and talked too much in class. It may be that a new start would be the right thing for her.'

Mum gave him the kind of look that would have knocked a weaker man to the floor. 'Are you saying that her work and behaviour was so bad that you would have expelled her? Would you have told her father and me that she wouldn't be allowed back to this school?'

Blakemore looked shocked. 'No, of course not.'

'So it's not really relevant that her teachers said she could have worked harder. I imagine they say that to most students. You're just confusing the issue.' Mum had got her confidence back and more. 'You're not saying that she can't come back because her work isn't up to standard. You're saying she can't come back to this school because you can't – won't – have a disabled student. Have I got that right?'

'Mrs Starling, please.' He could hardly get the words out. 'It really isn't as simple as that. I don't want you or Libby to feel . . .'

'Feel what?'

'That all things being equal, we wouldn't have loved her to complete her schooling here.'

'Unfortunately, things aren't equal, are they? After all that Libby's been through she needs as much stability as possible. That's why we wanted her to come back here. I don't think there's any point in continuing. We need to go home now and talk about it with her father. I'll be in touch soon.' She stood up and nodded at me to go. Her presence seemed to fill the room. Ms Benjamin followed us out and scurried down the corridor, and Blakemore put his hands on the desk as if he was going to stand up but then sat down again.

'That's fine,' he said, determined to have the last word.

'I'll expect to hear from you soon. But do go and have a look at Wembley College and let me know what you think.' Mum didn't even bother to reply.

Outside the door she started shaking so much she couldn't get the car keys out of her bag.

'I'm not sure I can drive home.'

'Mum. Mummy. Sit down for a second until you calm down. He's not going to come out again for quite a while.'

'You were great in there,' she said to me. 'So calm and strong.' I felt more numb than strong.

'Hi you guys. How did it go?' I don't know how long Cleo had been hanging around there, or why she wasn't in class. 'Dance,' she said, reading my thoughts. 'I'm supposed to be doing library research into classical ballet. Well, tell me what happened?'

'He more or less said I couldn't come back here,' I said, the penny finally beginning to drop.

'What!?'

'He said it would be too dangerous and too difficult for me to be in school. He said that they'd have to make too many changes and the teachers wouldn't have it.'

'That fascist pig,' she exploded in a typical Cleo fashion. 'What did Ms Benjamin say? I saw she was in there.'

'She didn't really say anything. I think she was a bit scared of him.'

'That mealy-mouthed pathetic wooz. I'm not surprised. Where are you supposed to go to school then?'

'He suggested a special unit at Wembley College. At least I think that's what he suggested. He said I wouldn't

240

be able to be in the same year as you anyway and my report was so bad it would be best for me to have a new start.' The feeling was beginning to come back along with Cleo's anger. Like after you've been to the dentist and had an injection.

'He said that!? The miserable bastard.' She said it so loudly, I'm amazed he didn't hear her. Perhaps he did. 'No way. Absolutely no way. It's not fair. We can't allow him to get away with it. Why should you have to go somewhere else – your work was a million times better than half the kids in our year. I'm going to call you later.' She hugged me and ran.

When we got home Mum was in such a state, I made her lie down on the sofa and brought her in a cup of tea. It wasn't easy because everything in the kitchen was too high for me, but I managed it without spilling too much. I even made a couple of sandwiches by balancing a tray on my lap and organising everything from there. Neither of us was hungry but it felt like an achievement.

'I'm sorry I'm being so pathetic when you're being so strong,' she said.

'You're not being pathetic; you were great in there.'

'Did you mind that I did all the talking?'

'No, I wouldn't have known what to say.' I didn't even know what to think.

Cleo rang not that evening but the one after.

'I've talked to people at school and everyone thinks it's disgusting. You should be allowed to come back; it's terrible what he said to you. They want to start up a petition or something. What do you think?'

I wasn't sure. I knew Cleo meant well but I'd been hurt enough over all that business at Anita's party. I didn't know whether I wanted a whole lot of people involved in what was essentially my business.

'I don't know, Cleo. We are doing things at home. Dad's going to ask some people in the Teacher's Union and Mum's talking to some people who've started a group that doesn't want children to have to go to special schools,' I said, unsure of how this sounded.

'People really do want to help though,' Cleo said persuasively. 'At least come round my house on Sunday afternoon and we'll talk about it. Please?'

'Okay, but don't let too many people come. I don't want a great big crowd.'

Mum quickly regained her energy. Through someone she knew, she got in touch with a group and started talking to other parents who had children who were disabled in some way and who wanted them to go to ordinary schools. 'We call it segregated schooling,' a woman told Mum on the phone. She had campaigned to get a lift put in her son's primary school. 'We believe that separating children from their brothers, sisters and friends because they are disabled and making them go to what they call "special schools" is a kind of apartheid. It's like what they did in America and South Africa, where they segregated children and sent them to inferior schools because they were black.'

I knew that was wrong. It was terrible to exclude children just because their skin was a different colour. But what if the Head was right? What if I really was a danger to other people in school? Perhaps it wasn't fair to ask everyone to change the way they did things just because of me. I didn't want anyone else to get hurt. I couldn't get it straight in my head. When I remembered the meeting with Blakemore I felt furious and betrayed, but when I thought about what we could do about it I felt deep-down sad.

When I spoke to Barbara on the phone she wasn't nearly as surprised as I thought she'd be.

'It's bloody typical,' she said. 'But you can't let him get away with it.'

'But what if he's right?'

'What do you mean?'

'What if it is dangerous for everyone else for me to be in school? He talked about all these health and safety issues and what they'd do if there was a fire.'

Barbara gave me one of her reassuring laughs, although I wasn't sure what was funny. 'That's what they always say when they don't want you around. Half those teachers would probably have a heart attack on the stairs in a real fire, but they don't sack them. I get it all the time, especially when I try to have some fun. Like at the cinema. In some places they're really helpful and the people who work there offer to carry me up and down great flights of stairs and get me popcorn, and in other places they tell me I'm a fire risk and I'm not allowed to buy a ticket even if I've got someone with me. There's loads of cinemas and theatres that don't allow people in wheelchairs in even if there aren't any stairs. And they almost never allow you in on your own. It's got nothing to do with you being a fire risk; it's just their prejudice.

The last time this happened to me I said, "Are you banning me because I'm black or because I'm disabled or both?" You should have seen his face; I thought he was going to choke!'

I laughed with her at the awfulness of it, but I wasn't entirely convinced that it had anything to do with school. 'He did seem to come up with a lot of good reasons, though. The classrooms are in two different buildings and the science labs are upstairs. I mean, I hate him but you can't really blame him for the way the school was built. He said it just wasn't designed for wheelchairs.'

'Libby, listen to me,' Barbara said firmly. 'IT'S − NOT − YOUR − FAULT.' She pronounced each word as if it was in a sentence of its own. 'Don't let them make you feel as if you are to blame. You are not a wheelchair; you are a person who uses a wheelchair, and that person deserves to get a good education. I agree it's an old building but if you decide that you want to go back to that school at least to do your GCSE exams, there will be a way to do it. He's the one who has to find the solution.'

'What if he doesn't want to?'

I could almost hear Barbara smiling at the other end of the phone. 'I know you. You'll find a way. And don't forget my motto.'

'What's that?'

'Don't let the bastards grind you down.'

Talking to Barbara always made me feel stronger. 'The problem is not your inability to walk,' she had said. 'The problem is the way the buildings have been designed to shut you out and their lack of imagination in finding a way to let you back in.' I tried to tell myself that this was true, that she was right. But I was sure that Blakemore hadn't gone home that night thinking this was his problem and he had to find a way to solve it. It was me and my family who couldn't talk or think about anything else.

Chapter Fourteen
Use Your Imagination

I only went round to Cleo's house because I couldn't bear the thought of people being there talking about me while I was at home. I couldn't really see what a bunch of fifteen- and sixteen-year-olds could do if Blakemore was determined to keep me out. I'd begun to have dreams where I was trying to get into school but Blakemore, with his big shiny face and his great big body, stood in the doorway, blocking my entrance.

Mum had been very keen for me to go and in the end it seemed easier to just agree. I'd gone very quiet since the meeting at school and I didn't have the energy to do anything except stay home watching the telly. Granddad had started bringing his mates round to have a look at the house and measure up the garage, but I couldn't get up any enthusiasm about it. The whole school business felt like another great burden for me to carry round, another thing I was powerless to change.

I'd decided that if I was going to go, I'd get there on my own, so that was a first for me. Cleo and her mum lived two streets away and if I went the long way round, I didn't have to cross any roads. It sounds like I'm a baby when I say that but it wasn't the traffic I was worried about. It was those things I'd never given a second's thought to before, like the millions of unramped or too-steep kerbs that suddenly presented themselves as enormous obstacles. Not to mention the dog shit, the uneven pavements and the up and down of people's driveways. I'd always thought that where I lived was flat. I was wrong.

It felt like quite an achievement by the time I got there, a bit like climbing Mount Snowdon in a pair of canvas plimsoles. What I'd forgotten was that there was going to be a step between me and Cleo's front door so that the doorbell was unreachable. I sat there in front of the house thinking about what I should do next when Jesse came along. I hadn't seen or spoken to him since that time at Barbara's. He seemed pleased to see me, not especially pleased but nice and friendly like he always was. Anyway, I'd made up my mind that I was going to just act cool and remember that we were there to talk about me getting back to school, nothing else. He pressed the doorbell and helped me over the step in his usual easy way. None of the 'How do I do this? Am I holding it right?' stuff that people usually did when it came to me and my wheelchair.

Cleo's house was like mine but even scruffier. They let rooms out to students, which Cleo hated, and every now and then one walked through the room to get to the back part of the house. We'd been the last to arrive. Ben, Esther, Asfah – who I'd known well in Lower School – and another friend of Ben's, Anil, were all waiting. I couldn't help but be pleased with the group Cleo had got together. I started off by going over what Blakemore had said to Mum and me in the meeting. I didn't need to exaggerate it; it was bad enough already.

'How do you think we should begin?' Cleo asked after indulging in a gory fantasy about what she'd do with Blakemore's private parts after she'd garrotted him. 'Shall we all make some suggestions about what we think?'

'The best thing would be to get them to put a lift in the old and the new building, then Libby could get everywhere on her own,' Ben said.

'Don't be stupid,' Cleo said. 'That'd cost a fortune. Anyway, even if they agreed to do it, Libby'd be collecting her pension by the time they got round to putting it in.'

'Well, I still think we should try,' Ben said sulkily.

'Yeah, we shouldn't give up on it completely, just because it would cost a lot,' I said, seeing Ben looking hurt. 'But we should think of that as a long-term thing. If we stick on that one, they'll just say I can't go back to school until there's a lift and there probably won't ever be one.'

'We ought to have a really big demonstration,' Cleo said. 'Invite all the papers, even the telly. We could make big banners and posters. Discrimination Against The Disabled. That'd look good.'

'I know what we should do,' Jesse said, catching her

enthusiasm. 'We ought to stage a sit-in like they used to do in the seventies. Like, outside the teacher's staff-room or somewhere. I could easily get Libby upstairs in the wheelchair.

'We could get the whole of our year to sit in front of the staff-room at break when they're all in there drinking coffee and smoking their fags and say we're not going to let them out until they let Libby back into school.'

'I've got another idea,' Anil said, butting in. 'If we could get hold of some wheelchairs, a whole load of us could all go to school in wheelchairs and refuse to get out of them. You know, to make the point it could happen to anyone.'

'Where you gonna get wheelchairs from?'

'I dunno, a hospital or something, it can't be that hard.' I felt my heart sinking.

'Hang on, please,' I said. 'I don't think we're on the right track. I know everyone's trying to help but I really don't want to be carried up and down stairs like I'm some sort of dummy. I don't want to be the centre of attention like that. If you carry me around, it just proves I can't do anything for myself.' Jesse looked a bit crushed and I felt awful although I knew I was right.

'A sit-in, or whatever you call it, wouldn't work anyway,' Asfah said. 'It'd just turn the teachers against us. You know what they're like, they're always going on about how you should sort things out by talking about them, not by violent action.'

'This wouldn't be violent. It'd be a peaceful demonstration to show we're on Libby's side.'

'I know, but they'd just come out and be all patronising

to me and tell us all to go away and they'd have a meeting or something. It just wouldn't work.'

'What about my idea about borrowing wheelchairs?' Anil said.

'I can see what you're getting at but I think the teachers will just see it as a stunt, like a gimmick or something,' I said. 'You know – like when people go round pubs to raise money for charity, they wear army uniform or bandages like they've been in the war and they get pushed in the wheelchair or they dress up like babies and go in a pram.' I thought of what Barbara had said about how people loved raising money for charities because it made them feel better about themselves. 'And you know what people are like,' I added. 'They'd all want to borrow the wheelchairs and race around the corridors in them and act stupid. It'd all just be a joke to them. I'm not a joke and I'm not a charity.'

It was like sticking a pin in a balloon; everyone looked deflated. I carried on. 'Look, Blakemore doesn't want me back in the school. He says it can't be done because it's too complicated to ask teachers to reorganise their lessons downstairs and the teachers' union won't let people take me upstairs. He used all these excuses about my work not being up to standard and it would be a good idea for me to go somewhere else and make a new start.'

'That's just rubbish. Everyone wants you back at school,' Asfah said hotly. The others nodded in agreement.

'Isn't it against the law, to ban you from school just because you're different to how you were before?'

'Apparently not. My Mum found out that when they passed that Act that was supposed to be for disabled people they didn't include schools.'

'What does that mean?' Anil asked.

'As far as I can understand, the law says you've got to make public buildings accessible for disabled people, where it's reasonable to do so. But they didn't mention schools or colleges, so they can just say the building's not suitable so I can't come back. And they can say I'm a safety risk so it wouldn't be fair to other people.' That just started everyone off again. I felt we weren't going to get anywhere.

'What do *you* think we should do?' Esther asked kindly. 'You know best.'

'The trouble is, I don't know. I wish I did. I keep thinking of what Barbara said – you know, Jesse's aunt who works in the hospital.' Jesse looked at me. 'She said that they're the ones who'll have to find the solution, but we might have to find a way to help them do that, because they haven't got any imagination.'

'Can I make one more suggestion then?' Jesse asked, half amused and half shy.

'Yes, you can.' I tried to smile back.

'Why don't we use that as our campaigning slogan? You know, throw it back at them. Let them see that it's their responsibility.' He put his hands together in the air and drew them apart as if we could see the words in front of him.

USE YOUR IMAGINATION – THIS IS LIBBY'S SCHOOL TOO

'That's brilliant,' Cleo said.

'But that doesn't really tell people what it's about,' Ben said. Everyone groaned.

'Duuh . . . That's the whole point, Dumbo,' Cleo said. 'People will be asking what it means. Teachers will ask the Head. Kids will ask teachers. Parents will ask their children. Someone might even ask a newspaper.' She looked at me. 'Alright, no-one will ask a newspaper. But someone will have to provide the answers.'

'Oh, I get it,' Ben said, nodding in agreement. We all laughed.

Cleo produced some paper and an assortment of biros and half-chewed pencils and we got started. Asfah was going to work out a design we could use on posters and leaflets on her computer at home because she had a good graphics programme.

'Do you mind if I put a picture of a wheelchair in the middle with USE YOUR IMAGINATION above it and THIS IS LIBBY'S SCHOOL TOO underneath?' she asked me.

'No, that'd be fine. After all, that's what it's all about.'

'I'll do it tonight. Can I come round to you tomorrow after school and show it to you?'

'It's important to keep it simple and not try to do too much. We don't want to take on more than we can do ourselves,' I said, although I was already becoming aware that they'd be doing it and I'd just have to observe.

'Yeah, and we don't want lots of other people, like teachers and our parents muscling in and trying to take over,' Cleo added. I wasn't sure how my mum and dad would take to this, but I thought they'd understand. Probably.

'I think we ought to get going as soon as possible,' sensible Esther said. 'Because our exams start not long after Easter and we won't be able to do much after that.'

Anil pulled out a small Filofax. We all laughed and groaned.

'Oh. Ya,' Cleo said. 'There's a yuppy in the making, a budding city accountant.'

'Ha, ha. At least I'm organised. And anyway, do you know that's a racial stereotype?'

'What is?'

'Asians? Accountants? That's what they think we all want to be.'

'I didn't mean . . .' Cleo started, but Anil just laughed at her without any malice and Asfah joined in. He turned over the pages of his diary.

'I'd say we have three weeks till the Easter holidays and a couple of weeks after. At the most. If we haven't made them agree to let Libby back to school by then and worked out a proper way to do it – we've failed.'

'We're not going to fail,' I said, suddenly confident. 'We're going to succeed.'

'What are we going to do about money?' Anil asked. He looked at Cleo mocking him. 'That's got nothing to do with being an accountant. It's just being sensible.'

'What will we need money for anyway?'

'You know – paper, photocopying, that kind of thing. Everything costs money.' That stopped us all in our tracks. I felt embarrassed at the thought of asking people to give money to help me.

'Don't worry,' Jesse said cheerfully. 'Malcolm will give us some paper, we've got loads at home. He buys it cheap.' People raised their eyebrows questioningly. 'Malcolm my dad, stepdad. He does freelance work, helps companies out with computer problems. I know he'd want to help. But I don't know if he could do the photocopying.'

'My Mum works in a nursery school and she told me you can buy a card there and it'll give you 1,000 copies for £10. That's really cheap. If we do some small, we could print two leaflets on one sheet of A4 paper. I'm sure she'll do it if we give her the paper and a tenner,' Asfah said.

'I'll give you the money tomorrow, Az,' I said.

'Are you sure?'

'Yeah, I've got nine months' pocket money owing.' Everyone laughed.

'It wouldn't cost much to enlarge it into a small poster size. You could do that on a photocopier.'

We talked about who was going to do what and how we were going to set about it. I didn't like the feeling inside me when I thought of them all buzzing around school talking to each other about how things were going, but they all promised to keep me in touch and we agreed to meet every Sunday.

'Do you think we should put names on the leaflets, so people know who to ask what it's all about?' Esther asked.

'No, I don't think so,' Ben said, having caught on to the idea of it being a mystery. 'We should make them work at it. Anyway, most people will know who to ask. They know who Libby's friends are, or they can find out.'

Who Libby's friends are. I'd never seen myself as having a group of friends like this who would support each other and work together. It felt good.

* * *

We were all getting ready to go when Jesse suddenly broke in.

'I've just had a brilliant idea of a way to start it all off.'

'Yeah?'

'You know how at school, when you use the computers, every time you put in your passcode, a message comes up, and then you can press any button to clear the screen? At the moment it says, `Year 11, remember that the last day of April is the last day for your coursework`.'

'So?'

'Well, wouldn't it be brilliant if I could change it, so that every time anyone turned on the computer, the message `Use Your Imagination, This is Libby's School Too` flashed across the screen? I mean, it wouldn't just be the kids who saw it – it'd be the teachers, the secretaries, the Head, everyone.'

'But how could you do that?'

'I know that it's Mr Ferguson who puts that message in because he's the administrator of the whole computer system. It'd be like code-breaking. I'd have to work out what his passcode is, because that gives him access to the whole computer network in the school. Once I find that out, I can get access into the message facility. Then it's simple. I just have to delete the stuff about coursework and type in our message about Libby.'

'Would you have to break into his room?'

'No, I'm pretty sure I could do it from any of the computers in the school.'

'How do you know all this?'

'He told me about it once when he was showing me

how the data operating system worked. He asked me when my coursework deadline was and he said, "I'll put that in as this month's message, shall I?"'

'Did he tell you his passcode?'

'No, of course he didn't, but I did see how he got into the system. I know he changes it every half-term.'

'How could you possibly find it out? It's a chance in a million.'

Jesse looked rather smug. 'Let's just say, I've got an idea about it. It might not work, of course, but I could try it on Tuesday after school. You know, when we get let off early and the teachers go to a staff meeting. Will you let me have a go at it?' He turned directly to me. He probably knew I'd be the last person to refuse him.

'Won't he spot it first thing in the morning, as soon as he turns on his computer?'

'The brilliant thing is that the message doesn't come up on his screen.'

'How come?'

'Well, everyone else gets the message automatically as soon as they try to get into the network, but because he's the boss, he has to call it up specially, otherwise he doesn't see it. We'll probably get away with a few hours. We might even get away with longer.'

'*If* you can do it.'

'*If* I can do it. I'm going to have to do a bit of research. Just give me till Tuesday evening. If it works, we'll let it run on Wednesday or until they discover it and start what we agreed on Thursday. If not, we'll start the rest of the stuff on Wednesday.'

'Jesse, you could get into real trouble over this,' I said.

'I don't want you to . . .'

He cut me off. 'Naw, I won't,' he said confidently. 'First of all, I'm not going to own up, not unless I think someone else'll have to carry the can, and secondly, even if they find out, he won't do anything much. I'm his favourite student.' He picked up his things. 'I'm out of here, everyone. Libby, I'll speak to you soon. Bye.'

Everyone had agreed we'd only tell the people we really needed to — at least at the beginning. We wanted it to be as much of a surprise as possible and we didn't want any of the teachers getting in the way and blocking what we were doing, even if they meant well. I wanted to talk to Mum and Dad about it, though. It wasn't fun to me, it was deadly serious, and I didn't want them to think we were being stupid or say that it was too important an issue to be handled by a bunch of kids. I told them everything — except about Jesse and the computer password. I thought I'd wait and see how that worked out. They listened seriously and even smiled as I began to get all heated up with excitement. When I stopped, they looked at me carefully.

'I think it's very brave of you all,' Mum said. 'I just hope no-one gets into trouble about it. Not with their exams coming up and everything.' I didn't want to think about that side of things.

'Will it spoil what you're trying to do?' I asked.

'I don't think so,' Dad said. He had a really soppy look on his face. 'Your mum and me, we're both very proud of you. "Use Your Imagination. This Is Libby's School Too." That's brilliant. I bet you thought that one up, didn't you?'

257

The following evening, Az came round to see me with the design that was going to be the centre of the campaign. She'd done a border round the outside, a symbol of a wheelchair in the middle and the words above and below it. I thought it was great even though it still made me feel a bit funny to think of that symbol – the one you see on toilet doors, by ramped entrances and all over the place in hospitals – representing me. I gave her the money to give to her mum. She was going to buy the photocopying card and, with the paper from Jesse's dad, make loads of copies – some small, some big.

By Tuesday evening, I was practically busting with anxiety and curiosity and nervousness. At about six o'clock the doorbell went. It was Jesse. And Cleo.

'What happened?' I asked her. I couldn't look at him.

'I don't know. He wouldn't tell me a thing till we got here,' she said through clenched teeth. Mum was cooking in the kitchen and we crowded in the back part of the sitting room, my sometimes bedroom. 'Come on, Jesse, we're here now. Tell us.' A great cheesy grin spread over his face.

'I did it,' was all he said.

'C'mon you bastard, tell us how,' Cleo said, sticking him in the ribs. He took his time, just to annoy us.

'I need a drink first. All that code-breaking's made me thirsty.'

'God, I hate you sometimes,' Cleo said affectionately, and went into the kitchen to get him one. He looked at me and I wanted to say something now we were on our own, but I felt stupid and shy.

'Tell us now before I kill you,' Cleo said, coming back into the room. He sat down on the bed I'd slept in the night before.

'And tell us the whole thing, right from the start,' I said, finding my tongue at last.

'Okay I will. Well, I asked my tutor if I could use the computer in our room after school when she was at the staff meeting and she said that'd be fine, but if I finished before she came back, I should just shut the door behind me. So I knew I didn't have all that long, probably an hour, an hour and a half at the most. I already had an idea about what Ferguson's passcode could be from that time I was telling you about when I was working in his office, but I only had a really vague idea.'

'How d'you mean?'

'You know when you hear a song or a tune, you might not be aware that you've even heard it but it gets inside your head and you start singing it yourself?'

'What's that got to do with the passcode?' Cleo asked impatiently.

'Listen and you'll find out. Well, old Ferguson's always humming something under his breath and I must have caught it too because just after Christmas when I was in his room, I was working away and he says, "Oh, you're a Springsteen fan too, are you? I didn't think people your age liked him." And I said, "What?" and he says, "Bruce Springsteen. *Born in the USA*. You were singing it just now." He's such an idiot sometimes, he didn't realise I'd caught it off him. Anyway, I didn't want to be rude so I said, "Yeah, brilliant. *Fifty Seven Channels and Nothing On* – Malcolm listens to him sometimes." And he looks really pleased and he says, "*Human Touch*, his best album ever in my humble opinion." And I go "yeah", not knowing what to say next and he says, "Bruce Springsteen, King of Rock. I always knew you were a man after my own heart, Jesse." He thinks I'm going to do Computer Studies at A level, poor deluded man. And then, as if he'd almost forgotten I was there, he says, almost to himself, "That's a good idea. I think I'll use his songs for my passcodes this term." I thought it was funny at the time, that he'd told me even that bit of information, but I didn't see what use it would be to me.

'Anyway, I got to school really early yesterday and hung around outside his office humming bits of Springsteen songs to get on his side. I wanted to get there before he'd got into his files. I'd thought up a really brilliant problem to ask him about working with a database, where you . . .'

'Spare us the details, please.'

'Okay, okay. He never lets you see him punch in his passcode but I thought I'd have a much better chance if I knew how many letters he used because it could be anything between six and twelve and it would be impossible to find it if you didn't even know how many. So when he got in, I told him about this problem and he says, "Hold on a second and I'll just set things up." And he takes his coat off and sits down. Then he tells me to turn my back and I listen very, very carefully and I can hear the keys clack. Eleven times. That's once for ENTER and ten letters in the passcode.'

'That's brilliant.'

'Yeah, but it was only the start. I'd already done some

260

research. Malcolm knows someone who's a Springsteen fanatic and he's got every CD he's ever made and he went round to collect them Monday night for me.'

'You didn't tell him what you were going to do, did you?'

'Yeah, he's cool about things like that. He was a bit of a lunatic when he was at school; he thought it was great. We didn't tell my mum, though. Anyway, I didn't know whether Ferguson used the titles or the first lines so I'd had to get the first ten letters of both of them. The titles were alright but the first lines took forever. We were up till two in the morning doing it. I had a plan. I was going to start with *Born to Run*, the first album Springsteen ever made, then the most recent and then back and forward. But because he'd said that album *The Human Touch* was his favourite, I thought I'd start with that.

'It was so easy. It was brilliant. I turned the computer on and it says `please enter your passcode`. So I typed in the first ten letters of the title of the first track, `humantouch` and it says `incorrect message` so I type in the first ten letters of the song `youandme`. `incorrect message`. So I carry on and there it is. I could hardly believe my luck. The fourth track, song title `crossmyhea` – and I'm in there. Bingo. Easy peasy japanesy, wash your face with lemon squeezy. I'd worked out over a hundred possible codes and it was the seventh one I typed in. So then, the first thing that comes up on the screen is `administrator's name – conrad ferguson`.

'Conrad? He doesn't look like a Conrad.'

'Then immediately a set of icons appear. I pressed MESSAGE and I was in. I just deleted the old message and typed in ours. Then I press EXIT, DOCUMENT TO BE SAVED, PRESS ENTER, REPLACE, YES blah blah blah and I'm out of there. The whole thing only took ten minutes.'

'Thanks Jesse,' I said simply. 'I hope you don't get into too much trouble over it.' He looked at me and my stomach turned over.

'It'll be worth it. It's my present to you.'

Chapter Fifteen
The Campaign Continues

It was infuriating to have to sit at home whilst so much was going on at school. But I never had to wait long; someone rang or came round most nights. Not Jesse, though. After his success with the computer he took a back seat and waited for the shit to hit the fan. Amazingly, it took until the following week before they got to him, but before that lots of other things had happened.

On Wednesday morning of that first week, whoever turned on the computer read our message. No-one knew what it meant, but lots of people started asking each other questions. On Thursday morning, Asfah's little sister, Shurma, took in hundreds of the 'Use Your Imagination' leaflets and quietly gave them out to her friends in Year 7 and they distributed them around their tutor groups. For the whole week, every time anyone in Year 7 handed in their homework books, they tucked a leaflet inside.

On Thursday afternoon, Cleo and Esther stayed behind and ducked into the staff-room while the cleaners weren't looking and put an A4 leaflet in all the teachers' trays, and posters began to appear all round the school. On Friday morning, our computer message changed to the bland `only two more weeks until easter holidays`. Everyone at school seemed to be talking about it but no-one had been hauled in front of the Head to explain what was happening. We didn't trust this silence; we knew it was a matter of time.

When we met that weekend, at my house this time, everyone was excited but edgy. We couldn't quite believe the teachers' silence. We had expected non-stop questions and recriminations.

'Why do you think they're being like this? Why are they ignoring all our stuff?' I asked.

'P'raps it's 'cause they're all thick and don't understand what it's about,' Ben said.

'Naw, it's you who's thick,' Cleo said.

'Shuddup.'

'I think they're just stalling for time. Maybe they don't want to talk to us because they want to see how things work out.'

'What d'you mean?' Cleo asked.

'You know like when Ms Benjamin was at that meeting with me and the Head and she didn't say anything. I don't think it was because she agreed with him. I think it's because she didn't know what to do.'

'Well it's not very helpful, is it? If all the teachers just keep waiting for someone else to do something, nothing will ever get done,' Anil said.

'Maybe he's put the frighteners on them,' Jesse said.

'Who has? What're you talking about?'

'Blakemore. I think he's told all the teachers that they've got to keep schtoom and not ask us any questions. Otherwise we'd all have been in deep shit by now. I just can't believe Ferguson hasn't said anything about the computer. He must have a pretty good idea it was me who did it.'

'It's true,' Asfah said. 'My little sister told me that the first day the Year 7s put the leaflet in their homework books, her teacher asked her about it, but after that, no-one's said anything.'

'Yeah,' Esther chipped in. 'The only teacher who's asked me about it is a new Australian supply teacher and she only started on Monday.'

'But why would Blakemore do that?'

'Because he's worried that if we talk to the teachers and they find out what he said to Libby and her Mum, they'll all be against him.'

'Or p'raps he's testing the water. See how many teachers agree with him that she shouldn't come back to school and get them on his side.'

'I think that's probably right,' I said. 'I bet he's getting his own campaign together, like getting the support of the Fire Brigade about the safety risk and the teachers' union about having to reorganise their classes. You know what he's like. Once he's decided on something, he's not going to change his mind.' I felt really depressed.

'Don't look at it like that,' Cleo said. 'We haven't failed yet. If the teachers don't want to talk to us, we'll have to talk to them. Anyway, I know they're talking to each other, because Dave in Year 12 went to The Green Man on Friday night and heard a bunch of them.' I watched a pale blush spread over her face as she mentioned this new name.

'What were they saying?'

'Nothing terribly interesting as far as he told me. Just about what had happened to you and about seeing the poster everywhere. Then they saw Dave's group of sixth years and changed the subject.'

I couldn't help but feel worried. Things weren't going as we'd expected. I tried to cheer myself up by thinking of all the phone calls I'd had from girls at school who'd never called me up before and how many people were on my side. Not all of them, of course. More than one person had rung me up to ask, 'What exactly did happen to you?' and wanted me to give them lots of gory, medical details before saying something infuriating like, 'But it's not the school's fault it has steps, is it? Isn't there somewhere that has special places for people like you?' Cleo said they were just stupid bitches and I shouldn't take any notice and I knew she was right, but the pleasure I got from each nice phone call was always outweighed by the pain I was left with after remarks like that.

We decided that for the second week, we'd have to go about things in a more direct way. It obviously wasn't any good waiting for the teachers to come to us. We'd have to go to them. Cleo thought that we should still use the 'Use Your Imagination' slogan but since they didn't seem to have as much imagination as we hoped, we needed to spell things out for them.

'If we had something written out clearly, then everyone could have the same answer and we could go up to teachers and say, "I want you to read this and tell me what you think."'

'You'll have to say it nicely,' Esther said. 'You know what they're like.'

'Don't worry, I'll say PLEEEASE,' Cleo said a bit more sarcastically than was really necessary.

'I better do that,' I said. 'After all, it is about me.'

It was strange writing about myself as if I was writing about someone else.

```
      use your imagination -
   this is libby's school too
You  may  have  heard  that  Libby
Starling, who used to be in 10
EJ, has been away from school for
some time. She became very ill
with an unknown virus and she now
uses a wheelchair to get around.
She is ready to come back to
Dupont High to continue her GCSEs
but the school says this is
impossible. We say they need to
find a way because it isn't just
their school, it isn't just your
school, it's Libby's school too.
if you agree, tell a teacher,
tell your parents, tell the head.
```

'If that doesn't get you into trouble, nothing will,' I said to Esther when she called in for it on Sunday night.

'Don't worry about that, it's not your problem. We can handle it.' I hadn't realised how much more confident she'd become. She was looker older, too. Her glasses had been exchanged for contact lenses and she'd had her hair relaxed and wore it tight against her head, tied back by her neck.

'How's everything going?' I asked her. Sometimes I had to make myself realise I wasn't the only person with worries. She immediately knew what I was talking about. 'Are you going out with him now?'

'I'm not sure Ben understands the concept of going out exactly, but he does talk to me in school from time to time. I don't really know what's going on.'

'Well, he's always been a bit, how shall I put it – lollopy. But he does like you; I can tell by the way he looks at you.' This was a lie. I'd completely forgotten about her and Ben until that moment.

'Do you think so?' She looked really pleased. 'Why is Cleo so rude to him? He's quite clever really, in his own way.' She paused for a second. 'Do you think I should ring him or something?'

'Sure,' I said as if I was the expert on this subject. 'Don't leave it to him. You know what boys are like. Give him a call when you get home and talk to him about what you're gonna do about this leaflet.'

In the second week, things began to hot up. Apart from my statement, the others had got a petition ready and almost all the students wanted to sign it. The teachers were still strangely silent but more and more kids were getting involved. Some took round the petition; others offered money to help with the photocopying and things. Joyce got Ben a T-shirt made with the 'Use Your Imagination' slogan on it in huge black letters. In PE he told the teacher he'd forgotten his kit and asked if he could wear his own shirt. 'Just this once,' he'd been told. When the teacher saw it, he thought he was in for it – you know what games teachers are like about kit – but instead, he looked at it for quite a long time and said, 'Well, young man, I hope you will also "Use Your Imagination" to run round the pitch ten times.' Ben wore it under his blazer all afternoon and no-one said anything.

One of Cleo's friends (interestingly, someone who'd completely blanked me for the last four years even when I was sitting on the same science table as her) went out off her own bat and got a whole load of round yellow stickers made with our slogan on them – the peel-off kind the dentist gives you when you're little with 'tooth decay – keep your distance' or something like that on them. She gave a bunch to Cleo and they sold the rest of them at breaktime. Ms Benjamin was on duty and when she saw a whole crowd of kids huddled in the corner of the hall, she went to find out what was going on. Cleo was sure she was going to get it then. Not that she cared; I honestly think she'd have gone to prison for me by this time. Instead Ms Benjamin took a sticker and even gave Cleo a pound for it. She put it in her pocket, not on her jacket, but she asked how I was and told Cleo to send me her best wishes. Then, just as she was going, she said, 'I want you to keep this to yourself, but you might like to tell Libby that a number of teachers have asked the Head about what's going on and he's agreed to hold an extended staff meeting next Tuesday after school so we can all have the opportunity to discuss it.'

The Tuesday she was talking about was three days before they broke up for Easter. We'd obviously been right. The teachers had been talking to each other even if they weren't talking to us.

Just when it seemed Jesse was going to get away with the computer stuff, his moment of reckoning came. At the end of school on the Friday of the second week, ten days after the message had danced across all the screens in the school, Mr Ferguson came into his tutor room and, without speaking, crooked his finger in a way that told Jesse he had no option but to follow. He didn't say a word until he'd got into his office and shut the door.

'I see you're still pursuing your campaign,' he said, eyeing Jesse up and down. The 'Libby Stickers' had become a fashion statement, and Jesse was wearing them up and down his tie and all over his bag.

'Yes, sir.'

'And I suppose your commitment to it is sufficient reason to drop me in it right up to my neck?'

'No sir, I'm sorry, I . . .' Jesse had prepared a speech for when this moment arrived but he wasn't allowed to finish it.

'I took the rap for you boyo,' Mr Ferguson said furiously. 'And do you know why I did it? I did it because despite the appalling way you've behaved, I happen to share your belief in the cause.'

270

'You do?'

'Yes, I do, but couldn't you have asked me to help you with it, instead of abusing my trust?'

'We all thought it would be better if we did it without involving the teachers,' Jesse said honestly and then, unable to stop himself, 'Does the Head know it's me who did it?'

'Yes, indeed he does.' Mr Ferguson stood silently and enjoyed watching Jesse's reaction. 'It's only because computer technology is uncharted water to our dear leader that you got away with this at all. And if you repeat that observation to any of your little cronies I will take great pleasure in personally removing that carrot-topped head of yours from its neck. Lucky for you, I was away from school all last Wednesday on a specialist computer course which is why you got away with an extra day. The first thing on my return, when you were so carefully avoiding me, I was called into the Head's office and asked to explain what was going on. You can imagine how pleased I was to discover your little message whilst sitting at our great leader's leather-topped desk. It didn't take me long to work out who must have done it. There aren't many people clever enough. Or disloyal enough.'

'I'm really sorry,' Jesse said again. Then, foolishly, 'Can I ask what you told him?'

'Can you ask what I told him?' Ferguson repeated sarcastically. 'Is this a saving-your-skin question or one of pure intellectual interest? If you must know, I told him that I'd been explaining to you some of the functions of the data operating system and must have accidentally called up the message file onto the screen. His secretary rang me to get some urgent A level statistics – this part at least was true – and while my back was turned, you must have typed in the message. I said that you wouldn't have realised it was the message file, you would have thought that you were just messing around on the operating system.'

'And he believed that?'

'Yes, he believed that.'

'Thanks for covering for me, sir.'

'I didn't do it to save your slimy little skin, you can be sure of that. I did it because I'm not going to make myself look an even bigger fool by telling them about me and Bruce Bloody Springsteen, am I? Nor that a very able student set out to make me look a fool. Of course, the staff who know anything about computers know that this explanation couldn't possibly be true, but most of us believe that Libby Starling's future education is more important than one kid who has delusions of being a great hacker.'

Jesse flopped back on a chair when he'd finished telling us this story. We were all round at Cleo's for our weekend meeting.

'Do you think he's going to take it any further?' I asked. I knew that Jesse still had to have his coursework marked by Mr Ferguson and I didn't want anyone else's education to suffer.

'I don't think so. He's a good bloke really; he was just letting it out. I've offered to help him clear out his office when we all go on study leave.' He screwed up his face in a half smile.

'Did he accept?'

'He said that as long as he didn't have to look at my ugly face while I did it, he would accept this gesture as an apology.'

'The teachers all seem to be coming round,' Esther said. She was sitting next to Ben on the sofa. 'Mrs Aljabar, that young history teacher, said she thought you should be allowed to come back to school and asked me to tell you that.'

'You know Mr Peacock?' Ben asked. Everyone groaned. Mr Peacock was the Deputy Head of Science. A thin, beady-looking man with a smart line in sleeveless striped jumpers and a voice that could cut through you like a razor. 'Come on, he's not that bad.' Science was Ben's best subject. 'He called me back after class and produced our last leaflet. I thought he was going to tell me off, but he didn't. He didn't even ask me if I was involved.'

'Well, what did he say?'

'He said that there were probably schools that were more inaccessible for disabled people but he couldn't think of many.'

'Oh, great. That's really helpful.'

'No listen. He said that we were right to campaign to get Libby back if that's what she wanted but what we'd done is just the first stage – getting people to be aware of what happened to you. He said if we wanted to overcome their opposition . . .'

'Ooh Ben, big words.'

'Shut up and be serious for a second. He said, what we needed to do was draw up a list of points, like a charter or something. Things that needed to be agreed by the teachers so that Libby could get back to school. He said the trouble with most teachers is that they didn't have any imagination.'

'Mr Peacock said that?!'

'Yeah, funny, isn't it? But he said that we ought to start by making a list of what needed to be done.'

'Like what?'

'Well, he said that one lesson it would be hard to teach downstairs would be science but he was sure there would be teachers and some of the older kids who could be trained to get Libby upstairs. He said it wasn't enough just to get her into the room. The teacher would have to make sure she could use all the equipment because the work-benches and stools are high.'

'God, I'm impressed. But what about all the fire risk stuff?'

'He said he had a nephew in Scotland who was disabled, muscular something or other.'

'Muscular dystrophy?'

'Yeah, that's right. He said, as far as he knew, he'd never internally combusted.'

'What's that mean?'

'Blown himself up. He thinks that people just use this as an excuse when they don't want disabled people around. As long as everyone's aware of the safety issues, there shouldn't be any problems.'

Life was full of surprises. If you'd asked me to name the teachers who would be against me coming back to school, Mr Peacock would have been near the top of the list. With some help from the others, I wrote my own charter.

Use your imagination –
this is Libby's school too
Charter for Libby Starling

1. All her lessons (except science) to be held downstairs in the Old Building.
2. A team of teachers and older students who volunteer should be trained to help Libby up and down stairs.
3. One science lab should be adapted so that Libby can use all the equipment.
4. Libby should be allowed to leave lessons five minutes early to avoid the crush.
5. The girls' toilets should be adapted by knocking two toilets into one and putting in a grab rail. Libby should be allowed to use the visitors' toilet on the ground floor if this is not done by the time she comes back to school.
6. Libby should be allowed to use the Sixth Form Common Room even though she is coming back to Year 11.
7. There should be a teacher allocated to help Libby sort out any problems in school. This should be someone who has personal experience of disabled people.

8. The school should start campaigning for lifts to be put in as soon
   as possible.

We thought we wouldn't hear anything until after the
staff meeting, but then we'd never really understood what
was going on inside Blakemore's thick skull. At break on
Monday, not long after the charter had started circulating
around the school, Ms Benjamin had gone up to Cleo
and told her that the Head wanted to see them in his
office immediately after school.

'What, me personally?' Cleo had asked.

'He didn't ask for you by name. We all know who's in
your group, or at least we think we do. If I were you, I'd
talk to each other and send two people along. And if it's
going to be you Cleo, may I suggest that you take out the
nose stud and try to borrow a regulation brown pleated
number rather than the latex tube which you seem to
think passes for a skirt?'

Cleo rang me at lunchtime in a bit of a panic to tell me
this. I wished I could have just said, 'Don't worry about it,
I'll come in and see him myself,' but that wasn't possible.

'I think Esther and Ben should go.'

'Why them?'

'Well, you can't go; you've been in his office too many
times for the wrong reasons. I think Anil will be too shy.
Az, I'm not sure about. Jesse is still seen as a bit of a new
boy. Esther and Ben are our best bet. Esther's safe. They
think of her as a star student and none of the teachers
really know what to make of Ben.'

'But will she be able to take it if he gets really angry?

276

You know how scary he can be.' Everyone had been getting on so well that I'd forgotten how Esther and Cleo felt about each other.

'She'll be fine, really. She's grown up a lot recently and there'll be the surprise factor. I don't think Blakemore will realise she's been involved.'

Esther called me that evening to tell me what had happened. Blakemore had been incandescent with rage. On his desk he had a pile of signed petitions and was holding all three of our leaflets in his hand.

'I take it you're prepared to accept responsibility for these,' he'd said, waving the papers in front of their noses.

'Yes sir,' Esther had said simply.

'And you think it's right to spread disinformation and downright lies, do you?'

'I'm not sure exactly what you mean, sir.' Esther had looked at him open-eyed.

'I mean,' he'd said, spluttering with rage, 'that you have taken it upon yourselves to imply that I have forbidden Elizabeth Starling to return to this school. You weren't in the meeting I had with her parents so you know nothing about it. Look at this.' He was jabbing the second leaflet so hard that his finger made a hole in the paper. 'It says here that the school has said it's impossible for her to come back, when you know very well that I have said no such thing or made any such decision.'

'Can Libby come back to school then?' Ben had asked, as if he was asking whether the tuck shop would be open at break.

'If she does it will be absolutely no thanks to you. You

have gone in way beyond your depth. Having a disabled child in a building as old as this one is a serious matter with implications you know nothing about. You have absolutely no right to send round a petition without asking my permission.'

'But sir, in our PSE lesson last term, you taught us that in a democracy, the petition is a very important way to get people in power to change their minds,' Esther had said innocently, knowing the effect this would have. Blakemore immediately changed tactics.

'This so-called "Charter". I suppose you thought you were being very clever. I take it you've done all the research I've done?' he'd asked with heavy sarcasm. 'Spoken to all the headteachers with handicapped children in their schools I've spoken to? Enquired about specialist provision nearby? Done a building inspection? Talked to the teaching organisations? Mmm. Well have you? Have you?'

'No sir, we haven't. But we have tried to look at ways to sort out some of the problems. We just care about finding a way to get Libby back to this school, which is where she wants to be.'

'Oh, you've spoken to her about it, have you?'

'Yes, of course we have. It's her campaign. It's her Charter.' For some reason, that had seemed to fluster him.

'We all have Libby's best interests at heart,' he'd said rather lamely. 'This is far too important a decision to be taken by students. I'm surprised at the pair of you getting involved in something like this.' Esther and Ben had looked at each other and sensed that they were now on a winning streak.

'It's not just us two. Most people we've talked to think that if this is where Libby wants to be, we should find a way to get her back.'

'You speak as if nothing is being done about it,' Blakemore had said, regaining his anger. 'As it happens, there is a staff meeting tomorrow to discuss this very matter and until that time, I would be most grateful if you could stop acting like this school is Hyde Park Corner and start doing what you are supposed to be doing – studying for your exams.'

'I felt like jelly when I came out of there,' Esther said to me over the phone. 'And do you know what Ben said to me? He said I was really brilliant and then he kissed me, a great lipsucking kiss right outside Blakemore's office! I think he's great.' I was pleased that an offshoot of the campaign was the effect it was having on other people's love lives.

I wish I could have been a fly on the wall in that staff meeting. Whatever was said, teachers obviously wanted a decision one way or the other, because at seven o'clock that evening the telephone rang and it was Blakemore. Dad answered. All I could hear was the one-way conversation.

'Yes, I see . . . Well, we'd rather not leave it until next term, because Libby's going to be away for a few weeks and I'm sure she'd like to have it sorted out before she goes . . . Any time on Thursday or Friday would suit us fine. Look, if you can't make it during the day, we'll be quite happy to come before school or at the end of the day . . .

Don't worry about that, we'll just fit round you . . . Friday at nine . . . Yes, Libby will be with us. We wouldn't dream of leaving her at home . . . No, I don't think we should have this discussion without her being present. After all it is about her needs . . . We hope that a decision will be made . . . Fine. Thank you very much. We'll see you then.'

Mr Blakemore was waiting for us outside his office, squirmy with politeness. He smoothed his hand over the greasy strips of hair on the top of his head and then reached out to shake Dad's hand. Ugh!

'Thank you so much for coming,' he said. 'Do sit down.' When we were all organised his secretary brought in cups of coffee and a plate of chocolate Hob-Nobs. Quite a difference to the last time I'd been there.

'Now, as you know, since our last meeting I've been looking at ways we can make Dupont High accessible for Libby.' What a liar. I'd guessed he wasn't going to say anything about our campaign, but I didn't think he'd get as low as this. 'I've talked to my staff and we feel it would be possible for her to receive most of her lessons on the ground floor. People are being very accommodating.' He directed a sickly smile at Mum. 'Minor adaptations to the girl's lavatory shouldn't be too difficult or too expensive. I think we could justify financing them out of the school budget.' I suppose he expected us to thank him at this point but there was silence in the room. 'However, there are still a few difficulties that cannot be solved so easily.'

'Oh yes, what are they?' Dad asked evenly.

'With the best will in the world, we cannot cater for all Libby's educational needs on the ground floor. If we could, we'd be more than happy to welcome her back. However, science cannot be taught anywhere other than on the first floor, and this makes it impossible to fulfill the Government's curriculum guidelines.'

'Could you spell out for us exactly why this is a problem?' Dad asked. Blakemore looked at him as if he was a complete idiot.

'There are two reasons,' he said slowly. 'First, the teachers' union will not allow their members to undertake an activity that could be dangerous for them, and taking your daughter up and down stairs may be construed in this way. Second, fire regulations will not allow someone in a wheelchair to be in a building where there are no easy exit routes in the case of fire.'

'I think you'll find that's not quite right,' Dad said, producing a wad of papers from his bag. Blakemore's jaw dropped open. He hadn't realised he was dealing with a hobbies man and that Dad's most recent hobby was proving Blakemore wrong. 'I've been in touch with all the major teaching unions and there is national agreement that where teachers want to be involved in assisting a disabled student, they can volunteer to do so. From what you were saying just now it sounds like lots of your staff would be very happy to help Libby, and she's the best person to show them how to do it properly. It should be only a couple of times a week anyway.' Blakemore's jaw dropped even further and he seemed about to say something but Dad sailed on.

'Now, about the business of the fire regulations banning wheelchair users. This seems a common misunderstanding often used in a prejudicial way.' I couldn't believe it. This was my dad speaking. My roll-me-over-and-tickle-me-on-the-tummy Dad. 'I've been in touch with our local Senior Fire Prevention Officer and he assures me that as long as any building is fitted with half-hour fire-safety doors, and apparently your school is, there is no problem at all with having either a member of staff or a student who is disabled. Now of course, we hope that by the time Libby does her A levels, there will be a lift in this building.' You could see Blakemore make a conscious decision to close his mouth. 'But until then, I think you'll agree that this is a pretty good compromise.' Blakemore reached out silently and took the copies of letters from Dad. 'I'm sure you'll want to look through these at your leisure. But can I take it that we've agreed that Libby will continue with her options in Year 11 starting next September?' Blakemore's mouth was now opening and closing like a goldfish in a bowl.

'Of course, I'll have to look at all this thoroughly,' he stuttered.

'Of course. But you do agree, don't you?' This was the first time Mum had spoken. Blakemore looked at her in surprise.

'Well, yes. I know the staff will. That is to say we all want to . . .'

Mum put him out of his misery. 'Thank you so much,' she said in a sweeter-than-sugar voice, standing up and putting out her hand. 'I'm sure we'll speak to you again about the details but I know how much Libby is looking forward to coming back to her school.' Blakemore looked like a broken man, but the ritual of hand-shaking seemed to restore some of his senses. He now looked at me for the first time.

'By the time you start next year, you will have missed a lot of school,' he said, standing too close over me. 'Bearing in mind your last report, I suggest you get down to some hard work straight away.'

Even the nastiness of that last remark couldn't spoil my pleasure. As we left his office there wasn't just Cleo waiting for me but what seemed like half the school. Everyone cheered and hugged each other – it was like winning the Cup Final.

Somehow the local paper got hold of the story and that weekend they came and took a picture of the six of us outside school. They printed it under the headline 'Local Girl Wins Battle to Return to School'. It didn't feel like the last time I'd been in the news. And the photo was okay; I still have it on my pin board – Az, Esther, Cleo, Anil and Jesse, with me in the middle coming to just below their armpits.

Part Three

Chapter Sixteen
Pinner

April was a very different month, just as busy in its own way but less sociable, too. Dad planned to spend the Easter holidays converting the garage with Granddad and his team of unpaid helpers, and I was booked to spend a few weeks doing some rehabilitation in Pinner in a unit specially for people who had spinal injuries and used wheelchairs. Barbara said I was lucky to get a place there because it was always full and these days they had to watch every penny. It was where she'd been for five months after she'd broken her back. I wasn't exactly looking forward to it, but there were still a lot of things I found hard to do and now I knew for sure that I was going back to school in September, it felt like I had something to work towards.

On the Saturday after we'd met up to have our

photograph taken for the local newspaper, Cleo suggested that we go down to McDonald's for a kind of small-scale victory celebration.

'The entrance is completely flat – I checked,' she said. All of us were beginning to develop a new awareness of our surroundings.

'What about getting home? Will you be alright?' Dad asked me. I was cross with him but tried not to show it. It was true that I still got very tired if I had to push myself a long way and I was pathetically afraid of things I'd find on the way – like building works which meant that I'd have to find a way to get down the kerb and wheel along the road. It was a bit like my childhood fear of abandoned houses and the shadow of tall trees. My centre of gravity was now in a completely different place, and even when there were ramped kerbs, I couldn't always tell how steep they were until I was halfway up them. Steep slopes made me feel like I was going to tip backwards and land on my head unless I had someone standing behind me.

'Don't worry, we'll make sure she gets home okay,' Ben said to Dad. I wondered who 'we' meant.

It had been ages since I'd had a McDonald's and it felt good sitting there with six friends. I tried hard not to see other people looking at me and then not looking away again until they realised I was staring back. Jesse raised his chocolate thick shake.

'To Libby. Congratulations on defeating the wonderful Colonel Blakemore, winner of the "Stupid Bastard of the Year" award, and welcome back to Dupont High in just a few months' time!' Everyone raised their Cokes, Fantas and milkshakes.

'It's thanks to you,' I said, raising my own. 'I'd never have done it without you.'

'Yeah, we were pretty brilliant, weren't we?' Anil said, and everyone grinned in a happy, self-satisfied way.

I told the others about Blakemore's parting shot. 'He's just a big bully. He only said that because he knew he'd lost.'

'Maybe. But by the time I go back I won't have done any proper work for months. I can hardly remember how to help Robbie.'

Jesse put down his hamburger and looked at me. 'How long are you going to be in the new hospital for?'

'Three or four weeks, I think. I should be home by the end of April.'

'I can come and help you with maths if you like.' Then, modestly, 'I'm not brilliant or anything but I like explaining things.'

'But won't you be revising for your exams by then? You'll only have a couple more weeks.'

'They don't start till the beginning of June. Anyway, it'll help me with my own revision. It'll be a way to go over things.' For a moment I forgot about my resolution to see Jesse as just one of the crowd – nothing special.

'Thanks,' I said. 'That would be great.'

Pinner was very different from my last experience of hospital. Once again I was the youngest patient, but it was nothing like those weeks in the ward with Olive and Mrs Gates. For a start it was all on one floor and most of the rooms led out to a central paved terrace and garden. I didn't feel so trapped, and when I had nothing else to do

I could take something to read or listen to my Walkman outside. One of Mum's friends had lent me a whole pile of decorating magazines, and I was starting to get excited about the idea of my new room. Not that I had much time to myself; every weekday was organised for me like a school timetable.

Mum and Dad had promised me that even if the house was in absolute chaos, I could still come home every weekend. The hospital was only about fifteen minutes away and the brown car still seemed to be going strong, apart from its reluctance to start on wet mornings. This was just as well since, even with all this volunteering, the renovations seemed to be costing a fortune.

All the patients were in wheelchairs and, to my amazement, one of the doctors was, too. My bed was in a section called 'Self Care' for people who could be pretty independent. This meant we had to get ourselves up and ready, change our sheets, make our beds. There were four of us. Me, two guys in their early twenties – both with tattoos on their arms – and an older woman. The woman, Jackie, had been disabled for a long time and was back for some kind of treatment, and the guys were getting ready to go home, once they'd found somewhere accessible to live. I didn't have much in common with Jackie but it was interesting to see her getting ready in the mornings. She'd always get up before anyone else to make sure she could have a shower, and then there would be a thirty-minute ritual. First she'd put her hair in heated rollers, then while it was cooking, she'd carefully apply her make-up: foundation, eye-liner, mascara, lipstick, the lot. Next, she'd get back on the bed and put on her clothes, usually matching tops and gathered skirts with elasticated waistbands, tights and soft, flat leather shoes to match her outfit. Then she'd take out the rollers and back-comb and lacquer her hair in a kind of Margaret Thatcher style. Lastly, she'd take a deep breath and say, 'Now I'm ready to start the day' and wheel off for her breakfast.

The men were completely different. They practically fell out of bed into their jeans and T-shirts. I never saw them wash. They spent their days chatting up the nurses and trying to persuade them to take them down the pub in the evenings. Steve, the older one, had fallen off his motorbike while taking the corner too fast on a wet day, and no-one really talked about how Kevin had had his accident. It was rumoured that he'd been illegally stripping a roof of lead and had fallen off. It seemed a pretty extreme punishment to me.

The first morning I was there, I woke up with that familiar, sinking, hospitally kind of feeling, but I was in for a nice surprise. A young nurse showed me the way to the Gym. There wasn't any question of her taking me there, and nobody tried to push me. The whole feeling of the place was that you would do everything you possibly could for yourself. I hadn't been in a Gym since the dreaded days of Pauline Blood. The one in the spinal unit looked much like the one at Queensbury except there were loads more wheelchairs and the same kind of exercise equipment you see on the telly – rowing machines and those kind of big bars you pull apart. Everyone working on the benches or on the floor seemed to have their own physiotherapist.

'Hello, Libby,' a cheerful, hearty voice called out. I wasn't sure where it was coming from. 'Don't you look well? I bet you don't even remember me!' I turned my wheelchair in the direction of the voice and met the same grin as my own.

'Trudy! Course I remember you. Do you work here now?'

'Yup. Hard though it was to leave, they offered me the job of deputy boss woman here and I had no choice but to take it. I've only been here a week. How would you like to be one of my first patients?' I was so pleased. The thought of a replacement PB had been haunting me, and I knew I'd be okay with Trudy.

Even the first assessment wasn't too bad. She was gentle and firm at the same time and she made me giggle, too. I was a bit worried that she'd tell me off for not doing more 'walking', but she was fine.

'You're doing really well,' she said as I wobbled my way up onto the parallel bars.

'Really well?'

'Yes, you are. Being able to take weight through your feet, even for a couple of seconds, is useful, especially when you're not at home and need to get into a small loo or you want to transfer into another chair. And standing is good for your posture and your kidneys, even if you need support to do it. But a wheelchair can be a great way to get around and whilst you're here, that's what we'll work on. There's lots of things I can help you with. I'll have you wheeling up mountains before you go home.' She laughed, then stopped for a second and gave me an ironic look. 'You'll be pleased to know that the OT's don't do jigsaw puzzles and basket-weaving here.'

'They don't?'

'No. They do cooking, cleaning out the bath, wheelchair maintenance and stripping down the car engine.' I giggled but wasn't sure if she was entirely joking.

She held the chair steady while I sat down again. Then, quite unexpectedly, she said, 'Pauline Blood gave you a really hard time at Queensbury, didn't she?'

I wasn't sure what to say. 'Yeah, I s'pose so.'

'Do you still feel angry about it?'

'It's not really anger. It's just that she made me feel such a failure about everything. She seemed to think I wasn't trying hard enough to walk. To her, any kind of walking was better than using a wheelchair, but that's ridiculous because I can't do anything for myself when I'm standing up clinging onto a frame.'

Trudy nodded sympathetically. 'I've thought a lot about you since I started working here. It wasn't all Pauline's fault.' I pursed my lips together but kept silent. 'A lot of it is to do with the way we're trained, all of us – physios, doctors, nurses. We're trained to make you better, and getting people up and walking is a major part of that. We feel we've failed if we don't achieve this goal.'

'I don't think she thought *she* was the failure; I think she thought *I* was.'

'It's hard in a case like yours where it takes a long time to work out what's actually happened and what you can and can't do. Since I've come to work in a Spinal Unit, I look at things differently. We have to define "getting better" in a different way. Very few people leave this unit walking, but lots of them go home to an independent life – like you will.'

As the weeks went by, I began to feel more comfortable and more confident about myself. My first waking thought was usually still a surprised 'how could this have happened to me?', and I didn't like being away from home, but I was learning a lot. Surprisingly, it was Robbie I missed the most. He could still be difficult with Mum but it was me he told his troubles to, and I was the only one he'd let hear his 'reading book' every day. He didn't really understand why I wasn't like I used to be, but it didn't seem to matter to him at all. I was just his big sister and as long as I was around when he wanted me, that was enough.

Meanwhile, I looked to people like Steve and Kevin to see how to manage life from a wheelchair. I learned how to do a wheelie, how to mount a kerb and push myself up it all in one go, and how to fall out of it onto the floor and get myself back in again. In the Gym, Trudy had me training like a maniac. Twenty minutes on the rowing machine, three sets on the Lateral Pull Down and four sets on the Pec Dec. 'Even crips go for the burn,' Steve said to me one day, bending his arms and showing me how, when he flexed his muscles, he could make the bosoms of his naked lady tattoo grow.

I didn't hate being there or anything; I knew it was important for me. But it was strange to look at Steve and Kevin and the others on the unit, even Jackie or the doctor who went around the wards in her white coat and stethoscope, and know that for the rest of my life people would see me like I saw them now. As someone different from the rest.

The hospital was set in enormous grounds – it had started out as an isolation hospital for people with infectious diseases – and whenever the weather was nice, Trudy would take 'her gang' on arm-aching excursions which seemed miles long. Our treat was a Cornetto or Choc-Mint Feast at the hospital shop, and we took it in turns to pay. I was like the Spinal Unit 'pet', but I didn't mind it too much. At least it meant I was saved from the earnest, intense conversations about bladders, bowels and the problems of finding somewhere to live that I heard going on all over the place.

Trudy hadn't been entirely right about the OTs. There were still plenty of craft activities going on but they also taught me a lot of useful stuff about looking after myself. Sometimes they were really small things, like remembering to put out all my clothes for the next day, so that I didn't waste any energy getting on and off the bed. Or it would be things like how to get in and out of the bath or where to place the wheelchair after you'd got on the shower seat so it didn't get soaking wet. Like Trudy, their approach was that I would be completely independent as long as I got my surroundings right. The nurses were helping me get into what they called a 'routine with my waterworks', which hadn't worked properly since I'd been ill. A polite way of showing me how to get to the toilet in time.

There was a complete little flat at the back of their part

of the unit, and one day I cooked lunch for Trudy, my OT, Mum, Grandma and Robbie. I made a chicken casserole with leeks, carrots, baby onions and celery with tarragon and a jacket potato, followed by apple crumble and ice cream. I laid the table myself and served everything. Grandma had tears in her eyes, which she insisted was early hay fever, and kept saying it was the best meal she'd ever eaten. I felt pretty pleased with myself.

One day, I had just come back from the Gym and was about to eat my lunch (tinned ravioli and salad — a hospital favourite) when one of the friendly nurses told me that someone had come to see me and if I wanted to, she'd keep my meal and warm it up for me later. (Warmed tinned ravioli and salad?) I wasn't expecting anyone and couldn't imagine who it could be at this time of day. Then I saw the shock of red hair and heard that unmistakable voice.

'Hello Libby, what are you having for your lunch? Is it those square things with that tomato stuff on top of it? I like those ones but we don't have them at our old hospital do we? Are you going to get a pudding? Is it going to be a nice pudding?'

'Hi, Brian. Hello Brian's mum,' I said, running my hand over his head. He had had it cut really short and it felt like stroking a Siamese cat the wrong way. 'What are you doing here?' For once, he looked at his mum for an answer.

'We've changed our doctor, he needs a different kind of operation now and this hospital has a specialist orthopaedic unit for Brian's condition. We should have come here years ago really.' She seemed worried and tired but when she looked at Brian she gave him a big, reassuring grin.

'Have you got a plaster jacket on now?' I asked.

'No', he said pulling up his T-shirt to show me. His little chest was very pale and you could see all his bony ribs. 'But I'm going to have an extra big one and I've got to keep it on a long, long time haven't I, Mummy?' He turned his face towards her.

'Yes, love.'

'And you're going to be in this hospital?' I asked.

'I don't know.' This was the first time I'd heard Brian sound unsure of anything. 'It's not the same hospital is it?'

'Yes, it is the same.' She turned to me. 'He's a bit confused because this hospital has lots of different buildings. It was quite a long walk to get here; his ward is right the other side of the grounds.'

'Well, while I'm here, I can come and see you every day. The exercise will be good for me. Would you like that?' He nodded again. 'And I promise to tell you everything I've eaten or will eat, although the food here isn't very interesting. Except of course when I cook it.'

He stood very still looking at me. He seemed to have lost some of his old sparkle and confidence.

'Do you remember the taxi rides I used to give Robbie? Would you like one?'

'What, now?' His face lit up like in the old days.

He gave me some imaginary money and climbed on my lap. I took him all over the unit. When we got to my room he said, 'Where's all your nice pictures gone?' He was remembering all the cards I had on my wall.

'I haven't got any cards this time.'

'Why not?'

'I s'pose because I'm not ill any more. I'm just here to learn new things.' I had been sent a few cards from Grandma, Joyce and a nice letter from Barbara, but nothing to get excited about.

Brian was entranced by the little flat in the Occupational Therapy Unit, especially with the kitchen with its low cupboards and pull-out worktops. But he wasn't his old self. He wore a new, grave, over-serious expression on his sweet freckled face.

'What's the matter, Brian?' I asked gently.

'I don't know,' he said in a small, quiet voice.

'Are you worried about your new operation?' His mum had told me he might have to stay in hospital for several months. He was silent for a minute.

'I don't think I like it here. I just like the other hospital with . . . ' I looked into his face. It felt like I could see his little brain working but he had already learned to be more cautious about what he said. He gave out a big sigh as if he had the troubles of the world on his little shoulders. 'I don't want to eat those ravly-only things,' he said at last. 'I like the chicken and the munchrooms we had in the other hospital.'

I tried hard not to laugh. 'You won't have it every day,' I said and then, lying absolutely, 'Sometimes we have really nice food here.' I took him all the way to the Gym and showed him to Trudy, who remembered him, of course. No-one could forget Brian. I told him about how my dad was making me a new room of my own and all the things I wanted to do with it. He was all for putting my old cards up again all over the walls.

'When you come out of hospital, would you like to come and see it?' He nodded again. 'I'll get your mum to bring you over. She's got our phone number.'

'Do you really, truly, really promise?'

I gave him a kiss on the top of his head. 'Yes I do really, truly, really, honestly promise. You can come over for my birthday if you're feeling well enough. It's only a few weeks' time.'

I kept my first promise to Brian and went over to see him whenever I could. It was a long way – up and down lots of slopes and uneven paths – but the weather was warm and light, the best of early spring days, and the trees were full of pink cherry blossom. It was a challenge to get there and I was proud of myself when I did.

Someone from the family came to see me most evenings, but no-one from school. I'd spoken to Cleo and Esther on the phone but usually by the time I'd got through the day, I was so knackered I just wanted to go to bed. Not that I slept much with all the noise of the hospital going on.

Dad and Granddad were making great progress with the conversion. Dad had sold Nellie, the red MG, which was just as well, even though they kept trying to reassure me that they were hardly paying for anything. The first weekend I went home, they'd already taken out the garage doors at the front, put in a big window and bricked up the rest of the wall. I was surprised at how big and clear the space was, about four and a quarter metres long and three and a half wide.

Granddad was in his element. He was still really strong and fit and he'd never got used to being retired, even though it was three years ago. He hadn't wanted to sell the shop at all but it was hard to make a living in a small family business these days. The shop was in West Hampstead, one of those parts of London where ordinary working people used to live and work, but over the years it had become really fashionable and expensive. All the shops like Granddad's selling useful things like electrical goods or fruit and veg began to disappear, and in their place there were fancy restaurants and the kind of clothes shops that were painted all white inside, with just one dress hanging in the window. If you wanted to buy a kettle these days, it would have to be a French designer one in stainless steel and green enamel, rather than an ordinary Russell Hobbs.

When I was little, I used to love going in the shop. It was crammed from floor to ceiling with all kinds of dangerous and interesting things. Paints, brushes, screwdrivers, nails, drills, all manner of spare parts, shiny buckets, brooms, pen knives, measuring tapes, scissors. After Dad had left to go and train as a teacher, Granddad had tried to keep the business going, but it was hard. Eventually he'd had a good offer to buy the lease from a shop called Allegra, which sold overpriced body oils and fancy bathroom fittings, and he had no choice but to accept it. Starling's Hardware Store had been losing money for a long time. They managed to buy the upstairs flat, which had been their home (then our home, then their home again), so at least they had somewhere secure to live.

* * *

When you came in the front door of our house, the kitchen was straight ahead, the door to the sitting room on your right and the garage on your left. By the second week I came home, they'd put a door in on the left-hand side, raised the floor to get it all on one level (with a slopey bit at the back so the water could drain away) and put a little round window with frosted glass in the back wall and a partition with sliding doors to make a tiny bathroom. Mum told me that Granddad had concreted the floor in one day with three of his mates from the British Legion. They all brought their sandwiches and flasks and spent the whole time singing songs from their army days. 'Mademoiselle from Armeteer' or something, 'Inky Pinky Parlez Vous'. I was glad I'd been out of the way.

Both Dad and Granddad were completely obsessed with their new project. Dad spent the whole of the Easter holidays working on it and could hardly tear himself away long enough to fetch me from hospital on Friday afternoons. Mum wanted to join in, too. She was a dab hand with a trowel or electric drill, but they hardly allowed her a look in on all this 'men's work'. Although they had a lot of help from the volunteer force, there were still lots of things they had to buy, and Granddad thought nothing of driving all the way down to Hertfordshire to get a set of cheap tiles or a specially raised toilet. Barbara and Trudy had been to visit and given us some advice on how to arrange things. I wanted it all to be as spare as possible – just what I needed, no more. It's amazing how much room a wheelchair can take.

By the end of the third week, Dad was back at work

but the bathroom was all in place. Along the back row, evenly spaced – one, two, three – there was the toilet (or lavatory, as Grandma insisted on calling it), a little sink with a glass-fronted cabinet above it and a pull-down shower seat. On one wall there was a neat shower fitting and a rack for my shampoo and soap, and on the other side there was a little grab rail and a roll for the toilet paper. We'd put grey speckled tiles on the floor that Granddad had picked up from one of his mates as a 'job lot', and plain white tiles halfway up the walls. I had to swivel myself round into place before I pulled the sliding door shut, but once inside I could do everything for myself. No more bringing down things for me to pee into or waiting for someone to help me into the bath.

The bit left for my own room wasn't enormous but it was big enough. I'd really wanted a wooden floor like Barbara's – carpets are hopeless when you use a wheelchair – but that was too expensive. We bought cork tiles, which had the same kind of look and colour, and Granddad gave them six coats of varnish to protect them. Poor thing, he could hardly stand up afterwards; he wasn't quite as fit as he thought. We brought my bed down from upstairs and arranged it by the far wall, with a little shelf above it to hold my light and a few things. Mum painted the walls a colour I chose – a pale, chalky, greeny blue like the colour of the sky on a spring day – and we painted the rest of the bathroom the same colour. Dad cut down an old, plain, wooden door he found on a skip and put some tubular metal legs on it. It made a long, thin desk that stretched along the wall under the window. We painted the desk the same colour as the walls but darker, a warm, sagey, bluish green. He brought home an old, wobbly bookcase they were throwing out from his school and spent a whole weekend gluing the corners and sanding it down to its original pale wood. I helped with this and rubbed until my hands blistered. Robbie and I swapped wardrobes. I had his little, pine, children's one, which was fine because I could reach the top shelves, and he was going to have the one fitted into my old room. I couldn't think that I'd need long, hanging-up spaces now. Trousers and T-shirts were still my uniform. I brought down my old pin board, cork with a wooden frame, and I made a collage of all my favourite cards and postcards from those early days in hospital.

If I'd accepted everything people wanted to give me, my room would have ended up looking like a car boot sale. Mum handled that by saying, 'Thank you very much' to everyone and taking the frilly cushions and autumn-leaves rugs straight to the nearest Oxfam shop. We did accept two nice things, though. Joyce gave me a plain, pale, cane armchair, slightly battered, and another of Mum's friends offered me a white 1970s style angle-poise lamp for my desk.

After four weeks in hospital I came home and found my room ready to move into. Grandma had made me a white blind, and Mum had made me some cushions for the cane chair, old velvet she'd got from somewhere – pale blue on one side and caramel on the other. It was a perfect room. Cool and delicious and all mine.

Chapter Seventeen
Birthday

This euphoria didn't last long. I suppose I should have seen it coming. All the intensity and tension of the school campaign, immediately followed by my time at Pinner and the pleasure and excitement of getting my own room, together had taken me onto a great high. I suppose there was nowhere else to go but down.

I think I would probably have been okay if I'd just been allowed to have a quiet time. I wanted to just *be*. I wanted Mum and Dad and Robbie to be around when I needed them and I wanted to spend time on my own when I felt like it. I wanted space to be unhappy and miserable. I suppose that's selfish, but just because I had a room of my own and a school to go back to, it didn't mean everything was back to normal. Things weren't all better again.

I'd thought Mum and I were never going to go back to

the kind of arguments we used to have before I got ill. But the thing is, we were still the same people we'd always been, only now I had an extra-sensitive, easily bruised layer. The big showdown happened over my birthday, which was in the middle of May. Mum had been getting on my nerves, always suggesting things for me to do when I didn't want to do anything. Well, I didn't know what I wanted and it made me feel worse thinking about other people's ideas of celebrating and having fun. She was dead keen on me having a party. I hadn't had a birthday party since I was in the infants and I couldn't imagine what sort of party I could have now. When I thought about it, all I could see was loads of people standing up way over my head.

Esther had been on at me to have a party, too. She wanted a proper teenage party, the kind she'd read about in *Sugar* and *Just 17*. I think she just wanted a reason to get Ben to take her somewhere. Their 'going out' together still consisted of the occasional chat at school; he still hadn't quite got the hang of what a girl expected from a boyfriend.

'We've got to mark your birthday somehow, Libby darling,' Mum said. 'You're going to be sixteen, sweet sixteen. We can't let that just pass by without some kind of celebration.' I looked down at the book on my lap although I wasn't reading anything. I knew she was getting irritated. 'It doesn't have to be a great big do or anything. Just the family and a few people, your friends too. We need to say thank you to all those mates of Granddad's who helped out.'

'Oh for God's sake,' I snapped. 'Do I have to go through my whole life being grateful to people?'

Mum's eyes changed and she bit her bottom lip. 'They did do a lot of work for nothing. I know that Bill's son put off a paid job they had so he could do the bricklaying for you.'

'I thought they did it out of the goodness of their hearts,' I said nastily. 'Because they felt sorry for the poor crippled girl. Doesn't it make people feel better about themselves – hearts of gold and all that?'

'Libby, that really won't do,' Mum said. I almost didn't recognise the tone of her voice. 'Those are just straightforward nice people who helped us out when we needed it.'

'Need, need, need,' I repeated. 'I shouldn't have had to need them. The council should have done it for us and then I wouldn't have to say thank you to anybody.'

'That's as may be, but things aren't always fair and their help got you a lovely room. You're a lucky girl. There's not many people your age who've got their own room and bathroom with everything just as they like it.'

'A lucky girl,' I said incredulously. 'A lucky girl? Is that how you see me? I'm lucky because I can get to the toilet on my own, am I? I'm lucky because I can wash myself? I wonder if you'd think I was lucky if you had to spend one day in my body, just one hour. Then you'd know what it feels like to be me.' As I said it I had a picture of Dad working all through his holidays, covered in plaster, swearing under his breath as he tried to fit the door. And Mum, sitting Robbie in front of yet another video so she could get my room painted for the weekend I came home. A bit of me knew I was out of control. All of me felt wretched and miserable.

'I hate you. I hate everybody. I hate myself. No-one understands what I go through every day. You can't just make everything better with a party. Why doesn't everyone just leave me alone? I'll go back to the hospital, shall I, and you can have your party. Then you can have some fun because I won't be there to make everyone miserable. You'd all be better off without me anyway.'

Mum looked at me and I felt like a stranger. She didn't try to comfort me. She didn't say anything. I wanted her to say she still loved me and it didn't matter what I said, but we were both beyond speech. She got up and busied herself in the kitchen, turning her back towards me. I went into my bathroom and pulled the door shut behind me. I looked at my face in the mirror, watching myself cry. I used to like my face crying. I thought that being sad suited me: my eyes looked bigger and the tears and sadness gave me inner depth. I thought it made me look more interesting and intelligent.

Now I looked at my face and saw something different. For the first time I could see that I'd been right and wrong at the same time. Life was hard, and there might always be a bit of me thinking 'Why me? Why me?', but it was hard for Mum, too. I couldn't always expect her to understand how I was feeling, especially when I didn't know myself. She'd always wanted to protect me from everything bad but she hadn't been able to protect me from this. I splashed my face with water and blew my nose. In the kitchen I could hear Mum doing the same. As she heard me come in, she crumpled up a bit of kitchen paper and threw it in the bin.

'Mum . . .'

'I didn't mean to say that . . .'

We both started at the same time, then stopped and smiled. She came up behind me and put her arm round my shoulders. I leaned my head against her and she kissed me. I put my arms round her waist.

'Let's not say sorry,' I said.

'Let's make tea instead.'

Ironically, we had three goes at a birthday celebration that year. On Thursday night we had the volunteer league round for a drink or two to see their work (Granddad and Bill bought a crate of beer between them so Dad was happy), and I was on my best behaviour. I smiled when they all went on about how wonderful I was. I even kept silent when Bill patted me on the head and called me a 'brave wee lassie' and his wife, Beryl, gave me a bottle I thought was perfume but which turned out to be holy water from Lourdes. 'You must never give up,' she said sweetly. 'God works in mysterious ways his wonders to perform. I've cut out an article for your dear mother about a miracle that happened in America. It was a young mother. The doctors said she would never walk again but her faith proved them wrong.'

On Friday we had a family meal with birthday cake and candles, and on Saturday night we had a party. Not exactly a rave or what Dad called an 'everybody must get stoned' kind of party, more of an old-fashioned get-together. I expect everyone would've been singing round the piano if we'd had a piano. It probably wasn't very cool to be sixteen and have a party with your mum and dad and their friends, but it seemed the safest choice. I don't think I'd have been very good at the kind of do with drink and drugs, all the lights turned down and everyone dancing so close they shared each other's sweat. And hand jiving wasn't my scene.

The family gave me their presents on Friday, my real birthday. I didn't think I was going to get anything more – everyone had already spent a lot on me – but they must have dug even deeper in their pockets. Mum gave me some money for new clothes, and I don't know where Dad had found the time but he'd used a special machine at his school and made me a leather rucksack specially designed to hang on the back of my wheelchair. I thought it was brilliant. I'd just received my new chair – lightweight, black and sporty like Barbara's. It was amazing how much easier it was to get around in after the cumbersome grey NHS job I'd been using. It was like driving a Rolls-Royce after a Fiat Panda. We'd been able to pay it off using one of the allowances I got for mobility. By the time it was paid off, I'd be seventeen and could think about leasing a car through the same scheme.

Granddad, who was a great fan of car boot sales, had found me a tiny square fridge and an elderly electric kettle and reconditioned them.

'It's for your room. I thought you might like it when you have your chums for a cup of tea,' he said, coughing in embarrassment. It amazed me to think that he saw me as an independent person, almost an adult. I'd thought he still saw me as his little granddaughter. Or perhaps he thought I was always going to be at home now, living with Mum and Dad. Robbie (with Mum's help) gave me a set of mugs, blue, mauve and green – one colour on the inside and a different one outside. They were really lovely. He was grinning from ear to ear, proud of keeping a secret. He gave me a home-made card. 'TO THE BEST BIG SISSTER IN THE WOLD.'

'And you're the best little brother,' I said, forgetting the non-stop arguments I'd been having with him, trying to keep him out of my room.

Grandma sat at the big table in the now-restored back part of the sitting room. She didn't speak until everyone else had finished.

'Here you are darling,' she said, handing me a soft, flat parcel. 'Do you know what it is? I made it for you myself; I looked at the colours in your room and chose something to go with it. I hope you like it.' I guessed it would be a new duvet and pillowcase. I hadn't had a new one since the days of My Little Pony, and I'd seen a couple I liked in the Habitat catalogue – big, flat, beige stripes or a thin, pale-blue check on a white background. 'I knew you wouldn't want anything babyish and I thought your room is so plain, it would be nice to have something to brighten it up a bit.'

I opened it up. Grandma had sown frills of material all the way round the duvet and the pillowcases and made a frilly valance to go with it. It must have taken her ages. The background was bright, slightly acid pink and there were trellises of flowers and leaves – pansies, violets and roses in purple, baby blue, green and fuchsia. It had a kind of sheen on it like cheap wrapping paper. It was like a seed catalogue gone mad. I thought of my beautiful, perfectly co-ordinated room and the lovely, natural colours – aquamarine, tan, cream, white. Then I took a deep breath and smiled.

'Thanks, Granny. It must have taken you ages to make.'

She looked at me anxiously. 'Do you like it?'

'It's really lovely. It's so . . . It's so bright and colourful.'

She beamed. 'I'm so pleased, darling. I thought you'd like something to brighten the room up a bit.' Mum stood up and brushed past me closely as she went towards the kitchen.

'Well done,' she whispered, and went to fetch the cake.

Cleo's present was more to my taste. A week before my birthday she arrived unexpectedly with two circles of transparent plastic cut out in the middle like car tyres and an assortment of paint cans.

'What are they for?' I asked.

'They're spoke guards,' she said knowledgeably.

'They're what?'

'You put it over your wheels for a bit of colour, that individual touch. You attach it like this.' She showed me the small holes punched in the edges and the small tape to tie round the spokes. 'I thought we could do them now. Something outrageous. We could even do your name.' We laid them out on the kitchen table. We painted sharp zig-zags round the edges, red and green outlined in black, and Cleo showed me how to mix the paints with oil so that in the middle there was a rainbow effect like oil and water in the puddles on a rainy day. We tied them onto the spokes and as I wheeled backwards and forwards, the pattern spun round like a psychedelic trip.

'Where did you get these from?' I asked, surveying the results.

'Oh, contacts,' she said, grinning. 'I don't see why you should be invisible just 'cos you're in a wheelchair. Get noticed, that's my motto.'

My next problem was what I was going to wear for the party. Cleo and I didn't exactly have the same taste in clothes but then again, I didn't know what my taste was these days. At least she didn't get her knickers in a twist about being tactful. If I looked awful in something, she'd tell me.

We went to Brent Cross on Saturday morning. I think Mum was pleased to have me out of the way. Apart from my room, our house was always in a mess and there was a lot of clearing up to do. Cleo came round early and we waited for the Dial-a-Ride bus, a special minibus for disabled people. When it arrived, there were already two other people in wheelchairs on it. There was an old woman with her middle-aged daughter and a grey-haired man with his equally elderly wife. It made me feel a bit peculiar, like I didn't want them to be there. It was that uncomfortable kind of feeling where you know you shouldn't think like this and it doesn't make you feel good about yourself but you can't stop it.

In the few times I'd been out near where I lived, I'd always felt that people were surprised to see someone as young as me in a wheelchair. Like it was alright if you had permed, grey hair and a tartan blanket over your knees but weird if you were only fifteen. It occurred to me that when I was Grandma's age, people would think I'd just started to use a wheelchair because I was old. They wouldn't realise I'd always been like this. Funny thought, that.

I'd always loved Brent Cross. When I was little it would often be my birthday treat to go there with Mum and have a look round and eat chicken and chips in Rivoli's while Mum ate pick-your-own salad. I didn't mind if we didn't buy anything else. Now I liked it all over again, although I'd forgotten how big and noisy it was. There were so many people in wheelchairs that I was nothing special. The floors were smooth and even, the big, glass lift took you smoothly from level to level and I could get in all the shops without having to ask for help. It was the first time I'd been out in public without feeling like I was on show in a big human zoo. Usually, the cage around me might be invisible but everyone still stared.

Mind you, I wouldn't have been surprised if people had stared. We were a bit of an odd couple, Cleo and I. I was still rather thin, bordering on skinny, and a bit pale. I'd had my straight brown hair cut shorter, shoulder length, parted in the middle. Cleo had been right when she made that comment about how I shouldn't try to hide away just because I was in a wheelchair. I still dressed in a kind of anonymous way, which I knew made me look as if I wanted to disappear – big grey T-shirts, baggy trousers, plain trainers. Cleo, on the other hand, had now dyed her hair jet black and wore it in two high pigtails with gingham ribbon, Björk-style. She had a round, almost child-like face and was wearing pale lipstick and lots of black eye make-up. She wasn't fat, although you certainly couldn't call her skinny, especially in the bosom region, and she had on a very short pinafore dress, citrus-yellow satin T-shirt and black canvas shoes with thick, high heels.

Cleo was dismissive when I said I thought we should

313

start in the big department store, John Lewis. She thought it was a shop strictly for wrinklies but she went along with me. To tell the truth, I had no idea what I was looking for. I browsed through some skimpy, brightly coloured tops and big, checked shirts.

'What do you think about this, if they've got it in a bigger size?' I asked, holding up a plain black top with a silver star in the middle.

'It's okay. I'll go and ask someone, shall I?' She wandered off in the direction of the jeans to find someone who could help. It wasn't hard to hear the shop assistant's stagey whisper.

'Your poor little friend. What's the matter with her?'

'Sorry?'

'The one in the wheelchair. Was she born like that?'

'How the fuck should I know?' Cleo snapped. 'Never seen her before.'

'Oh,' said the assistant, covered in confusion. 'I'm sorry. I thought I saw you talking to her.'

'Yeah. I was asking her if she did drugs. I've got some Es to sell. Want any?'

'Oh no. Oh dear. I . . .' The assistant backed off quickly, colliding with a rack of oversized tops for pregnant women, knocking them flying. Cleo and I fled in hysterics.

'Cleo, you shouldn't do things like that,' I said between breaths.

'Stupid cow. She should mind her own business.' I'd never have had the nerve to say it myself, but she was right. It was true. Complete strangers did seem to think my business was their business these days.

We stopped for a cappuccino and a sandwich in Ed's Diner and talked about everything except what I most wanted to talk to her about. I was dying to ask her about Jesse – what he was up to, what she thought he felt about me, what she felt about him – but I'd kept silent for so long that I didn't know how to start. So we talked about clothes and other people and her new boyfriend, Dave from the sixth form – he sounded a distinct improvement on the last one – and we talked about what everyone but me was talking about these days, their exams.

We must have gone in every clothes shop in the place, Miss Selfridge, Kookai, Jeffrey Rogers, Morgan, Top Shop. All I could see were little satin dresses that scarcely covered your knickers or tight shorts to show off your legs. Everything seemed to be clothes for standing up in. Clothes that were supposed to lie straight over your hips rolled over my stomach in wrinkles. The only thing I could see that might be alright were long, floaty, flowery things in shops like Monsoon. I was only sixteen; I didn't want to look sixty. Cleo looked at my face and took over.

'Come on, I know what would suit you.'

'I'm not trying anything else on.' The thought of all those tall girls in the communal changing rooms made me feel queasy.

'You don't have to. I know you'll look good in this.' She took one hand and half pulled me into one of those smaller shops down the side turnings.

'Cleo. Look at the prices.'

'Come on, you haven't had anything new for ages. Say to yourself – I deserve it.' She pulled down a pair of black trousers in a wonderful material which stretched without you seeing how it did it and a white, sleeveless polo-neck top with thin black edging, ribbed but quite long. It was a slim, tight fit, and automatically I started pulling it away from me.

'Don't do that,' Cleo said. 'You've got great boobs, you ought to show them off.' I made a face. 'I wish mine were like yours, all firm and upright. Mine are so big they're gonna be down by my waist by the time I'm twenty.' She pulled the top down again but it was too long for me; it rucked up in the middle. The assistant showed me how to wear a thin belt round my waist and pull some of the top over it so that it covered my stomach but still looked tight and fitted. It did look good. In another, less expensive shop, I bought a pair of flat patent pumps. I knew what Mum would say.

'That's gorgeous, so retro. It's just what I wore in the seventies.'

The party went okay. It wasn't brilliant but it was better than okay and I was glad we'd had it. Mum had made the usual kind of party food – sausage rolls, sandwiches, crisps and nuts. We'd borrowed Joyce's 'gelato' machine and made some wacky ice-creams – peanut butter and fudge, orange and bubblegum, blackcurrant jam and cream cheese – and Robbie and his friends served them in cornets to everyone.

Barbara came with the man I'd seen at her house that day, the tall, good-looking one. I assumed he must be her new boyfriend now. I took her to show off my room.

'I don't know if you need one of these, but I thought you might like it,' she said, handing me a package. 'You can just chuck it over a chair or sofa if you don't use it as a bedspread.' It was a large piece of soft, Indian cotton, patterned cream on cream with a short fringe round the edge. It didn't seem just a coincidence that Barbara had bought me what I wanted. I'd always felt she knew what I was thinking before I even thought it. I unfolded it and threw it over the bed. Now the riotous, hideous flowers of Grandma's duvet could snuggle down, unseen.

I spent most of the party waiting for Jesse to arrive. Esther and Ben came together and sat on the sofa not talking much or touching each other but looking quite happy. Cleo came with Dave, some beer and a collection of CDs, and he hung around looking a bit awkward until he struck up a lively conversation with our next-door neighbour about using the Internet. The rest of the crowd came – Az, Anil, even Joanna. We stayed at the front of the room with the music, with Mum and Dad and their friends down at the other end, by the door to the garden. Barbara had gone home a while before. Perhaps because she wasn't quite sure which end she belonged in.

Some of the oldies were just beginning to go home when the doorbell rang. My body had given up jumping out of its skin every time I heard it go and I was resigned to the fact that he must have decided not to come. He came in with Jason, a tall, loose-limbed boy from school. We'd never actually spoken but I remembered him as someone very confident about himself and his chat-up lines with the girls. He was the kind of boy who was always on the borderline of trouble at school but usually managed to pull it off with a perfectly timed smile which

317

charmed everyone except the most humourless of teachers. Now he seemed shy and slightly awkward, very polite to Mum and Dad. So was Jesse, but then I expected that. He was good with adults.

They were both wearing trainers, outsize shorts and looked slightly sweaty.

'I'm sorry we're so late,' Jesse said, pulling up a chair and sitting down close to me, as close as you could get without actually touching. 'We had the basketball tournament. It went on so late, we didn't even go home to change. I didn't bring you a present or anything. I hope I don't smell too bad.' He pulled his shirt away from his body and smiled. I could feel his warmth. His look went straight into my stomach and flipped it over twice.

'How did the game go?' Ben asked.

Jesse shrugged, trying to look modest. 'We thrashed them.' He was talking to Ben but looking at me. He had lovely hazel eyes, green in the middle and orange round the outside.

'What? You got right to the finals? You beat Preston Park?'

'They weren't the problem. It was the Stonebridge lot,' Jason interrupted and began to describe the game ball by ball to a captivated audience. Jesse didn't take his eyes off me.

'You look great tonight, Libby. How are you, have you been okay?' He put his hand on the wheel of my chair. Usually I hated people touching my chair like that, but now it felt okay; it was just a way of being close.

I remembered why I liked him so much. It was because when he talked to you, he made you feel he really wanted to listen to what you had to say. He wasn't waiting for you to finish so he could carry on talking about himself.

'I'm fine,' I answered routinely and then, more honestly. 'Well, up and down. Winning the school thing was great and then I was busy getting my room together but since then things have been a bit quiet. I suppose I've had too much time to think about myself. It's a bit scary, thinking about the future, it makes me tired. Everything I want to do, it feels like I have to invent a new way to do it.'

He seemed to know what I was talking about. 'What do you do with yourself in the day?'

'Things are pretty quiet. My Mum takes me swimming a couple of times a week and I'm trying to get through some of the course books Ms Benjamin sent me but I find it hard to concentrate.'

'What about after school?'

'Not a lot. Everyone's busy getting ready for exams. Cleo comes round sometimes, and Esther. Not together, of course.'

He laughed, knowing what I meant without having to explain.

'D'you remember what I said about coming round to help you with maths? I meant it; I'd really like to. It'd be good for me too – it would help me to revise.'

'I don't think so, not with the standard of my maths. It would be more like helping out in Year 7,' I said, trying to sound light. I wondered if this was another of his sincerely made promises which would come to nothing, like when he'd spoken to me at Barbara's. But then I thought about the risks he'd taken for me since and the way he was looking at me now.

'My exams don't begin for a couple of weeks and then we could carry on right through the summer. I could come on Wednesdays at about five o'clock. If you want me to.'

Chapter Eighteen
Love and Mathematics

Snogtastic

I'd really like to snog my boyfriend. The trouble is I don't know what to do. I mean, does it involve tongues, or do you just kiss? Is it something you do on a walk in the country, or do you cuddle up in the back row of the cinema?
Totally confused, London

Dear Totally Confused,
One of the greatest, snogtastic advantages of the big smooch is that there are no rules. Just shut your eyes and go for it. Or open them if you prefer! Use your tongue if you feel like it, or keep it safe on home ground if you don't! Explore every nook and cranny of the inside and outside of his mouth, or if you'd

rather, explore just his lips, gently and cautiously. It's your mouth, it's your boyfriend and it's your choice. Everyone likes different things when it comes to snogging, but it's pretty much all pleasurable. You should just do what feels right.

I'd abandoned Jane Austen's *Pride and Prejudice* for the problem page of Esther's copy of *Sugar* in the hope of calming my nerves, which had been fluttering in my throat all day, making it impossible for me to eat or drink. I'd obviously picked the wrong issue.

I'd arranged my desk and rearranged it. I'd got some fizzy drinks off Mum, filled the kettle, put milk in the fridge and pinched some biscuits from the kitchen. I'd tidied my room until there was nothing else to put away and arranged Barbara's throwover in the hope of making my bed look less bed-like. I tried putting some music on but couldn't decide what kind and anyway this was supposed to be work not play. I'd changed my top three times and now there was nothing, absolutely nothing else to do but wait. When the doorbell rang at two minutes past five, my body still started with the shock.

Mum had taken Robbie to his swimming lesson and they wouldn't be back till six, so I went to answer the door myself. Jesse had changed out of his uniform into jeans and a dark-green shirt and was standing on the doorstep with a whole lot of books under his arm.

'Wow. This is a brilliant room,' he said as he followed me in. He'd missed the guided tour on Saturday. 'Did you choose all the colours and everything yourself? It's brilliant.' I smiled, hoping I didn't look too nervous, and offered him a drink. He accepted a Coke, pulled the top off, dropped it back into the can and took a long gulp all in one, easy movement.

Then I remembered I hadn't got anywhere for him to sit – there was only Joyce's cane armchair, and no chair at my desk. I sent him into the kitchen to fetch one and re-arranged the pencils and rubbers and the maths text-book Ms Benjamin had sent, trying to look busy – and cool.

Jesse pulled up the chair beside me and rolled up the sleeves of his shirt. He already had quite a golden tan and the light, auburn hairs on his arm were the same colour as his skin. I wanted to put my hand on his arm, just above the wrist, and smooth them all in the same direction. I forced myself to concentrate.

'I thought we'd start with basic algebra, if that's okay with you. Then we can work through the book, slowly or quickly, however you want. You'll have done most of this stuff already – last year.'

He was a good teacher, near enough to learning all this himself to remember to explain each stage of the process and to let me talk it through myself until I knew I understood it. He made maths seem interesting and logical. It was only when I heard Mum's key in the lock that I realised an hour had gone. He stood up and ran his fingers back through his hair.

'I'll see you this time next week, shall I? Give me a call if you want to go over anything.' No kiss, no hug, just that smile.

I didn't telephone, although I thought about him all week. He'd written his number on the back page of my notebook and I doodled all around it, an intricate pattern of hearts, leaves and corkscrew circles, with his name and my name until I had to tear the page out and crumple it up in the bin. It didn't matter; I knew his number by heart.

The whole week was about waiting for Wednesday. From my stomach right up to my throat there was a nervous, quavery feeling that was all about seeing Jesse again, and either I didn't eat at all or stuffed myself with Mars bars until I felt even sicker. By Wednesday afternoon I had an ache in my right shoulder that I knew must be from tension because it was the feeling I used to get when I knew that Pauline Blood was coming.

Mum left to take Robbie to his class and I was glad that I had half an hour on my own before he was due to arrive. I put on one of Mum's kd lang records to calm me down. It was soft and soothing. When the bell rang, ten minutes early, the palpitations were controlled enough for me to answer the door and smile sweetly at him.

It was better once we started working. I could feel myself loosen up. It was great working together. He was like a best friend, easy-going and easy to follow. For the first time all week, the knot inside me began to loosen and I started to enjoy myself. We went through the work I'd done in the week and began on a new topic, quadratic equations.

$$2x - 2y = 17. \quad 2x - 3y = 13.$$

'First of all you have to make the co-efficients of y equal. You can do it by multiplying the first part of the sum by 3 and the second part by 2. Now if you subtract the two rows, you can make the ys vanish.' I was getting

324

my xs and my ys in the wrong places. Jesse moved his chair a bit closer to mine to show me how to change the numbers and leant over me, his arm on my arm, his hand on my hand. I felt the electric tingle of warm flesh on flesh. He stopped talking and I put the compass down. We looked at each other, not smiling any more, deadly serious and still. He moved his chair round towards me and I pushed myself away from the desk with my right hand and pulled the right wheel forward so that we were facing each other. He moved his chair a fraction forward and leant over and touched my face.

It was a long, warm, gentle, dry kiss. I wanted it never to stop.

It lasted until the sound of the key in the door. We sprang apart instantly and I started to straighten up, pulling my hair back into a ponytail and smoothing it down.

'Now a normal quadratic equation starts with an x squared,' Jesse said, trying to sound serious. 'But to factorise a co-efficient, you have to put 3 in the first bracket and 1 in the second.' We both exploded into giggles. I could feel rather than hear Mum walk past the door, stop, hear the laughter and move on.

I began to clear up, ready for him to go. I wanted to say something to him but I didn't know what. Next week was the half-term holiday and after that his exams started. I couldn't bear the thought of him going now; I didn't know if it had meant anything to him. Perhaps it was easy for him to kiss and forget.

I felt desperate that he would go without saying anything. I put my face up so that I could look at him and he leant down and gave me a sweet, soft kiss.

'Are you okay?' I nodded.

'I'll call you soon,' he said, and left.

I stayed in my room until Mum called me to come and eat. I was glad of the time to be alone and live it all again in my head. I went into the bathroom and looked in the mirror, splashing myself with water. I smiled back at my reflection like I had smiled at him, letting my hair fall onto my face, and made a kissing shape with my mouth. I could feel him still with me. I hoped that he had seen what I saw now, a smooth oval face, big green eyes, my mouth full and my hair smooth and shiny. I was in love with this new idea of myself.

Mum looked at me strangely as I came into the kitchen but she didn't say anything. After our meal – fish, potatoes, vegetables, ice-cream – which I ate like a normal person, I asked Robbie if he'd like to come into my room and we could start to make a card for Grandma and Granddad's golden wedding anniversary in a few weeks' time. I wanted to be nice to everyone and I thought I'd enjoy cutting out shapes and sticking shiny paper onto card.

'That's very nice of you, Libby,' Mum said drily, looking at me intently as if she was trying to read me from the inside. She'd been asking me to do this with Robbie for ages and I'd always found an excuse.

Poor Robbie. I wasn't much use to him. He wanted me to be in the land of scissors, glue, gummed paper and stencilled letters, and I was in the land of Jesse's touch and Jesse's kiss.

* * *

On Thursday morning I woke up early, surprised that I hadn't dreamt about him. I could hear the sounds of Dad in the kitchen and Mum calling up to Robbie to come down for breakfast. I sat up and swung my bum onto the chair, followed by my legs. I shifted around until I felt comfortable and wheeled into the bathroom. In the mirror, my face looked plain and uninteresting. My nose seemed big and pudgy, my lips too thin, my hair straight and lank. Perhaps I was just tired.

I was glad to think of him at school all day because when the phone went, I knew it couldn't be him. Mum had told me that when she was a teenager there was an unwritten rule among the girls that if a boy phoned you on a Thursday to ask you out, you were supposed to say no because it showed he'd just been waiting to see if something better turned up. Monday and Tuesday were good days, Wednesday a bit iffy, Thursday not really and Friday a definite no–no. I didn't care when Jesse rang me; I just wanted to hear the sound of his comfortable, friendly voice. I thought about phoning him myself; there were lots of reasons I could have given but I chose to wait.

He didn't make me wait long. On Thursday, just before five, at exactly the same time as he'd arrived at my house the day before, it rang and I knew it would be him. I carried the portable phone under my ear as I pushed myself into my room and shut the door.

'Hi,' he said, his voice warm and familiar and a bit uncertain. 'Are you okay today?' I nodded and then realised he couldn't see.

'I'm fine. I'm great.'

'So am I,' he said. 'I was wondering. Your birthday. I didn't get you anything. I wanted to but I didn't. Would you come out with me on Saturday?' I thought about all the problems of getting me anywhere and didn't know what to say. 'Don't worry,' he said, as if he knew the reasons for my delay. 'It'll be okay. I promise. I'll arrange it all. It'll be a surprise – I'll call for you at seven.'

First dates are supposed to make girls nervous but not in the way I was nervous. Girls on their first dates are supposed to think about what they're going to wear, how they'll do their hair and make-up, what perfume is most alluring and how far they'll let him go on the one-to-ten scale of teenage sexual progress. They're not supposed to worry about how they're going to get wherever they're going because they can't use the Underground or buses and they're both too young to drive. They're not supposed to get their knickers in a twist about whether there'll be a toilet where they're going or think about how damp their pants will be if they don't get to one on time.

I knew he'd said that he'd make all the arrangements because he wanted to save me this worry, but it made me feel even more out of control. Mum didn't help. From Thursday evening to Saturday morning she kept up the battery of questions. Where were we going? Had he checked it was accessible? Did I want her to give me a lift? How was I going to get home? Did I want dad to come and collect me? She even threatened to ring his mum but I threw such a fit of the screaming ab-dabs that even she was silenced. In the end it was dad who shut her up.

'Claire, the girl's sixteen. She knows where we are. If she needs us, she can just give us a call and one of us will come and get her. He seems like a nice boy to me. I'm sure everything will be fine.' He reminded her how her dad had been waiting at the bus stop to collect her from her first date and how much she'd hated it. She smiled at him but pressed her lips together to stop herself from saying that it wasn't quite the same for me.

I'd told Cleo and Esther I was going out with Jesse and they were both dying to know more but I didn't want to say anything. Well I did, but I couldn't. Both of them had told me details about their sexual lives (not that there was anything for Esther to tell), but that one kiss felt like a special, private, grown-up secret between Jesse and me. I knew that boys were supposed to blab to their mates about their conquests, but I didn't think Jesse would do that. Anyway, I was hardly a conquest.

Girls on their first dates are supposed to spend all the afternoon getting ready. In all the books I'd read, the heroine holds different clothes up against her in the mirror and then throws them on the floor in despair. Then she tries on loads of different outfits before deciding on the right one. Even if I'd had loads of outfits, by the time I'd got on and off the bed to try each one on, rolling from side to side to get them off again, I'd have been exhausted. In the end I wore what I'd had on for my party. He said he'd liked it then and it was the best I had. I borrowed a plain, little black jacket from Mum and hoped that the weather didn't turn cold.

I didn't know what to do about make-up; I never usually wore any but like most girls, I had some sort of collection. I put on some coloured lip gloss and a bit of mascara, fastened the top half of my hair back with a tortoise-shell clip and brushed the rest down so that it curled up a bit at the end.

'You look lovely darling,' Mum said. 'I'm sorry about all my silly questions. I can't stop being a worry guts. I'm sure you'll have a lovely time.' I guessed she must have rung Barbara and been reassured, but I couldn't prove it.

Chapter Nineteen
Häagen Dazs and Taxi Rides

Jesse arrived exactly at seven. It was wonderful how reassuring his punctuality was. Still is. He was wearing jeans and a pressed white shirt with a button-down collar. His hair was clean and shiny and he gave me a really cheesy grin. Malcolm followed him up the path. I'd never seen him before but there was no mistaking Barbara's brother. They had the same warm brown skin tone, intelligent laughing eyes and bright, open smile. He wasn't very tall — Jesse had a couple of inches on him — but he looked fit and strong.

Malcolm shook hands with Mum and Dad. I'd made them swear not to ask any questions and they didn't. I had my suspicions that they knew more than I did, but they just stood at the doorway together and waved us goodbye like I was five years old, being collected by a friend's parent to go round to their house and play.

'He's going to give us a lift Up West,' Jesse said once I was seated in the front of the car with my wheelchair in the boot and Jesse on the back seat. We drove down through Kingsbury, along by scruffier Willesden and Kilburn, past Maida Vale and the canal and into the smart part of Edgware Road, with its banks and leather shops and cafes with Arabic names. We swung round Marble Arch, through a whole maze of smart backstreets and London's green squares until we reached Oxford Circus. It was a lovely, mild, late-spring evening and the streets were full of all sorts of people sitting on the grass, walking along hand in hand, and groups of young people talking and laughing. In quiet, suburban Kingsbury, you could stand by our front door and not see a soul pass from seven o'clock at night until the next morning and even if you did, it wouldn't be anyone interesting.

We drove round Oxford Circus, down elegant Regent Street past Liberty's, full of beautifully coloured fabrics, Hamley's toy store with its giant teddy bear in policeman's uniform, and round Piccadilly Circus. The Trocadero and the neon signs flashed in techno colours and the statue of Eros was full of tourists taking each other's pictures. I thought it was all wonderful. I'd been here before with Mum and Dad but it had never seemed so noisy and alive.

Malcolm stopped just before we got to Leicester Square.

'This is where you two get out, isn't it?' he said. Jesse brought my chair round and I swung myself into it, holding on to the strap above the car door.

'Be okay, will you?' Malcolm asked, winking at me. He took out a flat, black leather wallet and pulled out a couple of crisp notes. 'Make sure you look after her. Treat her like a lady. I know you think it's out of date but they love it.' He winked at me again and drove off. Jesse was blushing and laughing.

'He seems very nice.'

'Malc? Yeah, he's great. Got really old-fashioned ideas about women, though. He gave me a whole lecture on good manners before I came out. And how it was important to iron your trousers.' We both laughed. 'I got a real blasting when he found out I'd turned up to your party without changing my clothes.' He folded up the notes and put them in his shirt pocket. 'He's just landed a new job, developing computer programmes for Southwark University. It's good money too. He's really generous anyway, when he's got it. I told him I didn't need money but he gave me it anyway. It means we can get a taxi home.' I had no idea how I was going to get into a taxi and I just added this to my list of things to be worried about.

Leicester Square was full of life and activity. There was a little open garden in the middle and the whole area was paved over. All round the outside were cafes, restaurants, cinemas and stalls selling hot dogs, pizza slices and brightly coloured helium balloons. It was packed with people. A few were a bit sad and scary looking, but mostly there were groups of tourists, families and young couples hand in hand. He still hadn't told me what we were going to do and I raised my eyebrows quizzically.

'I thought we might go and see a film. Actually, I

booked something at Warner's but I haven't paid yet and there are loads of other films showing there as well. Only Barbara said that the Warner Cinema was good – you know, loos and everything. What do you think?'

'That's fine,' I said, hoping I sounded more enthusiastic than nervous.

'I booked the James Bond film but we can go and have a look what else's on.'

'No, that's fine.' God, I must have sounded stupid. I promised myself I wouldn't say 'fine' anymore. Great, wonderful, okay, safe, brilliant, cool, fit, ace, but not fine.

He came back with the tickets.

'We've got about forty-five minutes. What do you want to do? Do you want to get something to eat?'

I felt slightly panicky. I imagined some smoothie waiter handing me a menu with a hundred different choices on it and I knew I'd never be able to make up my mind.

'What about an ice cream?' I said, casting around for ideas and catching the name Häagen Dazs from the corner of my eye.

'That's a good idea. Where shall we go?' He followed me out of the cinema to the ice-cream place right next door. There were three steps to the entrance. I knew Jesse was going to offer to get me up the stairs and I didn't want to have to say no. Sometime, yes, but not now.

'You can sit here if you like,' the young waitress said, indicating a table on the pavement. She brought us a menu. There were still fifty choices but it was easier to choose an ice-cream than worry about whether you were going to order spaghetti with some sauce you've never heard of or chicken a la whatsit.

'It's nice here,' I said. 'A bit different to Kingsbury.' I looked at the crowds and he looked down at the table. How did you get a conversation going? It was something my grandma was great at. She struck up intimate conversations with total strangers; I'd often seen her do it in parks and on buses. Dad always said she could get a butcher talking about the price of herrings.

'You haven't lived there long, have you?' I asked. 'Do you like it at Dupont?'

'Yeah, I do. I think it's a great school – apart from Blakemore, of course. It's really friendly, people get along together and don't mess about too much in lessons.'

'Where were you before?'

He twiddled his spoon about in his ice-cream and looked uncomfortable. 'I was at private school – boarding school in Sussex.'

I was dead surprised. 'What was that like?'

'It was okay. There were good things about it. It was a beautiful place, right at the bottom of the South Downs, and the sport was really good. They had everything there – cricket pitches, football, hockey, tennis, swimming pool – and the other kids were okay, not really snobby or anything, it wasn't as bad as you'd think. A lot of them came from abroad. I missed my Mum and Malcolm though – and girls. It's weird being locked up with all those boys.'

'Why did you leave there?'

'I'd never planned to stay forever. I wanted to come home and starting GCSEs seemed to be a good time. I'd only been there a couple of years. I'd had a bit of trouble before – in my last school in South London.' He bit at his wafer and looked at me as if he was trying to see whether he could trust me enough to tell me the story.

'We used to live in Streatham, me and my mum, until a couple of years ago. Malc wanted to come back to North London to be nearer Barbara and his family.'

'Didn't you know your real dad?'

He gave a low grunt. 'Yeah, I knew him. He lived with us until I was about two, then Mum chucked him out. He was hardly there anyway. I haven't seen him for a long time. I'll probably get a card next birthday – he usually remembers once every four or five years. I'm not like him – except for the hair; I got that off him. I don't even call him Dad, sometimes I say, "my father". Malcolm's my real dad. He's the one who looks out for me and shoots baskets with me in the back garden. He's the one who comes to parents' evenings and gives me advice.'

'What were you saying about school?'

'I liked primary school. I had lots of different friends there, everyone just mucked in together. You know, played together in the playground and kicked a ball around the park after school. I don't remember anyone getting bullied or anything. A lot of us went from there to the same secondary school. Dad thought I should go to the boys' school because it had quite a good reputation, you know, strict uniform, homework policy. He thought it'd be hot on discipline and there'd be a better standard of education. It was alright for the first couple of terms and then I got into a bit of a race thing.'

'What do you mean?'

'I'm not saying that in primary school we didn't notice

that we weren't all the same or it didn't matter what colour you were or any of that crap. Of course it mattered, but it wasn't a reason not to be friends with someone in school. There was a gang of us, boys and girls, and we were friends.

'Secondary school was different. People fancied themselves as tough and there was a lot of bad feeling about race. Some white kids didn't like the black kids. Some black kids didn't like the Asian kids and so on. Everyone started hanging about with their own groups and I didn't know where I was. The white kids thought I was white and they didn't like it when I told them what I thought about their stupid racist jokes. The black kids didn't want a red-haired, freckle-faced, what they thought was a posh kid in their gang, and they made that very clear, especially when they found out Malcolm was black. I suppose it might have been easier if I looked mixed race. I don't know. I didn't fit in anywhere. Some of the kids started to push me about, I was on my own, no-one to sit with in lessons, no-one to hang around with at break.

'When Dad found out, he told me I had to learn to stick up for myself, otherwise they'd always get the better of me. So I started getting into fights. Everywhere. All the time. Of course he hadn't meant me to do that but I was only twelve and I could hardly stand there and give them a *Guardian* lecture on equal rights. So then I stopped going to school altogether. First of all I used to pretend I was going to school. I'd put on my uniform and take my lunch money and then just hang around the streets. They found out of course. So then I said I was ill and they started taking me to all these doctors. In the end I had to go and see an educational psychologist. He gave me millions of tests where you had to tick things in boxes and finish off pictures he'd started. Stuff like that. He said it would be a good idea for me to get right away from the area. I think he had his own prejudices; he thought it was hard for a kid to have parents of different races, which is crap in my opinion. But he was right about me leaving that school. Things had gone so wrong, I could never get them right again.'

'How did you manage to pay for it?'

He gave me one of his wry grins. 'I got a scholarship. It was more of a sporty school than an academic one, which was just as well because I'd missed practically a year of school. I got in because they wanted me in their football team. There were quite a few kids like me from London. The school liked to win.'

I wanted to put out my hand and hold his but I felt stupidly shy. 'It must have been horrible for you. Kids can be cruel.' I remembered my own first year and hoped that one day, I'd be able to tell him about it.

'You're the first person I've told. That's one of the things I liked about it when came to Dupont – people seemed to accept me without hundreds of questions. It's great going to a mixed school. Going to a boys' boarding school in the middle of the countryside – I haven't had a lot of experience with girls.' He looked straight at me for the first time since he'd started talking.

'That's alright then. I've always been to mixed schools but I haven't had a lot of experience with boys.'

'Really?' He opened his mouth to say something else but stopped and looked at his watch. 'We better get going.' I offered to pay for the ice-creams but he wouldn't let me, reminding me it was for my birthday. 'I'm pleased I told you that about the school. It's hard to talk about it.' He smiled at me and I reached over and touched his hand.

We bought a big carton of popcorn and some drinks. At the lift we were told we had to wait until an attendant came. I don't know why we couldn't have gone in by ourselves; it couldn't have been beyond our capability to press a lift button. My next problem was the thought of asking where the 'disabled toilet' was, but the attendant made it easy for me.

'The special ladies is straight ahead of you, right down the end. You'll see the sign.' I pushed myself along the heavy, resistant carpet, feeling embarrassed. It didn't help much to think that most females went to the toilet when they went out, even if they weren't called 'special ladies'.

'Follow me,' the usher with the big torch said in a loud whisper. The adverts and forthcoming attractions were just starting. She led us down a steep carpeted slope to the front row. I held on tight to the metal rims of the wheels, nervous that I was going to roll away straight through the screen. 'Now, do you stay in your chair or get into a seat?'

If the height of the seat was good, the arm solid and in the right place and the floor level I could have transferred, but it was dark and I was nervous. The idea of falling splat on the floor was too horrible to contemplate.

'I think I'll stay in my chair.'

'Right. You just hold on and I'll get someone else and

we'll take the seat out. I'll be back in a tick,' she said in an even louder whisper.

I suppose taking out the seat wasn't that difficult or time consuming but I wished they could have done it before I arrived. Even in the dark, it felt like everyone was looking at me.

'Sorry,' Jesse said. 'I thought they'd already have done this.'

'You sit down.' He put the drinks in those circles you get attached to the arms and held on to the popcorn. I manoeuvred myself into the space they'd now made for me and put the brakes on. Instead of snuggling down together in the back row like the girl had suggested in the magazine, I towered above him, stiff and upright.

'Oh.' It wasn't what Jesse had been expecting either. 'I know what I can do.' He stood up and let the seat flip back and sat on the five-centimetre hard rim of the chair. It must have been incredibly uncomfortable but at least we were the same height.

'Excuse me. I can't see a thing,' the man behind whispered in a loud, irritable voice. Jesse let the seat go and sat back down. I kept my eyes straight ahead; I didn't want him to see the look on my face. I didn't want him to see me trying not to cry. He tried to hold my hand but it felt all wrong and soon he let it go.

I spent the first half of the film attempting to focus on the screen, which felt like it was only inches from my nose, but after a while I forgot how awkward it was and began to relax. We laughed in the same places and in one really exciting bit I instinctively put my hand out to him and he squeezed it in return. By the time the lights came on, I realised I'd enjoyed it.

It was dark when we got outside. Leicester Square was even more packed with people. Jesse held one hand and I steered myself along with the other. We went all around the square. The first bit was downhill and it felt like running together. Going back was harder and he stood by me and pushed one side while I pushed the other.

'Shall we go back now?' I nodded. I couldn't imagine how we were going to get home but he seemed pretty confident.

'You've been in a taxi before?'

'No, not since I went to the pantomime with my grandparents when I was about nine.' He began to look nervous.

'I think the ones we need have a wheelchair sign on the front, where it says For Hire. They're supposed to have ramps they can put down and a special place for the wheelchair.'

We walked down a bit towards Piccadilly Circus. Lots of taxis went by but only a few of them had that wheelchair symbol and they didn't all stop. It took us a while to realise that the For Hire sign had to be shining yellow, otherwise it meant they already had someone in the cab. The first two who stopped said they couldn't go as far as Kingsbury. 'Not worth my while.' I didn't know they were allowed to do that. The third one said he was sorry but he'd left his ramps in the garage, and I began to feel like I must have some contagious disease. The fourth one was more cheerful.

'Right you are my darlin', I'll just get these ramps like this and up you go. Now, mind your 'ead. Ooh, I bet that

'urt, you should've ducked as we went through the door.'
I rubbed my forehead, pretending I wasn't really in pain.
He fitted me into a corner with my back to the driver's
seat and clamped me down with a complicated
assortment of safety belts. Jesse sat opposite me.

I'd always thought of being in a taxi as really romantic.
Snuggling back into that black leather seat far from the
driver, watching the lights of London go by. It wasn't like
that at all. Perhaps I could learn to do these transfers
when I felt a bit more confident.

'Has this been a success?' Jesse asked doubtfully.

'Yes it has,' I said, trying to sound convincing. 'Thanks
for being brave enough to organise it for me. Not many
people would. It's been really, really important. It's my
first visit to the pictures. My first taxi ride. My first
Häagen Dazs ice-cream sundae. My first date.'

'Do you mean your first date since you got ill or your
first date ever?'

'My first date ever.'

'No. Honestly?'

'Yes. Honestly.'

'Mine too.'

'No. You're kidding?'

'I'm not. Remember all those years at that boys' school
miles away from civilisation?'

'Well, well.' I wanted to kiss him so much that I ached.

Getting out of a taxi wasn't so bad – going down is
always easier than going up. I opened the front door
while Jesse paid. Mum and Dad were in the front room
watching the television and Dad stuck his head round the
door.

'Have a good time love?' he said as if I did this every week. I'd already seen Mum's anxious face at the window looking up and down the street.

'Yeah, great thanks. Jesse is here, we're just going to have some coffee.'

'Well don't be too late. Mum and I are going up soon. Goodnight love. Goodnight Jesse.'

'Goodnight Mr and Mrs Starling. Thanks for letting me take Libby out.' This must have been part of Malcolm's old-fashioned advice and it worked a treat. Dad stopped looking as if he was about to tell him it was time to go home and obediently followed Mum back into the sitting room.

I turned on my desk lamp and aimed up the light towards the ceiling.

'Green with blue lining or purple with lilac?' I asked, handing him one of the mugs Robbie had given me. We both blew on the hot coffee and sipped it slowly as if we were waiting. There was silence in the room. I put my cup down on the desk. He put his cup down. We listened to the sounds of Mum and Dad turn off the light, close the door and climb upstairs. There was no sound above us.

Without speaking, Jesse pulled my chair towards him and, still sitting, moved his legs either side of my chair. He put his hands on my knees and I leant towards him.

It's a funny thing about kissing. How even though you've never done it before, you know exactly what to do. I suppose that had something to do with waiting for such a long time to kiss anyone and then being with the right person. I thought I'd feel all awkward and it would be all noses getting in the way and sloppy wetness but it wasn't. It was soft and warm and wet and dry and exciting and hard all at the same time. It involved lips and tongues and teeth and arms and hands and touching faces and stroking hair.

Neither of us wanted to be the first to stop. When we finally pulled apart it was at the same time and we both looked at each other and smiled.

'Wow,' Jesse said, breathing out. My smile spread to a grin. Suddenly I knew he wasn't with me because he felt sorry for me or because he felt guilty or because I was Cleo's second best. He had kissed me because it was me he wanted to be with. Otherwise I knew it couldn't have felt like that.

'Do you know how long I've wanted to do that to you?'

'Since last Wednesday?'

'A bit last Easter when I sat at your table in maths last year. A lot that day at Littlehampton and more or less non-stop ever since.'

'What about that thing with Cleo then?' I didn't want to spoil it, but the words were out of my mouth and I couldn't swallow them back.

'Oh that.' He groaned, half amused. 'I thought you must have heard about it. It . . . it was a mistake.'

'A mistake?'

'Well, not exactly a mistake. It was one of those things that happen when you're at a party and someone's stoned and someone's drunk a bit too much and the music's loud and the lights are low.'

'Oh, very poetic I'm sure.'

344

'To be honest, I didn't really know what hit me. Cleo was very . . . She was very . . .'

'Very very?'

He laughed. 'You know what I mean.'

'Did you feel sorry you'd done it, afterwards?'

'No, not really,' he said honestly. 'I would've done if anyone had got hurt or there'd been any misunderstandings but Cleo isn't interested in me. I was just a shoulder to cry on.' I raised my eyebrows at him. 'Well, p'raps a bit more than a shoulder. But she was getting over someone else and I was there. She wasn't thinking about me, I could tell. Anyway, if you want to know the real truth, I imagined I was kissing you.'

'Oh yes?'

'Yes, I'll prove it to you.'

I opened my mouth to receive his kiss. I let my tongue explore the inside of his lips and then reach down into his mouth. Small, soft, dry kisses. Long, deep, wet ones. He put his fingers onto my lips and I kissed them. His hand touched my chin, down over my neck and flat across my breasts for just one magical second and then away as if we both knew that neither of us wanted too much to happen, too quickly.

'I wish I'd have known you liked me all the time I was ill.'

'I'm sorry. I didn't know what to do. I was such an idiot that day at Littlehampton. I wanted to ask you out then, but I didn't know how to. And you seemed a bit, you know, cool about me. I didn't even know how you asked a girl out. I could hardly ask Ben, he knows even less than me. Look at the way he goes on with Esther. He still hasn't actually asked her out, he just keeps trying to bump into her.' We both laughed. 'When I heard you were in hospital, I felt really bad. You know, I told you, I thought it could be my fault you'd got ill. Then I thought it was best to wait till you were better and start again.'

'I'm not going to get better,' I said softly. 'This is how I'm going to be, there's not going to be any miracle cure.'

He looked shocked. 'I didn't mean that. I meant better like you are now. I don't want you different.'

I opened a drawer and took out a folded-up square of dry paper. 'I bet you don't know what this is.'

He took it from me and unfolded it carefully, examining the small grease spots where the paper had turned translucent.

'Do you remember in Littlehampton when we went for that walk together along the sea front? You bought me a doughnut from that funny van. That's the bag it came in.' I could remember that walk as clearly as if it had been yesterday. The day before I was ill.

'You've kept it all this time? I wish I'd known.'

'What would you have done?'

'I dunno. Probably something stupid. I'd have felt . . . I'd have felt I could come round and see you this year, instead of feeling I'd only make things worse.'

'You did do things for me. You came and visited me in hospital, you bought me a present.' I pointed to it sitting on my shelf. 'And you took a lot of risks at school.'

'Yeah, but in between I've been a complete prat, haven't I? I haven't done much to help you.'

He took my hand in both of his, then turned it over and looked at the palm as if he was trying to read it.

'I won't be able to see you very much in the next couple of weeks, with the exams coming up. Then I'm going to Ireland to help my mum's sister and her husband. They've got a farm, well a smallholding really, and I promised I'd help them ages ago. June and July are their busiest months. But I'll be back for the end of the holidays; we can do things together then if you want to. You can come with me to Barbara's when I do her garden. We could go when she's out at work; we'd have the place to ourselves for a bit. What do you think?' He looked at me anxiously, earnestly.

'That would be great.' I could already feel myself missing him. 'Shall I write to you when you're there? I like writing letters – not that there'll be much to tell you.' I kissed him to seal the promise.

'Next year, when you come back to school, it might be hard for you being in a different year. I haven't forgotten how it feels to start again. I know you've got lots of friends but I really want to be there for you. I want to take care of you. I want to look after you.'

'I don't want you to look after me, Jesse. I've had enough of people looking after me to last a lifetime.' He looked like I'd just taken his lolly away. 'You can look out for me if you like. You can help me, you can be my great friend. I just don't want people taking over anymore.'

'Fair enough. I'll look out for you. You can tell me what you need and I'll do your bidding.' He put his palms together and bent his head down until it touched them, as if he were obeying my orders. We smiled at each other. I didn't know that in just one night you could feel so close to someone, so warm as if you'd known them forever.

'And what do you think about the term "going out together" or the word "boyfriend" – are either of those terms acceptable to you? Can I tell people we're an item, in a relationship? Unless of course you're planning to dump me before we've even begun.'

'I'll be very, very pleased to tell people that you're my boyfriend. I'm sure Malcolm will be impressed with such an old-fashioned term.'

I put my arms up around his neck and he put his around my waist. I looked over at the bed and thought, I'll put some cushions on it, make it look more like a sofa. Then we won't have to think about metal wheels and spiky brakes. We could hear Dad making elaborate coughing noises at the top of the stairs.

'I've never been in this situation before, but I reckon that's my cue to go.'

'I expect it is.' We went together to the door and I kissed him goodbye.

'Thanks. Really, it's been a fantastic evening. I know I'm not the easiest person to take out.'

'I haven't got a lot to compare it with, but it seems pretty successful for a first date.'

I felt the long tunnel of missing him, even before he had gone.

'Good luck with the exams. I bet you do really well.'

'I'm not getting out of your life just yet,' he said. 'I'll ring you tomorrow.'

'And I'll ring you the day after that.'

One last kiss. He stuck his hands in his pockets and walked in long, easy steps away from my house. I watched him go down the quiet, dark, empty street with its identical semi-detached houses, paved front gardens and straggly rose bushes and I could see his white shirt, bright under the street lamps, and the reflection of the yellow light on his shiny copper hair, until he turned the corner and was gone.

Chapter Twenty
Libby

Jesse has been in Ireland for over a month. I write to him a lot and he writes back, not quite so often – quick, funny postcards with little cartoon drawings of himself, feeding the pigs or pulling up radishes. He sent me a photo his uncle had taken of him, leaning on a spade. He looked tanned and fit. I really miss him but it's a comfortable kind of missing because I know he'll be back soon and we'll be able to spend some time together before school starts again.

Cleo's been around all summer, mostly round the corner with her mum. We've spent a lot of time together, chatting and mooching around. Her mum seems a lot brighter these days. She isn't working but you can tell she's looking after herself better and Cleo's helping her do the house up a bit. Every night they go through the *Evening Standard*, looking for a job for her mum. It's a lot of responsibility for someone Cleo's age.

My mum's going back to work after the holidays. She's got a paid job as lunchtime helper in a school. The money's lousy but she wants to be able to take me to school and be home in the holidays, so it'll suit her for now. She's thinking about doing an Open University degree. She's talked to Barbara and decided she wants to be a social worker. I hope she does it, even though she's over forty. She deserves to do something for herself.

Brian and his mum came round to see us. He missed my birthday because his operation didn't go as well as they hoped. He's still as cute as ever, but perhaps he's a bit more serious now. Actually, he's always been serious, but now he's quieter, more reserved. He doesn't tell you everything that's going on in his funny little brain.

He was really excited about coming to see me. He was never the sort to jump on my lap – his new, big plaster cast, which went from his neck to his hips, would have stopped him doing it anyway, but he gazed up at me with his adoring, puppy-love look which always made my heart melt.

He was fascinated by the idea of me having a fridge in my bedroom. He opened it up enthusiastically but was sadly disappointed to discover that it was empty except for the end of a bottle of milk and half an old Kit Kat. I wished I'd thought to put a treat in for him – a chocolate teddy or some strawberry ice-cream.

His mum was holding a square cardboard box with a lid.

'I bet you can't guess what this is?' he said.

'A chocolate cake with black cherries and whipped cream.'

'No!'

'A chicken and munchroom pie with green peas and yellow sweetcorn and chips.'

'No!!'

'A baby tiger,' I said, clutching at straws.

'You nearly guessed it! You nearly guessed it!' he shouted with delight, opening the top of the box. I hadn't noticed the air holes punched in the sides. I looked in. Out popped the head of a small, timid, anxious, cute-as-anything ginger kitten.

'Oh, Brian.' I looked at his mum and I looked at mine. She was smiling.

'It's for your birfday really,' he said triumphantly. 'You didn't know did you? I can keep a big, big secret, can't I?'

'Yes, you can.'

Mum's smile told me it would be alright to keep it. Everyone had known but me, even Robbie. They'd already organised the litter tray and the cat food.

'Our big cat had five baby cats and I chose this one for you. It's – how old is it, Mum? It's seven weeks so it doesn't need the big mummy cat now.'

'It's adorable,' I said, holding it on my lap. 'Its fur is the same colour as your hair.'

I had a bit of trouble choosing a name. At first I wanted to call it Brian. Brian is a great name for a cat, but I couldn't really. Apart from anything else, Robbie wouldn't have liked that at all. I thought of all the names I could call it. Ginger. Rust. Copper-nob. Sienna. I thought about that one for a while. I liked the sound of it, a hot, sunny word – Sienna. Terracotta. Ochre. Umber.

You can't call a cat Umber. Syrup. Tangerine. Marmalade. Treacle. Carrot. In the end I settled on Pumpkin. It's a wonderful, round, orangey word. Pumpkin.

Pumpkin's grown so much in the last few weeks, I can only just pick him up with one hand while I hold on to the chair with the other. Soon he'll have to learn to jump up on my lap on his own.

Life isn't going to be that easy for Brian. He's only four and his mum is already talking about the problems of finding the right school for him, somewhere mostly on one level where the teachers understand that he'll have to have a lot of time off school for operations and treatment. I hope he'll be able to stand up to the questions and teasing of the other kids. I think he will. I want to be a special friend to Brian as he grows up. Like Barbara is to me.

I'm practising pushing myself about longer distances so I'll be able to get myself to school on my own sometimes. I keep trying to imagine myself there, but I can't. We've had to get permission to adapt the stupid school uniform. In our school you have to wear skirts in the summer with a shirt and school tie and you're only allowed to wear trousers when the temperature drops below ten degrees. (I mean if you're a girl; boys can wear trousers all the time.) Unless you're a Muslim girl; then you get special dispensation. Now it's unless you're a Muslim or a disabled person. I think I will try wearing skirts again one of these days, but it won't be brown, pleated ones.

It'll be funny being in a different year from all the others. I know they've said I can use the Sixth Form Common Room but I'm not sure if I will. I'd like to make some friends with kids in the new Year 11, otherwise I'll feel even more left out. With a May birthday, I'm quite young for my year, so there won't be a huge age difference. I am looking forward to going back to school though. The everyday routine of school life, the sociability, the getting on and doing something after this year of hanging on by the threads. I'm even looking forward to having homework and doing exams, which is hilarious when you think about the kind of student I was before.

I'm not sure whether I'll stay on at Dupont High to do my A levels. Jesse and Esther and the others will all have left school a year before me, so there's no point in being there just for them. I might try to find a college or an accessible school which does A-level courses. I'd like to be in a place where I'm not the only disabled student.

I still think about Jesse all the time, but it's different now. I imagine having conversations with him, telling some of the new things which keep popping into my head, and I'd like to find out more about him. Since he's been away, I dream of us being together, kissing, touching. That feeling for him goes right down deep inside me.

Of course, I don't know what'll happen to us in the future. I mean, we're both only sixteen, we'll be lucky if it lasts a few months. On the other hand, who knows? We might become lovers, go to university, travel round the world together. My grandparents met at sixteen and they've been married fifty years!

I think I'll always be friends with Cleo and Esther, at least

I hope I will. We'll always be separate friends, never a trio — those two have irreconcilable differences. Esther is serious, studious, thoughtful. You hardly ever see her lose her temper. She's not going to set the world on fire but she's the most loyal, dependable friend anyone can have and I hope I'll stick by her like she's stuck by me.

As for Cleo — well, she's one on her own. Against all the odds, she studied hard for her GCSEs and I hope her grades are good enough for her to stay on for A levels. She's very bright under all that defensive play acting. If you'd asked me last July, I'd never have believed we'd have got this close, so that's one of the good things that's happened to me this year. She'll never let me say, 'I can't do that, it's too difficult.' Like when I said I wasn't coming on their end-of-exams trip to the big leisure centre out past Watford. She just said, 'Don't be such a boring wooz, Libby. You're bloody well coming and that's that.' And I did. They got me in through the back of the school minibus whilst most of the others went on a big coach, and she practically stripped me off and *made* me go in the swimming pool.

Cleo needs me, too. She needs all of us. If I let her, she'd spend hours in the kitchen talking to Mum about her problems at home, listening to her advice in a way I never do. She loves my dad too, even laughs at his stupid jokes. And when she's in the mood, she'll get down on the floor and play long games of snakes and ladders with Robbie.

I have good days and I have bad days. At the moment they seem to balance each other out. People are still a bit funny with me, even people I know really well, and presumably strangers will be funny with me for the rest of my life. People can be oversensitive about things that they think might upset me and then without realising they've done it, they'll say something really stupid which will hurt me quite deeply.

Like the other day, when Esther and I were talking about what we'd like to do when we leave school, I told her that I'm going to learn to drive as soon as I'm seventeen and I can lease my own car through a government scheme. She said, 'Oh, it's alright for some. I don't think I'll ever be able to afford a car of my own.' And then, immediately, 'God, I'm sorry. That was a stupid thing to say.'

And I said, 'What's stupid?' genuinely not understanding what she meant.

And she said, 'You know, when I said it's alright for you – after everything that's happened to you. Sorry.'

People don't realise that on the whole I don't see my life stretching before me like a tragic wasteland. I see interesting, exciting things to do.

On a bad day I wake up crying. I still have days when I'm bone weary, every muscle, every joint aching from head to toe. I get fed up with how long it takes me to get ready and how difficult it is to do ordinary things that other people take for granted, even things that sound silly, like getting to the shops to buy someone a birthday card.

On a bad day I imagine Jesse and Ben and Esther and Anil with the school 'Outsider's Club', camping and rock climbing and cycling up mountains, and there is a sad, heavy feeling inside me. 'Outside' means something different to me. Outside is where things are unpredictable, uncertain, beyond my control.

On a good day, I realise I probably wouldn't have wanted to go mountain climbing anyway. I was never exactly the sporty type.

On a good day, I know I'll find different things to do. I don't know what they are yet.

I saw a programme on the TV about a man who uses a wheelchair. He travels round the world setting up workshops to make strong, cheap wheelchairs using local materials for disabled people in developing countries. In Cambodia, where people are still getting their legs blown off in land-mines, they make wheelchairs mostly out of wood and bicycle wheels. In Bangladesh they make wheelchairs for village women only a few inches off the floor so that they can cook and look after their children. It would be great to do something like that.

Or maybe I'll be an environmentalist or a scientist and do research into pollution in the rivers and the sea and try to get new laws passed to make sure our waters are clean. Dad would be very proud of me then.

On a bad day, my first waking thought is Why me?

On a good day, I'll look in the mirror and I'll see a pale, interesting face, not beautiful but unusual and strong. Big, sad-looking eyes with long, dark eyelashes. Nose too big. Well-shaped mouth. A face that can light up with a smile.

On a good day, I think it doesn't matter that I can't walk. It doesn't matter about the things I can't do. I will find other things that I can. I can be clever and nice and funny.

I am Elizabeth Alice Starling. I'm sixteen years old. I'm going to have a good life. A different life.